SANCTUARY
FOR
INNOCENTS

by
ISOBEL KELLY

Also by Isobel Kelly

Epidemic (ISBN 978-1-84685-217-6)
A Cutting Affair (ISBN 978-184685-482-8)

SANCTUARY OF INNOCENTS by ISOBEL KELLY

British Library Cataloguing In Publication Data
A Record of this Publication is available
from the British Library

978-1-84685-544-3

First Published 2007 by

Exposure Publishing, an imprint of Diggory Press,
Three Rivers, Minions, Liskeard, Cornwall, PL14 5LE, UK
WWW.DIGGORYPRESS.COM

My appreciation goes to those who have supported

And encouraged me – you know who you are

And my love, as always, to my family -

I could not wish for better Cheer Leaders!

Best Wishes

Isobel Kelly

CHARACTERS

Captain Luke Fraser	United States Air Force
Captain Mike Whitman	" " " "
Colonel Martyn Schafer	" " " "
William Meredith	Highland Shepherd
Jessica Meredith	Granddaughter to William
Henry Fowden	Finance director Merchant Bank
Elizabeth Meredith	Jessica's mother
Charles Welland	Merchant Banker
Mark Welland	His son
Warren Seager	Merchant Banker
Annabel Seager	His daughter
Colonel Phillip Haskins	Mark's Co in the Royal Air Force
Comm. Harry Patterson	Scotland Yard Policeman

And others pertaining to the story

The Wheel of Fortune turns, and the self-centred plans and pipe dreams of restless human beings, veer in a different direction. Tiny particles of life's kaleidoscope change, the game plan alters. Apart from the mischievous whims of the Gods, men are still hostages to Fate; sometimes by their own choice but more often because there is nowhere else to go.

PROLOGUE

WEATHER conditions fair next 24-hour period. Preliminary Practice authorized. Pilots and Air Defence Personnel to attend final briefing – 16:45 hrs Command Centre.

Take off 06:30 hrs. All planes grounded except for those detailed. Unauthorized traffic excluded over Barra, the Sound of Sleat, Loch Carron, Dingwall and the Moray Firth.

*   *   *   *   *

Under the cirri-cumulous sky, Luke Fraser felt the adrenaline race hotly through his veins, sparking a fire in his belly. He glanced back at Mike Whitman, his wingman, who was flying on his left, and raised a hand in happy acknowledgement to his friend. Before long when the two Tornados reached land, Mike would fall directly aft of his tail as they played follow-my-leader through the Highland glens. They knew each other's ways intimately since they had first met, for they had trained, qualified and flown together for a long time. The pilots, each as perceptive as the other, interacted in close accord. Even off duty they were rarely far apart. Harmonious in friendship, they required no more than to fly together.

Their recent studies had been strenuous in learning the dynamics of a strange plane. As guests of the RAF, and luckily chosen from a number of US pilots, they were about to gain direct knowledge and flying ability of TIALD (Thermal Imaging Airborne Laser) and to take part in a NATO exercise planned for later that year with NATO Forces. After hours on the Tornado Simulator, familiarising themselves with the controls, today was decided for a preliminary flight in the chosen planes then a Tornado fitted with TIALD would be available for them both to gain further tuition to take part in the exercise..

Luke caught sight of Mallaig. Glancing at the map, he banked a degree off the huge, dark mountain chain, which lay to the right, followed by Mike, a constant shadow. It would be tricky flying low through the glens and he looked forward to using the latest device to highlight ground contours that would show every hill and indent on the flight path, but being airborne was the love of his life and this preliminary flight was no more than a walk in the park. Ahead lay the island of Skye on his radar screen. His eyes veered to the right to locate the Sound of Sleat, the wide waterway he was looking for. Exactly on time and in the right place. Weather as good as it could get for clarity in this part of the world. No sweat; this should be a piece of cake!

They descended to the altitude designated and for a brief second he glanced down at the sea below. The glittering early morning sunshine on the water momentarily blinded him and he blinked his eyes to get rid of the glare, hastily realising his visor was up. He remembered he had tipped it when he turned to wave at Mike.

9

An instant later, he opened them and his attention immediately fled to a pulsing light on his Radar panel. Scarcely believing what he saw, he immediately stared out of his Plexiglas cockpit.

Jesus! For an instant, Luke thought the plane over on his right, heading for him on an intercept course, was a strange reflection of his wingman, but the size and shape of the plane and pilot dispelled the illusion. Luke had a glimpse of something white draped round the man's neck but his brain concentrated on things that were vital. What the hell was he doing in their sky? This was no mirage. The trespasser was not supposed to be there, was not in their briefing. Nobody had mentioned a word that a single aircraft would be waiting for them so far south though they understood they would have to reach a certain point of the compass to avoid the ambush set up near Cape Wrath. However, if the powers-that-be had thrown them a counter-attack they would have to run with it. Their training meant they must be prepared for any event and this was a test, albeit a preliminary sortie, where faultless attention to detail was paramount.

The pilot appeared rigidly set on a course of destruction. Luke estimated there was only bare seconds to take evasive action. Didn't he know this wasn't a fight to the death? Friend or foe - it was only a game – or was it? What was going on under that helmet that he was not even trying to avoid the on-coming planes? This is for real, you louse; it's collision time! Where the hell are you going? Up? Down? Where? Jeez – make your damned mind up!

"Break left, Mike! Break left-t-t-t-!"

Too late! He knew his cry came too late even as he yelled. Luke felt the short and snappy shudder of impact as his instinctive reflexes, honed to perfection with years of flying, led him to precipitate an evasive spin to the left. It had been either that or a head-on collision between him, the intruder and the possibility of implicating Mike. Despite his natural reaction to save himself from destruction, in the following moments of hindsight Luke felt the latter ought to have been the better choice and he should have accepted the penalty of total wipe out. The last thing in the world he wanted was to put his own buddy in danger.

Mike's response was slower, though only by milliseconds, but the distance between the planes not enough. Hellfire! Savagely Luke pushed his ejector handle as he watched the jagged splits tear towards him along the wing. He lost sight of Mike but hoped to God the man would eject. As for the stranger - whoever he was - may he roast forever in H-h-h-e-ell!

Before he could ascertain if Mike had ejected from his plane and was safe, Luke was instantly dislodged with inescapable violence. He was drawn mechanically headlong out of his cockpit which had immediately angled the other way after the impact and now rocketed him not straight up but sideways far out into the sky. The force of the ejection pulled the blood from his head, stunning him into temporary oblivion. His senses rallied briefly moments later to the realisation that he was dangling from a parachute and over land instead of sea. Below him the ground rushed up to meet him at what seemed an inordinate rate.

Of course they had been low. That was part of the planning to avoid the radar. Was it too low to get out of this alive? Somehow he thought it was.

His flagging senses registered a sound of an explosion and he guessed it was either his plane or Mike's. Too much to hope for that it was the stranger's; but for God' sake, he prayed, don't let it be Mike; please not Mike. If it was, he surely deserved his own forthcoming death. So without a shred of emotion leaching through his brain, for hadn't fate always given him the roughest of paths to follow, he resigned himself to total extinction as he plunged too swiftly into the topmost branches of a pine tree in the depths of the Scottish hinterland. The rough sound of breaking of branches as the intrusive package tore itself through the canopy faded to utter silence as the inert body swung slowly back and forth, suspended high in the air amidst the trees.

ONE

"Me? Oh no, I couldn't. I've never done anything like it before. I really couldn't."

Consternation filled Jessica's face and her eyes, the colour of blue hyacinths widened anxiously at Henry's proposal.

"Of course you can," Henry Fowden began again, racking his brains to find the right words to persuade her. "Look how well you organise me - this department. Sorting out one evening should be easy," he shrugged his shoulders scornfully. "You have to be a darn sight better than Miss McEwen. Her idea of a wine and cheese social does not bear thinking about, especially in this case. Anyway, her rule is over, she is retiring. She won't ever do it again."

"She's done them for ages; people are used to her ways even if this is a special event."

He grinned beguilingly at her. "Think of it as a normal office party. Look, if it will help, I'll choose the wine. Just make sure we don't get dry old biscuits and mouse-trap cheese!"

Jessica laughed at his words knowing exactly what he meant as she gazed fondly at his floppy jowls that reminded her of a beagle, though the rest of him was immaculately dressed. It filled her with great pleasure to see his dapper frame clothed in a dark business suit and elegant tie, his greying head combed with not a hair out of place. She liked orderliness in her life as her own neatly dressed figure in a plain navy skirt and white blouse attested. Henry had proved to be her ideal of a chief to work for and she looked forward to her daily efforts with eagerness and bliss. They were a good unit in the firm; both well satisfied with the other's routine. He really was the kindest of men, she reflected, and considering how he had helped her attain her present position, it would be churlish to say no. A tingle of excitement was nestling deep in her brain. Could she do it? Not easily, - it never was - but she would give it her best shot; she would accept the challenge. It was, after all, just another step along the path of her ambition.

TWO

The sun shone brightly that late May afternoon, on the Georgian building that stood not far from the Mansion House in the City of London. Its lancing rays cut through the old windows in sloping gold bands, laying burnished gleams over the mahogany furniture in the boardroom. It lit ornately framed oils of the long dead founder and chief partners of a Merchant Bank; their darkly, painted portraits staring down from buff-coloured walls on the pleasing scene below.

Jessica Meredith walked the length of the room, her eyes on every detail of the buffet laid out on the impressive table. It was a view worth looking at in shades of peach and green, the food specially chosen to match the china and napery. She'd finished arranging the flowers but bent to give a last tweak to an errant blossom. Heaving a huge sigh of satisfaction at the result, she heard the clock in the hall chime six. The caterers had left and soon waitresses would take their stations and attend to the firm's staff and guests in celebrating the 50th year of Welland and Davies' existence. All at once the door opened and Henry Fowden entered, smiling broadly as he saw her.

"Ah, there you are, Jessica. Everything ready?" he said, before turning to the table. "Good gracious! Doesn't it look sumptuous? It looks a banquet, my dear girl. I hope you've done your sums, for Sir Charles is sure to ask the cost. He's too used to Miss McEwen's frugality,"

His normally severe face twitched in a humorous smile. "Well? Confess to me right now, is this madly over budget? I had better know beforehand, for it is my neck that will suffer. You know what he is like when it comes to spending on the staff."

"Not by a penny, Mr Fowden. I did the flowers myself and I managed a super deal with the caterers, well within the sum allocated. They were pleased to get the job, as they are new to the catering business. Sir Charles should approve. At least I hope so."

"It looks a grand job to me but he's bound to say something, particularly looking at this super spread. Well it can't be helped. Anyway, he ought not to criticise the miracle you've achieved, especially as it's for his benefit and the guests he'll bring along. Right, my dear, it's getting late. You go and pretty up, or are you staying like that?" He eyed her plain navy dress and matching pumps with concern. He had never seen her in anything frivolous as long as he'd known her. She rang the changes but they were always severely practical and neat.

"No sir, I'll try and do justice to the occasion. It won't take long; I've brought my things to work ready for tonight." Jessica followed Henry out of the room to get changed.

With a glow of excitement, she headed for the women's staff room and the new dress she had bought. In the shop she tried it on reluctantly, hoping it wouldn't fit rather than admit it was too expensive for her pocket. She didn't need the persuasive voice of the salesgirl to tell her it was exactly right, she knew it immediately. The soft coral pink warmed her pale complexion and fair hair, which she wore in a long bob curling inward to her face also emphasising the deep violet blue of her eyes. Softly gathered drapes revealed the rise of curving breasts under a low neckline before swirling in flamboyance around slender hips. The salesgirl went with her to the make-up department to choose matching lipstick and blusher and then they decided on dainty high-heeled sandals to complete the outfit.

"You look wonderful. This dress seems to be specially designed for you." The girl said
enviously as she gazed at her client. "I do hope you have a lovely time."

"Thanks for your help and good wishes. I hope so too. I'm sure this dress will be lucky for me. To tell you the truth I've never worn anything like it in my life. If it weren't such a special occasion I'd never dream of buying it now, but I'm so glad I have."

She left the shop with a smile on her face and a strange feeling of excitement that almost threatened to spill over like bubbles from shaken champagne. It had stayed with her all the time she had been working on decorating the boardroom. Now she fervently hoped she'd have the cloakroom to herself, so she could change in privacy and enjoy the moment. Happily no one was around when the quiet, unassuming duckling became a beautiful swan.

THREE

Fine words of congratulations for the firm's Golden Anniversary began the evening; spoken by those well used to elegant rhetoric. The phrases echoed in the high-ceilinged room to mark the special occasion. The Chairman and his wife and those directors who felt they had rather more prestige than the rest of the firm, enjoyed the good wishes; basking in the reflective glory. But most ignored the speech, for having set their eyes on the food and drink they couldn't wait to begin.

Eventually Jessica stood to one side, a fruit juice in hand, watching the stylishly dressed throng gather round the table. She hadn't mixed with her associates, only speaking to a few of those she saw from day to day, content to watch in silence. Graduating from a junior clerk in the typing pool to personal assistant of the Finance Director in three short years, she had learned to ignore the snide comments of her contemporaries who yearned for the same chance but did not have her sheer determination and ability. Knowing that only she was responsible for the party and that it appeared to be a success turned her elation into a secret triumph.

"You've done well, Miss Meredith. My wife and I are most charmed with your efforts. You must tell me later how you managed it." Charles Welland appeared suddenly behind her, a smile on his lips but missing his eyes, which held their customary appraisal.

Nevertheless, she glowed inwardly with the Chairman's rare praise, ignoring the reference to cost. Unassuming and innocent in behaviour, the nuances of subterfuge usually went over her head. The rest of the senior colleagues were surprised with the difference in quality of this array, comparing it with the food usually presented by the Chairman's former personal assistant, Miss McEwen, who had recently retired at sixty.

"What magic did you work to make things so tempting? Old Charlie will be after your bones over the bill, you know." Jibed one junior chartered accountant in a whisper, who had once rubbed the chairman up the wrong way and been severely chastised for his presumption.

"I found a firm newly starting up, they were pleased to give me a low price just for the prestige of doing it...I arranged the flowers myself, which saved pounds...it wasn't too hard." Shyly she depreciated her efforts, retreating from the limelight in great haste lest her fellow workers might think she was boasting too much of her achievements.

"How about a glass of bubbly, Jessica? I'd say you've earned it and more. Sir Charles waxed most eloquently even if he did remind me to look carefully at the bills, as of course I will. Everyone is saying what a superb party this is. You must realise you'll have the job for life after this display tonight?" Henry Fowden chuckled gently as he stood by her holding out a glass of champagne. He was full of pride and pleasure for her efforts.

She declined gracefully, and held up her glass of fruit juice. Refusing the champagne was no pretence for she had never acquired the habit of alcohol, and in any case, she felt she ought to keep a clear head.

"Have you seen Mark Welland? Sir Charles is looking for him. I'm surprised he's not here today of all days. His father will have plenty to say when he does turn up. Heaven help us when he finally joins the firm." Henry Fowden pursed his lips gloomily at the prospect.

Jessica quickly masked a disquieted frown as she thought of the chairman's son. The words tall and handsome suited him to a tee for he was indeed good-looking. What his many girl friends did not see until too late, were eyes which lay too close together and cruel, sulky lips, which tightened warningly if he was prevented from having his own way. Jessica rarely had contact with him, for her work for Henry was solely concerned with his affairs in the finance department. It was how she preferred it. Her personal life was too committed to hang after him, even had she wanted. Quite unlike the other office girls, dangling their charms in an effort to get his attention. They did not know or even guess how clearly he saw through their obvious wiles and despised their puny efforts to attract him.

"No I haven't, maybe he's still abroad. I expect there's a good reason for his absence." she said soothingly, knowing her boss didn't like Mark. "He's unlikely to affect us when he does join. He'll be working with his father, I presume. Oh look, your wife is signalling to you and I'd better see if anything needs replenishing on the table. Off you go and enjoy yourself, it is all working well. No need to worry."

Giving him a quick smile she turned away; quite aware that Henry Fowden's wife was jealous of his regard for her. Jessica couldn't help but notice when Julia rang to speak to him, how off-hand she was with her and how haughtily she spoke. Jessica had tried to ignore her actions knowing there was no basis to her jealousy, for Henry was ever the perfect gentleman, but it hurt nevertheless.

Having confirmed all was in order with the catering, she had just finished replenishing her glass at the bar when a voice in her ear made her jump in surprise.

"My God, girl, you're not drinking that horrible stuff? Champagne's what you need, not piss water!"

Turning sharply, she found Mark Welland behind her. His lazy look that had previously held scornful contempt turned to intense speculation as he stared down at her.

"No, thanks all the same, I have a drink..." before she could protest, her drink was taken away and a glass of bubbling wine thrust in her hand. To save a fuss she smiled and toasted him before taking a tiny sip. It tastes quite pleasant, she noted with surprise, feeling the bubbles on her tongue. A little bit like lemonade but not so sweet. Then she decided it was not something that she wanted to get used to, considering its price, even had there been the slightest prospect of that happening in her life at present.

Mark Welland tossed his head derisively in the direction of Miss McEwen, who sat with friends. "This beats her wine and cheeses by a mile! And doesn't she know it. *And* her cronies are rubbing it in with salt! Now, more champagne? Drink up, there's plenty here. Tch! No, I'm sorry, that other stuff will not do. No, I insist. We've got to celebrate our fifty long years of robbing the poor to line our pockets, haven't we?"

Jessica caught a strong whiff of alcohol on his breath interlaced with his aftershave as he leaned over her, surprising her with his height in spite of her high heels. His face had a strangely sardonic twist, and his smile wore more than a cast of villainy in the look he gave her. Then his features relaxed and he became the familiar debonair man who roamed the banking house now and again but he continued to gaze down at her petite figure with searching relish, his eyes alive to every detail.

"You're just like a butterfly emerging from a chrysalis. I can't remember you looking quite so...so attractive, so gorgeous. You hide yourself very well around the office."

"Have you seen your father? He was looking out for you," she interrupted, ignoring his obvious attempts to flatter, wishing he wouldn't be so extravagant, it was embarrassing.

"Yes, yes," he replied impatiently. "I saw him when I arrived. Irritable as usual. Can't be a minute late with him; Lord knows how it will be when I'm here all the time," he swayed a little as he topped up her glass, and then leaned forward to whisper in her ear. "I'll need heaps of holidays to weather the strain of this place or I'll die of sheer boredom." he grinned at her and
the bright blue eyes twinkled with humour.

She couldn't help but laugh back. There was no doubt he had sex appeal. He'd put it to good use when he'd failed university, at once enlisting in the Air Force and rising quickly to the rank of Captain after a brief time, more by amazing good luck than having a particular expertise. Strangely and quite inexplicably, after a short-lived period, he'd bought himself out, announcing to his parents he had decided to join the family firm after all, but first he was taking time to relax and have a holiday. His mother agreed with him, saying he looked tired and overwrought. He must have a rest after his strenuous time in the service. That had been ages ago and the so-called holiday had extended far too long a time, much to the dismay of his father as he watched the bills increasingly mount up.

But cleverly, Mark had mastered the art of treading a fine line between doing exactly as he wished without tramping too hard on the toes of parental rectitude, or so he thought. His mother adored him with a maternal blindness to any of his shortcomings, but he knew full well his father hoped he would shoulder his responsibility to the firm and enter the business as soon as possible. Charles was keeping an acute and mostly irritable eye on his wayward son so he had planned his next move with care.

"Are you starting soon?" Jessica asked; having overheard through her open office door Sir Charles tell Fowden Mark was playing games with his future. He'd sounded concerned about Mark or was it merely because he was taking too long to buckle down to work.

"Time the lad knew how to earn money, Fowden; he surely knows how to spend it," he grumbled. "God only knows when he's going to join us."

"What is he doing?" asked Henry carefully. He was always careful with his words when he spoke to the Chairman; for he never felt completely comfortable with the man.

"Gadding about Europe with idle layabouts, that's what! Plus wasting his time in pursuits that are frivolous and of no use to anyone. Frankly his mother is getting quite worried about him. Some of the places he visits are quite disreputable."

"Sowing his wild oats no doubt." said Henry quietly.

"Wild oats at his age! He ought to be bloody well over that by now. It's just plain idle to my way of thinking." Charles retorted. "About time he settled to some honest work like the rest of us." he said disparagingly.

Henry found himself wishing it would be anywhere but at the firm. His initial meeting with Mark betrayed the fact they had nothing in common and never would have.

Their voices had drifted off down the corridor but Jessica too was left with the idea that Mark was aiming to keep his playboy life and her opinion of him dropped accordingly

"Yes, the dreaded hour is coming ever closer." Mark's eyes closed in fake distress at the thought. "I'll be locked up in the vaults never to see the light of day. Will you come and feed me through the bars, fair Jessica? For I vow I'll languish forever forgotten if you don't." he grinned mockingly, "Then I'll always be on your conscience, won't I?"

"Idiot! This place isn't a prison. I'm sure you will do very well." she laughed again at his daft play-acting. After a few minutes of small talk she left him to ensure the waitresses were clearing the remains of the buffet, for most of the guests had already taken their leave and the rest were making ready to go.

Well pleased with the evening which had turned out to be more of a success than he had anticipated, the Chairman made a mental note to keep his eye on the young woman who had arranged it all. His replacement secretary was irritating him and would need changing soon. He might poach Fowden's PA in her place. Perhaps he would investigate her background and see if she would suit. After saying goodbye to the few that remained, he and his party left; Charles having a quiet word in his son's ear that he would see him in his office early next morning.

Jessica caught the not so subtle exchange and noticed a vicious scowl of anger on Mark's face as he was forced to listen to his father's orders. Afterwards he returned to the bar then disappeared. She wasn't in the least concerned he had departed without a word, in fact she was glad. A little of him went a long way she decided, feeling rather as her boss felt.

FOUR

The next hour for Jessica was hectic as clearing took precedence and by the time the last person had gone and she turned off the main lights, all the elation vanished to leave her drained of energy. She'd never known the place so quiet like this before. During the day the firm was constantly crowded with staff and clients as the busy bank conducted financial business. Earlier she had confidently assured Henry she didn't mind in the least being the last to leave. She would ensure the main door was secure and all the alarms set as usual, for unfortunately the timing of the event had coincided with the resident caretaker being away on his annual leave.

Henry had been livid when he found out that Hutchins wouldn't change his holiday dates. The caretaker had promised his wife a holiday abroad and the date had already been fixed in January long before there was any mention of a celebratory party. Despite hard persuasion Hutchins was adamant. "She's dead set on going abroad, sir. And it's her first time. I can't disappoint her, it's our anniversary and she'd be really upset."

"I'll stay until the end and see the place is locked up." Henry had said crossly once he realised what the situation was. Julia would be furious but it couldn't be helped.

"No, of course you won't. You know your wife won't like staying late. I'll be all right, I promise. There's bound to be someone around to keep me company." But for once there hadn't been anyone. The catering staff had vanished as soon as their jobs were done and the few young bachelor accountants who lingered a short while to drink the last of the wine, had made plans to go on to a nightclub. With a cheery wave in her direction they left without so much as a thought that Jessica would be on her own, not even a "Will you be okay?" as they slammed the main door shut behind them.

Wearily spent, her adrenaline now at low ebb, she was making her way through the huge hall to the staff room at the back of the building to collect her case of office clothes when all at once she felt a *frisson* of fear. Although unused to being in the old London house by herself she was far from being a nervous person but in these circumstances the shadowy nooks and corners and loudly echoing stairwell filled her with alarm.

Anxious to quit the place as soon as possible she decided not to change into her office clothes, retrieving instead a light raincoat she kept folded in her bag. Slipping it on she picked up her case and headed for the door to the corridor switching out the cloakroom light as she went, knowing the main lights were on in the hall. However, the lamp in the passageway was off and suddenly she found herself in darkness.

The shadowy figure that showed itself in the dimness was heart stopping. For a moment all her childhood fears of the dark rose up in one huge nightmare and Jessica couldn't stop the terrified scream that echoed through the building or stop her heart pumping with fright. Then reason prevailed and swiftly catching the odour of his aftershave she identified who it was. The light flicked on again and Jessica, completely taken aback, stared in amazement as she saw Mark Welland leaning lopsidedly against the wall, a devilish grin on his face, his tie hanging loose and his hair unusually awry. Her chest still heaving with fright at his stupid attempt to scare her, she forgot where and who she was and enraged with his stupid trick, she yelled her displeasure at the chairman's son:

"Mark Welland! What the hell are you doing here? You scared the wits out me. I'm locking up ready to leave. Everyone else has gone home, why not you?"

"Waiting for you, sweetie, what else?"

"Waiting for me? Whatever for? I thought you'd left the party ages ago."

"Nope. I decided to stay behind and show you a surprise. I like surprises and this is a real humdinger, you'll see."

"Oh?" she said curtly, then belatedly realising who she was talking to, tried to modify her tone, even to smile; though it took a tremendous effort. "What's the surprise?"

"Aha, secret. Tell you in a minute. Come with me."

"Mark, I really must go, it's late, and my mother will be worried."

"Shit! Does Mummy still control your life?" abruptly his voice changed tone. "How old are you anyway - Ten? Does diddums have to ask permission for everything?"

"No! Certainly not! I'm twenty-one, but that doesn't mean I come and go regardless of her feelings. We live happily together, just as we have always done. She is very dear to me."

After her father died Jessica was obliged at an early age to take over the reins and make hard decisions that would have been tough for an older person let alone an eighteen-year old, but she had grimly fought through with tenacity. They no longer had a house and the flat was a second-floor walk-up, but apart from the pink dress, which had cost more than she normally spent on clothes, they were out of debt. Though their existence was frugal, they had survived.

She pictured her mother and the rented, cheerless flat in Streatham, which was all they could afford since her mother found out her Dad had cashed their insurance policies earlier for one of his pet schemes. A would-be inventor, he was forever going to make his fortune with something special; except his strange gadgets inevitably failed. Finally, his heart failed and he bestowed on his wife, already frail, a mountain of debts to cope with. It had taken Jessica a long time to sort things out but eventually they had become solvent again.

That it was all due to her better job was again to her credit. She had worked hard to get where she was, spending time and effort in extra-curricular education to acquire knowledge that would enable her not only to hold her own with other better educated young people but to rise in the job she had chosen. This she had done to her satisfaction and already her nimble brain was planning her next step on the career ladder. To become a financial director before the age of thirty, she thought, was not entirely out of reach. She'd have a good try.

Recently, she had noticed her mother seemed thinner than usual, with a yellow pallor to her face. She said she had been to the doctor and nothing was wrong, but somehow Jessica didn't quite believe her. She was resolved, now the firm's party with its obligations was finally behind her, she would find the underlying cause of her mother's poor health. Though she was not robust, she had never looked quite as down as she appeared now.

There was silence for a moment then Mark mockingly smirked. "Well, what's it to be? We can't stand here all night. Come on, it's make your mind up time. Or do I take it, despite the fashionable dress; you are just an infant pretending to be grown-up?"

"All right," she said impatiently, ignoring his sarcasm, "show me your surprise, then I really must go or I will miss my last train. It is late already and I can't afford a taxi home."

Smiling again like a schoolboy who had got his own way, he made her drop her things in the front hall, slipping off the raincoat despite her protest, and then holding on to her arm he pulled her up the main staircase to a suite of rooms on the first floor. Not certain at first where he was heading she didn't try to resist, until, opening the Chairman's door he made to draw her inside. At once she protested. "I can't go in there, it's private. It's Mr Charles' office and unless personally invited it's off limits to all the staff."

"Of course you can go in. You're with me. And I'm certainly allowed in here. Don't fret, it's perfectly all right, really it is. Come on, hurry up, the surprise is in here."

She hesitated, torn with indecision. Apart from innocuous dating at Business College she steadfastly turned her face away from any involvement with men knowing she was the sole breadwinner for her mother and must concentrate on her work. As a result, she was genuinely innocent of the wiles of men and yet instinctively she felt threatened with her situation. Reason told her he was up to no good. Normal people didn't act this way, at least not in her world they didn't. How did it concern his father? Had he arranged some surprise for Charles and wanted to know what she thought? Possible, but hardly likely. Then what was it? More to the point, she was aware she was on her own with him in the empty building. How was she to extricate herself from the situation she now found herself in without arousing his anger?

Mark solved the issue by pulling her bodily into the room, then twirling her around he wrapped his arms around her while his foot slammed the door and his hand turned the key. Immediately he held her captive his lips descended on hers and he commenced kissing her more thoroughly than she had ever been kissed before. At last, frantic for air, she began to struggle and pressed hard against his chest to free herself.

When that didn't work her struggles grew wilder and somewhat reluctantly he released her mouth. "For goodness sake, Mark, if you'd wanted a kiss you could have done it downstairs. Why come up here? It's not right and I'm not happy with it. I'm sure we're trespassing."

"So tomorrow when I'm carpeted for being late for the party I'll think of making love to you and shut my ears to the bellyaching. Besides, the old skinflint has the only decent couch in the place." he leered at her and at once a shiver of panic went through Jessica.

"Look, Mark, a joke's a joke, but I'm not staying any longer. It's late, I'm tired and I'm going home. Now leave me be."

Backing away from his encircling arms she reached for the door but in an instant he swiftly had her arms pinned behind her back.

"That's where you're wrong, young woman!" he scowled down at her.

"Please, Mark," she begged, "Don't be stupid, this isn't a silly game, and I **am** going home right now. Please understand I don't play about in this stupid fashion. Your father would be furious if he saw us in here and rightly so. I don't know what you've been used to doing in the past with other women but I assure you we don't get up to tricks like that here."

She thought he would listen to reason but the look on his face filled her with fear.

"Oh no, you bitch, you're not going to cock-tease me all night with your pink dress and just walk away...I am not having that...I haven't waited all evening to be put off now. Keep still, you are not running away from me...you can't anyway, I've got the key. You might as well relax and enjoy what I'm going to do now." Mark held onto her firmly.

"I wasn't...whatever you said...I was doing a job for your father...the firm...really and truly you're mistaken. I'm sorry...Ouch! Let go of me! Mark! For God's sake what are you doing? Are you crazy? MARK! Let me go!" she stared at him, aghast with fright.

His eyes glinted with evil as he gripped her wrists in one hand while the other unzipped his trousers to expose himself to Jessica's horrified eyes. "Don't even think of turning me down." he warned. "I've wanted you all evening and now I'm having you. Understand?"

She felt his hands on her breasts and hit out swiftly, screaming at him to leave her alone. He quickly fended off the blow and shoved her up against the door laughing cruelly as the back of her head hit the wooden panel. The blow was hard enough to cause a wave of blackness to sweep over her and she reeled with dizziness. Pulling herself together, she tried to kick him, but because of her panic any strength she owned was weakening fast, until, gasping for air, she was at the mercy of his brutal and utterly overwhelming power.

She had no more fight left in her as he threw her towards the couch. She staggered and as her foot slipped the flimsy strap of a sandal snapped and she fell to the floor. In an instant Mark was on her and tearing away her underclothes he held her down. She shrieked as he violated her, the pain of the assault leaching through her body, then screamed again as his fist connected with her face. Previously, at school, she'd acquired a brief knowledge of sex between two people, but she had never been intimate with a man, nor had ever imagined how dreadful it could be or that this terrible act was happening to her. As she sobbed bitterly he savagely took his pleasure.

Utterly devastated, she was too helpless to stop him.

"Well, well, Jessica, a sweet little virgin?" surprised, he smirked at her "Lucky old me! Now stop crying you stupid idiot, I've done you a favour, think of the fun you'll have..."

He broke off as a violent hammering suddenly lashed the door to the office.

"Open up! Who's in there! Open this door at once, I say!" an enraged voice cried out.

"Oh Christ! Go away, whoever you are, I'm busy!" Mark scowled angrily.

"Open up or I'll fetch the police!"

FIVE

With a sigh of exasperation Mark stood up, tidied himself then turning the key in the door opened it to find Henry Fowden standing there with his fist raised to bang again on the door.

"What in hell's name is going on?" Henry yelled at Mark. Then his eyes went past the grinning man he disliked so much to the figure that still lay sobbing on the floor. "Jessica? Oh my God, what's happened to you?"

But there was no answer from the recumbent figure who continued to sob heartrendingly in terror. "What the hell have you done to this girl? Christ, Welland! You've raped her, haven't you? You are a bloody awful scoundrel! You'll answer for this, just see if you don't!"

"Don't worry about her, Fowden, she only started crying when you banged on the door, enjoyed it really. Take no notice; she's making too much fuss over a very minor incident."

"I heard her screaming from downstairs, you rotten devil. We'll see if **YOU** enjoy it in the morning when I tell your father. I'll give you minor incident! It's a bloody hanging offence in my book. Now get out of here, you despicable wretch. You are not fit company for this place and I'll see to it you never come to work here ever, or your father will."

"I wouldn't make too much of a fuss if I were you, Fowden. Say too much and **I'll** see to it your assistant is labelled as your **tart**. Mud sticks you know, old darling." he said grinning maliciously, then he saluted Henry derisively and left the room.

Enraged, Henry moved a pace to go after him then paused to consider. It would do no good to tackle a man as physically strong as Mark Welland, for in every respect he topped Henry both in height and physique. No, there were better ways of mastering that unpleasant wretch and make him pay for his crime. Let's see how the police would view such appalling behaviour; they'd arrest him for sure. But first things first.

Sympathetically and carefully he helped Jessica to stand up. Spotting the wisp of torn underwear on the floor he picked it up and stared at it for a moment scarcely realising what it was, then his face colouring with embarrassment, he shoved it into his pocket.

Opening the chairman's top drawer of his desk he found a few paper clips and fastened the huge tear in her dress, picked up the ruined shoe, helped her take off the other one before guiding her out of the door and switching off the light.

"I'm going to take you to your doctor now, child. He will help you more than I can."

"No! I don't want a doctor; I want to go home away from all this. Please take me home, I can't get on a train looking like this." she cried bitterly

Doubtfully he stared at her white set face, and the purple bruise that was just beginning to darken the side of her cheekbone. "You really ought to have medical attention at once, Jessica," he began, feeling embarrassed with the whole affair. "In fact the best thing is to visit the nearest Police Station.

They will have a doctor to attend you who has experience with these affairs. Believe me it's the best thing to do."

After the party he had driven his wife home, then, conscious of a strange sense of unease he decided to return to the city to make sure everything was in order. His wife's protests were vociferous. She said he was being unnecessarily protective. The girl was, after all, just an office assistant, why make a special journey just to make sure the premises were locked and she'd gone home? But whilst he felt confident in Jessica's ability to do as she had promised he had seen Mark at the bar drinking steadily all evening and his eyes had been on Jessica. It must have been some sixth sense that had triggered the uneasiness. Thank God it had. He had been appalled when he saw her things scattered at the foot of the main staircase. Lord knows what else might have happened to Jessica had he not come back? Nonetheless guilt still struck him deeply as he recognised he had not come in time to save her from rape.

They stopped to collect her things and she put on her other shoes while Henry briefly wondered if Jessica had begun to struggle at that point or had gone willingly to the Chairman's office. Not that it mattered. The deed was done and the repercussions would be formidable. Arrogant swine! Henry would see he paid for it. A long spell in prison was what that rat needed. It might teach him sense, though Henry doubted Mark would benefit in the slightest. Unless of course, he was given a taste of his own medicine and raped in the same brutal style he had used on Jessica. Henry smiled to himself at that hopeful thought.

The streets were reasonably empty of traffic and it didn't take Henry long to drive Jessica home. He peered inquisitively at the three-storied typically square Georgian style house built like the rest of the street in London Stock bricks with a shallow grey tiled roof over all. He tried to imagine the number of people that lived in an area like this and at once felt claustrophobic. Thank the lord for his pleasant house, well spaced out from his neighbours in a quiet residential road in North London not far from his local golf course. Not as pleasant as Yorkshire, where he had been born, but much nicer than this place. Then he pulled himself together and helped Jessica out of the car.

"Wrap your coat round you to hide your dress; I'll carry your case. I'm coming up with you. No, I must insist. Your mother at least, has to have an explanation and I can't leave you to face her on your own. Don't fret, I'll be tactful, I promise. She'll understand I'm sure."

Jessica felt too numb to argue as they walked up the stairs to the flat on the second floor. But no sooner had she opened her flat door than a bang came from below and a woman came rushing up the stairs from the ground floor flat in a tearing hurry.

"Jessica! She's not there! Yer mum's gorn off to the hospital! They've taken 'er off to St. James." she peered down at the tightly held raincoat Jessica was wearing.

"Watcha got on, ducky; it ain't raining, is it? Loverly evening I thought. Good weather's really set in. Wouldn't have thought you'd need a mac..."

"An unfortunate spill of wine," interjected Henry quickly. "Where's St. James and what's happened? Jessica, you get changed while I find out what's wrong." he urged her on through the door. He had no qualms about being with Jessica outside office hours but he had to redirect the woman's attention from Jessica's appearance lest it lead to more scandal. This was a hell of a business. It was going to cause no end of trouble, for him as well as her.

For a moment he regretted going back to the office then relaxed. He couldn't think badly of her especially after that shady bastard's actions. Despite Mark's sly innuendoes he didn't for one moment believe she had incited the brute. He'd known her for a long time; liked her shy retiring manner, air of quiet innocence, which covered a sharp brain and able competence. It was the reason he had encouraged her to organise the buffet. He had thought it would do her good, give her a chance to shine in public rather than hide her talents in everyday matters of commerce. How wrong he had been.

The woman gabbled at him for some moments, her nasal Cockney understandable from his years in London. It turned out Mrs Meredith had collapsed in a local Supermarket that morning and was taken to a hospital in Balham. They had decided to keep her in for further tests and sent a woman constable round to the house to tell her relatives. Mrs Watts had promised to inform Jessica when she returned from work that evening.

"I couldn't think where she was, regular as clockwork usually, never late like this." Her bright inquiring eyes peered at Henry. "*Looked like a lord, e' did, in his toff suit an' spoke ever so nice.*" she told her husband later, relating the event with glee. "*Called me madam, too.*"

"We've had an office party, that's why she's late. Thank you, madam; it was kind of you to take so much trouble. I'll see Miss Meredith gets to the hospital and no doubt she will let you know what transpires. Please don't let us keep you up any longer. Good evening, madam."

He turned to Jessica's door hoping his action would persuade the inquisitive neighbour to leave. Luckily she took the hint, bade him goodnight and retreated downstairs. He closed the door, leaned against it and breathed a sigh of relief at the fortunate escape.

"Can I come in?" he called from the small hallway.

Jessica emerged from a bedroom looking exhausted, hairbrush in hand. She had quickly changed into her usual dark navy clothes, wiped the tears from her face and blood from her legs, replacing the torn tights with fresh ones.

"I'm ready Mr Fowden, but please, you've done enough. I'm really grateful for your help but I'll get a taxi to St. James, it's not far. I'll be all right, really I will." She tried to speak in her normal tone but her voice sounded unnaturally tense with strain.

He shook his head. "I'll take you, Jessica. You've had more than enough to cope with on your own tonight. Perhaps when you get to hospital they could look at you, just to see if you really are all right? One never knows...he is not a nice person...he's been to all sorts of places mixing with god knows what kind of people..." he couldn't find the words to explain what he meant and her blank stare told him she was ignorant of his meaning.

"No! Please no, I couldn't bear it." she said harshly.

"Take it easy, nobody's going to make you do anything against your will. It was only a suggestion. Perhaps tomorrow you'll feel able to visit your doctor. Meantime we'll see how your mother is and I'll phone my wife. She'll wonder where I've got to."

"There's a pay phone in the hall."

"No. I'll ring from the Hospital." Henry imagined the temptation for listening ears in the flat below. "Right, if you are ready, let's go. Probably we'll find it's something simple like a fainting turn. At your mother's age they'd would want to make sure she's okay."

SIX

When they reached the hospital, they were told that the consultant in charge of the case would see them presently; he was tied up with an emergency and couldn't come straight away. Would they take a seat in the waiting room? Henry fetched some coffee and for a while they sat in silence. Gradually the place cleared of people until they found themselves alone. The large clock on the wall sonorously ticked out the seconds, sounding like the heartbeat of the building itself. Henry felt fidgety so to take his mind off the waiting he began to talk to Jessica; asking questions about her life with her mother and her younger days. Questions he would never have dreamed of asking had they been at work. In the office he had never felt the need even if there had been time to indulge in idle gossip. Owning a reticent nature he was rarely inclined to get close to people and supposed others were equally the same. Perhaps that was why both he and Jessica got on so well.

In the event, she answered his questions matter-of-factly, speaking like an automaton; precise, expressionless words coming out as though her mind was elsewhere and she physically gone, not connected with the present world; a robot in name if not in fact. She replied to his questions, and when prompted, revealed some of the details, but Henry imagined he was prying into an empty house while the owner was absent. He fell silent after a while, saddened with the knowledge of the struggle her life had been, wondering how he would have coped had it been him. His brain was now empty of queries; he only longed for this terrible night to be over and get to get back to the normality of his daily life. Jessica, feeling bewildered with the happenings of what was supposed to have been a triumphant day, had stopped thinking, her mind a blank, unable even to pray that her mother would be all right. So in that fashion they sat together, listening to the ticking of the clock on the wall, temporarily suspended in time, knowing there was nothing they could do to change matters or make it pass more swiftly.

Both of them rose with relief as the doctor came into the room and with a swift smile of greeting he held his hand out to Jessica, at once taking her cold hand in his warm grasp.

"Miss Meredith? Jessica Meredith?" she nodded.

"I'm Geoffrey Williams, Consultant in Renal Disorders. Your mother has been my patient since yesterday morning when she was brought in after collapsing while shopping. We've stabilised her condition but she is still a very sick lady so we have her in the ICU ward. This is a unit where we monitor very ill patients continuously until they rally."

"Oh dear!" gasped Jessica, turning even whiter if that were possible. This was far worse than she could have imagined. Why oh why hadn't she done something sooner. She ought to have been more caring instead of concentrating on other things.

"Come and sit down and I will explain things to you." invited the doctor, his eyes going to Henry who stood protectively behind Jessica. The doctor raised his eyebrows questioningly.

"I'm a close friend of Miss Meredith's," he volunteered. "I brought her to the hospital as soon as we found out what had happened." Close or not he knew she was the only friend she had at that moment.

"Good." he said with a smile. "I'm glad you're here. Jessica needs your support. There's nothing like a friend at moments like this." he turned back to Jessica.

"Now, Jessica, if I may call you that?" She nodded again. "Your mother was unconscious when she was brought in and showing signs of internal haemorrhaging in the area of the kidneys. We sorted that out, and then when we had her blood pressure under control, we gave her a scan to find out what was causing the trouble. Unfortunately, my dear, we've found a carcinoma. This is a type of growth. It lies near the problem kidney and there are also secondary or other small growths near the liver. We shall be doing more tests to verify our findings but the outlook is not optimistic at the moment. Sadly she has left it too long for radical treatment, although we will review the situation in the coming days. For the moment though, she is far too ill for either chemotherapy or radiography." He paused and sat quietly surveying the young girl; trying to assess her reaction to his discouraging explanation.

Jessica listened to his words, her brain numb with horror. Her poor mum, why hadn't she said something to her?

"I'm so sorry to be the bearer of such bad news," the doctor was speaking again.

She made an effort to concentrate.

"In these enlightened times we find it is far better to get it all said in the first instance and know the worst then afterwards every improvement is a bonus. I can assure you that we'll make every effort to give your mother as long as possible. Pop in to see her for a wee while then go home and rest knowing we are taking care of her. Is there anything more you'd like to ask, my dear?" Williams studied her taut face, baffled at the strange bruise on her cheek, but sensing now was not the time to ask. Was she mixed up with this so-called friend? Had he raised a hand to her? No. He doubted she would have come to the hospital with him if that had been the case. He was intensely aware of compassion for her distress knowing what lay ahead, for there was no way her mother could survive for long. This was a part of his job he loathed; having to give kinfolk bad news was never easy. But he could sense there was deep strength of character in her gaze. Yes, she was upset, but she wouldn't break easily, which was the reason why he had been so plain spoken.

Jessica stared back at him trying to hide her despair. She had been numb with exhaustion until now but suddenly every nerve was alive, painfully aching with worry. All she could think of was that she had been away when her mother needed her; wrapped up in that damned party, which had ended so disastrously. Only concerned at the time, with the praise she would reap for her efforts, her triumph was now turned to ashes and it all seemed shallow and meaningless.

"How long?" she croaked, her throat unexpectedly dry. She tried again. "How long is she going to live? Oh please, can I hope she has a chance of recovery?"

Damn it. She hadn't taken in his words. Oh well, she would realise soon enough. Now was not the time to emphasise what was going to happen. "It's too soon to tell yet, Jessica. As I've said the tests are not finished. Let's get the next few days over and your mother rather better than at present. We shall give her the best of care. I think she will rally now she is nursed." he took up her hand again, patting it gently. "Come now, my dear, show a fine brave face to your mother, she's been more worried for you than she is for herself."

Jessica's eyes, dry until then, brimmed over with tears as the doctor turned to Henry. Of course she thought, painfully aware of her mother's nature, Mum has always put me first.

"Take her to the ICU ward so she can see her mother is being taken care of then go home. I'll get a nurse to give her something to sleep. When she's had a rest, things will look better. But forgive me please, I have to go, we are extra busy tonight. Can you find your way to the ICU ward all right? It's on the second floor."

"Yes, we'll manage. And I'll make sure Jessica gets home safely. She'll be all right, she's a brave girl." Henry half-smiled as though he knew Jessica intimately, all the while conscious of taking in so little of the stranger he had worked beside for over three years. Relieved, the doctor nodded then hurried from the room. Through the door Henry saw a nurse waiting impatiently for him, a sheaf of folders in her hand. The doctor glanced at them briefly then whirled off up the corridor, his loose white coat flying out behind him.

Mrs Meredith was laying quietly, her eyes closed, amidst the whirring and humming machinery monitoring both her and the other patients in the Intensive Care Unit. Jessica stood silent, gazing down at her beloved face. She perceived the illness in her features. Signs that had gone almost unnoticed before, and berated herself for her careless regard. Then, unwilling to disturb her mother's rest she touched her hand gently before leaving quickly.

Her tears had stopped; but apart from the odd sob or two she didn't speak as Henry drove back to Streatham along the empty streets to her home. Her mind felt disorientated and unable to collect her thoughts in her usual tidy fashion. What was she to do now?

"Don't come into work tomorrow, or the rest of the week. See to your mother and I'll be in touch. Okay?" Henry's voice was very firm, almost reading her mind.

"What about the work for Everson's, it's needed this week for their MD to sign. I'm almost finished but I still have to put in the final figures..." she began, memory returning. "I'd like to see it through to the finish."

"Don't worry, I'll sort it. In the meantime, you've had a hell of a bad shock with your mum so poorly. You need to stay at home, rest, take things easy. You'll want to visit her tomorrow of course. Spend as much time as you need with her, get over the shock, work can wait for now. It's never easy when one loses one's parents. I was in pieces when my mum died."

She was in shock, not only with her mother, he thought viciously, but with that bloody bastard Mark; realising he wanted Jessica out of the way while he had angry words with Charles Welland. He couldn't think what he would say but by God it would come to him. Oh yes, he'd find explicit words right enough. And if Charles failed to act to put a stop to his son coming into the business then he himself would tell the police. Jessica might not like it now but it would be better for her in the long run. After all what was to stop Mark from bullying her into a liaison with him. The very thought sickened him. Yes. Charles would be coerced into following Henry's plan of action. A bit of blackmail like threatening the Welland family with the police might do the trick. Even so Henry swallowed to moisten a sudden dry throat filled with apprehension. Tackling Sir Charles would not be easy.

SEVEN

Jessica woke at her usual time feeling leaden and heavy eyed. Perhaps a reaction from taking the sleeping pills, she guessed, never having had to resort to them before. Surprisingly, the disorientation returned as she rose out of bed and crept into the kitchen, all at once realising how quiet it was, for usually her mother was up and pottering with breakfast. Now it was silent, no one to chat light-heartedly to or gently tease. She was all on her own and the realisation of this made her weep as though her heart would break. After she finished crying, Jessica went to the bathroom to shower. She caught her breath as she saw the remains of the pink dress lying behind the bathroom door where she had tossed it the night before.

It lay there like a beacon of dishonour reminding her so vividly of the shameful act that'd been forced upon her. She snatched up the garment hastily and going through to the kitchen thrust it into the rubbish bin to be disposed of later. Whatever the dress cost was meaningless. She would not keep the hated thing any longer. Her blithe words that it would be lucky haunted her mind. If only she had known beforehand just how unlucky it would turn out to be she would never have bought the wretched thing. A few hours ago she had taken the pills and retired to bed and oblivion. This morning the pain was raw and piercing; there was no place to hide. It did no good to think what might have been; she had to concentrate on what was. She would only be able to bear it if she closed her mind to the dreadful memory and focused solely on her dearest mum. Please God, help her to get well, she begged, she's all I've got in the world. She doesn't deserve to die like this.

Jessica stayed in the shower for a long time, scrubbing her skin until it hurt, but nothing could erase the sense of filth that clung to her. Large blue bruises adorned the white skin of her thighs and there were scratches on her arms. I look as if I've been in a fight, she muttered to herself, as she looked down at the abrasions. Then it came to her she had indeed been in a fight, a fight for her innocence and moral integrity; and she had lost. If only she'd been able to fight back, even to kill the bastard. Fury filled her until she felt physically sick. But if she'd killed him all she'd have gained from the act would have been punishment for committing the deed. People would have thought she'd encouraged him. No one would know the truth. Even her boss had looked wary after seeing her things scattered at the foot of the stairs.

Thank goodness her mother hadn't seen her disgrace. The bruises would be long gone before she got home. That's if she did come home. Again it hit hard that her mother's future might be short. The tears streamed from her eyes to mingle with the water as she sobbed once again. After she got dressed, she made coffee, then disguising puffy eyes and bruised face with make-up, left once again for the hospital. Down in the hall she had a few brief words with Mrs Watts, who was keen to prise from her as many details as she could, but Jessica managed to escape as soon as possible.

Her mother was awake this time and anxiously waiting for her. "Jessica love, I'm really pleased to see you." Elizabeth Meredith wiped tear-filled eyes. "You look tired, dear. You mustn't worry, you know, they are looking after me beautifully."

"Yes I know." Jessica smiled and took a seat beside the bed. Grasping her mother's hand she tried desperately to think of something cheerful and light-hearted to say. But the words stuck in her throat like dry chaff. Any moment the tears would flood her eyes. Come on, you idiot, think of something!

"You should be at work, dear, I really wasn't expecting to see you until this evening at the earliest. Don't take time off for me. Your job is much more important."

"Nothing is more important to me than you, mum. In any case my boss has let me have the day off. He's a decent man and ever so kind." Jessica explained briefly, shying away from any other explanations. At least her mother wouldn't see the bruises that covered her body.

"How did the party go? Was it a success?" her mother asked eagerly.

Jessica almost gave herself away. Success? Oh brilliant! Success for one person only. She managed to tell her mother all the right things she wanted to hear, firmly shutting her mind to the horrible ending. She even managed to make her laugh with some of the details. Who was there; who said what and to whom. The kind words from those who mattered. Oh it sounded like a story with a happy ending.

"I always knew you would do well at that firm, it won't be so hard for you when..." her voice trailed away though Jessica knew at once what the next words were going to be. Ready tears sprung to her eyes. Surely, the doctor hadn't told her mother she was going to die. How could she find the words to comfort her mother, give her reassurance?

"Oh mum, you're going to get better. Don't give up hope, darling, the doctor will get you well again..."

Then the watchful nurse came up and said brightly: "I think we'll have a little nap now, Mrs Meredith. Can't have you looking jaded for Doctor's rounds, can we?" she looked at Jessica and smiled. "All right, my love? See her a bit later, will you? With any luck she'll be going into a ward soon and you'll be able to stay longer."

Jessica said her goodbyes and went home. She walked about the flat aimlessly until a hollow feeling inside reminded her she hadn't eaten since lunchtime the day before. She had a sandwich and drank some milk then dozed in a chair till it was time to go to the hospital again. She was just leaving when the pay phone rang. It was Henry Fowden.

"I'm glad I caught you," he said. "I was going to leave a message. How's your Mum?"

"She was awake when I called but there's no change. They are going to do some more tests tomorrow but I'm sure they'll be useless. She looks real poorly. Anyway I'm rattling around here with nothing to do so I'll come in tomorrow. Fixing my mind on work will stop me from brooding, apart from the fact it will be piling up ahead of us."

"No!" said Henry quickly. "Don't come tomorrow. This is why I rang. I'll come and see you this evening, about 6 o'clock. That okay? Will you be home? I shan't stay long."

"Yes." agreed Jessica, puzzled at the unusual fluster of his voice. He was invariably calm and matter-of-fact, seldom giving way to bad temper and certainly never the kind of tantrum she knew the other partners indulged in. She loved working for him, and in return, knew he relied on her painstaking attention to detail. He was probably disorientated with her absence, for he was used to having everything laid in front of him that needed attention. Jessica had rapidly absorbed his likes and dislikes, and together they had become an excellent team.

Today, he had to rely on other staff and fitting in with their methods of working wouldn't have suited. Usually she guarded his privacy zealously and being a healthy person never took time off for ailments so for a long while he hadn't had to resort to strangers. Still, he oughtn't to have sounded so ruffled and upset. Frowning, she replaced the receiver and ran to catch her bus; she must not lose a second of her time with her mum, for soon she might not have her at all.

EIGHT

Henry sat at his desk in a daze after his call to Jessica, unable to believe his orderly brain was not reacting as usual. He couldn't seem to piece together all the events that had led to this morning's revelations and their impact on his own life. What the hell was he going to say to the girl when he saw her? More than that, how on earth was he going to sort his own life out? Was it only yesterday his world had been normal and uncomplicated? It surely wasn't now!

"Sir Charles isn't seeing anyone at all this morning; he is engaged in private business. Can you make it some other time?" the chairman's secretary, Marie Enright, responded to Henry's request to see Sir Charles in her customary unsociable voice, which defied a visitor to even dare to imagine they would be allowed entry unless she said otherwise.

"Tell him," Henry enunciated clearly, "It is vital I see him immediately, it can't wait." After a pause the answer came back as he expected; her tone unwilling as though she had been made to feel she was to blame for his persistence. "Yes, Mr Fowden, Sir Charles will see you at 10 o'clock sharp."

While he waited for the appointment he had a strange feeling he was the one on trial. How very odd. He had nothing whatsoever to reproach himself for. On the contrary Mark was the one facing the music. The previous night, late thought it was, Henry had not slept at all well.

He continually turned over in his mind the conversation he was about to have with his boss and he heard a clock strike five before his brain shut down and he slept. When the alarm roused him at seven thirty he was groggy and ill-tempered. Julia said very little though she glanced at him warily once or twice as he replied to her questions in a surly tone. Mentally shrugging off his moodiness as she had an early golf match to get ready for she merely put it down to over-indulging in the cheap champagne. Serve him right, she thought, he ought to know better.

On his way into work Henry once again reviewed his tactics. He knew Charles was a man to be wary of and one he had never crossed before. Still, in the light of such dreadful evidence what could the man say? He couldn't possibly condone such a serious crime. However, the certainty Henry had depended on was swiftly dispelled the moment he walked in Charles' well appointed place of work filled with elegant antique furniture that belied the term office. It could have been written in stone, it was so obvious. Charles had been told about the previous evening,
for the glowering scowl on his face said it all.

"If you're going to speak about last night, forget it. I've already had the gist of it from Mark. There's nothing more to be said. Now if that's all?" he paused, clearly waiting for Henry to leave straight away.

"No, Sir Charles, it isn't all. I have some comments I wish to make on the subject," said Henry, determined to stand his ground. "Your son attacked Miss Meredith last night in your office. It was lucky I returned after taking my wife home to make sure all was locked up here. I was appalled to discover what had happened to Jessica. If it hadn't been that she was so shocked I had to take her home, your son would have been in jail today, facing charges."

"Come now, Fowden, you are making too much of this. It's merely a misunderstanding."

"Oh?" said Henry coolly. "How extraordinary. This is the first time I've heard the word misunderstanding used as a synonym for rape. One learns something new every day."

"Rape? Rape! What d'ye mean rape? That wasn't rape! The girl was perfectly willing. In fact I'm most surprised how two-faced people can be when they get drink in them." Charles' face reddened with anger. "Drunk and disorderly, that's what she was; incapable."

"Jessica doesn't drink. Not ever and particularly not last night."

"That's not what I heard. **She** was doing very well on champagne. **My** champagne if you please! Why there was even a bottle and two glasses in here this morning..."

"Unopened, and the glasses dry. Yes, I saw them last night, and I might add, if I'd been able to persuade Jessica to inform the police of her outrageous injuries, your son would have been arrested last night on charges of grave assault and rape, and facing a prison sentence. In fact I've a good mind to go to the station myself, right this minute, to report it."

Charles glared furiously back as he retorted: "Rubbish! Absolute rubbish! You'll do no such thing if you know what's good for you. I don't condone using my office, I made that plain to Mark, but we can't have affairs like this from the staff, she must go at once."

"What?" yelled Henry, "You're not serious? Mark commits a criminal offence that could get him years in prison and you sack the innocent victim? Bloody hell! That's talking right off the scale of decency. Why that's downright outrageous to even think of such a thing!"

"Come now, Fowden, aren't you exaggerating?" all at once Charles held up his hand as Henry opened his mouth to protest again and touched his intercom. "Marie, would you bring coffee for two. Also hold all my calls for now, thank you."

Charles turned his attention back to Henry, fiddled with his tie, straightened his jacket then cleared his throat before saying, "Now where were we?"

"Sacking Jessica Meredith." Henry's voice was caustic, his face a thundercloud.

"Let's change the subject a moment. I'm going to let you in on some secret negotiations I'm having with - shall we say - a kindred spirit. You'd better sit down, Fowden, and listen."

Well, thought Henry, about time! Better than standing like a disgraced schoolboy in front of a headmaster. The scowl was still obvious but without replying, he sat in a nearby chair.

"As you know, Oliver Davis was never replaced in the firm after his death;" continued Charles, "his wife merely gets a pension for life. They had no children and she's almost eighty now. So I've been the sole owner of this Bank, to all intents and purposes, for some time. My so-called partners in the firm are mere figureheads. They have no real authority in decision-making policies. They only control their own departments as indeed you do. I'm at the point when I have to think of my future, how long I should stay here and when to retire. Now as you also know, I want Mark to succeed me. Handled correctly this is a sound business and it will provide him with a decent living. However, Mark has for some time been dragging his feet. Furthermore he does not yet have the knowledge to come in and take over. The world is in a state of flux. Recession is again rumoured; businesses are failing for lack of finance; companies are dispensing with manpower and one has to be alert and ready to swing with the tide." Charles paused and rubbed a hand over his face as though he was tired. Had the shock of his son's treachery got to him or was it something else?

"In fact," he continued after a moment, "Things have been tough and we can well go to the wall if wrong decisions are taken. After considerable thought and involved negotiations I am proposing to merge with another merchant bank very similar to our own. The owner, a man like me, has good instincts and is well respected in the City. The bank has long-standing clients, a most reliable history of stable finance, and young, experienced staff to guide the fortunes of not only their bank but also this place. It has been proposed to run the two banks autonomously but sharing the work load and hopefully extending our own list of clients."

Charles met Henry's gaze face-on and the two men eyed each other silently across the desk. Henry could read no warmth whatever in the icy greyness of the other man's stare, no feeling of unity for a working colleague, no compassion or sympathy, and his heart sank to abysmal depths.

What kind of a man had he ended up working for?

"In other words, each bank will have its own name and staff but will amalgamate in all other respects." The secretary knocked. "Come in, Marie."

His secretary opened the door and entered, carefully carrying the tray of coffee before setting it on a side table and serving the two men.

What was this merger going to do to him? *More responsibility? Or much less? More salary or redundancy?* Was he going to be pushed out of a job into the street? He felt nauseous as he thought of what might happen, what had happened to thousands of others in the recent years. What had he unknowingly walked into?

"I'll go further, but this is only for your own ears," warned the chairman after his secretary had gone. "Mark has been dating a young lady recently and co-incidentally she happens to be the daughter of the man I propose to merge with. You see our dilemma?"

"Yes, I see." And Henry did indeed see. And much more than that he saw his wife, Julia, and their two sons, Roger and Michael. The eldest was due to go to university in the autumn while the other would embark on his A-levels. The family lived well, had good holidays; golf for both he and his wife. Nice cars, clothes, they had it all. What was going to happen to them?

Giving him a moment to think he took a large gulp of coffee and in an instant it burnt his mouth and throat. Tears at once flooded his eyes with the pain but he dashed them quickly away lest the chairman thought him weak and upset over the news. Always a quick logician his brain considered the reasons behind Charles' statement.

Henry hadn't been blind to market forces. His very job precluded ignorance. The effect the former recession had had on the firm was very much on his mind these days, the sliding down hill, the inevitability of decreasing profits. Whilst he had been aware of the vagaries of world markets he had relied on Welland's being sufficiently stable to ride out any future storm should another downturn become inevitable.

Like a blow to the stomach he recognised from his tone Charles had kept secrets from him. He had been less than honest. The business had to be in a parlous state if he were contemplating mergers. Henry acknowledged he was scared of being made redundant; he'd watched the cutting back of staff creep nearer his desk in an alarming way. It was one reason he'd kept a low profile, biting his tongue before answering back when unjustly blamed for errors caused by other people. Charles must have thought the proverbial leopard had changed his spots when he heard Henry's violent denunciation of Mark.

"What will the changes do to me?" he had to ask; had to know the worst.

"What do you want them to do?"

Ah, here it was. Not blackmail spelt out in black letters but sly, greyish innuendo. Words within words. *Make what you will of them Henry, for Charles can deny them with a wave of his hand. And believe it, for he will do just that if it suits him.* A grim peal of danger rang loudly in Henry's mind. *What if he lost his job?* He shuddered and rubbed his hand over his forehead. Christ, he was sweating. Must be the coffee; his tongue felt blistered and raw.

"Well, Fowden? What do you think of the scheme? Are you prepared to join us? You are a very able accountant. I should hate to lose you..." The threat was apparent now.

"What about Jessica." He had to know what would happen to her. It was, after all, the reason for him being there. Surely she should have some justice for her dreadful ordeal

And Mark? This meant Henry must agree to say nothing and accept the scoundrel's appearance in the firm. *Or be sacked.* Where was yesterday when all that was on the horizon was a party? How he had looked forward to the event; feeling as a long-standing director it was equally as much for himself as the Welland's. Why hadn't he foreseen the disaster that lay up ahead? His stomach turned sour as he thought of sharing last night's toast with this villain.

Belatedly Henry thought of the underhanded dodges Charles had pulled since he had joined Welland's. Oh so well disguised one could never accuse him to his face, and certainly not an employee; but nevertheless Henry had seen them and, to his everlasting shame had kept quiet.

"Miss Meredith? Oh, we'll give her a sum of money to leave with. Say a thousand. No. Make it five hundred pounds. She might get the idea we're buying her off." said Charles, in his usual unsympathetic manner and displaying yet again his miserly character.

You rotten bastard! Of course you're bloody well buying her off! Henry never voiced the words he longed to say but the implication of them hung in the air like a huge poisonous cloud. "I think a thousand would be better." Henry said firmly. "Any less would be an insult."

"I don't agree. If anything, she has insulted us by her behaviour. But if we allow it I never want to hear from her again. Not ever, or my son. Understand? Any hint of scandal or gossip and I promise you she will regret it and so will you."

"I don't think there is the slightest chance of that happening, Chairman. I think she will be only too pleased to leave and hopefully put the dreadful event out of her mind. Thank you for the interview and also confiding in me. It's been most illuminating. I'd also appreciate being further informed as your plans come to fruition and sincerely hope it benefits the firm and me." Henry's voice was stilted and cool. Then all at once he felt a tightening pain across his chest that he'd never felt before. What was it? Not his heart surely? Hellfire not now! Not just at this minute when his future and his family's future were in the balance. His tongue and throat burned with fire as darkness loomed and the world swung dizzily around him. He waited a moment to recover before rising.

"Thank you, Henry; I'm glad you are with us." For the first time that day Henry saw a smile on Charles' face. "We look forward to better times for our company and ourselves, eh what, Henry, old man? I'm confident this merger will prove a turning point in the fortunes of the firm. It wouldn't do to have the merest hint of scandal touching any of our staff."

"Yes, I agree, "said Henry, "Scandal is nasty for anyone to endure."

"We shall be under the limelight facing a discerning and particular man. Mr Seager is most exacting. But why not? He owns a flourishing company and will want to ally with an equally successful business." Charles ignored Henry's pointed reminder of Jessica.

Henry knew it was useless to refer to Jessica again. He saw victory written in Charles face. His boss had won, hadn't he? Now Henry realised how stupidly futile his display of anger had been. Going into the lion's den like a warrior and coming out a mouse.

Charles rose, came round his desk to shake hands with Henry. Irrelevantly, Henry tried to recall when Charles had ever called him by his first name, then, as he found himself at the door, and each man parted to go about their affairs, Henry felt an icy shiver of dread race down his spine. Had he just made a pact with the Devil? And Jessica? What had he accomplished for her? A mere £1,000 pay-off? For what she had suffered? Where had all his fine aims of justice and righteous indignation got him? Ending as usual, grovelling to a man who would kick him out of the firm without a backward glance just as soon as it bloody well suited him.

His conscience cried out in despair, you coward! All he had achieved was to abandon her, leaving her dishonoured and jobless. And if he had kept his mouth shut? Why, the same thing would have happened, but minus any financial help. Knowing Charles, as he did, the man had no compunction whatever in disposing of unwanted staff. As for Mark, he would never lift a finger to help a girl he had used so carelessly.

Henry tried to rationalise his actions. He had achieved something even if it were only a parting sum of money. A thousand pounds was not paltry; particularly to a girl in Jessica's circumstances. So why did his conscience still trouble him? Caught between his job and his deep concern for Jessica he could see it was like being between a rock and a hard place. He had often smiled at the maxim and had used it carelessly and in fun many a time. Now at this particular time he didn't find it amusing. It was only too true.

NINE

Henry left the chairman's office and went back to his room. He felt sick inside and wished with all his heart he was back in Yorkshire, safely working in a small business where the work might be tedious and badly paid but at least his integrity would be intact. He wouldn't have this feeling that he'd been a complete traitor. Selling Jessica's innocence to keep him and his family secure, how low could one sink? Except, he'd had no choice at all. To start looking for another job at his age and at the same salary was expecting too much.

He thought of a quiet, low-paid partnership, an old friend from up North had offered him recently. Amazingly, he'd considered the offer, wondering if he should make a move. It would entail returning to his native Sheffield. His boys wouldn't have the same freedom with money, and Julia, what would she say about it? Would she even consider it? The answer to that, he felt, was a very definite no. She'd have to leave her friends and the bridge club, not to mention her place in the women's team at the golf club. *And* their lovely house in Norwood. He groaned out loud to himself in sheer misery. He really couldn't do it to them, but then neither could he face working for a man he was unable to trust; who would, as soon as it was politically possible, rid himself of Henry, who now knew too many secrets.

*   *   *   *   *

He was on time getting to Jessica's and as he stood on the step waiting for her to answer the bell, he felt the second stressful surge of pain across his chest. He would visit the doctor tomorrow without fail and ask his advice; all he needed was to take precautions. In spite of everything, he thought, when this blows over I'll get back to my routine and all will be well.

Jessica greeted him with a welcoming smile, looking much better it seemed, or was it merely a desperate hope that she did look better?

"Hello, my dear, how are you?"

She smiled again, this time rather wanly, her eyes full of repressed pain. "Come upstairs where we can talk comfortably." she said, and turning, led the way up to the flat.

"Would you like some tea?" she asked him once he was seated in the living room.

"No thanks, I've dinner waiting," he replied, feeling he wouldn't mind a whisky to bolster him up and give him a bit of courage.

"So what did you want to see me about?" Jessica was business-like. "It's nice of you to call but I really would like to get back to work. I can't concentrate unless I'm busy. I need the regular discipline to keep my mind occupied. I see my mother at visiting times but apart from that I'm hanging about here with nothing to do and I hate it."

"I saw Sir Charles today and we discussed the - er- the episode of last night." Henry ignored her words and began his speech. Words that he had rehearsed over and over again. Feeling pent up with the effort of getting it all out he eased his collar reflexively. This was almost as bad as confronting Charles.

Puzzled, she stared at him, a frown wrinkling the fine smooth skin of her forehead.

"Jessica, he takes Mark's side, which I suppose is only natural. Anyway after a long talk he has decided – well quite frankly - he wants you to leave at once."

"Leave?" her mouth dropped open in stunned, disbelieving distress.

"Look, my dear, I know this is terrible but you must see how dreadfully embarrassing it is for you, and would continue to be that way if you return to work and face the staff. These things have a way of getting out and whispers behind one's back can be so damaging." *And it would make it just as awkward for me as well.* "I'll give you first class references - you'll get another job – an even better job - you'll see - in the long run - it will be for the best..." sweat prickled his skin, bringing itching discomfort, adding to his embarrassed stress as he stumbled inanely over his words.. Oh dear this was every bit as unpleasant as he thought it would be. He seemed to be making as bad a job of this as at his interview with Charles.

"GET OUT! Get the hell out of here. Right now! I won't listen to you any more. Just get out." she turned away from him, hunching up her shoulders as though to avoid a blow.

Abruptly Henry stood up, taken aback at her vehemence. She had never spoken to him like this before. She was turning into a stranger before his very eyes. He felt marooned in the sea of emotion that ebbed and flowed around her. Never in his life had he been able to cope with irrational female behaviour, avoiding any confrontation like the plague. He paused, undecided, wondering how he could disentangle himself from what was turning out to be a messy situation, one he should never have involved himself in. He thought again that he shouldn't have returned that night. Then he wouldn't be implicated in this nasty affair.

"I've brought this for you. It's the best I could do. It's here on the table." He tapped the envelope. "It'll help till you get a new job. I hope your mum gets on okay. Goodbye, Jessica - I'm -I'm sorry about this but there wasn't a thing I could do...you can't possibly understand how things are...the changes that are to come...what I've had to agree to..."

She didn't reply, stood silent, rigid, as though he was invisible. Oh well, he had done his best. He couldn't do any more, could he? He'd tried hard to sort her out. And now she would have to come to terms with it herself. He fled abruptly downstairs, almost falling over in his haste. Back in the car he heaved a sigh of relief. She'd come around. People usually did in the end. Anyway, his part was over. He had to get on with his own life, protect his own family. He drove home almost with a feeling of light heartiness. Considering the circumstances he'd done quite a good job. She was really very fortunate; in his memory nobody had ever left Welland's after a sacking with money in their pocket.

Julia voiced her customary: "You're really late tonight, Henry, what is it this time? Why didn't you call? I hate not knowing where you are."

"Oh the usual problems. Too much work, not enough staff. I've had no end of trouble today." *Well that was true at any rate.* "But I'm turning over a new leaf, going to take things easy for a while. I'll have a check-up with the doctor, maybe take a holiday. That's a good idea; we'll both take a holiday. Go somewhere warm, how about it?"

She snorted derisively. "Take a holiday out of season? You? Why, you always wait until July. I'll believe it when it happens." they laughed amicably at the usual family joke.

"Seriously, Julia, there are big changes afoot. Can't say much at the moment but I have high hopes of great improvements in the firm."

"How interesting, Henry. I hope you are in for a raise. Just the thing we could do with. The house does need one or two things doing..."

"And if I'm out on my ear?" Irritated with her selfishness he scowled angrily at her.

"Don't be silly, dear. Charles is forever saying he can't do without you. What's up? Have you two had a spat? Is that the cause of the dismals?"

"Well, yes and no." He didn't want to tell Julia about the events of the previous evening. He hadn't rung from the Hospital and she'd been soundly asleep when he returned home. In any case he knew she'd be totally unsympathetic towards Jessica. Moreover, he would have to relate exactly all that had happened and she would chew it over piecemeal. He was too tired to indulge her. It was finished. At least, the part he had played in it, there was no more to be said.

"What does that mean? A yes or a no?"

"Oh, just over dry old accountancy."

"Huh, is that all? I'd forget it if I were you. You're always worrying about something.

Now I wonder if we can afford new curtains for the lounge?" she mused, hoping for a good response. But the acid reply warned her that now was not the time to indulge her fancies.

"Let's wait for the raise to come before you try to spend it all."

"Of course dear, I was merely daydreaming. I'm sure a holiday would be much better."

She retired to the kitchen to wait for his mood to change. Fortuitously she had cooked his favourite meal that evening. He'd be in a different frame of mind after he had eaten. Her mind roamed freely as she laid the table for dinner. Tomorrow she would visit the shops and look at curtains - just in case. The outside of the house also needed a coat of paint. All the other houses in the road had had their annual spring redecoration; it would not do to be labelled niggardly or lacking in *amour propre*. After all, she did have a position to keep up in the neighbourhood.

Henry went upstairs to change from his business suit to the comfortable casuals he wore at home. As usual he emptied his trouser pockets before hanging them up. He got a nasty shock when he pulled out Jessica's torn panties. Hastily glancing at the bedroom door in case his wife appeared, he crumpled the delicate garment and then shoved it in a trouser pocket before heading downstairs and out into the garden.

"Where are you off to? Dinner's ready for the table, I'm just going to dish up." Julia called out in an irritable tone, wondering if he was going to be difficult all evening. Charles must have upset him more than usual. He didn't reply and she watched him walk down the path towards the greenhouse and beyond, then with a sigh slid the plates back in the oven. She would give him a moment or two before she called him back. Tch! The neighbours must think he spent all his time at the bottom of the garden for she was forever calling him to come in for a meal.

Once out of sight of the kitchen Henry held the flimsy material to his nose and caught the scent Jessica usually wore. The floral fragrance reminded him he would miss her friendship. Unromantic as he was, he now and then had dreamily visualised other scenarios than married to Julia. Dreams of a different life, which could never have taken place anyhow, and now, with Jessica gone, would vanish, like smoke, from his mind.

He pushed the cloth between the sticks of garden rubbish he was going to light later that night. It would finally spell an end to the whole affair. A pity because he'd really liked Jessica. Henry little knew that far more problems were coming his way than losing his secretary.

TEN

The days passed slowly for Jessica who devotedly visited the hospital as many times as the nursing staff would allow. She was as loyal to her mother as she'd always been. She only came alive when she was sitting by the bed hoping to tease her into a smile. She knew it was no use, she could see the changes each day which showed the cancer was gaining ground and her mother slowly slipping away. She hardly cared about anything else at all; mail piled up unread, not even opened, housework was left. She only did the bare essentials to keep fed and clean. Sometimes she laid her head down on her mother's bed and snoozed while her mother slept the twilight sleep of the dying. The nursing staff left them alone, the curtains drawn round the bed. They knew it wouldn't be long and ached with sympathy for the poor sad girl who would be left bereft.

Two months after her admittance into hospital the phone rang at midnight, waking Jessica out of the light doze that was all she allowed herself at the flat. It was the night sister from the hospital. "Sorry to disturb you, dear, but I think you ought to come now."

"Yes, at once! I'll get a taxi. Be with you in about 20 minutes." She arrived in time to hold her mother's hand for only a few minutes before the sister ever so gently touched her arm.

"She's gone, my dear, be happy for her, she's free of pain now. She's slipped peacefully and easily away, as quietly and uncomplaining as she's been these last weeks. We've not had anyone as sweet-tempered as she was. You must have had a happy childhood, Jessica, she was a lovely person."

Jessica thought back to her early life and realised how lucky she had been. True, they'd never seemed to be free of money worries but as her mother sustained and loved her father, so she supported Jessica when she took over the role of maintaining the two of them. Sometimes, Jessica had railed against her fate, wanting to stay a child when the bills came in and there was no money to pay them, but one look at the crumpled, sad face of her mother and the angry words would die on her lips. She would hug her mum close and mutter consoling words.

The sister was still speaking and she had to wrench her attention back from memories that were painfully bittersweet and try to concentrate on what she was saying.

"Yes, I understand." and knelt down at her mother's side to pray. She looked at the dearly loved woman, lying so still. Her had face changed, the winkles smoothed out; free of pain and illness, assuming a freshness of youth not unlike her daughter. She looked serene and, Jessica devoutly hoped her spirit was now free to go to a better life. She would not weep for her mother, for tears could not bring her back, nor would she weep for herself, for she had shed too many already. She felt numb, frozen of thought. There was nothing left in her life, not a soul to care whether she lived or died, and she cared least of all.

She went later to the top floor where there was a low-lit chapel, silent and empty, but it gave no comfort. For the one person who'd loved her through childhood and onwards, guiding and urging her to a better life. was gone forever. She had lost her mother and there was no comfort for her anywhere. Even the gentle religion fostered by her mum was useless; no one knew how she felt, how angry she was with God to treat her mother so badly. That's if there was a God. However, she doubted it. Surely she wouldn't feel so desperately alone if there had been? Surely he wouldn't have been so cruel as to heap her life with so many adversities?

Jessica barely remembered the funeral. There was only her and the downstairs neighbour Mrs Watts to see the body laid to rest. There was no service apart from the local vicar saying a few words at the graveside. Even the pall bearers sloped off once the coffin was set down and the two men employed to lower the casket sat nearby talking of football scores. Jessica could hear them arguing as she tried to concentrate on what the vicar was saying. Not that it mattered, she thought, Mum will go to heaven anyway, if there is such a place. She'd been a good woman, gentle and kind to all. Always ready to help anyone. I'll miss her ways, her sweet loving friendship, she mourned, and then, as bitter tears slid in a torrent down her face, she watched the coffin slowly disappear from sight.

Jessica and Mrs Watts returned to their flats together.

"Course, most times one 'as a do after a funeral. Can be quite good, an' all." Mrs Watts sniffed, "Not much of a wake with only us two is there?" When Jessica didn't reply she went on. "Going back to work I 'suppose, now she's gone. They been ever so good letting you off all this time. Tell you what, ducky; you come into our place an' 'ave a sherry. Do you good, perk you up a bit. You bin looking right peaky lately. Course it's natural, you've had a bad time, but you gotta put it behind you. Get back to work and forget yer worries, that's what 'ol Watts says. Not that 'e 'as any worries, not as long as he's full up with beer!" She nudged Jessica and tittered exuberantly. "He's a one for a wake. Life an' soul o' the party, he is."

ELEVEN

Jessica felt stifled; she just had to get away. "Thank you so much for coming with me but I'd rather be on my own now if you don't mind. I think I'll take a nap; I didn't get much sleep last night. I feel dreadfully tired now it's all over. Yes, bed really is a good idea. See you later." her hurried words burst out spontaneously, completely ignoring the startled look on Mrs Watt's face. She had intended to indulge in long eulogies of the deceased imbibing her favourite drink.

Jessica raced off upstairs without waiting for an answer; not even caring it was only four in the afternoon. Her neighbour was left standing with her mouth open in comic dismay watching her disappear up the stairs.

"We-ll she's a rum 'un and no mistake; shouldn't be surprised if she goes round the bend or does something silly. Fancy not wanting to toast the dear departed." she muttered as she went to her flat. Very soon the sherry bottle was opened and she drank to her neighbour with fervour. Though truth to tell, she knew no more about the women upstairs than she knew when they had first moved in. Secretive they were, even old Watts remarked on it, and it took a lot to get his mind off football and beer. Mrs Watts poured a third glass of sherry, feeling the heat rise in her face and began to sing, "Here's to the dear departed. Long may they rest in peace. They were ever so nice when we knew them. So here's to their happy release."

She carolled raucously knowing there was no one close to hear a voice that grated on her ears, let alone anyone else. Still, who cares? She could always remember her mother singing those words or something like them. She tried to repeat them but her voice cracked. After another sip of sherry she found she had forgotten the words completely. Oh well, did it matter? She had sung 'em once. Nobody could say she didn't do things right, not nobody. Old Watts would laugh his head off when he heard there was only her at the wake.

*   *   *   *   *

Once inside her own flat Jessica leaned back against the door as she locked it. Thank heavens the world was outside and she was safely away from people telling her what to do, prying into her life where they had no business to go. Thoughts coalesced in her mind, thoughts that had slowly taken shape during her mother's illness, hiding themselves in the deep recesses of her mind until at last she would put them into practice. She had nothing to live for, nobody to care about and for sure nobody to care for her. Why struggle? Why not end it all? Simple all round for everyone. Perhaps by now the two casket men had resolved their argument and they'd deal with her. At least she would be beside her dear Mum.

She pushed herself away from the door, tossed her coat and bag onto a chair then hurried into the bathroom. Once there she searched a medicine cabinet taking out all the pill bottles she could find. Then she hunted through the kitchen cupboards where she recalled seeing a packet of aspirin and a few pain killers. What else did she need? Ah yes of course, Alcohol! The stronger the better; she ought to have that too. She had read somewhere it was supposed to add potency to the action of the drugs. She opened one cupboard after another but only found a tiny drop of sherry and a small bottle of Kummel. Perhaps she should have joined Mrs. Watts and drunk herself silly before actually taking her life. Not that she could bear Mrs Watts' chatter at the best of times and this definitely was not one of those. Then an idea came to mind and she went to a sideboard in the living room to investigate.

Ah, this is more like it – she was on her knees searching the recesses of the sideboard. At the back, hidden behind a pile of knitting wool she found a large bottle of brandy. She recalled her mother saying it was for emergencies only when they had moved into the flat. It had never been opened. Well this was an emergency if ever it was.

Jessica gathered the pills together in a heap. Bright red ones belonging to her mother - I wonder what these are for? I can't remember her taking them. Aspirins - unfortunately only a few. Plus odds and ends of long forgotten pills, which should have been thrown away ages ago. She tipped them all into a pile on the table. Assembled they made quite a multicoloured heap and for a moment she wavered in her intention. Was there enough to cause the oblivion she craved? Was she doing the right thing? Then deep grief rose up in her throat and hardened her resolve. There was nothing in this life for her from this moment on, nothing at all. The future stretched out before her filled with despair. No job and no mother. Without further hesitation she fetched a tumbler and opening the brandy she poured a large amount into the glass, filling it halfway. She smelt the heady spirit as she poured.

"Cheers!" she said ironically, before taking a deep swallow. Instantly she choked and coughed till the tears ran down her face. God! How dreadful! Her throat stung with the spirit and it was a moment or two before she could breathe properly. Incredible! She couldn't believe people actually enjoyed drinking this stuff. It was vile.

But soon, in spite of her reaction to the spirit, a strange intriguing glow began to spread from her stomach through her body, and her taste buds, unaccustomed though they were to the strong drink, relished the flavour. Gingerly she took another sip; hmm, not too bad if one took it slowly. She drank a little more as she eyed the pills with great disfavour. Oh well, no sense in prolonging it so she took up an aspirin. She had never liked taking tablets. When she was young her mother would crush them on a spoon and add jam to make them slide down easily. Even so she had hated the process. Later on, she avoided them altogether.

It took several swallows of brandy before she was able get down the first pill and she stared with dismay at the rest. This wouldn't do, there must be an easier way of committing suicide. She drank more of the brandy while she considered; enjoying the light-headed warm feeling. The best thing to do was to grind the pills together, mix them with plenty of water and pour the whole lot down her throat. It wouldn't taste nice but she must put up with that. Then she could swig the brandy until...well, until she fell asleep. At least that was the idea.

Jessica suddenly surprised herself with a giggle. Where did that come from? Shhh! This was serious! Mushn't laugh! Hic! Oops! She drained the glass as she muttered to herself then refilled it again slopping some on the table. Careful, musthn't waste it! She leaned forward to blot the puddle with a piece of paper lying close by then noticed the pile of letters that had lain untouched for ages, strewn untidily on the table.

She stared at the miscellaneous heap with bleary eyes. What were these? Letters? Bills? "Mutht leave my affairs in order, p-people think I-I not cap-able-ble" she said crossly. Then, "Whoops I shud have drunk brandy thish morning, feel mush better, don' min' whash happens. Hic!" she tittered foolishly. "Why did I say I d-don't dink – drink? S'wonderful! I'll sort these silly things out then..."

Slowly, fortified with sips from the glass, she began to go through the mail, putting bills to one side, tossing the junk over one shoulder to the floor. At the bottom of the batch was a thick, official-looking envelope. Jessica undid it slowly, swaying slightly with the effects of the drink. She'd never been drunk before, had no idea of the result of so much liquor on an empty stomach, or that the warm, light-headed feeling spelt dire trouble. Glancing at the envelope Jessica saw it wasn't addressed to her. Forget it, throw it away, you have to focus on important things, taking the pills, for one. Then something made her open it up and read the typed page inside, and then start all over again trying to concentrate on the dancing words:

Messers Parker, Rowe & Macfarlan
Queen Street
Glasgow
GA2 3JP
Scotland

28th May 2005

Dear Sir,

With our deepest sympathy, we beg to inform you that your father, William Angus Meredith has sadly passed away on the 30th March 2005. Unhappily, his death was due to an accident whilst engaged in exterior repairs to his property. The will he left with us some years ago now comes into effect and therefore you, his son, James Brunton Meredith, of 5 Fairhaven Grove, Chiswick, London are now his heir. You will inherit such monies and property as are his at the time of his death and after due legal process of probate has been granted. We would therefore be most grateful if you could contact us as soon as possible so that his estate can be finally brought to a close.

We respectfully remain,
Your faithful and humble servants,

M. D. Macfarlan
Messers Parker, Rowe & Macfarlan

This was a letter to her father. She giggled again as she thought of the postman tapping on his tombstone in Brompton Road Cemetery trying to deliver it and her father's hand rising up to take it. How amazing! After all this time of removal from their old house, the people who now owned it had actually remembered where to forward the letter. She shook her head in wonder at their thoughtfulness then wished she hadn't as the room swung around alarmingly and abruptly the ground rose and fell in sickening lurches. Oh this was awful. What was happening to her? She tried to stand up thinking that if she could open a window a breath of fresh air would revive her. Getting to her feet was a big mistake as she felt her stomach start to heave. She just made it to the toilet to throw up and spent the next long while being thoroughly sick. When she felt able she washed her face then decided she felt too ill to be bothered with anything at all.

Desperately tired and worn, Jessica crawled thankfully into bed, pulled up the covers and at once drifted off into the first peaceful and dreamless sleep she had had since the night of the rape. All was quiet in the house and street outside and gradually her mind relaxed from the anxiety that had filled her days and nights. From some inner core a process started to take place, soothing the traumas and fears. She would need all of that strength in the days to come but for now, asleep and unaware, her unconscious mind welcomed the therapy and began to heal itself. The rage and terror of the assault, combined with the awful grief of losing her mother ebbed from a mind that was naturally ordered and composed, and sleep did the rest, helping nature to accomplish the healing.

TWELVE

The next morning despite a dry throat and a suspicion of a headache, she rose bright and early and walked into the kitchen to make breakfast. The kettle had only just boiled when she felt sick again and had to dash to the loo. "It's that wretched brandy, she thought. I'll never touch that stuff again. She soon recovered and was able to enjoy her breakfast without more upsets. After clearing she walked into the living room and immediately saw the pile of tablets. A deep chill shuddered through her as she realised how close to death she had been. In fact if it hadn't been for getting drunk with the brandy she would have surely died.

"Only one place for you." she said out loud, and with grim determination swept them quickly up on a magazine, dumped them in the toilet and fiercely pulled the plug. 'How could I have been so utterly senseless? So I'm on my own? Well, tough, Jessica Meredith. You can manage, you know you can. You've done it before, you'll work; get a good job without anyone's help. Don't let Mum down with suicide!' She was ashamed at her fall from grace, not only for the attempt but getting drunk too. Yet if she hadn't made herself drunk she'd now be dead.

Putting the frightening thought from her mind, she began to tidy all her correspondence once more. Jessica read the one from the solicitors again, this time soberly and in the light of day. Unfortunately, she barely remembered the few scraps she had been told of her late father's background and her own early life. She recalled snippets of conversations she'd had with her mother who only enjoyed talking of her days as a dancer. Her father had been singularly uncommunicative about his early beginnings. All she knew was that William Angus Meredith was her grandfather, and he had quarrelled with his son James. Thereupon the son had left for London to find work and a new life. Once established James had met a young attractive dancer from one of the London shows and within a short while had married her, started a home, and soon a baby was on the way.

James was good with his hands so after a brief time of learning the plumbing trade with a local building firm he began to work for himself in maintenance, and then slowly advanced to general building work. The young couple moved into a small but pleasant villa in the suburbs, which had a large garden and a decent shed at the end from where James operated a business employing a few men, tackling larger renovations as he gained more experience.

For a long while, the business thrived and the three of them were a happy family during Jessica's childhood. When she reached her teens, James began spending more time in his garden workshop messing around with many short-lived inventions. All of which he was sure would rock the world but none got farther than the scrap heap outside. Frustrated, he began to neglect his business; lost orders; fouled up jobs; retreating more and more to inventing fanciful schemes and dreaming of being rich one day. He had never gone back home to Scotland to Jessica's knowledge, or indeed ever talked of parents or his early life.

Jessica had no idea where her grandfather's home was or whether it was suitable. To find out, she would have to go to Glasgow, sort things out there and then go on to William Meredith's place, which, she now presumed, by the laws of inheritance, belonged to her. Jessica wrote that day to the solicitors then waited with impatience for the reply. In the meantime, she did what she'd meant to do weeks ago and let slide, she called at the nearest Social Security to sign on and let them know she was unemployed. While she was waiting her turn she felt surprisingly sick again and had to rush to the toilet. It soon passed and she resumed her place in the queue.

I must have a bug or something, she supposed, presuming the effects of the brandy were over, perhaps a visit to the doctor's for a check-up would be sensible, and I'll throw out the rest of food from the fridge. Nothing but stale scraps left anyway. Maybe I've eaten something bad.

Doctor Malone was a kindly, overworked family man with beetling grey eyebrows, which he waggled at children to make them laugh. When he learned of Mrs Meredith's death, he had hoped Jessica would call at the surgery so he could tell her how he had suspected something was seriously wrong with her mother and had tried hard to persuade her to have tests. He prescribed for her but at the same time wanted her to go to the hospital for further investigations. But she'd been stubborn. Perhaps she thought it was already too late. He knew of cases where patients had known they were going to die ages before symptoms showed. His conscience pricked him as he had neglected to insist she saw a specialist straight away, but, as he reasoned to himself, his job was to give advice. If no notice was taken, what else should he do? He was overrun with work at the time and had said nothing more; neither had she returned. He made particularly sure this time he was meticulous with his examination and Jessica was quite surprised at his thoroughness. However, she so seldom had cause to visit a doctor she thought it was all part of the National Service treatment and a new way of conducting tests. She felt a momentary qualm that she may have picked up a virus that would be hard to get rid of.

"You've lost weight, Jessica, though it's quite normal in the circumstances. You must eat well, but sensibly and you will soon put the weight back. Though take care it isn't too much. It makes labour more difficult."

"Yes, I haven't been eating well." she admitted. "I spent such a long time at the hospital there wasn't time to cook meals so I made do with odds and ends, but I've bought some fresh food now." Then she paused, staring at the doctor. "Labour more difficult? You mean work."

"No. I mean labour. When you bring a baby into the world. You will have to look after yourself, young lady, for the sake of the infant, for I judge you to be around two and a half, maybe three months pregnant. Good wholesome food is what is needed to keep you fit."

"Pregnant? Me? Oh God, NO! Not that, please, not that!" she stared aghast at him.

He frowned at her then began to ask more questions till the whole sordid story was laid out in the open. Head bent, Jessica sat trying not to cry, turning and twisting a handkerchief in her hand. How much more could she take?

"Why didn't you come to me or go to the police?" he said gently; concerned at the amount of stress she was trying so desperately to hide. "You had every right to report him; he is a black-hearted unmitigated villain. Unfortunately the trail is cold, if you know what I mean? The man can and likely will deny it. You have no physical proof like semen to confront him with unless a court orders a DNA sample, and they don't do that unless there is a deal of legally responsible proof. Oh yes, you have proof of the pregnancy, but it could be anyone's child if he denies the fact. You follow?" He sat at his desk looking at her with sympathy. What a mess she was in. Where could she get help?

All of a sudden she nodded her understanding of the situation, her face pale, almost gaunt-looking from lack of food and the stress of her dying mother. Then she cried: "Oh, it's unfair!" Hiding her face in her hands she rocked back and forth in misery.

Malone looked at his watch; time for the next patient, and then visits to make. Thrusting a tissue at her he said in his usual rounding off tones: "Let me think about the problem for a while. I'd like to see you again tomorrow. Book an appointment with the receptionist as you leave. There is much to talk about and I haven't the time to spare at this moment. We need to discuss the situation thoroughly."

"I'm sorry, doctor, I've taken up too much of your time already. Thank you for seeing me." As though she could read the doctor's mind, which in the circumstances, had to be concerned more with all the difficulties that lay ahead, she recognised there was not much he could do to help her. So she rose and went towards the door. "I think hell happens on earth, not when one dies, don't you. It seems that way for me. I must be very wicked to earn this retribution."

She left him with a feeling of utter helplessness, which stayed with him all day. But he had an early call out to a child in the afternoon, a dying woman to attend to later and surgeries were full as ever, so it wasn't until four or five days had passed he thought once more of her.

"Did Miss Meredith make an appointment?"

"No, doctor, should she have?" said his secretary.

"Yes, I did ask her to return. I sometimes wonder why I bother to put myself out; no one takes any notice of me these days. I'm a pen-pusher not a doctor."

He shook his head in irritation. Maybe he'd give her a visit shortly. Silly girl, he could help her if only she would allow him. Fortunately, these days, he could solve her unwanted pregnancy, though it went against his principles. It shouldn't be a problem for Miss Meredith though she'd left it rather late and he'd have to make a good case for getting rid of the foetus. But when he was next in the vicinity of the flat and called to see her she was gone. Other tenants were busily moving their stuff in. There was no forwarding address.

THIRTEEN

Jessica returned home from the doctor's fully determined she was not going to let a baby ruin her plans. A new life lay ahead of her; nothing, if she could help it, was going to stop her taking advantage of the escape, which she could see opening up before her eyes. Where it would lead she did not know but take it she would and hang the consequences.

The day after her visit to the doctor a letter came from Glasgow with instructions to phone at a certain time to speak to the partner who apparently had charge of her grandfather's effects. Jessica made arrangements with him to go to Glasgow the following Tuesday which would give her four clear days to pack her things, pay bills and leave the seedy little flat that she and her mother had called home for nearly five years. She was more than glad to abandon it.

It didn't take long in the end; her mother's clothes went to Oxfam, larger items in a crate to be stored till she was able to send for it, and her clothes and personal things into two suitcases ready to leave. Only the landlord's possessions were left - furniture and such items that went with a rented flat. She and her mother had lost so much paying off her father's debts, losing the house and almost all their furniture that in the end few of their belongings remained.

Her grandfather's legacy had opened up another world. She was determined to move herself bag and baggage into a new life with a fresh beginning. The more Jessica thought about it the more determined she felt it was the right thing to do; no one would know her, she could begin once again to carve out a new future for herself. She gave not a moment's thought to her child's future, either bearing it or bringing it up. But Jessica wasn't stupid, she was sure there were plenty of finance places in Scotland where she would get a job. If her grandfather's place wasn't suitable she could always sell it and move where she wanted. The thing to do was to get the will probated then she would be free to decide. For the first time in months she actually felt excited at the prospect then a feeling arose that she was being disloyal to her mother. In an instant it vanished, she relaxed, her mother would never begrudge her any happiness she could find for herself and Jessica hoped she was happy too, wherever she was. She paid a last visit to her grave and after telling her mother all her plans she came away strangely comforted for the first time in ages. She didn't know when she would return but it didn't matter. Wherever she went, she would always carry her mother's love with her.

~ SCOTLAND ~

FOURTEEN

Jessica's head slid down from the headrest until her cheek touched the cool glass of the window and she awoke. She was getting used to the periods of acute tiredness when come what may, she had to close her eyes and rest. The last two days in Glasgow had proved particularly fatiguing so no sooner had she settled herself in the West Highland train than she had fallen into a sound sleep, the slight swaying of the train soothing in its regularity.

"Have ye had a guid wee drowse, hen? Ye must hae been awful tired, ye went off afore Helensburgh, ye've missed the first o' the mountains and look yonder, there's the top end o' Loch Lomond, visitors dinna miss yon picture, and it's such a bonny sight."

The elderly person, who sat opposite, had a cheerful smile on her red-cheeked face and a glint of curiosity in lively brown eyes. Jessica was glad she had woken up if only to hear the softly spoken brogue of the Western Isles, a dialect, which was so different from the rapid, sometimes, peculiarly unintelligible speech of the Glaswegian. Jessica had needed to strain her ears to catch all the complex instructions given her during the period she spent with the partner from the law firm, so by the time she left she felt it would have been quite appropriate to have had an interpreter.

Yawning self-consciously, she sat up and gazed at the magnificent stretch of water spread out before her, the sunlit ripples dancing and gleaming as though made of pure beaten gold.

"It's beautiful," she agreed, and then looked through the other window as the train skirted its way round a huge green and purple mountain that towered high in the air, a dark passing cloud giving it a sombre look. She saw rocky ravines, and stretches of grass with rhododendron and purple heather. Yellow gorse bushes on the steep hills clung tenaciously to the scant soil.

"Tha's Ben Vorlich, he's a big yin, but there's bigger than that to come, ye ken. You're into the mountains now, hen. They're a braw sight, ye ken? Ye'll enjoy yer holiday, nae doubt."

They talked the inconsequential chat of companion travellers, whilst the train pulled, every now and then, into tiny stations immaculate in their tidiness. The window was open and Jessica could hear the cheery exchange of voices of those being met from the train or those who recognised a friend and a pang of longing went through her. There was no one to meet her, no one who cared a tuppenny piece whether she lived or died. Jessica had never felt so completely

deserted in her life. For a moment, sheer desperation filled her mind then recalling the dreadful episode with the pills she shook off the feeling with determination. Courage girl! Come on, where's your courage?

They reached Crianlarich where the old woman was to change trains for Oban. She wished Jessica well and hoped she would have a happy holiday and enjoy herself. God, if only she knew, thought Jessica, - I'm unmarried, pregnant, all alone, I have little money of my own, - for she didn't count her grandfather's savings, nor did she reckon on the thousand pound cheque she had found lying on the table when she regained her senses. Vaguely she had recalled Henry Fowden leaving an envelope for her, but on opening it had been taken aback at finding such a huge amount. It was made out in his handwriting, but it bore the name of Welland and Davis.

She was about to rip it up and discard it, but with a grin she stopped; amused at the thought of Sir Charles biting his nails in anguish to part with so much cash. It struck her as comical and she laughed till the tears ran and the sobs took over. She opened a new account for the money, vowing she would have to be very desperate to touch a penny but at least once the cheque was cleared Welland's would never have the use of it. She felt a vindictive satisfaction for an instant then swept the thought from her mind and forgot about the money.

Holidaymakers replaced the old woman and Jessica turned her face to the window as the train proceeded slowly northwards, while she recalled her incredible visit to Glasgow.

∗   ∗   ∗   ∗   ∗

She arrived at Glasgow Central Station late on the Tuesday evening, and met by a junior clerk from the law firm. He dropped her off at a small hotel near the University, where she retired to her room too tired to take more than a glass of warm milk and a wheaten biscuit, which the night porter brought up to her. The bed proved very comfortable and it wasn't long before she fell into a sound sleep.

The next day Jessica lay luxuriating in bed, marvelling at the strange transition from the small cold flat she had left without a backward glance, to this supremely comfortable bedroom with an en suite bathroom, where she now found herself. Then the usual sick feeling warned her to use the kettle facilities and make tea and eat a biscuit before she did anything else. This time the morning sickness was temporary and she was showered, dressed and downstairs to sit in solitary splendour at a small table in a sunlit window, ready to eat whatever a young waitress could persuade her to take.

Ten o'clock arrived and so did Derek. Jessica was driven through busy streets lined with ancient buildings, pleased to be entertained by the light chatter of her attentive escort.

"You'll not have been to Glasgow afore this I would guess, Miss Meredith? Of course I know you are used to a big city but d'ye not think this is a braw old town?"

"Indeed, it looks very pleasant." She agreed, for politeness sake, but she was tired of cities with their dirt and hustle. Privately she longed for fresh air and open country. She hoped her grandfather's place was not in the midst of another town. A small village would be perfect.

Presently, after a short wait, Jessica found herself ensconced in a leather chair midst a dusty chamber, surrounded by law books that had never been moved in aeons. The grey-haired man she faced looked as wrinkled and dreary as the rest of the room. His black business suit shiny with age appeared tired and crumpled almost as though he had slept in it.

After shaking her hand and seating himself behind an old-fashioned partner's desk, Mr Macfarlan surveyed her quietly for some few moments then noisily cleared his throat.

"Now, Miss Meredith, have you proof you are who you say you are? We have to ask, of course," he clarified. "We live within the bounds of many rules."

"Of course. Here is my Birth Certificate and my parent's. A cheque book and this is my old rent book."

He examined the items. "I think that's quite satisfactory, unless you have photographs?"

"Yes, here's one of my Mother and I, and this is Dad as a young man." She paused as she passed over the photo of her mother but the solicitor ignored the emotional break in her voice. After a moment's study he glanced at her.

"Have you any other relatives?"

She shook her head. "No. There is nobody else. My mother was an only child and all her relatives are dead."

"I see. May I ask what your future plans are? Do you, for instance, intend to sell your grandfather's farm?"

"Farm? My grandfather has a farm?" Her voice was full of surprise.

"Yes, didn't you know?"

"No. I hadn't a clue. My father was very reticent about his parents or his youth, come to that; somehow we never discussed matters concerning his family. Your letter came as a surprise. But I am eager to know about my forebears, especially now my mother is gone."

Andrew Macfarlan rubbed his chin reflectively.

"I don't know a lot, I'm afraid, our senior partner, who is dead now, dealt with the original will which your grandfather rescinded then for some reason reinstated some years later, which was why we had a record of your old address."

"In fact, to my surprise, the letter was forwarded from there to our flat."

"I see. That was very fortunate for you and ourselves as we like to clear outstanding cases tidily. May I presume your father and grandfather reconciled their differences?"

She shook her head. "I don't know. Perhaps they did, but I was never aware of it. My father lived entirely in the present and was not given to speaking of his youth even when I asked him the odd question." How aggravating it was not to remember any past conversations. Though in the event there had been so few she was certain nothing had been mentioned in her presence about her grandparents, where they lived or why her father had left them. His head anyway was always in the clouds thinking of his next achievement which was always going to make their fortunes and her mother had never instigated talk of the past.

"Where is the farm?" Curiosity was getting the better of her. Why didn't he get on with it and tell her. This was going to be her future home. Lawyers were always damned long-winded.

"Miss Meredith, if I were to say 'the back of beyond' it wouldn't mean a thing, neither will Kinlochhourn, lassie. Come over here; let me show you on this map." He rose and went to a large wall map of Scotland, full of pinpricks, scuffs and stains but still reasonably legible, despite its deep yellowish nicotine stained surface.

"Here is Invergarry, you see?" He pointed to a large settlement between Loch Ness and Loch Lochy. "Now you take this road out of town and follow the track, which is only a narrow, mostly rough trail alongside Loch Quoich to Loch Hourn.   Where those tiny squares are, got it? Well that's Kinlochhourn, at the head of the Loch. All the area from there to the sea is forest, or in a few places, grazing land for sheep. One of the most lonely places in Scotland, I believe. Not many roads and what there are can be very difficult to drive on, especially in winter. I didn't call it the back of beyond for nothing!"

Jessica stood for quite a while looking at the map. The contours were plainly marked and she could see for herself there seemed to be vast areas of deserted land, either of water or forest but no habitations whatsoever. Was this where her father had been born?

"Oh." Jessica said doubtfully, and then she pointed out a spot, "Is that a village?"

"Lord Bless you, no. There's nothing but the farm or the odd shepherd's hut. Used to be a few houses at Skiary further along but that's mainly deserted, some of it in ruins, most of the folk there gave up and left because the living was so poor and the fishing dropped off. No, lassie, I'd forget all about it and sell it as quickly as you can."

"Who to? And why should I sell it without seeing it? After all it's the only home I have now. I won't do anything about it until I've lived there for a while."

"I see, but what will you live on, child? I noticed your account wasn't overflowing."

"What did my grandfather live on?"

"Well, he had his pension and the sheep..."

"Then I'll run the farm and learn to keep the sheep. Where are they? Just left to roam?"

"Good lord no, lassie. One has to keep track of these livestock. The chap who wants to buy the place is caring for them at the moment. Apparently your grandfather agreed to sell the farm to him just before he died but wasn't able to complete the contract. He would like to go ahead, if you are agreeable? It's a lot better prospect getting some cash in your pocket, and then you'll be able to live where you want. The highlands are no the right place for you, lassie, believe me."

The old devil, he was just getting round to persuading me to sell. Probably had his fee all ready sorted with this person. They will just have to think again because I am not selling. That is my inheritance and if it was good enough for my grandfather then it will be all right for me. And, Mr-Senior-partner Macfarlan, I think you are one tricky lawyer. Just don't play tricks with me. Aloud she spoke clearly leaving the lawyer in no doubt she was very determined on her own course of action. "Mr Macfarlan, I would like all the papers to do with grandfather's estate that you have. I'll leave tomorrow when I have the travel arrangements sorted out. I doubt I'll need to book a seat."

"My, my, you are in a hurry. There's the probate to finish, which hopefully will be ready for signing in the morning, if we can fit in the necessary typing, but I've a suggestion to make if you're intent on seeing the farm?" She nodded, wondering what other persuasions he would use.

"Go to the outfitters in Argyle Street, kit yourself out with practical gear and Fell boots. You are a smart young woman but Highland weather takes no notice of style. It is gie cold and wet even at this time o' year. You'll shiver even in the sunshine. Take my word for it."

"Thank you that is a very good idea." Jessica smiled at him.

"Your hotel is booked for the two nights. I'll see you back here at ten o'clock in the morning for your signature, in the meantime I'll phone Mr Fraser to meet you at Spean Bridge -"

"No, thank you. I prefer to make my own arrangements and travel in my own time scale. All I need are the deeds to the farm; you to be done with your probate and our business will be complete. I would rather wait until I have seen the property before making a final decision. I'll not do anything until I've had time to think."

"Very well, Miss Meredith." His lips were tight with aggravation; obviously his grim words of warning had not got through to her. "We shall leave things until you've had a wee look at the place, but, ye ken, a little nest egg wouldn't come amiss rather than you being marooned in the lonely mountains at your young age, hmmm?"

Jessica nodded her agreement and stood up. She hoped he was only trying to be helpful, after all he must know the situation at the place, and maybe he was just trying to warn her not to tackle the impossible. Whatever, she would find out when she reached the farm, but she would make her own mind up, not be coerced by someone else. If there was one thing she had learned in the last few years, and particularly just recently. It was to fight hard against being shoved in a direction which served someone else's interests, not her own; from now on nobody was going to take advantage of her, she'd see them in hell first.

FIFTEEN

Jessica had an early lunch then went shopping. It's not before time, she thought, for already her expanding waistline was causing discomfort. Picking out two pairs of maternity trousers, two thick voluminous sweaters and a pair of gloves, waterproof Fell boots and a padded rainproof anorak, which would keep out any weather Scotland chose to toss at her pleased her immensely. So did the finding of an underwear shop to buy a few more essential items. Then she invested in toilet preparations. Likely there wouldn't be a ready available chemist close by, which reminded her that she needed to consider another practicality. The warm weather was holding well and streets were filled with people in light clothing, some of them looking as if they were on walking tours, with their shorts, heavy boots and backpacks. It jogged her memory that she had no idea where she might end up and it was as well to be prepared. She decided she could do with a sleeping bag in case she was stuck for a bed. If conditions were primitive then she would be well prepared. Her shopping took most of the afternoon and when Jessica returned to the hotel she was exhausted. She rested until it was time for dinner then returned to bed shortly after, to sleep until the morning sun and an empty feeling woke her.

Following breakfast Jessica packed up the few toiletries she had used and leaving her luggage at the hotel to be collected later made her way back to the solicitors by herself, feeling freshly optimistic in the bright warm sunshine. She felt a thrill of anticipation run through her; this was an adventure and she had not encountered many of those in her young life, she was going to make the most of it come what may.

After a brief wait as a typist concluded the paper-work, she joined Andrew Macfarlan in his office to execute the final matters beginning with her going through a list of her grandfather's possessions, chattels, house and available land.

"When was this done?" She asked, having cast her eye over his hand-written will.

"Your grandfather probably did it some time ago when he originally made the will, or so I'm told by the chief clerk. He has been here many years and would remember."

"So you personally don't know if what is left is the same as in this previous inventory?"

"Och, it's bound to be, nothing much changes in the Highlands, Miss Meredith, not in these farming Crofts." He rambled on for some minutes about the farming traditions in that part of Scotland until Jessica stirred impatiently, interrupted and returned to the matter in hand. She learned her grandfather had left her about two thousand pounds after his minimal debts had been settled. The Croft was freehold and there were long established grazing rights in the surrounding countryside, secured for the farm for a lifetime, providing it stayed principally with sheep.

"What about funeral expenses, did you pay those?"

"Well, no, I believe they were paid from monies he had in the house, though I'm sure Mr Fraser would have had a hand in it as he was there at the time. They were very good friends, you know. Mr Meredith thought verra well of him. He was shocked with his accident, ye ken?"

Macfarlan appeared a tad uneasy, indeed became more so, shifting noisily in his chair, when she picked up a paper she recognised as being the Statement of Account from the law firm.

"What's this?" Though she knew quite well.

"Och, that's our fees for services rendered, it's all quite in order and doesn't come out of your money, it's quite separate, it's all been properly taken care of." he added hurriedly, bending forward to take the paper from her hand.

"But it's for fifteen hundred and forty pounds! That is a great deal of money!" She held on tightly to the paper, her eyes narrowing significantly with her knowledge.

"Aye well, that's the way of things."

"No, Mr Macfarlan, it is not the way of things! You have neglected, maybe for obvious reasons, to itemise your costs separately. Which, as far as you are concerned, are negligible, for apart from picking me up at the station and sending notification to London there is nothing else at this particular time your firm physically or monetarily carried out? Agreed? Or is there anything else you have omitted to tell me? You have not done a recent inventory nor compared results. You did not pay my hotel expenses, I did. Did you think I would be so naïve not to notice the fact? You had nothing to do with my grandfather's funeral and as for sending a letter to London, I'm sure you knew, or thought you knew, it might never be answered. You must have been rather taken aback when I appeared on the scene. I think we shall record these facts on the Statement of Account and send it through to the proper authorities. Following that, I am sure they will make a detailed search of all your records and come up with a few unexpected answers. Certainly a charge of fifteen hundred and forty pounds will be at issue. In addition, believe me, I will contest every penny. Furthermore my experience tells me that there may be other monies which you have knowledge of."

Macfarlan opened and shut his mouth several times but the words were stuck, unable to get out to refute the awful charges this woman was implying, which he knew to be true. He had no idea she knew so much, she could make a lot of trouble for him. He thought of an accusation from another client, which had earned him a warning from the Law Society not to transgress again, and hurriedly changed tactics. The sooner he got rid of her, the better for him.

"In view - er harrumph" he choked, swallowed and began again. "In view of the er - small amount your er - your grandfather left you, I'm prepared to forgo our usual – er - usual fees and - er just charge you thirty pounds. Plus VAT of course!"

"In that case our business can be finalised." She agreed abruptly, without a trace of a smile. She walked away from the solicitors feeling amazed that she had managed to outwit his greediness, thinking with great pleasure of the horrified look on his face. Serve him right. The final cheque included two and a half thousand pounds more than the lawyer had first mentioned. He had shrugged at her raised eyebrow but said nothing not even when she asked for a draft for the instant payment of money into her account. She had hastened to the nearest bank and a short while later arranged everything to her satisfaction. Despite the expert knowledge she had gained in her London job it had still taken all her courage to remain cool and contained, never once losing her temper even although she had given the impression of being very angry. That she had stopped the theft of precious money from the legacy was not as important as demonstrating to her satisfaction that she had the ability to survive. It gave her some hope for the future, whatever it might turn out to be.

SIXTEEN

The train wound its way ever northwards through the Grampian Mountains, filling the eye with the splendour of the surrounding peaks, tumbling waterfalls and fast flowing streams, with fascinating glimpses of huge lochs and areas of forest land. At Rannoch Moor the land opened out to a flat terrain which at first sight looked to be ideal for walking but was in fact a vast desolation of bogs, pools, lochs, stagnant water and squelching marsh that would be a nightmare to any hiker. It exuded loneliness under the cover of dark sullen cloud and Jessica shivered, suddenly oppressed by the brooding solitude. There was a great deal she needed to learn about this northern country full of unpredictable changes. How would she manage to cope by herself?

Her thoughts went back to Macfarlan and her final dealings with him. She had walked away from the office in a daze, filled with enormous surprise at her boldness in tackling him head on. She had been angry at his duplicity, which had given her the courage to face him but not so angry she had lost her wits. Instead she had beaten him at his own game of precise legal terminology and won. She hadn't served the last three years in finance without picking up a great deal of legal knowledge, especially as she had been lucky enough to handle work for local law firms. It helped to convince Macfarlan she knew more than was the case and because he was caught blatantly overcharging, his other sins of omission were written clearly on his face for all to see. By rights she knew his services, such as they were, should have cost her more, but she was unrepentant. Serve him jolly well right.

It meant, with the legacy, the extra money squeezed from Macfarlan and the four hundred she had brought up from London, which was all she had in the world after her mother's funeral:

less the hotel bill, the shopping and rail fare which took it down to a mere hundred and seventy pounds, she had in total, four thousand, six hundred and seventy pounds to live on till she had the baby, learned how to farm sheep and maybe keep chickens? No need to worry. I am rich! And I might even get social security money as well, she speculated, though maybe perhaps one doesn't if they consider I'm self-employed, if I really can manage to cope with sheep. Anyway, I'll think about it later. Contented, she stared out at the range of sternly forbidding mountains as the train chugged slowly up the pass between their soaring heights, lost in admiration at the scenery. I really am having an adventure; she thought with glee, almost hugging herself with excitement, it's improving all the time. I can hardly wait to see my grandfather's house.

Jessica left the train at Spean Bridge and joined fellow travellers on a bus to Invergarry, the nearest small town to her destination. The time was getting on for five when they reached the white painted houses, dotted here and there with grey-brown granite, lending a pleasing contrast. She was feeling exhausted again and knew it would be wise to seek a meal and a bed for the night as she still had a long way to travel and as yet no idea how to do it.

The tiny cottage that offered a room was pure heaven. That there were still some pleasant people around was proved in no small measure from the highland welcome her hostess, Mrs Fiona Stuart gave her. Later that evening, she curled up in a cosy bed, after a meal of Scotch broth and a Mutton Pasty, served by the garrulous motherly woman who chattered happily on without stopping. When she went to bed that night she felt comforted and the loneliness retreated to the edges of her mind and was soon lost in the depths of a feather bed. She fell asleep in the tiny low-ceilinged bedroom feeling safe and happy.

*　*　*　*　*

"Ye're going whaur? Kinlochhourn? Whit ever for? Thon's one desolate place, lassie, ye mon bide here awhile with me. There's mair than enough to see round this toon o' Invergarry."

"The farm there is mine, Mrs Stuart; I inherited it from my grandfather."

"Wully Meredith? You're Wullie's granddaughter? Well I never! I knew he was dead, but I thocht his partner was taking the place, well I never! Whit a surprise, lassie! Why ever didn't ye say before? But for goodness sake, darlin', ye dinna look old enough to inherit anything."

There it was again, this unknown man seemed to have wormed his way into everything. Who was he anyway? Someone who thought they could take advantage of an old man? Partner indeed! She must speak plainly about partnerships when she eventually got to see this stranger. She listened to Mrs Stuart's suggestion of how to get to the farm caught between feelings of weird surprise that she couldn't just get a local bus to take her where she wanted to go.

"So I'll hae a word with Andy Keiller," she continued, "he runs the country post, does all the deliveries round here, fetches and carries like a hero. He'll take ye, never fear, he won't mind a passenger, he does it all the time. .Now we have to get you sorted with a box o' groceries, for yon young man out at Kinlochhourn wil'na ken apples from pears in a pantry. Likely he's aye living on thistles and tatties. I will send to Maggie at the shop, she will do an order fer ye, hae it ready fur ye ta gang awa with Andy. Now I canna mind what Wullie did fur the bedding' - I'd better find you something comfortable, ten to one he never bothered for himself."

"Don't worry, Mrs Stuart, I'll manage, I've bought a sleeping bag with me as I didn't know how things would be. Truly, I'm fine, but you're so kind to ask. I do appreciate it."

"Think nothing of it, lassie, I'm pleased to help. You look kind o' peaky to me, still, you mon be too long there, come back and stay with me, I'll feed you up."

There was no turning off Mrs Stuart so Jessica held her tongue and let her ramble on asking and answering her own questions till she waved her goodbye from the safety of the local mail van, which was nothing like the smart red vans of the London Postal Service. It was piled high with crates and boxes of all sizes leaving very little room for passengers. She squeezed in beside a woman from a house a few miles away who had come in for a tooth pulling. In a way Jessica was relieved her mouth was so swollen she could not ask Jessica any questions. The poor woman sat in misery holding a cloth to her face, rocking with the motion of the bumpy van.

Jessica was tired and glad to stay quiet and listen, as Andy Keiller recited scrap after scrap of all the gossip in the district for the benefit of her neighbour. He had such an inexhaustible amount it rolled out like a news bulletin. After the woman was dropped off he looked over at her with an enquiring eye and began to talk again, this time with an end in view.

"You're from the South aren't you? What brings you way up here?"

"Mr Meredith was my grandfather." Her accent had obviously given her away.

"Come to sell the family home, have you?" He grinned at her cheekily.

"Why should I sell?" Her voice was terse. Perhaps something was wrong with the place?

Why did everyone expect her to sell?

"Come away, lass, ye're never goin' to live there?" He scoffed, still in a teasing voice. "Way out in the backwoods miles from anywhere? Thon's a gye lonely place."

"Why not?" Jessica parried; a tiny worm of disquiet chilling her at his description.

"Well, there's nothing to dae, only sheep to watch, nobody to talk to 'cept Luke an' he don't talk much, you'll go daffy in a month. Och no, it will only tak' a week at the most," he grinned again, amused at the thought. "Ye'll be clamouring to get back to civilization."

"We'll see." She replied briefly. No one was going to make her give up now. No way.

The postman went silent for all of five minutes before he began again. While the van bumped over the ruts Jessica learned of how it had once been a road through to the Isles but had been bypassed and forgotten by the new road to the north of them. At one time there had been an old staging post at Tomdoun, now vanished like so many of the notable spots. Some had been erased by the severe clearances early in the nineteenth century and later by the advance of the technology and chances for the Scots to leave their land to seek prosperity elsewhere.

"This place is full of history, isn't it? Almost a complete civilization banished and cheated of their birthright through the greed of their so-called English landlords. No wonder there was so much fighting in the past in this area. The Scots were always being blamed for being unruly and warlike but I can understand now I've seen this area what it must have meant to them to be driven from their land. And now it's left desolate when it could have been a thriving area." Jessica replied contemplatively, remembering the lessons she had at school.

"Aye, but people can only fight for so long. When they starved and their bairns were dying then choices had to be made. Only one choice in the end, and that was to vacate the land. Many did well for themselves in the Americas. But many died, of course."

He stopped the mail bus to allow her to look over Loch Quoich and the beautiful view across the water to the wild heights of Knoydart and Morar, with the tall pyramid of Sgurr Na Ciche, holding its head up to the heavens. She had listened with deep intentness as the wild outlandish names rolled off his tongue, scarcely meaning anything to her yet but striking some buried chord in her blood that set her heart racing with the beauty and magic of it all. Her English blood protested at the solitude, missing the roar of London traffic, the closeness of people, but Jessica had learned there was no protection in numbers, no safety in the midst of people she had grown up with. Something in the wildness of it called out to her, welcoming her home like the lost soul she was.

"We best get moving, there's rain coming in afore long." He started the engine again and picked up speed; the rackety van travelling the bumpy road as best as it could.

"How can you tell?" She was surprised. The day looked clear and sunny.

"See yon roll of cloud out there to the Southwest?" He pointed the way. "You can see the rain falling down, and look there now, a braw wee rainbow, curving over that brae. That's lucky for you. It kens ye're a very welcome visitor."

She laughed at his dialect, enjoying the soft accent. "You make it sound very romantic."

"Och, away with you! It's no romantic for me, I've a mile or twa to gang afore I see ma supper this bonny nicht. And I see these roads every day, don't forget."

"Andy? I suppose you know everyone all round here even Luke Fraser?" As she expected, the ambiguous question set him off without a moment's hesitation.

"Luke Fraser? Oh aye, that's right enough, it was your granddaddy who found him when he parachuted down after the accident to his plane. He was hurt and he stayed here a bit until his unit picked him up. He was based with the American Air Forces up here, you see. They were doing an exercise in these hills and there was an accident. Part of their War Games practice or some silly nonsense like that. They think because the place is remote it's all right to do it but there's some folk around here get scared out o' their wits when a plane goes over at zero height. I'm one o' them. Ruddy fools they are, to be sure. I've seen a flock of sheep scatter all over the place in sheer panic.

Anyway Luke is'na American, he's a Canadian. Chose the wrong service I expect. He was pretty cracked up when your grandfather found him. The old man got him back to the hoose and looked after him until his unit turned up to take him back to base. Dinna ken what happened after that but next thing we knew, the lad's left the force an' makes his way back here to join your grandfather wi' the sheep. William was right pleased to see him, he'd grown fond of the boy, he said. Luke was really cut up when your granddad died. Now he wants to settle here. Ah canna get much outa him, he's no the talking' sort if you see what I mean, but ah ken't he was fixing to stay an' mebbe buy the farm from the old chap, but of course you'd know all about it," he added confidently. Expecting a wee titbit to augment his knowledge. "You being the heir an' all."

"Hmm," she muttered, "If there is a change I'll be sure to let you know," she said, looking sweetly innocent, hoping he would not discover that she too was ignorant of the facts.

65

She felt him glance over at her then look back to the road. When he began to speak his voice was serious without a hint of the previous humour and then apropos of nothing at all said:

"Its gye lonely in these parts for some auld folks, they canna afford newspapers, some dinna even have a radio. They don't get to the town often either. I like to cheer them up with wee bitty news the now, just to make 'em feel they are part o' the neighbourhood, ye ken. But I dinna spread any scandal, that is agin ma principles, just wee snippets o' people's lives, it helps to keep everyone together, ye ken? There's no so many o' us live around here the now. Most folks gang off to the big cities if they can. So what's your business is yours, I'm no one for probing."

"I understand you, Andy, but you have to realise I've come up from London where it is a matter of survival. One has to keep very private and self-contained, or you would go mad with interference. There are streets and streets of people bored with their own mundane lives who get a kick out of picking over other people's problems, so one keeps things to oneself."

"Ye must be awful glad you've escaped, then, to a fresher place where a body can breathe." He had the last word on the subject and Jessica smiled to herself as she recognised the truth in his riposte. More truth than he realised. Yes, she was glad to have escaped.

Finally, they made the rough descent to Kinlochhourn where it lay hidden at the end of a long stretch of water. If Andy hadn't told her, she would never have known, as there was only a cluster of sheep pens, barns and a small stone quay. Further on, perhaps a quarter of a mile away he pulled up outside a granite croft, which blended into the hillside as though it had been there since the dawn of time. She shivered suddenly. How quiet it was now the engine had stopped. Staying where she was she stared out of the window, uneasily anxious to see her new home but conscious of the deathly hush enveloping the glen. A quiet sinister atmosphere enshrouded the place. It seemed lonely beyond belief. How could she survive by herself?

Abruptly she shook herself free of nervousness and climbed out of the van to join the post-man busily shifting her bags onto the stony path. Then something jogged her memory and she clapped her hands to her mouth,

"Oh! Fool that I am, I forgot to bring a key with me. How am I to get in? Don't tell me I have to go all the way back to Invergarry? Or even worse – to Glasgow?"

Andy laughed at her expression.

"Do what anybody else does round here, look for the key outside." He went to the door and stretched his hand out. After a moment's search he produced the door key from a niche above the lintel. Jessica stared at him in round-eyed surprise. How had he known?

"How's that, hen? I'll mak' a good wee bank robber by an' by when I retire from being a postie. I know the way in to every croft for miles around." He chuckled at the look on her face.

"Oh, Andy, you're a marvel. I would never have found it for myself. Could you do one more favour and wait while I go inside and have a quick look to see if all is okay for me to stay." She pleaded softly. "I'd hate for you to go and leave me stranded."

"Aye, well be quick, I've got twenty miles to drive afore I get to ma next call. Luke will likely be up in the hills, ye mebbe will not see him afore Saturday, like as not. He usually comes into toon fer his groceries and a dram, Whisky, ye ken? But ye'll be safe enough here, so dinna worry yersel' about being on yer ain."

He turned the key in the lock and began to carry the luggage into what looked like a large kitchen-come-everything. It seemed dark after the sunlight and she hurriedly drew back the curtains from the small deeply embrasure windows. It was all very tidy and clean and she began to feel reassured.

Andy went across to a sink in the corner of the room and turned on the tap. "There you are, ma'am, running water, fresh from the spring. Cold and pure." He tried a switch on the wall but nothing happened so glancing round the room he spied a cupboard near the floor and putting in his hand threw a switch and a low voltage centre light lit the room.

"Oh!" She cried, "There's power to the place?"

"Och aye lass. We have the electricity, ye ken, we're all modern in our ways here. Even the Stone Age caves have lights. Though the voltage gets a bit frisky now and then." He gazed at her with amusement then went on; "Your grandfather had the place modernised when your grandmother took poorly, but it was too late, the poor wee biddy had worked herself to a full stop and I think she died with excitement o' not having to get a pail o' water from the burn. She lived here in gae hard times."

"Andy, what do I owe you for the trip?" She interrupted what promised to be another item of gossip about the family she didn't know. Sometime when she was settled she would get him talking of them but for now it was enough she had arrived and was about to begin her new life.

"You can bake me a mutton pie for when I come next time; I'm awful fond o' mutton pies. Now, I'll be awa' or ma customers will think I've fallen in the loch." He tipped his hat and went off to the van shouting something behind him,

"Dinna forget to warm the lum."

"Wha-at?" She yelled after him.

"The lum! Chimney to the Sassenachs!"

She shrugged unable to understand. Maybe he was talking about the mutton pies. The van sped up the rise and Jessica was left alone in the eerie silence of the glen. She stared across the water at the trees on the other side; the woods seemed ominous and almost as forlorn as she felt herself. 'Come on' she chided, this is where you wanted to be. Don't groan if it is not as good as you dreamed. He did say you didn't have to be scared you were on your own.' She reminded herself. 'Small comfort when I am terrified!' She smiled at the exaggeration then turned back to the croft. 'Well, it's mine; I might as well take possession.'

SEVENTEEN

Briskly Jessica turned back into the cottage and began to sort her things. She found a dresser on the extreme right near to the sink which held matching cups, saucers and plates on narrow open shelves at the top and everyday mugs and dishes her grandfather probably used daily in a cupboard underneath. Nearby was a cabinet with a rusty mesh door that she presumed was used for fresh food and she stacked away the perishables Mrs Stuart had ordered for her. No fridge worse luck, but she would remedy it later seeing as the place had power. Making herself a cheese sandwich she ate it as she inspected the rest of the room.

A large range was set back in an inglenook, the pots and kettle nearby blackened with age and use. A high mantel over it was laden with photos and souvenirs of the past years. Jessica spotted her father as a young boy. She fancied it was a standard school photograph. The rest of the snaps were unrecognisable in the growing dimness and she realised with a shock that the sun had gone and all of a sudden it was cold and raining. This was Scotland's changeable weather, no doubt. Running outside to see if there was a fuel store, she found it at the end of the cottage, which, she understood from the solicitor she had to refer to as a croft in these parts. The large barn-like area had a pile of logs in one corner. There was also a heap of dark brown brick-sized lumps she thought at first was coal but then intuition told her was probably peat.

Fetching the empty grocery box she filled it with the dried wood then scraped up small twigs to go under the logs to start the fire. Her first attempt at lighting the stove filled the air with dense smoke and she had to race to the door before she choked. It took some while before she understood she had to open a vent to let the smoke go up the chimney. Jessica went back for more twigs and began again. The rain was coming down in earnest and the sky was dark so she put on the light, which flickered and danced as though it was about to go out. The supply of matches began to dwindle and she was in despair at getting the fire to light and cold and scared at staying in the dark in what was a frightening and lonely place. Depression came on her like a dark cloud. How was she going to manage if she failed at the first obstacle?

After a few moments of panic she spoke very firmly to herself, rose from the floor and fetching one of her warm sweaters returned to kneel in front of the recalcitrant stove. "Damn stupid thing! Why won't you light? What the hell am I doing wrong?"

She had just bent forward to begin again, when the door burst open with an almighty crash and she screamed in fright as a tall male figure burst in and loomed menacingly over her.

"What in hellfire are you doing here?" He shouted fiercely, as she gazed in terror at him. Oh God help her, this was her worst nightmare coming true. To her horror, the man continued to lean over her, a bleak, threatening glare on the dark unshaven face, his eyes steely bright in anger, his brownish hair wet and tousled from the rain.

"Who the blazes are you? This is private property." His glance went quickly round the room then returned to where she crouched terrified and speechless on the floor in front of the stove, her face blackened with smuts from her attempts to try to coax a flame from the wood.

"Have you warmed the chimney?" The unexpected question he threw at her numbed her into silence until she become aware his voice held a milder level of gruffness.

"What? Er-no." She whispered at last, still completely unnerved.

"Oh shit! No wonder. Come on, move out of the way."

She watched while he twisted a sheet torn from an old magazine into a taper, lit it, and then held it under the chimney flue letting the flames go up. After a moment or two he thrust the rest of the lit paper under the sticks and to Jessica's astonishment the fire immediately began to blaze away merrily. Piling on more wood and then some larger logs completed the job. The fire lit. The stove was in action.

"So that's what Andy meant."

"Andy? Do you mean Postie Andy? What's he got to do with it?"

"He brought me here in his van, and then just as he was leaving he spoke of warming - I think he said lum and a sassa - a sassa - oh I don't know, it sounded like a foreign word. I'm still trying to get used to the different dialect. I feel as if I'm learning a new language. It sounds like English and yet it's not, if you know what I mean?"

"Sassenach?"

She nodded and he laughed for the first time, showing very white teeth in a brown face. Somehow the smile made her relax a little. "Oh I do indeed know what you mean. You have come a long way if you're a Sassenach - it means you're English. So, my little waif and stray, what brings you to this outlandish spot to trespass where you are not supposed to be? And why here of all places? Miles from anywhere."

*   *   *   *   *

"I'm Jessica Meredith, but I doubt I'M trespassing. Why don't you tell me how YOU came to be here?" An impish grin exposed a dimpled cheek but she had to face him with it sometime.

"Bloody Hell! A Meredith? Macfarlan didn't tell me he was in contact with anyone yet or even that there was a relative to contact. I suppose you are the new owner?"

"Yes, that's right." She listened to the deep crisp tones of his Canadian accent.

"I see. Why didn't you let me know?" His brows met together in a frown as he indicated an old-fashioned phone on the wall, which Jessica had never noticed before. Not that he would have heard it up in the hills, she thought.

"I didn't realise I had to - let anyone know, I mean. As far as I was aware I am the only direct Meredith around and consequently I've inherited this place."

"I'm Luke Fraser, I run the - used to help William Meredith, your grand-pappy. I was very sorry he died; he was a good friend of mine, one of the best. In fact he saved my life...once."

"Sadly, I never knew him, my father never visited."

"I know." She felt the bite of his censure and was angered briefly then reason stepped in and she realised she was more angry with her father who had deprived her of any relationship with her grandparents. Why hadn't he written to them? They were his parents, after all.

"We can't all be perfect and love our relations," she said sharply feeling a need to excuse him. He must have had a good reason. "Anyway, my father died five years ago and my mother possibly felt she wouldn't be welcome. She is dead too, so there is only this property and now me. The 'back of beyond' the solicitor called it. I didn't believe him but I can see what he meant. It's out in the wilderness and scary, especially learning how to light a fire." Her cheeks dimpled again for a moment and he grinned, thinking of the first sight of her smutty face.

"So, now you are here, let's get you comfortable. What about something to eat? I'm afraid my stores are a bit basic though. The shops are back in Invergarry."

"Mrs Stuart packed some groceries for me, I hope it's all right, I've put them in that tin cupboard over there seeing there's no fridge."

"That's what I like to see, female domesticity."

"Well that's all your going to see, I'm no cook, I warn you. My mother did all our cooking, I was too busy working. What did you do before you came here?"

It was as if a shutter came down over his face. His smile vanished and his eyes grew cold and grey like an arctic sea.

Jessica felt the cold chill of his manner even before Luke answered her briefly: "I won't bore you with my unexciting past, let's talk of other things, like who's going to scrub the spuds?"

"I think it should be you. I expect you have plenty of experience." Her voice told him she had recognised his snub and was prepared to give as good as she got. Reviewing the hardness of his reply he thought he would amend his words.

"If you must know I used to be a pilot," he said tersely. "I crashed my plane near here. Your grandpappy found me in the trees and he brought me back here and looked after me till my buddies picked me up. I left the service soon after. Came back here to help him with the sheep."

Jessica knew at once that there was a lot more behind his brief explanation but now wasn't the time to probe. Changing the subject she said brightly, "Is the oven okay to heat up the pie?"

"Pie? One of Mrs Stuart's mutton pies? Holy cow, you are the best visitor I've had this year, I love 'em." She forbore to point out the food was her rations and what would he have eaten if she hadn't come? Her mind had gone hazy again and all she wanted to do was eat and sleep. Curse this pregnancy; it was going to take over her life if she didn't watch out. While she had been busy, Jessica ignored the warning signs of nausea creeping over her until it was almost too late. Now she knew she must act, or she would throw up suddenly, right in front of this stranger.

"What does one do for a toilet here?" She gasped.

He stared at her quickly then pushed a door open to the rest of the croft. "In here. You're lucky, you know, at least it's not a mile away. Willy spared no small expense putting this in. It even flushes. More than you can say for some Crofts around here. Make yourself welcome."

Jessica took him at his word and hurried through the door into a short passage where there were two further doors, one of which was the bathroom. A large old-fashioned bath almost filled the area. There were two ordinary taps sticking out from the wall above it, also a small basin with a plughole and pipe outlet but minus taps and praise be - a toilet. She was just in time as her stomach heaved alarmingly.

The absence of tiling, and walls painted a dark, depressing yellow spoke volumes; it was obvious William had not been blessed with a surfeit of money. He'd probably saved a long time to afford even this makeshift bathroom. Torn newspaper served as toilet paper, adequate, but hardly comfortable but Jessica did not care as long as her stomach gave her peace. When she felt better, she used an old bowl on the floor beside the sink to draw water from one of the taps over the bath and filling the basin, washed, and then used an old twill towel to dry off.

Then she came out into the passage and peeped through the end door to see where it led.

At that moment, Luke threw the kitchen door wide open and the light shone into a bare, cold room holding a rusty spring bed with wooden ends, a small wardrobe and an old chair. The window had meagre curtains hanging askew on a rusty wire and altogether the place smelt damp and airless. Jessica wrinkled her nose at the fusty smell of an unused almost abandoned room.

"Old Willy never used the room again after your Granny died. He moved into the bed closet in the kitchen," said Luke as he watched her frown in dismay. "He never said much but I knew he missed her a great deal."

"A bed? Where is it? I never noticed." Jessica followed him back into the kitchen and he opened a pair of doors on the opposite side of the fire to the dresser, exposing a space large enough to hold a smallish bed that was topped with a feather mattress and two pillows covered in faded striped ticking. A folded counterpane hung on the bed rail.

"Oh my! What a surprise! I've not seen a bed like it before."

"It's very popular hereabouts, for when the snow comes you need to keep warm and being next to the fire it's always cosy. I'd sleep here tonight, if I were you. You will be very snug."

"Yes, I will." She shuddered at the thought of sleeping in the other bedroom. There would need to be more than a few changes before she could bring herself to use it. She would also have to learn how to decorate. But at that moment it seemed another mountain to climb. She would try to get through the next few days and see how she felt about staying.

"Feel better now?" He looked at her discerningly, almost, thought Jessica, as though he could see the small embryo growing inside her, yet she knew the enveloping jersey hid signs of her swelling figure and was glad. She didn't want him to know, at least not until they had struck a bargain over the farm. For the black depression had overtaken her again, bringing with it a feeling it would be absolutely impossible to stay by herself in the isolated glen, she could never manage on her own.

"Well food's ready. You probably need to eat for I'm sure it's been a long day for you. You won't have had anything since breakfast. Come and get it."

The food and the warmth of the room helped enormously to cheer her up and it was only when she gave a huge yawn that seem to come from the depths that made her realise she was dead on her feet.

Luke stood up and said firmly, "Come on, young lady, it time you were in bed."

He swiftly cleared and washed the dishes in record time then banked up the range to keep it quietly burning during the night before bidding her farewell.

"Where are you going?" She asked sleepily, suddenly aware she was going to be left on her own but she was too tired by now to be very much concerned. All at once her eyes were drooping heavy as lead and it was all she could do to keep them open.

"To the Bothy, it's a shepherd's hut down the way. Wully let me have the use of it as my own place. I presume it's still all right to sleep there?" His eyes twinkled at her in amusement.

"But of course. Where else would you go?"

"Where else indeed, on a night like this." He replied unenthusiastically thinking how sorry he was to leave the cosiness of the croft for a cold bed in an all-be-it weather-proof but very drab lodging which up to now hadn't bothered him in the slightest to use.

"There are some blankets in a chest, but I should have got them out earlier as they might be damp. Trust me to have a brain like a sieve. Can you make do for tonight?" He said ruefully.

"It's all right, I have a sleeping bag, and I'll put it on top of the mattress in the bed closet. I'll be just fine. No worry; I can cope with things like that. It's only chimneys that defeat me."

"Right then, I'll leave you to your sleep, see you tomorrow evening. So long, sleep well."

He went out of the door and Jessica was conscious of the wildness of the night, the teeming rain and rising wind. Losing no time she hurried up and got into bed, scarcely giving another thought to the day's events before sinking into a deep sleep.

EIGHTEEN

It was the early hours of the morning and pitch dark when she next stirred, conscious of the weight pressing on her. She found she was trapped and hardly able to breathe with the pressure of someone lying over her, hurting her as they had done before. She couldn't see anyone, could only hear the breathing in her ear but she knew it was Mark. He was going to rape her again; she would never be free of him. "No, no, go away; you've done your worst, leave me alone..." She screamed for all her worth trying to free herself from his clutches...then the figure spoke.

"Jessica, it's all right, it's me, Luke, you're having a nightmare, Jessica, take it easy, you're here with me." Luke shook her until he saw her eyes open then held her close as the sobs jerked her slight body with a frantic abandonment. As she slowly calmed down, comprehending where she was, that the light was now on and there was no one in the room except Luke, she realised it was only another nightmare that had come upon her. She was filled with embarrassment in the close embrace of this stranger who was kneeling on the bed trying to soothe her wild struggles.

"Yes, yes, all right, I'm awake. Oh dear, I'm so sorry to have disturbed you. I can't think what brought this on. I haven't had anything like it for ages." She blushed shyly, and then quickly freeing herself she nudged the hair from her eyes and pulled open the zip of the sleeping bag. As she did so she noticed in the dim electric light his chest was bare under a loose jacket. A faint line of body hair ran from the hair on his chest down to where his trousers were loosely buckled together. Elsewhere his skin was smooth and faintly tanned. She blushed even more at the untamed thoughts that raced through her brain and sitting up reached for her dressing gown.

Luke backed off the bed and went to the sink to fill the kettle. "A hot cup of tea is just the thing for shock. That nightmare was a real humdinger. Do you get them often? Poor old you if you do. They can be kinda scary. I know, I've had a few."

Jessica was about to reply when a long black nose pushed open the door but ventured no further. She gasped and instantly Luke glanced back at her to see her eyes fixed on the door.

He grinned with assurance. "Come in Cladagh, don't be shy. Come and meet our new friend. Would you believe she is William's granddaughter come to see how we are getting on in this wonderfully forsaken place? No, I guess not, but come in anyway." He pulled the door wider and a superb specimen of a sheepdog trod gently over the threshold and stopped by the bed looking up enquiringly.

"Ah, she wants introducing. This is Cladagh, your grandfather's sheep dog. She's accepted me to help her, thank goodness, for I'm sure I'd be hopeless on my own for she's a marvel with the sheep. Cladagh, meet Jessica, she's the one you heard making that din and who's just roused us out of our warm beds. She ought to carry a health warning." He grinned teasingly at Jessica.

"I'm so sorry for causing you a problem. I don't know what started it; I haven't had it for a while. The nightmare, I mean." Pausing abruptly she bit her lip, looking embarrassed again, then bent down to hide her face as she stroked the black and white Collie, who immediately reacted ecstatically, wagging her tail excitedly and wriggling as close as she could get to the bed.

"Would you look at that, it took me months to get her to respond to me, the memories of your grandfather were too strong. You do it in a minute. You females sure do stick together."

She did not laugh as expected. Perplexed, he gazed at her worried face in speculation, wondering about the nightmare. She was a strange one, quite unpredictable.

"I don't suppose you're used to sleeping bags, they can be quite constricting, I expect you got tangled up in yours and it triggered something." While he spoke he finished making the tea and handing her a mug, took the other one, and held it up to toast her before drinking deeply. Then he glanced up at her again with a speculative look on his face.

"How would you like to come to Barrisdale with me tomorrow? I've a couple of sheep to doctor, but we can do a spot of fishing for our dinner. I'm nearly out of food and yours won't last long but we should manage quite well for the next couple of days. Also the weather should be reasonable. You'll enjoy the scenery. Are you up to it? What do you say?"

"Oh yes, I'd like that if you're sure I won't hold you up, I don't want to get in the way."

"No, you won't be in the way and I'd like the company. But it's a bit of a hike."

"I bought fell boots yesterday in Glasgow and protective clothing but the boots are still new, they're not exactly walked in, I mean. I'd hate to be a nuisance. You know what new shoes are like with blisters. I'm hoping these will be okay. They fitted me very well in the shop and I've two pairs of thick socks..." Her voice tailed away as she waited anxiously for him to change his mind and say in that case they would make it another day.

"Don't worry, we'll Landrover it through to the bay, then only a couple of miles climbing to do from below. Give me the boots, I'll stuff them with wet paper now and they will start to soften by tomorrow. Wear your thick socks and they should be okay. Where are they?"

She pointed to her baggage still on the floor against the wall. He retrieved the boots and began to work on them. After a moment or two he said, "Okay, that's done. Well I'm off to bed, ma'am, shall I leave Cladagh with you?"

She looked at the dog curled round in unaccustomed luxury before the fire, her nose buried in her tail. "I heard somewhere it's wrong to have sheep dogs indoors, but if you don't mind...?" She pleaded with her eyes, knowing she would feel safer with the dog beside her.

"Go on then, it won't hurt if we'll spoil her just the once. Night Jessica, sleep well, see you early in the morning. In three hours to be exact." He grinned, looking at his watch.

"Oh God, that's six o'clock!"

"If you want to be a sheep farmer, you have to get up before then, I'm afraid. You have to be on the hills before sunup. I was merely making allowances on the first day, you being a city-dweller an' all." She heard him chuckling as he went off into the dark. She settled herself down to sleep determined to put the fear of a nightmare from her mind. Now she only had to think about waking up at five thirty. Inexplicably the memory of a broad bare chest pressed close to her body and the aroma of his masculine scent intruded. She fell asleep wondering at the fickleness of fate. Nowhere in her past existence would she have come in contact with a man like Luke. And even if she had come across him it would never have even got to first base. After her episode with Mark she thought she had forsworn men forever, but she conceded, not everybody was as bad as Mark. Might she make a friend of this man?

NINETEEN

The dog awoke her early so she was dressed and had the tea made as Luke came down the path whistling. The day had dawned with the promise of sunshine and outdoors it smelt freshly cleansed by the rain. Jessica watched a couple of sea ducks dive into the calm limpid water sending ripples chasing across the surface of the loch. Her night terrors seemed merely a figment of her imagination and she revelled again in the beautiful scenery.

"Tea? Oh boy, you must have read my thoughts, I'm not used to such luxury, eh Cladagh, we mustn't get to like this spoiling or we'll never let you go."

"Who wants to go? Not me," she cried joyfully. "I'm here to stay!"

"Hmm." He eyed her thoughtfully as he drank. How the hell am I going to persuade her to sell this darn farm? Then it occurred to him that he was going about it the wrong way. He ought to have left her all on her own then maybe she would have been scared enough to sell the place as soon as possible. Not come to her rescue like a shining knight in armour. Well maybe taking her off for a day's outing with the sheep would put her off.

"Ready? Okay, let's go." Luke led the way back to his hut where the Landrover was parked alongside. They climbed in and he drove back past the farm, round by the quay and along the south side of the loch pausing briefly to show her the abandoned village of Skiary, where the ruined Crofts looked dismally abandoned and drear. Then he carried on towards the seaward end of the waterway. Reaching a point where a spit of land from the north almost cut the loch in two, he reversed neatly into a lay-by.

"This is as far as we go in the Landrover, we have to walk from here, are you fit?" He smiled as she said she was ready for anything, then as she and the dog got out he grabbed a hold-all from the back seat and pointing to the path ahead said: "We'll keep low until we get further round the point then we can climb higher where the sheep are grazing. The views are lovely up there on clear days and today is one of the best. Now and then one gets sea fogs, so that one can hear the foghorns up the coast sounding off, then it's a bit grim and miserable but mostly, even in the winter, it stays clear."

"It's so pleasant today we won't even think of the bad weather in case it changes." She said cheerfully, determined to keep to a happy note.

They walked along a beaten path by the shore of the loch between woods of birch and scrub oak, with here and there, a Scot's pine to lend a darker contrast. The sky came down to touch the high peaks on all sides of them and Jessica thought she had never seen a more beautiful sight in her life. The yellow of birch leaves taking on their autumnal colouring; the fragrant deep green pines and over all, a blue, which went on forever roused her artistic eye. A painter would be in seventh heaven trying to capture the area on canvass. For a moment she yearned for the ability then her thoughts took a different path as gazing skywards she noticed a build up of white fluffy clouds way out to sea, which Luke said, looking with a keen practised eye, would bring rain before nightfall.

"Oh blow the rain. Isn't there any poetry in your soul? You're too practical round here."

"Needs must when one is out on a cold windy brae with a sick sheep and its raining torrents or one is frozen to death in a snow storm. There's no poetry then. It's just you against the elements and misery. All you want is to get in out of the wet."

"Hmm, I can see you are determined to tell me the worst. How about we save it till later?"

"Have you decided yet what you intend with the farm? Did the Solicitor tell you I was interested in buying it? I had discussed the matter with your grandfather." He had to say it.

"Yes, he did, Luke. It came as quite a surprise, but now I appreciate the situation and can see how it came about. But give me some more time to think about it, after all, I have only just got here. I can't make any decisions yet awhile."

He pursed his lips but did not reply; then changing the subject began to point out things to please. A clump of fiery coloured rhododendrons. Shady places where violets hid, wild orchids nestling in damp moss, the delicate blossoms unseen unless one searched very carefully or knew their hiding places, and a spring trickling from a hillside which had carved its own rock pool. It was obvious though when he reintroduced the subject that it still preyed on his mind and he was reluctant to let the moment pass; but containing his anxiety he merely said, "Okay. I shan't say another word till later then I'd appreciate talking things over with you. But you are right. The day is too beautiful to spoil. Look at this, see this small waterfall. Taste the water and tell me what you think."

She cupped her hands and filled them with the ice cold water, which ran fresh and pure after its journey from within the rocky hillside and took a tentative sip at first then went back to drink more. "Gosh, it's deliciously cool and refreshing. I have never tasted water like this. It would sell for the price of champagne in town. Londoners haven't a clue what real water tastes like." Jessica laughed delightedly. "I guess I've never known myself what it's like after being reared all my life on London water. Most times it's absolutely awful. I usually drink herb teas and disguise the flavour."

"I guess there are compensations in every place, but one thing we don't lack here is water," Luke sighed. "It is either falling on your head or you're up to your neck in it. See, over there where the grass is growing high?"

"Well that's a swampy marsh. You walk there and you're in a muddy, sucking bog before you've gone two yards. I lost a sheep back in the fall last year, when it decided to come off the hill in the wrong place and fell right into mud. It was strange because they usually know what they are doing. My guess is he was scared silly by a cat. Sheep can sometimes be spooked by those creatures."

"A cat? Do you mean an ordinary cat?" He had all her attention.

"No, a wild cat, they're bigger'n the usual domestics but twice as hungry and if they get an animal scared enough they'll even tackle a sheep. This one lucked out for the sheep disappeared into the bog while we looked on. Me down here by the loch and him somewhere up on the hill. I never saw him but I sure 'nuff heard him growl. They usually keep away from humans unless they think they are big enough to take 'em on."

Jessica didn't care for sound of that, she hadn't reckoned on animals around here being so wild they would tackle a sheep or a person. She hunched herself up in the sweater and strode on keeping a more alert look out for anything, which might attack them. Cladagh roamed back and forth, along the path and through the trees, now and then putting up a rabbit but making no attempt to go too far and once even walking alongside Jessica touching her hand with her cold nose to comfort her. It felt very reassuring to her and she said as much to Luke.

He laughed. "Typical sheepdog trick that is. She's herding us and making sure we stay together. She won't let you stray far, Jessica, that's for sure, she'll come along and chivvy you right back to where she thinks you ought to be."

Jessica had never owned a dog or even a cat. Her parents never wanted them and as a child she had never been one to whine for anything. All at once, she realised what she missed. To have an animal to love and care for and who gave love in return seemed almost miraculous. Perhaps...if everything worked out...Oh forget it Jessica, you are building dream castles in the air again. Keep your feet on the ground and stick to reality.

After a bit Jessica relaxed and for the first time in ages she felt at peace with herself and the world. They turned the corner and Jessica could see the Loch was very much wider here and banded with a grey shingle all along the edge. It was quiet and impressive with the mountains hanging over them from every side displaying a wild grandeur that Jessica felt was awe-inspiring. She hardly dare speak above a whisper when she asked Luke who owned the cottages she could see in the distance on the far side of the loch.

"That's Arnisdale; only a few elderly fisher folk still live there now and eke out a living. It's a poor life for them. But I suppose they are used to it and don't want to change."

"Why do you want to live here? I heard from Andy you've been a pilot. It's a big change from flying to sheep farming. What made you change your life and come to this place?"

At once his face altered, became austere, the mood of good humour fading at her words.

His eyes turned chilly steel with bleakness and his lips tightened as though he was angry.

Oh lord, I've done it again, she thought. He certainly doesn't care for people to ask questions. She watched his eyes that suddenly held deep grief in their depths and the face that instantly paled under her frowning gaze, the sunburn on his face so oddly strange. It was all quite different from the moment before.

"I suppose I might as well tell you, or Andy Keiller or anyone around here will, if they get the chance," he said, his voice filled with bitterness. "I crashed my Wing-man's plane when we were flying combat practice up here. I got away with it because I ejected. He was not so lucky. There was an inquiry and it was put down to pilot error; mine. I got grounded, of course, and I couldn't see any future ahead. I knew the only thing they'd let me fly after that would be a desk job unless I was shipped to the ends of the earth, so I bought out. Your grandfather found me after I baled out. He took care of me till the base sent to pick me up, so I came back to see him and stayed on to help. Rightly, I guess I should have shipped back to Canada, I'm from Calgary, that's in the Rocky Mountains, but there's no one back home now, my mom's dead and my pa...well...he ain't around any more. I really liked these mountains instead and I got on well with William. I can't think why the hell he chose to go up on the roof that day to mend a leaky patch. It wasn't as if it was a major crisis or anything. If he had waited till I got back from town, I'd have done it for him in a jiffy, no trouble." He shook his head sorrowfully at the memory of returning to the Croft after a visit to Invergarry and finding the old man lying quite still his neck broken; the ladder in two pieces on the ground beside him.

Jessica squeezed his arm in sympathy and sighed quietly,

"I know all too well what it's like to lose someone dear, you wonder how you are ever going to live without them, then you pick yourself up and your life goes on." She looked at him curiously and went on, "How long has your mother been gone?"

"My pa killed her, way back when I was sixteen. He was handy with his fists and used to get drunk; then she'd get upset when he belted me and he'd give it to her twice as hard. One day he went way over the top...he got life imprisonment, which freed me up, and I made out on my own until the American Air Force took me a tad earlier than the age they figured I was. I kinda looked older, I guess. I'm just thirty, but I feel twice that. It's a hard world out there, an' I guess I've plumbed every rock waiting to trip me up."

Jessica winced sympathetically as she tried to understand the story he glossed over as though it was nothing. Of a young boy, desolate at losing his mom and his home; having to fend for himself, then much later struggling to achieve a good career and succeeding, only to find it had all blown up in his face and he was back on the scrap heap again. Back to existing, merely living on the edge of life. Written in his sombre face the deep canker of disgrace was still eating away at his soul. Embarrassed, he spun away and picking up a stone, sent it skimming over the placid water, watching it hop seven times before disappearing, his face set hard in a glowering frown. Was he frightened to be friends with her in case she rejected him? Had everyone else rejected him except for her grandfather? If William had not, maybe it was because he did not think Luke was guilty. Somehow, her instinct told her that the hardness of her grandfather's life would make him unsympathetic with anyone who was unworthy of his regard.

"I can't understand the reason they found you guilty of pilot error? Can you explain?"

"You sure don't pull your punches, lady, being so curious. Why not go further and ask how I murdered my buddy? I bet that's what you are really thinking."

"My grandfather didn't think you murdered him. Otherwise, you would not have been accepted here. Neither do I...think you murdered him, I mean." She spoke positively taking a chance his anger wouldn't alienate him altogether from her. He was obviously very touchy about his past. He stared at her as though mesmerised, a wry expression on his face.

"No," he said slowly. "Willy didn't. Damn me; are you Meredith's screwy or something? He didn't because he happened to see the other plane up there and knew I took evading action to miss it and tipped the wing of my co-pilot by mistake. That third plane should have been way up in the north of the country. A stupid bloody Limey who didn't know his own neck of the woods. Unfortunately, by the time I got back to base, he had pitched his own story and it sure as hell didn't tally with mine. He screwed me to the floor. Well, the hell with him. What do I care?"

He thought bitterly of the interview with his Commanding officer, Martyn Schafer after his release from hospital. The colonel picked up Luke's report from his desk where he had been studying it intently as Luke entered the room. He handed it back to Luke with a scowl.

"I want you to tear this up, Fraser, and write me a new one, and this time, tell me the Gospel truth. It is bad enough losing Mike Whitman, but to pin the error on someone else is crap in my book. You talk of a third plane but the squad all booked in as being over Cape Wrath on the turn round; that English captain - what's-his-name..."

"Welland, sir, Mark Welland."

"Yes, Welland. He was certain of his position over Loch More and his radar transponder verified it. Adrift a little bit, I admit, but it was his first time on manoeuvres. Anyway, he was nowhere near you, as he will swear. In addition, I am not about to offend the Brits here, got that Fraser. We get far too much opposition being in England anyway; we have orders to keep our heads down. A new report, Fraser, and let's have it right this time."

"But what about Grandfather giving evidence?"

"I didn't realise he had seen what had happened until I came back here a second time, it was too late by then, I'd no one else to verify my side of the story. All I was concerned about was losing Mike. It should have been me if I'd played things right. Ah well there's no use griping about it now. Water under the bridge as they say. Always move on and move out. But if ever I get that bastard in my sights...sorry, Jess, don't mind me, I get carried away."

She laughed then. "Oh, you called me Jess. My dad liked to call me that when mum wasn't around, she always told him off, she preferred the posh name."

"Posh? Oh, you mean fancy. I guess I like your dad's version too. It suits you better, it's softer. Gee, I'm sorry to bore you with my troubles, guess you've enough of your own."

"Yes," she gave a deep sigh, "Enough. But let's not spoil the day. Do we fish now?"

"Sheep first, then you can get smelly with the fish."

"Thanks for nothin' pardner! Come on, I'll race you to the top of the mountain." She ran up the hill for a few yards before she began to wheeze. Hell, she thought, I'll only be able to waddle before long. I loathe you, Mark Welland, I really loathe you.

TWENTY

They carried on up the lower slopes of Beinn Na Callich and as they climbed higher, Jessica was able to see a long way over the water to Skye on the other side of the Sound of Sleat. Soon they were amongst the sheep and Luke began herding small groups together to see if they were healthy. Cladagh was invaluable, obeying every command with amazing talent. Jessica could imagine her grandfather doing the same thing for having examined the photographs she knew what he was like. A tall spare man, thin-faced, grey hair and with deep wrinkles round his eyes denoting humour. She recalled her dad having the same wry look as though the world hadn't yet realised how clever he was. What had made her grandfather stay in this out of the way place? She would never know now, it was all long gone and buried.

"What are you looking for?" She asked Luke as she caught up with him at one point. He had pulled a ewe out of a bunch of sheep, turned her over on her back and was applying a black substance to her leg. "What's that stuff?"

"She's got foot rot. Look here, it's all open and full of pus. I'm putting on a Coal Tar medication, which will protect the area while it heals underneath. If that doesn't work then she'll need an antibiotic. It can get very nasty if it's neglected."

She stared at the inflamed foot and crusty lower leg.

"Yuck! Does it often happen like that?"

"Yes, it sure does, that and Enterotoxemia, Liver Flukes, Blackleg, Tetanus, Dysentery, Tapeworms, you name it they get it, want me to go on?" She shook her head and he was stunned at how green her face had gone. In a flash she disappeared behind some bushes and he heard her retching. She emerged some moments later looking pale and fragile-looking.

"Hey there, I didn't mean to make you throw up."

"It's all right, it's just me, I haven't been too well lately, that was why I came up here. I felt the fresh air would do me good and let me recover." She tried to grin but still looked chastened and her spirits seemed as if they had taken a real nose-dive.

"Then you bump into a mad sheep doctor like me! I'm really sorry, how about we go down for some lunch? We can have it by the loch. I've got bread and cheese. Will it do till we get back to the house?"

She nodded, still unsure of her stomach but knowing she must eat soon or she would be sick for the rest of the day.

They were climbing down the hill towards the loch when Jessica put her foot on a patch of wet moss on the sloping ground. In an instant before she could recover, her legs flew from under her and she lost her balance. Unable to gain control of her stability and with the slope against her she tumbled headlong in a flurry of arms and legs and rolled some way down the hill before a stand of gorse bushes abruptly halted her descent.

Startled, Luke dropped his bag and raced after her.

"Gee Honey, let's do it the easy way and walk, huh?" He knelt beside her and ran his hands over her arms and down the length of her body and legs to check for damage. Suddenly he saw her sweater had hitched way up, exposing her stomach. The stretch trousers she wore hid nothing; the rotundity of pregnancy extending beyond her natural slenderness was plain to see. The significance of the bout of sickness was not lost on him as his fertile brain instantly put the two together. His eyes met hers, and he guessed at once that Jessica had tried to keep it secret. His face darkened with rage. What the hell was she up to? Why hadn't she been honest with him from the start and declared she hadn't the slightest intention of staying on at the Croft? Or was it the other way round? Who was going to join her if she kept the farm? There had to be someone else or why was she pregnant?

So who was going to look after the sheep? She certainly couldn't in her present state. What devious plans were brewing in her brain? Nothing to benefit him that's for bloody sure. No wonder she had been evasive. How despicable - She didn't have the integrity of a weasel!

"Where's the other half then?"

"W-What?" She stuttered, frightened by the look on his face. He appeared to be so enraged she was almost too nervous to speak.

"The husband - or boy friend! Whoever was guilty for this prime event? Or is it by chance Immaculate Conception? You have heard of that little myth, I suppose?"

He was staring at her, the expression on his face stiff and unrevealing. How did one explain the real truth to someone so unapproachable? For the first time she allowed herself to think of her condition and the impact it might – did have - on others. Oh it was so unfair. Just when, after such a long time, years in fact, she wanted to make friends with someone, this awful humiliation hung over her head. She felt soiled and ashamed all over again.

What was he thinking? What did this mean for him? Her anger rose, replacing the fright of the fall. How dare he assume...well what? Exactly what was he assuming? She saw outraged fury in his face. So she hadn't told him, that wasn't a crime; it was her business anyway, wasn't it? I'll give him Immaculate Conception! How could he be so sarcastic about that terrible event? He hadn't a clue what she had suffered, nor was she going to tell him, she would rather die. Or was that strictly true? She had been quite determined not to reveal to another soul about the dreadful thing that had happened to her but somehow she couldn't bear him to think so badly of her or look so severe and disproving. Would this be everyone's reaction?

"How dare you! No it wasn't bloody Immaculate Con...con..." her voice faltered, "It was rape, if you must know. Bloody, vile rape! Do you think I got this way on purpose?"

"Rape! You were raped?" He looked even more annoyed, furious, in fact. "Why the blazes didn't you say? Is that the reason you came up here, to hide yourself?"

"Why should I explain? You were a complete stranger until yesterday. No, I didn't come here to hide. I wanted a new life – to get away from all that was sad and abhorrent to me after my mum's death. I did not find out that I was pregnant until that happened. Then unexpectedly I found out I'd inherited my grandfather's farm. I'd never met him; I had no idea what kind of a place it was. It seemed the obvious thing to come and see for myself."

"And the baby, what about that little dilemma?"

This time there was no doubting the scorn in his voice.

"So I'm having a baby! What the hell do you think I do, go around getting pregnant by any man that's available? No, I'm not m-mar-ried. I was raped. By the boss' son, who's a right nasty piece of shit! That evening, at the hospital, I find out my mother dying. Then I come up here to be insulted by a...by a sh-sh-sheep...who...b-believes I'm a l-liar..." she burst suddenly into tears, then at once turned over and lay sobbing bitterly; her face pressed to the hillside.

Luke stared down at her appalled. Jesus! What a terrible thing to happen to anyone, let alone someone as sweet as she appeared to be, even if he had thought differently a moment ago. Then putting his feelings to one side he grasped her shoulders to pull her up into his arms. There he cradled her gently, rubbing her back whilst murmuring soothing noises to calm her, until finally her sobbing ceased, she reached for a handkerchief and sitting up, blew her nose.

"Oh leave me alone, I'm okay. I didn't want to tell anyone about the pregnancy. It's no one's business but mine. Don't touch me; I don't need help from anyone, least of all you.

I'm quite capable of sorting myself out." She pushed him roughly away from her.

"Have you thought where all this marvellous independence will get you? It would be very easy to die out here, you know. This is pure wilderness. I learned that a while ago suspended by the parachute straps in the trees. With a broken leg and no way of getting down by myself, I could have died up there in the branches and no one would have found me for years, if then. Think of your grandpappy. There was no one around to save him when he fell off the ladder. And just suppose you suddenly miscarry here on the hills and you're all by yourself? Where will you be then? You are miles from a doctor. Not a good thought is it?"

"Do you think I haven't realised all this before. I knew it the moment I walked into the cottage - the silence, the isolation. I've never known anything like it in my life before. But it seems I'm in disgrace, thrown out of my job for being a bad girl. I must hide, for I'm a fallen woman! Me – who's never had a boy friend in ages – God, how long - back at school probably. Much too long ago, to remember." Then abruptly she relented. "Oh I'm sorry. I guess you mean well. It's just I can't seem to get my head round things and plan like I used to."

His unexpected grin and spurt of deep laughter took her by surprise. His changes of mood were disturbing. 'Yes, by golly, you are a fallen woman, but only lying stretched out on the ground. Beg pardon for laughing, I love puns. Look, I'm so sorry if you thought I was judging you. I promise that's not the case. I'm real unhappy things have turned out so bad. It's just..." his face became serious. "Oh hell, let's get you up and see if you do need a sheep doctor. You can't go throwing yourself around in your condition. Put your arm around my neck and we'll take it gently. Come on let me help you up, if I can turn a sheep over I can manage you okay! That's my girl; gosh you're a right featherweight. You just wait till later. Whoops, forget I said that." He grinned again.

She couldn't help but see the funny side of things and began to laugh through her tears then with his help stood up unharmed. He breathed a sigh of relief as she began to move easily, showing no bad effects. Thank heavens she was okay. She didn't seem to realise what could have happened.

"Feel okay?" He said anxiously. "Anything hurt?"

"No, I'm all right." Jessica flexed her arm and right shoulder. "I'm lucky I guess, I seem to touch the ground with my shoulder first and my sweater protected me so no damage done."

"Well, take it easy. My nerves are tight enough with one accident; two is over the limit."

TWENTY ONE

When they reached the edge of the water Luke found a rock ledge high enough for Jessica to sit comfortably then he dived into his bag to fetch out their lunch. Handing her a sandwich he watched approvingly as she bit into it then he poured out a cup of steaming coffee. "One gets thirsty out here in the hills, but I've got a coke here, if you'd rather drink something cold?" He went on, "The hot coffee will be refreshing, I think, though it's just black of course, the way I usually have it. Willy used to use powdered milk but I didn't think to bring any."

"No, this is fine, it tastes wonderful, helps the sick feeling no end."

He nodded agreement and taking a sandwich, ate it hungrily. "My tongue runs away with me at times." Luke said, by way of apology. "It was a bit of a shock, thinking you might be married, I mean, not having a baby. You must be pretty choked at the way things have turned out for you. Did you take out a warrant against the guy? Is he in the slammer?"

"No, his father fired me the next day. That night the man I worked for took me home. We walked straight into my mother's illness and somehow what happened to me didn't seem important. She had cancer, you see, she didn't live long. I've no idea what's happened to the son. My mother was in hospital by then and I spent all my time with her until she died. Shortly after her burial, I began to feel sick; it was only then that I discovered the result of the rape." For a second a vision came into her mind of a pile of tablets on a table and she shivered in disgust.

He noticed immediately and asked if she was cold. "No, I'm fine. I was just thinking of my visit to the doctor and his great news. I had put the ordeal of the rape out of my mind and he must have thought me completely dumb for not realising sooner. Events then seemed to come one on top of another and I was in a daze for most of the time." Never would she confess how near death she had been. It was a secret that would stay locked inside her forever. "There was no one in London for me so I came up here." She added.

"Tough luck. This was the reason for the bad nightmare, then? They can be pretty bad, I've had a few myself that are right humdingers and scary as hell."

"Yes. When my mum was alive I didn't get much sleep. I was always waiting for the phone to ring from the hospital. But it was only after I saw the doctor they seem to start up in real earnest. I haven't had many but you're right, they are scary when they come."

"Your grandfather had a saying about his farm and this valley. He reckoned it was a haven for someone unjustly accused or badly done by. He called it a place of sanctuary, especially after I turned up again. He told me that when he came to live here he was running away from a charge of murder. Oh, he was innocent all right, but it was seven years before the real killer came to light, by which time he had settled and married your grandmother, who was a girl from Invergarry, I believe. It seems William was born in the Orkney's of fisher folk. I gathered it was a feud between two families over fishing rights and a man was killed. Unluckily William was blamed and due to be picked up by the law. His father gave him some money and told him to escape to America, so he made his way across country heading for Glasgow to get a ship. He must have stopped a while in the village, for once he set eyes on your grandmother he never went any further. Of course he would have taken care not to get caught, hence the fact they hid themselves in this glen. They seldom went out into the main stream of life unless absolutely necessary, although local people would never have given them away to the police."

She listened intently to his tale, tears in her eyes.

"Hey there, don't cry, they were happy for Pete's sake, apart from when your father left. Though they realised he must make his own life, William said he was sorry he had married a Sassenach who would not know the Scottish ways. By golly gosh, he would have been right pleased at you coming back to his Croft, to his idea of a place of sanctuary. I can just hear him laugh about it. He'd say some things are meant to be."

"I'm not sure about that. If I thought there was a God up there making bad things happen so I would go in a certain direction I think I'd do the opposite just to be contrary. But seriously Luke, you've got to understand why it is so difficult to make up my mind what to do. If I sell to you I have some money to live on but I wouldn't know where to go, there is no one out there. If I stay here I can't run the place by myself even if I wanted to, it would be real stupid to try; I just haven't a clue how to be a sheep farmer, I'd turn sick at doing things for them. The way things are I suppose I'd better sell to you, it seems the only way. Or, at least, the only sensible way."

After being on edge for so long a time, Luke was surprised he wasn't more elated at the news and even more astonished when he found himself blurting out: "How's about if we're partners? I'll do the sheep, and you look after the house, do the housekeeping and all, and maybe keep chickens?"

She stopped halfway through a laugh as she stared at the expression on his face.

"Why not? I'll be more than happy to do the sheep. You can keep ownership of the land and we'll share the profits. How's that for an earth-shaking proposal?"

Completely stunned Jessica stared at Luke open-mouthed for a long moment trying to take in his generous suggestion, then gulping hastily she shook her head once more.

"Oh for goodness sake, Luke, it's not fair on you; you'd just be a hired hand. No, I really couldn't do that to you; it wouldn't sit right with me at all."

"Well, s'pose we divide the whole thing down the middle. We'll work out a value and I'll put that in as a share to improve the flock. I kinda want to experiment with new crossbreeds. There's lot of opportunity to specialise, particularly in good fleece for the wool industry." His eyes were alight with ambition. Such a change from the previous hard stare, which Jessica now perceived, had been hurt dismay.

"You wouldn't be stuck with me either if you wanted out of it. It might take a time but I'd buy you out, if necessary. The same goes for me, though at this moment I can't see me giving up without a struggle," he grinned disarmingly. "What do you say? We could have it all drawn up nice and tight. Legally, I mean. Every safeguard you want. Think about it - a readymade home for you, a safe place to have your baby." He watched the light die out of her eyes and fell silent. Perhaps it wasn't the right time to mention the baby, to remind her that it was because of her assault she had ended up at the back of beyond, bur hellfire, it had to be thought of.

"It sounds fine, Luke," she said slowly then as she recalled her last visit to a Solicitor's she added quickly, "But I'd never want to go back to my grandfather's legal man, I didn't trust him an inch and I was right too. Let me think on it. We'll decide after dinner, for I'm sure you came up with it on the spur of the moment and you need to give it the same thought as I do. It is totally earth shattering when all's said and done. We didn't even know each other yesterday let alone begin to make a plan to become partners. You might live to regret it and hate me after a while."

"I might; but then again we both have an objective to make a success of things. Hell, Jess, you stepped into the unknown to change your life when you were in despair so you must possess some grit and strength of mind to even start out. You don't strike me as someone who gives up at the first hurdle."

She thought fleetingly again of the suicide attempt then decided she would put it behind her. Luke was right. She must make up her mind if she was going to fight or go under.

"I won't even consider it unless it's fair to both of us."

"You are quite a girl, you know that?" He interrupted her quickly. "Anyone else would have jumped at the first suggestion without any further thought, seeing it would do you the most good. Where did you learn to be so reasonable, for life hasn't exactly been fair to you so far?"

"Just you wait till I start adding up the profits or you want to spend too much money on your flocks. I'm a whiz kid with finance, you know. I've not mentioned it before but when I was in London I worked for a bank. I was second fiddle to the Finance director."

"Were you now? Well, doggone me, if that don't beat everything," he enthused eagerly. "I ain't the world's best mathematician; in fact I had a real job passing some of my exams when I was at school. I guess it was only when they saw me in a cockpit they knew I was a natural to fly and let me through..." he broke off abruptly and scowled then went on. "That's all in the past now. Here's where I belong - on the ground - minding the sheep and my own business."

Jessica instinctively kept silent though she was tempted to commiserate. She guessed he was not the sort to accept pity, particularly from a stranger. And that was all she was, just a stranger who had come to the Croft only yesterday. Could she resign herself to living in it? What else was there? Working in an office until the baby was due and she took time off. Living in a pokey flat, just like the one in London, scared to get to know strangers again. Somehow the day of wonderful freedom on the Scottish hillside, breathing fresh air, enjoying the views made the thought of working inside claustrophobic.

They were both silent as they returned to the Croft. Each of them had a great deal to think about. Once back Luke stoked the fire and set some potatoes to bake in the side oven while Jessica filled the kettle for tea.

"How about fried eggs and baked beans to go with the potatoes as we never stopped to fish?" suggested Jessica, thinking of her supplies and the problem of getting more.

"You've just read my mind." Luke said with a smile. "I'll fetch a can from my place, it's the least I can do after eating your food." He dashed off with Cladagh and Jessica sat down with sigh of relief to relax. She felt pleasantly tired and if it were not a fact her mind was in turmoil, she would have thought the day was the nicest she had spent in years. Nevertheless, time was passing; she had to make a decision about her future. To delay longer would not be fair to Luke.

If only she knew what direction to choose. Supposing they didn't get on with each other? Luke had shown a rough side, which could set up barriers. He might be determined to have his way regardless. She could not face a situation of quarrels and dissension. He was nice enough now he understood her reason for coming to Scotland but sharing her life with him? Could she do it? Once she agreed to be a partner that was it; she would have to stick to their agreement. One couldn't back out back out of something like that on a whim.

Jessica roused as Luke came back with a box full of food tins, dumping them in a corner of the room. She blinked sleepily at him and murmured. "Is that what you normally live on?" Her voice was teasing. "No wonder the pie was such an attraction."

"Yes and yes. And you are tired, young lady. A quick meal and then bed for you. In your condition..." he paused as she grimaced at him, then frowned, though Jessica did not know if it was at her or himself, before continuing, "As I was saying, you mustn't overdo things, specially at this time of the trimester, what are you, three or four months?"

She nodded, surprised he knew about pregnancies, "About. Let's not talk about it."

"Okay, but it has to come into the equation sometime. Right! Plates at the ready? Spuds done! These beans are hot enough. How do you like your eggs, shirred, easy over, sunny?"

"What a great choice. Sunny please if it means the yolk stays on top."

"Coming right up, ma'am. Sunny it is."

TWENTY TWO

After they had eaten and cleared the meal, Jessica sat down by the fire with Cladagh at her feet. She had quite recovered her energy after the food and was disinclined to go straight to bed. There was too much on her mind to let her sleep, she knew things would go round and round in her head without answers. Oh mum, what am I to do? Just tell me; I'm too confused to even think of a future here. I need Luke or someone to look after me without strings attached yet let me go when I want. I'm tired of always making decisions. Why can't I just close my eyes and let the next few months drift until I get rid of this burden? I'll be finally free then to leave the past behind and make a new life once more.

"Let's talk a while, Luke; it's too early for bed."

"Okay, suits me, what do you want to talk about?" He balanced himself in William's old rocking chair, extending his legs to the glowing log fire and sighed contentedly. The kitchen was comfortably warm and redolent with the smell of the aromatic pine logs.

"Well, us, I suppose. Do you think we would get on? Tell me some of your likes and dislikes. What do you do for amusement for instance?"

He ran his fingers through his dark hair and grinned a sheepish kind of grin, as though the embarrassment of talking about his feelings was the hardest thing he had ever had to do.

"I'm a kinda quiet sort of a creature. I've ploughed a lonely furrow for much of my life. That is why I do not mind being with the sheep on the hills. I like reading, classical music. Messing about with carpentry, car innards. That's about it. What else do you want to know?"

"Do you have a temper?" She watched him frown.

"Yeah, if I'm prodded. But I've never laid a finger in anger on a woman, if that's what you are getting at? You are safe with me, Jess, I promise you, God's truth, I'd never hurt you, not in a million years," he looked positively aghast at the idea, "Though I'd sure want to hurt that guy that...you know...hurt you if I came across him. He is one so-of-a-bitch"

She smiled tremulously at him. "Oh I believe you, but thank you for putting my mind at rest. I guess I'm still twitchy about...men...about people," she added quickly.

"That's understandable. Now my turn. You said you worked in a bank. Where was that?

London?' She nodded. 'So what was your job? You mentioned second fiddle. What's that?"

"Personal assistant to the Finance director. A miss-do-it-all. Sort of glorified secretary, but privy to confidential matters in the firm and able to liaise with clients. My boss was a really nice man and we got on very well most times. He was kind to me at the end, I think he tried to prevent the sacking but the owner was autocratic and I am sure Henry didn't stand a chance. It was not one of the High Street banks, you see, but a privately owned merchant bank. Good old Welland & Davis, the pride of the City," she said bitterly. "Too bloody proud to admit the son and heir was a rotten lecher. He got to stay and I got thrown out instead. How's that for justice? I want to spit in Sir Charles eye every time I think of it."

Luke's eyes suddenly narrowed in stunned disbelief and he slowly rose to his feet to stare at down at her. "WHO did you say you worked for?"

"Welland and..." startled, she tailed off at the expression on his face.

"Yes, I know the name. Is the son a tall, dark-haired, sort of good looking guy with shifty eyes and a sickle-shaped scar on his chin? Talks with a college accent and tries to impress everyone he meets he knows all there is to know. Was he ever in the Air Force, a pilot?"

Jessica remembered that scar, remembered how the sweat beaded on it as she fought the man who owned it. Her eyes widened in distress as she watched rage darken Luke's face. How could he know Mark? Where had they met? Yet Luke described Mark perfectly. Incredible! But then everything about her life since that night was unbelievable. For here she was, sitting in her own, all-be-it tiny croft by a Scottish loch, aeons away from her former life, waiting for fate to pitch her - where? She nodded her head in confirmation, utterly dumbfounded at the twists and turns of fate. "You've described him perfectly but I can't believe you actually know the same Mark Welland I do. It doesn't seem at all likely."

"Oh yes I do, if that's what he looks like then I know him very well. I ought to - he cost me my job and career. His name is written on my very soul."

"The third plane? Him? But here - in Scotland? It doesn't seem possible it's the same man, though he was in the RAF at one time a year or so back, or so I was led to believe." She said slowly, trying to think if she had heard anything about a flying accident. "It's just that it seems so extraordinary. Mark flying a plane? He never struck me as being that clever. We all thought he had an office job or just did accounts in the Service. But I do truly believe he was devilish enough to cause an accident. He's always had a 'couldn't care less attitude'. At least that was the impression he gave me." She fell silent for a moment trying to recall events.

"But him attacking me and then me meeting you?" She went on, her face frowning in sheer bewilderment. "I can't imagine such an extraordinary coincidence. Then again, he was supposed to have left the Service suddenly, rumour had it that it was because his father wanted him to take over the bank when he finally retired, even though Mark seemed extremely reluctant. It was a crazy idea anyway, stinking of nepotism. He wasn't cut out for the job, certainly not to become a banker. All he ever wanted was to play, have long holidays, enjoy life and to hell with whoever stopped him."

"You've summed him up pretty well, Jess, not that I found out anything of his background, or ever wanted to. But your description hits the type exactly. I keep trying to tell myself it's useless to think about it any more. He's a rotten swine and he'll get his come-uppance without my help. I just wanted out of it. But after your story, I look at myself and know I still have the acid eating my craw. Jesus Christ, Jess! That gives me two good reasons to kill him. I swear I will, if he ever comes near me again."

"No Luke, it's useless thinking like that. I felt murderous at the time so I know how you feel, but I'm damn well sure I'm not spending the rest of my life in jail over a rat like him. We both have to forget him; we can't change things and I don't intend him spoil the rest of my life. Now, shall we continue with our own plans? They are far more important."

TWENTY THREE

It was the evening of the next day, after they had dined well on a large sea trout caught that afternoon in the loch, with fresh fruit to follow, courtesy of Jessica's supplies, when they sat by the glowing stove once more to talk of the future. An equally shared partnership had already been agreed upon the previous evening and Jessica then introduced the idea of enlarging and modernising the farmhouse to provide them with more comfort.

"The shepherd's hut is awful, I don't know how you managed last winter, it's worse than this place, and that's saying something. The bathroom gives me the creeps, I hate the colour and it has so many spiders I'm frightened to take a bath in case one drops on me. Anyway, I cannot take over this place without consideration of you and your comfort. We have to share it, but not in its present state. If we extend it..."

"Jess, whoa a minute, I want to talk of something else that's been on my mind," interrupted Luke, "We'll get to this place later. Sorry to take you back to those evil times but do you think rat face Mark Welland knows you are pregnant?"

"Oh God I hope not!" She paled with fear. Then she recalled she had written to Henry Fowden before leaving the flat to thank him for the cheque, which she presumed, was his doing. Adding that it would give some support over the next few months. However, she was sure she had not said she was pregnant, in case someone else read the letter, yet hoped he would read between the lines. She decided not to divulge her action to Luke for she was convinced Henry would not repeat it to anyone. If ever there was a close-mouthed individual he was, frowning on all types of office gossip. "That's the last thing I need to think about, don't remind me."

Seeing the shock on her face Luke opened his mouth to interrupt.

"No, I never ever saw him again, or his father," she continued quickly before he could say more, "Neither was there a single inquiry as to how I was coping, not even from my old boss, that I must say did make me feel abandoned. It was as though the shutters had come down on my old life and I was labelled *persona non grata*." Yet hardly surprising, she supposed, after her angry snub the night he came to the flat. Still, she had been the victim; surely he could have made some attempt to inquire how she was doing. "It's none of their business anyway, it's my life and I'll run it any way I please. When I left the bank that was the finish of everything to do with them, or their nasty lives. No." Jessica repeated, "No one knows."

"Nevertheless, if by chance he did find out he might try and claim the child when it's born. The other thing is tittle-tattle. You've come into an area of strict moral ethics. Oh, people can lapse anywhere, even here, but I would like to spare you from gossip. You'll be going back and forth to the town same as I will and you'll soon be starting to show. We have to get you booked into the Doctor's as well, so..." he took a deep breath, "...how about if we got married?"

If Luke had surprised her with the partnership, it was nothing to the shock she experienced now. He saw her eyes widen in sheer bewilderment.

"Now hold on, hear me out. It can be an arrangement just like the partnership. I'll lend my name until we are certain that rat can't threaten you and take away your child. It will also make it right with some of the biddies around here who'll throw the Kirk at you as soon as look at you. I know I'm the last man on earth you would think of marrying but think of it as preventing a problem rather than creating one. What do you say? Speak now or forever hold your peace." He laughed at her embarrassment over the words.

"Luke...you are the kindest of men...but I couldn't...well...take advantage of you."

"I'll buy that; go on...why couldn't you? My feet don't smell, at least not when my socks are washed, I've not many bad habits, not so you'd notice, so why not? You have nothing to lose by giving it a go, have you? Or do you hate me that much?"

"Luke no, you know I don't. It's just that I can't put you under such an obligation..."

"It's my choice, you are not twisting my arm, and it's a partnership which either of us can break whenever we want. Just until the baby is born. Poor kid, he hasn't asked for any of this; you must give a thought him being called a bastard. This world's bloody cruel enough without that stigma to shoulder, he don't deserve it, poor little fellow, whatever his father is like."

"I hadn't considered that aspect at all. In fact, I have not given a thought to actually having this baby or what might happen to it or even, to tell you the truth, whether I keep it afterwards. There are so many people eager to adopt, I thought perhaps..." At the bleak look on his face her voice trailed away as she said slowly, "You think I'm wrong, don't you?"

"Let's take it one step at a time, Jessica. I know you must feel hate for what has happened but it's better to put it behind you. We want a contented babe not a squaller who hates everyone from the word go. Right? Okay, we can get married somewhere else, so no one knows around here, then we'll get you fixed up with a Doctor, what else, ah yes, we'll sort out the partnership, find a solicitor in Inverness, in fact we can get married there. How's that?"

Jessica laughed after shaking her head in amazement. "I never dreamed four months ago my life was going to change so quickly. I'm sure I'll wake up and find it's a nightmare."

"Hey there, thanks very much for the vote of confidence, I don't think I want to be classed as a nightmare..."

"Oh Luke I'm sorry, I didn't mean to hurt your feelings, really I didn't. I'm very grateful for your concern and regard," she said hastily. "You have thought of just about everything. If you're sure it's the right thing to do then I accept your generous offer and I thank you for it."

"Right, Jess, consider yourself engaged." He stood up and yawned, "Well, I'm off to the dog kennel." He looked of a sudden embarrassed. "Jess, I meant what I said, it's purely platonic, don't worry that I'll take advantage of you."

"I know, Luke, thanks for the thought. I shall sleep more easily tonight knowing the future is settled, but if you want out of the partnership at any time, you know...if you want to get married to someone else..." she paused, too embarrassed to put her thoughts into words.

"No, Jessica. When I make up my mind I stay with it. Very stubborn, that's me."

"Well, you might change your mind; you can never tell what the future will bring so I promise I won't hold you to anything. You will be free to choose."

"Right the same goes for me so now that's all settled, get to bed and rest. I see I'm gonna have to look after you firmly from now on, like no falling down hillsides or carrying heavy loads. Or over-doing things, right?"

"Right. Now if you've quite finished bossing me about I'll get to bed. Right?"

"Right ma'am." He grinned cheerfully. "G'night, Jess. See you tomorrow." Luke left the Croft whistling with a jaunty air and she heard his merry whistle as he strode along the path to his sleeping quarters. Jessica wondered if he had cheered up because of having someone to talk to and joke with. She realised afresh how impossible it would have been for her to stay in such an isolated place by herself especially now she was pregnant. Are you watching over me, mum? Is this your doing to make sure I'm all right? If so, you're doing okay. But don't think I'm going to fall in love with him and live happily ever after; this is only until the baby is born. Without warning, it hit her. She hadn't once given a thought to this baby she was expecting. Supposing she just stayed till it was born? What then? Mentally she shrugged. Well afterwards she could leave. 'Oh yes, after Luke getting settled and nice and cosy?' It was almost as though she could hear her mother speaking. 'Jessica, I'm really ashamed of you for taking him for granted.' Put like that she too felt shame and knew that despite her fierce vow of only looking after her own interests she would never let Luke down.

As Luke walked away under a starlit sky, his face fell into its accustomed gravity. Despite his cheerfulness he was under no illusion their relationship together was going to be a walkover. Indeed, they could end up hating each other in a very short time, still worse, although he had spoken of it being a temporary situation he found the idea disturbing. All he wanted was peace and permanence after a lifetime on the move. In this glen lay the seeds of safety, a refuge from the evil of the world. He knew the isolation would bring its problems. His fine brain was honed to perfection as a pilot, and he had been a good pilot. Would he decay in solitude till he was totally afraid to go back to the mainstream of life? What was he afraid of? Failing? Disgrace? Was that so surprising, for his life had been filled with all of those things, time after time.

Jessica's appearance in his life had heralded a new beginning, an exciting partnership that might grow into contentment. Then too, there was the child; how could she even contemplate giving it away? He must tread warily with her. Perhaps in time she would settle to the idea of marriage with him, perhaps they might even make a go of things on a long-standing basis. Naturally she was still shocked from the rape. Jesus, what wouldn't he give to have Welland before him and pound the living daylights out of the bastard? In the meantime, he would have to be patient with Jessica, court her gently, show her one man, at least, had respect, and cared a great deal about what had happened to her.

He laughed mirthlessly to himself. This will be a first, Fraser, caring about someone other than just you. Then he thought about Mike and the grief welled anew. What if he was the jinx that hurt others? Hell's teeth - to think that way was madness! He'd need all his wits about him in the coming months to cope with Jessica so he had better calm himself down. With an effort he shut down the fearful thoughts and soberly continued on his way to bed.

TWENTY FOUR

The hunter crouched in a rocky, gorse-shielded cleft high upon the hill, out of sight of his quarry. Dark fur, striped randomly with mottled bands, gave it the ideal camouflage for its stealthy activities as it melted into the stony background to become almost invisible.

Genetically bigger than the average wildcat, its mother was a black puma, a fugitive from private captivity in the South, who had made its way by degrees northward; chased from area to area by irate farmers, who more often than not thought they were hunting a large dog. The puma, mating with a large wildcat, eventually reared only the one male kit. Thereafter, the young cat, its large frame enabling it to tackle bigger and better prey, grew even larger and stronger, resembling its genetic puma parent.

The plump well-furred tail swung gently back and forth, as it eyed its victim from its place of concealment, the undersized roe deer, who had wandered foolishly away from the herd. The animal gently cropped the mountain grass, unaware of the danger from above. The tail ceased to swing and the body readied itself for the leap on to the neck of the roe, sharp claws clutching for a hold while its long incisors nipped the main artery in the neck. The roe struggled briefly then gave up as its life-blood gushed forth. The sudden intense scuffle caused the rest of the small herd to take flight but the wildcat was not concerned, he would hunt and kill again before long. Calling softly to his mate to join him in the feast he settled down to fill his stomach. Two kittens, safe in the sheltered cave-like lair would feast well tonight on their mother's enriched milk.

The cat felt satisfied with the kill, his skill was improving, so much better than dining on the usual fare of rabbits and voles. Yowling victoriously, he rubbed his face on the short springy turf before finding a place to rest. He was widening his territory and soon, before many moons passed by, although presently unaware of his intentions, he would trespass on another's ground, a hunter who would take great exception to the prowess of the cat; and at his recently acquired taste for lamb. As far as the cat was concerned he killed for food, but some food was easier to get than having to hunt for it. A flock of sheep was like an ever-open larder to the wily cat.

TWENTY FIVE

"Hullo, lass, how are you? You're looking very bonny, are you not?" "When's the baby due? Not so very long, by the look of it."

Jessica turned round to see Fiona Stuart bearing down on her. She was amused to hear Mrs Stuart still asking and answering her own questions.

"I've a while to go, Mrs Stuart, time enough yet to practice with my pies. But they won't beat yours. Your fame has spread throughout the district. You really ought to have a pie-shop."

"Och away with your blethering, I'm not as good as that. Let's get back to you. I still canna get ower the fact I didna ken you were marrit to yon Luke. He's a gye silent man and I suppose you being a Londoner an' all never thocht to tell me. I shoulda guessed; ye had a loving' twinkle in yer e'en that said yer a well-loved lassie. Luke was only tellin' me what a grand girl you are the last time I spoke to him. Puts me in mind o' my Sam. Gone now these five years and I still miss him. He was that tender at times you'd have thocht he was a poet. You treasure yon man o' yourn, they dinna last as long as we do. There's more widow wimman in Invergarry than men folk, ye ken."

"Yes, I'll mind your words. Now about the pies..."

"Ah yes, the pies. Ye mean yon mutton pies I make fer all and sundry? Och, them's easy, lassie, now listen here, I'll let you in on a wee secret o' mine, one I wouldna tell anybody else around here, but you are different. In any case a wee bitty help to a young wife is entirely in order. Now listen carefully. Put a wee sprinkle of rosemary and sage in the meat to bring oot the flavour. It does wonders for the taste. People are aye asking me ma secrets so dinna tell 'em, will ye?"

"Certainly not. It's between you and me, I swear." Jessica managed to get in.

"Now, what about the oven? You mon get the range right, lassie, for if your heat is wrong then the pastry wull not taste right. Have ye tested it with bread?" She rattled on, in her element at being consulted, having taken a real shine to Jessica.

"I'm fine with making bread and not bad with my cakes but either I scorch the pastry or it doesn't cook and just goes soggy." Jessica made a rueful face. "I think I've thrown away more than we've eaten. Though Luke, bless him, makes a good effort and doesn't complain much."

"No, no, I don't mean the baking of bread. Put a crust or two in the bottom of the oven and see how fast it browns. Too fast, then pull the coals back from that side of the grate. If it stays pale for more than twa - three minutes then build up the coal and try again. You'll soon get the hang of it and Luke'll love you forever." She laughed gaily and Jessica joined in as though it was true she had a devoted and loving husband and not the make-believe marriage it actually was.

Jessica had been pleased to divert Mrs Stuart's mind from the subject of marriage. For all had gone according to plan and no one in the district had even guessed that she and Luke had only known each other a short time, merely supposing Jessica had been in London until Luke was settled. She still felt uneasy in case she was caught in a lie, but the fact it had been Jessica's grandfather made things right, so consequently the two of them were accepted into the district without question. Jessica wondered if she owed anything to Andy Keiller. She had racked her brains to think of anything she might have said which was odd on her first trip to the Croft but as he made no comment about her being married she concluded he had accepted her too.

London-born and having absolutely no idea of farming had meant Jessica had to work twice as hard to assimilate all the duties she had taken on. Her store of how-to books increased by a score and Luke had built extra bookshelves to accommodate them. Books on Cookery, rearing Chickens, Interior decorating, Sewing, and dealing with recalcitrant cooking stoves were among the nightly studies. But she had only one book on Babies.

Luke had purchased this and he noticed how rarely she opened but made no mention of the fact. He had read it from cover to cover, committing every detail to memory just in case.

There were times when she wondered if she was doing the right thing by staying on the farm other times when she wouldn't have changed her life for anything else. It all depended on whether the cow they had purchased stayed still for milking and didn't tip the pail over, or the chickens laid their eggs in the nests and not in the nearby meadow or whether her back ached or her legs swelled. As she grew plumper the latter problems became more frequent till they were with her all the time and it felt as if she had been pregnant forever.

Putting together their savings had caused a long debate on how best to spend the money, which made Jessica reflect afterwards on how well they got on together, each very conscious of not trespassing on sensitive feelings. Each did their best to talk things through rather than bull-dose a suggestion, however strongly they might feel about it. As a result, their lives had settled into an amicable pattern that made them realise how lonely they had been before.

"I vote for a white tiled bathroom and taps in the right place." Jessica said when first they began on the list of renovations to enlarge and improve the property.

"How about a Fridge?" Countered Luke.

"Ooh yes, and maybe a Freezer as well?"

"Waal, if you really think so? Sounds as if you are going to stock pile food." He teased.

"Well you eat it. I wonder how I've managed up until now without one."

"Okay, but I get to buy my sheep, don't forget. And the budget still has to be stretched with all the rest of our plans. There's so much to be done."

"Wouldn't have it any other way." Impishly she grinned at him.

"You are a tease, you know, young lady. I've a good mind to..."

"To what?" Puzzled, she stared at him without understanding he was flirting with her. Luke regretted his spontaneous impulse to get close to Jessica and for a few days had been withdrawn and rather remote until the incident was forgotten as the alterations proceeded at a fast pace. Very soon the house was enlarged with a second bedroom, bathroom tiled, plumbing rearranged and a wood stove put in the extended corridor to serve the extra radiators as well as giving added hot water; finally the whole Croft was painted inside and out. What a difference it made as the place gradually became more cosy and comfortable. Best of all, a new cable had been laid from the small pylons which ran along the top edge of the glen and the voltage was now well balanced. No longer did the lights flicker and jump as though about to go out, one could use a higher wattage and read a book in the evenings instead of peering in the gloom.

The old barn had been moved further along in the modernising of the place, so as well as holding fuel for the stoves, had room for their newly acquired cow and a decent place for Cladagh to sleep. The dog was old now and had developed rheumatism, so it was not good for her to be kept outside in a kennel. She stayed with Jessica during the day but Luke insisted she sleep out at night so they had agreed on the barn. Jessica made certain her bed was sheltered from any draughts and fussed over her, much to Cladagh's delight and Luke's amusement.

Luke had bought a young dog and was busy training it. The dog hadn't yet acquired the skill of the older sheepdog or her keen instinct but Luke was proud of what he had done so far. He had also bought in a Border Leicester ram and six ewes to inter-mingle with his Black Faced Scottish horned sheep in order to raise the quality of the mutton and the wool. Most nights he pored over breeding and marketing books to learn and improve his knowledge of sheep rearing.

Jessica wasted no time in renovating all the things she felt necessary for a comfortable existence. She employed a local carpenter who added cupboards to the sink area to provide counter space and storage. She made new curtains for the windows and her crate of personal things was sent for to provide the huge kitchen with books, a small bookcase, two side tables and numerous knickknacks which was all she had left of her mother and her old home. The luxury purchase of an additional pair of comfortable fireside chairs, which could be moved in front of the range when all the cooking was done, was their final extravagance but Jessica appreciated them of an evening when the chores were over. She kept it all as neat as a new pin and learned to cook really well. Luke was glad to come home to a good meal and more comfort than he had ever known in his life.

At first, they behaved towards each other with great respect, each careful not to intrude on the other's privacy. But as her pregnancy advanced and Jessica increased in size, she suffered a cruel recurring fear the baby would look like Mark, would inherit his nasty ways. She grew depressed and quite bad tempered with Luke, associating his maleness with the wretched villain that had caused her to undergo such an uncomfortable situation. She knew she was being unfair. Daily promising not to snap or get irritable then weeping copiously as she transgressed.

"I loathe this lump inside. Things are never going to be the same after it gets itself born. Oh why didn't you let me make arrangements for it to be adopted? Then I'll be free forever from being reminded." She would cry in despair. But always the same answer came back:

He would nod slowly and tighten his lips before saying, "You would never forgive yourself if you did that and I certainly wouldn't forgive you." Then reaching out he would take hold of her hand. "Let's wait until the baby arrives then you can do it if you wish." It was his only answer and she had to settle for that knowing he spoke a lot of sense.

When she first felt the baby stirring she kept the news to herself for some time, unwilling to acknowledge the tiny life inside her. Then one day Luke noticed her flinch and immediately put a hand to her stomach. "It's moving, isn't it?" He said quietly. "Can I feel?"

Reluctantly she nodded, her face reddening with embarrassment. He never appeared to notice things then all at once, he would surprise her with an unerringly accurate analysis of the situation. She then said bitterly. "Yes, it's there all right. How I wish it weren't. I feel trapped, Luke, I really do. Why can't we contact the adoption services?"

He placed his palm gently on her stomach and waited for a moment or two then grinned with wry amusement. "What you might call a proper little kicker, ain't he? He'll be a lively critter when he's born, most like. How great to think he is healthy. I also have a hankering to see what he looks like before he's sent off without so much as a 'by your leave'. Don't you agree, Jess?"

"I suppose so," she said repressively, "Personally I don't think too much about it anyway." Luke was amazingly patient with her when she acted so distant, sensing her acute depression.

"How about a cup of tea?" He would say. "Well, coffee then. You sit down I'll make it, and then if you are very good I'll rub your back, twice even, if you make me an apple pie. There, you can't beat that for an offer, can you?" Teasing, cajoling, anything to make her laugh even tickling her unmercifully until she begged him to stop.

She would repent the bad temper and vow to herself she would try harder to be patient. But as time passed the strain showed in her face and Luke worried endlessly about her coping with the birth. Things would go badly if she didn't relax or let go of the deep depression and pent-up anger he sensed within. It could possibly cause her to give the baby away and part completely from him. This would be a catastrophe he couldn't bear to imagine. He said no more, unwilling to provoke her into something she would regret, but the way ahead seemed to bode great unhappiness. He did the only thing possible under the circumstances and became amazingly patient and tolerant, biting his lips at times when went wrong and he was frustrated too. Despite his own fatigue, he managed to keep up a good front and all his efforts went into making the croft a good home and caring for his sheep. And so the months went by and the two of them made progress in all sorts of ways, finding great contentment in every successful job accomplished.

TWENTY SIX

Leaving Invergarry one day, after a routine shopping excursion, they drove home along the twenty miles of track to Kinlochhourn and Jessica's mind went back to her Wedding Day, which was an unpretentious Registry Office ceremony in Inverness. It suited their needs exactly and later they dined at a pleasant hostelry nearby where Luke suggested they order champagne.

"No, not that, I really don't care for it."

"Why not? It's traditional isn't it?" He laughed. All the best weddings like ours have it."

"Well we'll be different. Order what you like but not that." Her expression left him in no doubt she was very serious. An inner perception alerted him that it might be associated with the evening she would rather forget so he hadn't disagreed.

"Okay, no problem. I think we'll have the *Beau Site,*" he said to the wine waiter. "You'll like this Jess; it will go well with our food. He was right; Jess had enjoyed the claret very much.

They spent that night at a guesthouse in separate rooms, Luke pretending his wife was a poor sleeper and he hated to be disturbed. The landlady was privately most indignant.

"He'll not get up fur the bairn when it's born," she said to her husband, "He'll never want to be disturbed, that yin. Yin folk dinna deserve us wimmin, you men are aye too fond of your ain ease to care a jot." Her husband merely grunted. He was too used to the ongoing nagging and turned the proverbial deaf ear to his wife.

The visit to the solicitor was smoothly concluded, and Luke, besides placing an agreed sum of money in her bank for his half share of the farm, bought furniture for the bedrooms at the Croft. He chose a double bed for her, giving her the larger of the two rooms and though she protested at the extra cost, he still insisted, knowing it would be far more comfortable.

"When children are little they always end up in your bed. You try getting to sleep with a kicking monster in a single bed. Besides, you take up more room now!"

Her indignation made him laugh when he teased her over the expanding waistline. Deep down, she felt frustrated and angry; trapped in the obligatory state she had to face. Not only carrying a child but she must face the pain of labour to get rid of it. However, when Jessica sank into the blissful roominess of the new bed she was delighted he had ignored her protests. The bed took up space in the small bedroom but now she had it she would never part with it.

"How do you know so much about children?" She asked him later on. At once his face reddened then paled, which, she had learned before too long, was a sure sign he was disturbed.

He gathered his thoughts before answering, his mind going back to a distant past.

"I was married once; had a kid too. It didn't work out and she left me." He shrugged as though it was no big deal but Jessica catching a glimpse of the pain in his eyes knew it had been one more blow in his life. How many other blows had he had she didn't know about. He noticed her frown and give him an odd questioning look and said hastily:

"Don't worry, I was divorced. I don't go in for bigamy. You are legally married, okay? I was a young idiot and it was such a long time ago I've forgotten how it came about. I guess if we had just slept together for a while, got the sex part of it out of our systems we would never have given marriage another thought; but she had her family to consider and I had my own crazy inhibitions like 'doing things the right way'. 'Marriage is for life' – well – you know how it goes. Trouble was there was no one around to tell me I was too immature myself to cope with a wife. So, we rowed and fought, made up and fought again, till eventually – well, you know."

She forbore to ask him why he had not mentioned it. What had happened to him before he met her was, she considered, hardly her business. She knew him well enough by now to realise he never told lies, merely kept silent on those issues which were not important in their daily lives

"I wasn't thinking about that, I was wondering if you missed the child? Was it a boy or a girl? I get the impression you like children, or am I wrong?"

"No, you're right. It's a girl; she'd be about eight or nine now. I never saw her again after I parted with her mother. Never mind, it's water under the bridge, Jess, another lifetime away and one I wouldn't want to resurrect. I've got all I want here, so don't fret, okay? Anyway, it's time I was off. I decided to move the sheep down from the high pasture today. Now the weather is closing in, it'll be a hard slog but better to do it now before it gets worse and we lose some of the flock. I have Jimmy Halverson and his dog coming to help me so it won't be so bad with two of us. See you later tonight unless we are pushed to stay in the Bothy. I'll take my sleeping bag and rations. Take care, Jess, mind you rest this afternoon, okay? Bye honey, be good."

They heard the sound of a motor coming down the hill so he collected his gear and headed into the cold air. It had snowed before Christmas but the weather turned mild and then had rained almost continuously for three weeks. Jessica watched his breath come out like smoke as he climbed into the van and saw there had been a heavy frost in the night.

Beyond tasks of feeding and milking the cow; seeing to the hens, which were warm and safe in their own quarters; collecting eggs and cooking, she had no chores to do. Luke had brought in plenty of wood for the stoves and inside, behind the thick walls of their home, she was warm and comfortable. Feeling energetic, she decided to turn out the wall cupboards where she kept dried goods and kept busy for most of the morning. She stopped for lunch at midday and noticed how dark the sky had become. Then, glancing out later she realised it had started snowing heavily and already the surrounding hills were whitened mounds, the soft snow gathering lightly like cotton wool on the tall-scattered pine trees, causing the usual outlook to become a different scene.

Luke will not be home tonight, Jessica thought, with certainty, rubbing her back to ease an ache. Being alone no longer bothered her. Civilisation was miles away and who would be daft enough to venture out in weather like this. Besides, she had Cladagh with her. She opened the doors of the bed closet where she usually had her afternoon nap and finding a book to read, lay down to rest. Cladagh curled up on the rug by the fire but every now and then she lifted her head and whined, a quiet almost inaudible whine, which made Jessica glance over at her, surprised at her unease.

"What's the matter, girl? Is Luke out in the snow? Never mind my lovely, he'll be home tomorrow. At least you are inside and that's where you are staying." She resolved to keep the dog in with her for company that night; Luke would not be around to turn her out in the barn.

TWENTY SEVEN

Heaving herself up on the horsehair mattress, she wriggled to get comfortable but the pain in her back persisted in a peculiarly intermittent fashion. She felt very tired and put her book to one side and sighed deeply. Time for a bit of shuteye; she said to herself, guess I should have left the cupboard alone, I've probably overdone things, but within minutes, all was quiet as she fell sound asleep.

Jessica awoke to darkness and silence, the fire only ash and embers, with no comforting glow. She wondered what had roused her, and then the pain came once more, a fierce grinding cramp that curled round from her back and flowed over her stomach before ebbing away as though it had never been, leaving behind the memory of a huge gripping hand.

She sat up clutching her stomach, waiting. Nothing happened. After a moment she rose from the bed and put on the lamp then closed the curtains. Outside it was snowing and she could barely see over the bank of snow on the window ledge. It had turned into a real Northerly blizzard and there was no doubt the farmhouse would be snowed in by morning. Jessica thought of the men and their enormous task with the sheep; she hoped that they had managed to get them down safely and were now safe in the Shepherd's hut, even if it was comfortless and cold.

Stirring the embers of the fire and throwing on some logs took only a moment then bright flames rose to light and warm the room. She was humming to herself as she began to fill the kettle when the pain hit her again, this time severely. Gasping, she held onto the sink until it was over. Oh heavens! Surely not. She was due to have the baby in about two weeks, or so the doctor said, booking her in at the Fort William Cottage Hospital. This pain must be because she was tired from cleaning out the cupboards. The next pain came again while she stood telling herself not to worry and this time she knew, beyond all doubt, she had more than enough to worry about. Luke could not possibly get home that night; the snow would be far too deep. In any case, how would he know she needed him? What was she going to do? She was alone and it was still only four o'clock. How long did a baby take to come? The book said around twenty-four hours for the first baby but supposing it came sooner. Supposing Luke did not come home tomorrow morning either. What if the snow was so deep it kept him away for days? Hadn't he told her that bad things could happen when one was so isolated?

She imagined him hurt, frozen. Stop it; she told herself severely, he would not leave you for long if he can help it...but what if?

Picking up the telephone Jessica tried to get through to the Doctor's surgery but all she heard was a hissing on the line. She tried the Hospital, then the Police, but it was no use, the heavy snow must have brought the line down. She thought about using the Landrover still parked outside, but although Luke had given her one or two lessons in driving they'd agreed to wait until the baby was born before she took her test. In any case the road was tricky enough to drive over on a clear day with an experienced driver; it would be madness to try driving to Invergarry all by herself.

Cladagh whined as Jessica crouched down beside her and scratched the back of her neck.

"You know don't you, girl? What do I do? Oh Cladagh, I wish Luke were here, he'd know what to do." Another pain kept her on her hands and knees and she recalled the lessons from the Baby Clinic she had gone to and panted fiercely while it lanced through her. She wasn't sure it helped. The pain was severe. The dog whined again and licked her face then went to the door.

"You don't want to go out in this, wait a bit till it stops snowing." Cladagh lay down again by the fire but she kept her eyes on Jessica, watching every movement as the next hour passed and Jessica timed the contractions. Finally, when the dog went to the door once more, she said in great desperation: "Cladagh, find Luke, fetch Luke back, fetch girl!" She opened the door and immediately the dog bounded out into the drifting snow and disappeared up the path.

Jessica stood looking out at the falling snow, watching it blow into drifts against the stone walls. Then an icy shiver made her go back in out of the cold to tend the kitchen range. She checked the stove at the end of the passage just as another pain overtook her, gamely gritting her teeth till it passed. Hours went by, well past the time Luke normally returned home so she knew he was staying in the hillside Bothy. What if Luke didn't come home tomorrow morning either? Again her imagination took flight as she thought of him marooned in deep snow. It might keep him away for days? Stop it, she told herself severely; he won't leave you for long if he can help it. Besides, Jimmy is with him as well.

Jessica longed for the dog, wondering if she had done the right thing by sending her to seek Luke. She was an old animal, the snow had become deep and treacherous; supposing the cold got to her and she died. Oh God, I'll hate myself forever if anything happens to her. Tears ran down her face and she sobbed at the idea of losing her. Then a thought struck her, even if she did find Luke he would have no idea what was wrong, he would merely think the dog had come to track him as she had done once or twice before when he left her at home. Fool that she was why hadn't she tied a note to her collar? Now it needed no genius to realise there wasn't an alternative. She was going to give birth on her own if this baby decided to come tonight.

Well Jessica, you had better prepare yourself before it gets too hard to move. Only, what to prepare? What did one need when you had a baby? Heavens above, she'd read about bathing and feeding but took it for granted the hospital would manage the rest. Come on think, Jess, you must have read about it somewhere! Where was that book Luke had bought? She searched everywhere for it but without success. She was not to know that Luke had slipped it in his pocket for a little light reading if he got a moment or two to rest after dealing with the sheep. Scouring the house for the wretched book had taken the last of her energy. Her brain seemed like cotton wool, unable to remember a single detail of instruction. What upset her most was the unfamiliar stupidity of her fright. Before this, she had always coped with emergencies. Why was this so different? Why couldn't she remember the things she was supposed to do? All at once sheer panic set in and she lay on the bed weeping hysterically.

Then unexpectedly she felt the urge to pass water and headed for the bathroom. Before she reached the toilet, water streamed down her legs and she remembered a nurse saying this would happen at a certain stage in labour. What stage? She tried to remember what she had been told but pain robbed her of coherent thought and she clung to the basin as another spasm tore through her. Was the baby ready to come? Should she lie on the bed? Oh God! Help me! What am I to do? What if my baby should die? She did not care about herself, only the baby. It would be a just punishment for being so neglectful of the tiny life now coming into a harsh and uncaring world. Oh, Jessica how could you have been so horrible to think badly of the poor wee soul? And how dreadful she been to Luke? She deserved everything that was coming to her but please oh please don't hurt my baby! Don't let him die!

Now she was completely ensnared in the hard pain as it surged through her body, intent on only one thing, to bring forth the wee scrap of humanity conceived in a moment of hatred and uncaring lust but for all that, innocent of blame, only completely resolute in its efforts to achieve life. She could only pray as she endured the agony of labour that neither she nor the baby would perish. That awful thought, brought not a shred of comfort. Confused; in pain; unable to reason properly; she could not guess that nature was having its own way again. She was about to bring forth a child and the fierce protectiveness of a mother, which is the main ingredient of life in its basic form told her it was hers alone to nourish and care for. Having spent months wishing for it to vanish from her body, now, all of a sudden she desperately wanted her child. Yes, nature had decreed, you are going to be a mother soon and you will find that forever you will fight with all your might to protect the child – *your child! Only your child.*

Now the contractions were fiercely strong, and it was as much as she could do to return to the closet bed. She sank exhausted onto the mattress, where a strong pain ripped through her making her cry out in distress. No chance to even gather a sheet to protect the bed or seek any means that would help her through the ordeal. Her brain, in a whirl over the volte-face, seemed unable to make up its mind. Jessica lost all sense of time, as one pain submerged her with grim intensity then another followed in quick succession.

Soon the pain changed its nature, Jessica was now conscious of a feeling she had to strain and push before she could be free of the torment. Mark, you horrible bastard, I hope you die shrieking in hell for what you've done to me. You are wicked and evil'. She screamed the words, cursing the very thought of him. How dreadfully unfair, she moaned. To go through his assault and then to suffer all this agony was beyond belief. She was going to die, she knew it!

TWENTY EIGHT

All at once, the door slammed back on its hinges. Luke stood there, the breath heaving from his body in a hot stream of mist. He had heard her scream as he was rounding the edge of the loch and ran the last hundred yards although he was already exhausted. He was completely sodden from the huge effort of fighting his way through miles of deep drifts on foot. It took only an instant to understand what was happening as a heartrending wail emerged from Jessica yet again. Luke shut the door hastily and heaved off his outerwear before going over to her.

"You have great timing, honey, what started you off? Did you fall? Have you had any kind of an accident?" He put his hand to her forehead. "Cool as a cucumber would you believe? All set to do the job without me? I guess you've been cleaning the barn to help things along!"

She shook her head and tried to smile. "No, I've been real careful, though I was cleaning cupboards. I didn't hurt myself, honestly, it started all by itself, when I was asleep."

"Good, then it's normal, earlier than we expected but there's nothing to worry about, we just do everything according to the book and it will be okay."

"Where is that damn baby book? I searched everywhere for it, not that I wouldn't rather have you instead." She groaned and tried desperately to pant again as another clenching pain hit her body. Oh, when was this agony ever going to end?

She smiled mistily at him through tears of thankfulness. How miraculous to have him with her, she had been more than in despair by herself. It was all right now; he would know what to do. And he did. It didn't take long to fetch a thick blanket and a large old sheet to cover the bed. Then he got her up, helped her undress, put on one of his large cotton shirts, and with more pillows at her back propped her up gently before tucking another blanket around her and giving her a hug.

"There! How's that, honey? You look snug as the proverbial bug? I'll be telling you to move over any minute now. I'm beat, my girl! That snow really is deep. I've never known it lie so thick round here before. One ginormous blanket. Sure does stop you in your tracks."

"I'm so glad you made it, Luke. I feel better now you're here; I really thought I'd be on my own for this, oooooh..." she tailed off as another contraction caught her and she tried to pant.

"That's it! Pant, love, keep it going! You're doing great, baby, just great."

She was but was he? It was all very well bringing sheep into the world, but a human baby? Could he manage? Suppose something went wrong and the baby died, or worse still Jessica. How the hell was he to handle it? His heart turned over as the truth struck home that he cared for her more than just as a partner. These past months had demonstrated just how lonely he had been before. How easily he had slipped into the feeling of homely comfort with her around. He liked the quiet determination to tackle jobs she had never done before; her ability to reckon their financial status and elect a policy that would give them fair profit in the future. He was an astute planner himself but he knew she had the edge on him. She never took advantage, merely went over the options and left him to make the final decisions. He always took her advice. He saw through the grotesque shape of pregnancy to the slim fair-haired girl beneath and liked what he saw. She wasn't glamorous in the flamboyant sense, but had a quiet beauty that was fresh and simple. Kindness shone like a beacon to him, even as she was now, swollen tear stained face, in torment from the deep agonising pain he wished he could relieve. Yet he had promised to keep his distance, treat her just as a partner, any advances were strictly taboo unless she gave a sign she was attracted to him too.

Leaving her for a moment, he filled the kettle, found a stout pair of scissors and string for tying the cord, and put them in a bowl with a drop of disinfectant and the boiled water. Then after washing his hands thoroughly he came back to sit with her on the bed. He dare not show he was anything but composed inside.

"Pant. Come on pant, like this, hah, hah. That's my girl, you are a real trooper!" And so it went on and on until the straining grunts told him pushing was inevitable. By then he wasn't aware of his inner fright so intent was he on the battle to expel the baby. To help her, he wedged himself against her bent knees and held her arms to encourage the effort she was making.

"That's my girl, you're doin' fine, pu-u-ssh honey, soon be over. Come on baby; give it all you've got. Time that little monster was out of there, you've carried him long enough."

"I can't, Luke, it hurts so much," she screamed at him as a pause came between the painful contractions. "Oh Luke it really hurts..." Her breath left her as another surge began.

"I know it does, it won't be long now. My God! I can see its head. Hold it now, Jess, let me help you. Whoa there, hold it! Pant for me gently. Gently now! Don't hold your breath, don't push any more, I don't want you to tear." He could see the top of the head distending the vulva to its limits; also, alarming him greatly, a section of the cord was emerging too.

This was trouble! He thought back to his experience with the sheep last spring and the long discussions with William over birthing them. William told him the cord sometimes got caught around the neck or shoulders, which could cause choking or death. A shepherd had to be ready to help or he could lose a lamb. It was far safer for the head to descend on its own. If Jessica pushed too quickly they might lose the baby. Gently he pressed back the skin of the opening to free the head and felt her tense with another huge surge of effort

"No Jess, hold it, baby. Pant for me. Don't push, there's my girl. Steady now, I'm just going to get this cord free." He worked desperately at the slippery coil to work it free.

"Nooo, I can't wait...it's hurting, oooooh..."

The next second Jessica gave an almighty scream and Luke felt a warm rush of liquid as the baby slid out into his waiting hands. Quickly checking to see all was right, he watched the little face screw up in unenthusiastic distaste at the cold world outside and his own tears fell like rain down his face as the cry of the new born baby filled the room.

"Oh, Jessica, we have a son and he's beautiful, quick love, open up your shirt."

She tore the shirt apart and he laid the baby just as he was, warm and sticky, on her bare stomach, to be instantly gathered up in her arms. Luke tied the cord in two places before cutting the cord then before she could protest he pressed hard on her belly. She groaned deeply and was about to yell in protest when almost immediately she felt another strong contractual pain and the afterbirth came safely away. Luke tidied away the debris before coming to hug the two human beings he loved most in the world while Jessica looked down in awe at the small creature she had nurtured inside for months.

"Who's a clever girl then? Isn't he great?"

Jessica lay exhausted but happy, holding the baby close. She had never imagined she could feel so utterly content with life and the soreness and aches faded away as she gazed at the crumpled face of her son. Not Mark's. Never his! The baby belonged only to her. Then she recalled Luke's excited voice as he was born, "Oh Jess...we have a son..."

Not you have a son, but we have a son!

"Oh Luke, he's gorgeous. But how did you know he would be a boy? You've been calling him he all the time. We might have had a girl, you know."

"Nah. Girls can't cope with the sheep. I had my order in for a son a long time ago."

She giggled in relief, partly at his sally but also in amazement at the rapt look on his face.

He really was pleased, just as she was. However, a disturbing thought struck her with dismay, of the long months of agonising and complaining over this birth.

"Luke," she began shyly, "I'm so grateful for all you've done, looking after me and all and now this...acting as midwife, no less. You are amazing, you truly are."

"*I* didn't do anything; you got through the worst all by yourself. I'm only sorry I wasn't here when you started. I can guess how frightened you felt." He pressed her hand warmly.

"Oh the dog! Luke, where's Cladagh, she went to find you? She seemed to know she had to fetch you. Is she out in all this snow? She'll die, Luke, she'll..."

"Calm down, Jess, it's okay. You don't need to fret about her. She made it okay. I left her with Jimmy in the Bothy. She was all run out; poor old dog, but she reached us in one piece, brave girl. Boy, am I glad she did, I guessed soon as I saw her, what was up but did not know if you had fallen or something, especially outside in the snow. Thank heaven it wasn't any worse. Did you try the phone? I could see the lines were down soon as I came round the top by the jetty. You know I haven't seen a snowfall like this since I left the Rockies, I tell you I fell into more drifts than I ever did as a kid, and I couldn't believe they got so deep in these parts. Now in Canada..."

he hugged her fiercely again, "No, forget Canada, I wouldn't go back even if I had a fortune to spend!"

He gazed searchingly at Jessica, more than a hint of fun in his eyes.

"You two look great but how about if I get you both cleaned up and looking respectable! Our son is kinda sticky...a bit like his mama..."

Jessica who had been gazing besotted at the scrap of a babe in her arms suddenly realised how naked she was, and what Luke had done for her. Colour rose in her cheeks as he watched. Guessing her embarrassment he pressed a warm hand over hers and said softly:

"Think nothin' of it, kid, I'm glad I was here, I won't say a word to anyone if you don't." She looked at him and smiled shyly, the smile became a laugh and soon tears of merriment were rolling down each face. It took a loud wail of angry displeasure from one small boy to remind them he too wanted some attention.

"I'm going to run a bath for you, then get this babe cleaned up, for he's gonna get awful hungry soon. Good job all his things are ready, he sure was in a hurry to be born."

She could hardly bear to relinquish the baby even for the short time it took to soothe her aches and pains with hot water. Soon the two of them were tucked back in the closet bed and she was attempting her first experience of breast-feeding. The baby seemed to be all wide, open mouth at first, and the yells of hunger were loud indeed. Jessica was alarmed to see tears of rage squeezing from tightly shut eyes as he blindly hunted for the food, which would sustain him. Luke cradled his head in one large hand and eased his face round to her engorged breast. At once the baby clamped strongly onto Jessica's nipple and she exclaimed at the baby's strength. Then after a moment when she got used to him sucking, she looked down at him and sighed with contentment. "Heavens, I didn't think it would feel like this."

"How did you think it would be?"

"I don't know, I've never let myself think so far ahead. Oh dear I seem to have been a real failure as a mother," she sighed heavily. "All I thought about was getting rid of a lump that was so awful I never thought of it as a human being. And now I realise this baby is a part of myself as well. Can I forget, Luke, that the other part is Mark's? Will I ever forget?"

"Yes, you can if you acknowledge our marriage and that this new-born baby is our child. I can't make you forget what has gone before, I can only say look to our future and believe we will be happy. Whatever has happened in my life before doesn't matter. It's this moment that counts. It is the beginning of a new life for me and I won't let it go. Your old life was sad and a great deal of the memories just that, memory. We have a new life here and I want it to be a good life for both of us. What say we forget the past and make a good future?"

"Yes, I'll go with that," she made a wry face. "At least it can't be as bad as before."

Luke would have preferred her to be more enthusiastic but at least things had turned out a lot better than his fears. They were still together and seemed likely to stay that way for a while. While the way ahead might be fraught with pitfalls he would take courage from the present and just hope things would turn out for the best. In one way at least he was indispensable. Jessica very soon found that Luke's early knowledge of having a child was helpful and once she put away her shyness and began taking instruction from Luke she was surprised how easy it was to both feed and attend to his needs.

Two days later the snow cleared sufficiently for the Doctor to visit. He pronounced them both exceedingly fit and healthy, though the baby, he thought, had come a little too early and would need to be fed on demand. Jessica didn't mind for there was nothing she liked better than sitting by the warm stove either feeding him or just gazing at him while he slept. She and Luke had decided to call him after her grandfather but reversing the forenames so he was duly named

Angus William, which Luke said was enough of a mouthful for anyone so small.

She'd wanted to use Luke for his second name but Luke had vetoed the idea immediately, suggesting instead with a dry chuckle that he would bestow his name on the next one. Jessica at once coloured up much to his delight and they looked at each other with new eyes, all at once conscious how far they had come and the depth of feeling slowly growing between them. How they had come together didn't matter for they were a real family now.

TWENTY NINE

"Your husband did very well, Mrs Fraser, under the circumstances. I would have expected you to tear much more with a first baby. Has he had any experience with childbirth before this?"

"Well, he was married, even had a child when he was younger. Though I don't suppose he helped with the birth; but he's very good with the sheep. I can only say how glad I was to have him with me; he helped enormously. I'm sure it was better than going to the Hospital."

"You were lucky it was straightforward, normally I would have said it was essential for a first birth to be in medical facilities but there you go, the world would be vastly under populated if we all chose that way. Give me a ring if you have any problems, and come in with the bairn when the weather clears up. I'll see your husband as I go. Good day to you, Mrs Fraser, take care now."

Jessica still found her married name a novelty, liking the status it gave her, for though it wasn't a normal marriage she enjoyed the comfort of being cared for; the quiet companionship without the stress of being tied emotionally. But what if Luke met someone else and wanted to be free of her? The thought disturbed her so much she felt tears rising in her throat and choked them back quickly as Luke came in the door. He raised his eyebrows questioningly at her.

"What's up, Jess? The Doc say anything. Is everything okay?"

"No, no I'm all right, just a bit tired that's all."

"I'm not surprised; you were awake all of last night. You'll be bound to feel a bit down after the excitement but you're still happy about the baby, aren't you?" His voice was anxious.

"Yes, of course, I didn't realise how much I would love him. You are pleased too, aren't you? I mean – you are still sure about being his father?"

"I'm over the moon, Jessica, I couldn't be more delighted if he were my..." he stopped, embarrassed at his gaffe.

"Your own son?" She finished for him. "There I knew you would feel some regret. I'm right aren't I? You won't ever forget how he was conceived." Her eyes shimmered with tears.

"Jess, he is our own, yours and mine, we fought for him, he's ours and never let anyone tell you different, okay? I guess I'm relieved you've taken to him so well, I was kinda worried now and then in case you'd reject him. You know? Because of how he was started. I don't want ever to say this again but it doesn't matter a damn cent to me how it happened. Or the fact I despise that son-of-a-bitch more than I can say, this baby is ours to bring up and love and make into a

decent human being with good values and...and...I'm gonna teach him baseball."

Jessica laughed in delight then said, "How about cricket?"

"Yeah, sure thing, if you teach me first!"

Some weeks later when the weather began to improve Luke and Jessica were in Fort William buying a pram, which could be dismantled for the car, and a large cot instead of the Moses basket Angus had slept in since his birth. Jessica was in a Fruiterer's stocking up with fresh fruit and veg. While waiting on being served she idly read an item from an old newspaper she had taken from a pile on a bench. Turning to the financial pages, her prime interest, she had been surprised to learn, that not only had Welland & Davis dispensed with the name Davis but they had also joined forces with another Merchant bank called Seager. Moreover, the paper noted, the two banks were further united, with the surprising marriage of Mark Welland and Warren Seager's daughter, Annabel.

Jessica stood in a daze gazing at the small print until prompted by the young assistant to make her wishes known. She was surprised how enormously relieved she was to read the news of the wedding. But when had it been? She looked quickly at the date on the front page. Last summer! August in fact, the rat! He had been courting this girl when he raped her.

Jessica experienced deep revulsion all over again until her common sense told her the episode was behind her. Gone, finished with. Mark had his own world and would never touch hers again, ever. She picked up her shopping and crossed the road to the Landrover where Luke waited for her with Angus, who was chuckling happily in his safe cocoon on the back seat. Luke noticed her joyful smiling face as she climbed into the car.

"You look like you've bought yourself a watermelon with that grin," he chuckled. "Do tell. Who or what has brightened your day?"

"Nobody and nothing in particular, I've just found a load of nice apples to make you a pie later on, when we get back home."

"Then what are we waitin' for, Angus, my boy, let's go home quick, Mommy's gonna bake me an apple pie! You know, Jess, I'm gonna regret the day when he's old enough to eat it as well! I'll bet a ten dollar bill I'll never get a look in when apple pie is on the menu!" He quipped with his usual teasing grin. "Let's hope he grows up hating apple pie."

"That all right, my lad, I'll teach him to like steak pie instead."

"Well of all things! That's one of my favourites too." Luke said quickly.

"Take your pick. It's either shares down the middle or you lose out on the steak."

"You know, I thought I was the tease around here, the trouble with you is you learn too fast. At least I have a breathing spell while he's still on milk to enjoy my food. I can see the prospects ahead are gonna throw up some real testing times."

Jessica glanced at him quizzically wondering if he was serious. "I'll always cook what you want, Luke, you know that. You aren't getting jealous all of a sudden, are you?"

She was rewarded with a roar of laughter. "Got you, my fair beauty. I thought I was losing my touch to tease you. But you rise to the bait like a beautiful salmon."

"Now see here, you rat, one of these days..."

The ride home was filled with laughter as the two of them elbowed for supremacy. Jessica thought later about the news from London and found to her pleasure that it touched her not at all. Her life was in the glen in Scotland with her family and all that had gone before was history.

THIRTY

Henry Fowden weathered the lonely months, after Jessica left, as best as he could. He had acquired a new secretary, but as efficient as she was, he missed the empathy he had enjoyed with Jessica, which had helped them to work in unison without him continually having to keep his eye on day-to-day routine. The transfer to the new job of amalgamating with the other firm brought its problems and he found he didn't look forward as he once had of setting off to work. Now it was a continually nerve racking task of changing procedures to fit in with the other bank.

Mark had married and was duly installed into the company with the titular title of PA to the Chairman, and it was common knowledge that he was being groomed to take over when Charles retired. Fortunately, Henry knew he would rarely come in contact with him except for the weekly board meetings Sir Charles presided over, but Henry had an inner feeling of unease that Mark would lose no time in causing trouble or getting rid of him as soon as he could.

"Right gentlemen," said Sir Charles, "Let us turn to item number three on the agenda. There are a number of financial questions to be agreed." There was a rustle of paper as everyone obeyed and Sir Charles paused to take a drink of water to clear his throat.

"Mr Mark informs me he is lacking the necessary funds allowed for the PR advertising. Mr Fowden, this is your problem, isn't it?"

Henry stared briefly at Mark who promptly smirked back. Crafty bugger he thought, he doesn't say anything to me but waits till he has an audience to have it brought up. He sensed the war of attrition was about to start.

"Permission for the transfer of funds for advertising lies in Mr Seager's hands. It was agreed he would have overall responsibility so that there was no clash in advertisements. We must present a united front between the two firms or the amalgamation doesn't make sense. Duplicating items in the media is a waste of time and money. It may be he has just temporarily delayed releasing them, but I have no idea why. He doesn't have to state his reasons."

"I see, but it was agreed at the last collective meeting that funds would be available and this delay is not good enough. Can't you negotiate with his Finance Director, what's-his-name?"

"Mr Richmond is powerless in the matter. I was aware of a time lag and I've already tried to speed things up. There is nothing more we can do. It is entirely down to Mr Seager."

"Hmmm, most unsatisfactory. Do you want a member of our main Board to intercede? Perhaps they could help?" There was a hiss of pity from those seated around the table. Poor old Henry was being carpeted and no mistake. Most of the board had seen Charles do this before.

Henry shrugged. "I think you will find Mr Seager knows exactly what he is doing. To intercede would only stir up trouble and cancel the funds completely. I was told Mr Seager had his reasons. It will be better to leave this item to be discussed at the next combined meeting."

"I disagree. We may be amalgamated but we still have to run this bank in a viable fashion. You'll have to work harder yourself to cool Mr. Seager's temper, if temper it is. We can't allow hold-ups to impede our progress. Mr. Mark has decided that advertising is vital to gain more business. Get the funds, Fowden, as soon as possible. Now, number four on the agenda..."

Henry felt the snub deeply in the lancing pain that sprang across his chest. How dare he! How could Charles impugn his work and suggest he was not trying. He had worked more hours than anyone else in the bank and kept things going almost single-handed during the extremely difficult amalgamation of the two companies.

The odd glances of pure hatred that had frequently been turned in his direction from Mark told their own story, Henry knew the board meeting was but the preliminary opening to more hostilities and there would be worse to follow. Once again he tried hinting to his wife that he would like to go back up north and settle into a smaller firm. When it eventually got through to her he was serious her response was immediate and dismissive.

"You're joking Henry! Go back to a scruffy area and leave my friends. Leave our house? For goodness sake think of the boys! Their lives are solidly established down here." He argued that the boys were mostly away at college and university and couldn't care less where they lived.

"They have their own lives to concentrate on, dear, not ours."

"Henry, I just couldn't uproot myself and start over afresh. I'm happy here, besides the house has just been redecorated. I am not letting anyone else have the benefit of that. I know things haven't been easy but have patience, Henry, you'll see it will all come right in the end."

In the end it did not come right, for after a particularly provoking board meeting when Henry was subjected to more telling remarks from the Chairman, obviously goaded on by Mark, he had gone back to his office and collapsed with a major heart attack. As the pain smashed through Henry's chest there was a brief illuminating instant when he thought of Mark and wished he could suffer the same agony he was going through, all because of Mark's evil spitefulness and enmity. It was a burning desperate curse, directed against an enemy who had rendered him powerless to fight back. For Henry, unfortunately, had been no match for the likes of Mark, a vicious opponent who spared no thought for others. Instead, Henry was a gentle soul who desired only to do his job and care for his family. As he stretched his length on the office floor he tried in vain to call for help, but nobody was near enough to hear. Then he died.

A few days later, after the funeral, Mark was walking along the corridor past Henry's old room, which was shortly to be redecorated for the new Finance Director, when the door opened and Henry's secretary emerged, carrying a large cardboard box.

"What's that you've got there?" Asked Mark nosily.

"Only odds and ends belonging to Mr Fowden, which I've cleared from his desk. I'll show Sir Charles before sending them on to his wife."

"I'll take them; I've got to see him shortly. No, it's quite all right, really, no trouble at all," he added, as she began to protest. "I can't have you breaking your back lugging boxes around."

Reluctantly, she handed over the box of mementoes and a folder knowing it was not the right thing to do but not daring to argue with him. No wonder, she reflected, her late boss had disliked Mark, for it soon became clear that there was hatred between the two men. She had never found out the cause and could only watch from the sidelines, as her boss grew more and more despondent. It wouldn't surprise her at all if Mark had been responsible for Fowden's heart attack or at least putting him under so much stress he became ill. 'Nasty piece of work and I'm not the only one here who thinks so.' Still angry with Mark she told a typist in the main office what had happened:

"Nosy blighter, he just wanted to see what Henry had left. I couldn't stop him although I knew they well and truly hated each other's guts. Pity it had to be Henry instead of him."

"What did Henry leave?" Asked the friend.

"Nothing much; just a load of useless keepsakes. Still that'll teach Handsome Harry; he saved me from hanging about till old Charlie was free. They make a right pair, those two." She said scathingly, wondering to herself if another job application elsewhere would produce results.

Back in his own office, Mark rummaged in the box.

He found a golf ball with a huge yellow cross on its slightly battered surface. A relic from golfing days, perhaps a Hole in One? A broken gold fountain pen with an old-fashioned nib; an old framed photograph of Henry's wife and the boys when they were young; an odd cufflink, a diary? Ah what's in here? Mark turned the pages over briefly and put it to one side to read later, having seen one or two references to himself that were better kept for his own consumption and not for the titillation of Henry's wife. The rest of the things were rubbish, but he supposed for the look of the thing he ought to return them to his wife. He opened the folder, nothing here as far as he could make out. Letters from City colleagues, referring to events over the years; items of no interest to Mark. But what was this? A letter from his former secretary? It brought to mind the tussle on his father's office floor and his groin tightened at the thought. She could have been a good lay for some time if only she hadn't kicked up rough. It might have been serious if he had had anyone other than old Henry to deal with but luckily, his father had believed his story rather than Henry's. In any case he had the old boy over a hell of a barrel with his forthcoming marriage. There had been too much riding on that to have it interfered with.

He opened Jessica's letter and read it several times to get the gist of it. Mark seethed at the reference to money. His father must have paid her off. How strange he had never mentioned it. I bet it was Fowden's doing, he thought, Dad wouldn't give away money so easily. Anyway, how dare the slut use it for her comfort? Why should she use it at all? She was smart enough to get herself a good job. Unless? Perhaps she couldn't work? Maybe she was ill, or ... was she pregnant? If she was ... was it him? Now there's a thing! Pregnant with his child?

His child! The thought of it excited him. Was there some feeling of paternity in his make-up? He was surprised at the sentiment. Mark Welland coming over paternal! What rubbish! He'd never given the idea even a token's thought before. Not ever! Freedom was his maxim, fancy getting all dewy-eyed over a brat? However the thought stayed in his mind, fermenting and curdling like a poison brew. Well, it was possible, given the circumstances. He knew he was a sexual man, there was no reason to believe he was other than fertile, despite his parents continually whinging over a grandchild and he had been the first with the girl!

Even Warren Seager had begun hinting it was time a little one made an appearance. What was he doing about it, because it could not be Annabel's fault? Not baby blue eyed, simpering, Annabel, whom he was sick of pandering to. Every time he didn't do as she wished there were tiny threats of telling Daddykins how badly she was treated. Well Annabel would just have to go to the Fertility Clinic and find out how *she* was doing in the baby stakes for he was damned if he would. Not that he could say anything about this, no sir, he would have to think very warily about things and maybe track down the girl to find out how things stood.

He had treated her badly, but what the hell, she would be as pleased as punch if he came back into her life, especially if she was fending for herself. Yes, that's what he would do, put a man on to finding Jessica and see if she was pregnant. He would have to be most careful. There would be hell to pay with Annabel and Warren if they found out. Except a private investigator was usually discreet; he would make damn sure of it. Anyway they had to be, or they'd never get work. No one would know, and certainly not his father. At least, not yet. And when he found her? Ah, that was another story. Let me wait until she is found then I can have some fun, he thought, a thrill of excitement creeping through his body. Maybe that was why he felt so low and gloomy. There was never a thrill with Annabel, no feeling oneself on a knife's edge. No pleasures from chasing down a victim and having them cry for mercy.

I will have to think up something outrageous, he told himself, stir the old spirits up, and get rid of the glooms. Thank god it's almost time to go skiing. The thought cheered him up at once. Without fail, Mark always went abroad every year to the best skiing resorts to indulge himself in his favourite sport. He was an able skier, always choosing the black runs or going off piste if he had a chance. Combining this with *après-ski lovemaking* filled him with exhilaration for weeks. Until the next mood of boredom set in and depending on the time of year, it would send him looking for other escapades. This year it was going to be difficult with Annabel around but he would soon find an excuse. He always did.

THIRTY ONE

Before Mark had time to instruct an agency to begin the search for Jessica Meredith, a blazing row blew up between he and his wife over his proposed skiing trip in the New Year. Annabel and Mark had only been married a short time, when he took to disappearing on small tours. A weekend here, a couple of days there, all business trips according to him and she took no notice at first being too busy spending money on the new house her father had bought them for a wedding present. A fortnight's stay in Zermatt in Switzerland was an entirely different matter. She wasn't at all happy.

Annabel was short and plump, not built for athletic games in any way. Neither, after an unfortunate attempt to learn to ski when she was younger, had she bothered with other types of sport. In fact she had set her mind firmly against most forms of exercise. However she soon realised she would have to rethink her attitude if she wanted to retain her husband's interest.

"Oh for Christ's sake stop moaning and come with me, then." Reluctant to have to say it he felt viciously irritated beyond belief, for his latest paramour had fixed for the two of them to borrow a friend's chalet and he was looking forward to some great sex, as well as enjoying his favourite sport.

"It's because I've never liked skiing," she grumbled discontentedly even though she had won. "Messing about on the nursery slopes for hours, falling over, cold, it's just not my scene."

"Only because you've not bothered to learn properly. Anyway, I go every year and I'm not going to stop because you don't like it...and don't go moaning to your father, he'll tell you the same, learn to ski properly. Even if you look a right clown on the nursery slopes it won't bother me, you'll be doing what you want and I'll be skiing where I want." He gambled that she would tell him to go to hell and do nothing about it. He was wrong.

"Why have we got to go to Zermatt?" She persisted. "The nursery slopes haven't the best of reputations; I certainly wasn't impressed when I went before. There are better places."

"Because I like it there and *I* don't need a nursery slope. Satisfied? As I've said, you don't have to come with me. Why not find some sun and sea somewhere else?"

"Is it too much to ask to have a holiday with my husband? I see you little enough as it is."

"Well, I've been working and you've had the house to tart up," he said shortly.

"Anyway make up your mind – Zermatt or nothing!"

"Book me up on your flight, I'll get kitted out. I'll learn to ski, Mark, just see if I don't, we'll get pleasure from this holiday together," she said, firmly determined he was not going to get the better of her this time. "We are not merely playing at marriage we are married and I want to enjoy it to the full." She was beginning to see how he went about getting his own way. He did it oh so very skilfully it wasn't until later that she realised how well he duped her to achieve his own ends.

Once they arrived in Zermatt and got organised, Annabel set foot on the snow to begin her lessons on the nursery slopes. By the end of the first day she was pleasantly surprised to make good progress and equally surprised to find she was enjoying it far better than her first attempt. She was fortunate to get a young enthusiastic instructor who was proficient and not yet jaded by would-be skiers who hadn't a clue and messed about rather than applied themselves.

Though it was late in the season the weather had stayed cold and the snow was still quite reasonable on the lower slopes. She found herself eager to learn and ended up getting almost one-to-one tuition. For the first couple of days Mark was free to enjoy his other female company without her knowledge, but as Annabel grew more confident she resented him going off to enjoy himself with experienced skiers and being gone for hours. After her instructor realised he had others to teach it left her at loose end and brought to a pitch her normal discontent.

A day spent idling around the shops in Zermatt was no consolation so it was not too long before she begged Mark to take her with him on the higher slopes. His angry protests that she wasn't proficient enough to use the steep runs fell on deaf ears. Annabel was no fool, especially now she recognized he would try to talk her out of anything that did not suit his plans. It was certainly obvious he would never join her where the area was crowded and the snow sparse, so she took the only course she had left and began to insist until eventually he said with biting antagonism:

"Annabel, you are the bloody limit, you need at least a couple of year's experience to use the ordinary slopes let alone the black runs. How the hell do you expect to ski up on the high piste? Be reasonable, you're still only a novice even if you have done well so far."

"But I've got you to take care of me. With your vaunted expertise what could be better?" She replied with honeyed sweetness, still hoping she could coax rather than bully him to stay with her. "We are supposed to be having a good holiday together, what's the use of me spending all day by myself, even if the instructors are dishy. I promise to do what you tell me, only I'm bored just going up and down on those nursery slopes, there's hardly room to move, I'll never learn to ski properly." Her voice was turning to its usual high-pitched whine.

Christ, he thought, you're bored! Try being in my bloody shoes, you bitch. How I ever got landed with you, Heaven only knows, I must have been gaga. Except that he wasn't mad or stupid. Shrewd and selfish and above all very greedy for the money that came with the deal, that's how he had come to marry the rich and spoilt daughter of Warren Seager.

Principally it was a sweetener to get Seager on the hook for a merger. His father, faced with financial ruin through one or two ill advised loans to companies that had defaulted, had managed to hide things under wraps but he needed the support of a sound ally to keep him monetarily afloat so Mark had been brought into the deal against his will. He hadn't cared a great deal for Annabel but he was greedy enough to know this was the best chance he would have to acquire serious money, a great deal of money. Warren Seager was a Midas man and Annabel was his only child. What more could a man ask for? Freedom? Not a chance of that now, he thought gloomily, she's got her claws well and truly into me and the only thing I can do is get her pregnant and then I'll be able to do as I please. Hopefully, at least it would quieten his father-in-law, keep his own father sweet and get Annabel off his back. Now the house was finished she was becoming a real pest.

The next day dawned blue and cloudless and Annabel made up her mind she was as ready as she would ever be. The sharply crested Matterhorn thrust its distinctive peak into the sky above them and the mountains around glowed in the early morning light; it was a beautiful day to be young and alive, the effervescent air sending the blood racing through one's veins. It was so much better than her earlier visit now she was more confident with her progress. Skiing was easy she decided. It was only a matter of knowing how. She had woken full of energy, quite able, she thought, with her head full of dreams and optimism, to manage to conquer anything, even racing full pelt down a huge and extremely dangerous mountain.

"I want to go high, darling. High as we can go, right to the top of the piste." Annabel carolled as she felt the fierce excitement of anticipation stream through her body just like bubbles in champagne. Why not? Now she had the chance to show Mark how clever she was.

Mark not only loved skiing he was very good at it so he felt there would be no difficulty in coping with the two of them. He didn't care that she wasn't experienced; if she had a couple of falls it might teach her a lesson. Nevertheless, he decided on the Schottdorf Piste where there was a run down to Areitalm that was gentle and not entirely beyond her capabilities. Purposely they left the hotel early, reaching the top of the run in good time before it grew crowded. It was while he was tightening her boots that he had the deadly notion. He had listened to her continual chatter as they ski-lifted all the way up the mountainside, of how his life was going to be busily organised when he was chairman, what Daddy thought he should do after that and so on ad infinitum. Between the pair of them, he realised, they were mapping his life out in detail entirely to suit themselves without a thought given to his basic needs. To his horror, Mark saw the years stretching ahead of him like a conveyer belt and flinched with dread.

How could he stand it for the rest of his life? But did he have to? The merger was now complete, what was to stop him getting a divorce? Only 'Daddykins!' He had got to know of the loans and hadn't been pleased, had even threatened to pull out or at least make life very difficult for the other firm. Charles had been at his wit's end to soothe things over; he would not only take issue with Mark screwing up all his finely crafted plans, he might change his mind at giving his son the Chairmanship. Mark had only seconds to make up his mind as he led the way to the start point.

"This is it!" He cried out, turning swiftly left to the dangerous off piste downhill run.

"Are you sure this is okay?" She said doubtfully. Now the moment had come, her legs felt like jelly. "Isn't this off piste? Shouldn't we be over there on the right hand side?"

"Please yourself. That one is merely a long coast downhill and there is a queue of people already forming. Now this one is clear, there's nobody waiting and besides it's really thrilling."

"But it looks steep. I'm not sure I can manage something like this."

Mark's anger spilled over, taking her aback. "I thought you wanted excitement? You're the one that wanted to come up here, I said you weren't ready. I'm fed up with your whines, Annabel: I'm going back to the hotel. You please yourself what you're going to do, I've had enough of trying to satisfy your wants." He bent and picked up his skis then turned to walk back they way that they had come.

"Oh I do, Mark, I do want a thrill. Don't leave me up here like this. I promise I won't argue again. It's just now we are here I feel a little wobbly. It's a lot higher than I thought it would be. But you will stay close to me, won't you. I don't want to fall over; it looks such a long drop." She begged, her nerve suddenly leaving her as she realised what she had to do.

He turned back and stared at her. "High in the mountains, you said. Right to the top of the world. Well I've brought you here. Its make your mind up time. Are we going or not?"

"Yes, I'll go, darling, but it looks a lot harder than the nursery slope."

"No it's not; it's dead easy if you keep your head. You will be okay. Think of it as a long glide home. I'll be skiing behind you anyway to keep an eye on what's ahead and see if you are tackling everything okay. It's no use you being behind me, I can't watch what you are doing. I'll soon stop you if there's a problem. Trust me. Once you ski this lot you'll never look back. You will never go on the nursery slopes again." Not if I get my way, she won't. This will serve her right in a big way. "Don't worry, I'll be close behind. Off you go."

She flashed a brilliant dare-devil smile at him and started down one of the most dangerous runs in the mountains; a black run that few people, unless very experienced, would attempt. "Right then Mark; let's show 'em how it's done!" She flung the words over her shoulder as she dug her ski poles into the soft snow and took off down the treacherous run completely unaware it was the most foolish thing she had ever done in her life, even more foolish than marrying Mark.

THIRTY TWO

Mark slid into his skis quickly and watched for several seconds to let her get far enough ahead, before he too began the long glissade down the slope. He wasn't troubled that he might be embarking on a course of killing the woman he had vowed to love and protect, if not scaring the wits out of her. His only concern lay in the fact she was in his way, and far too demanding. She was interfering with his freedom and he wanted rid of her. Nor was it the first time he had killed. A school friend committed a bad error in beating Mark too many times at sport. Mark had waited his opportunity and then drowned him in the school swimming pool.

The verdict was listed as accidental death for no one could provide a valid reason for the boy being in the pool late at night on his own. The autopsy found bruising to one side of the head and it was thought he had perhaps slipped on the edge of the pool, fallen in, and with no one around to help, had succumbed. Mark, his best friend, was thought to be safely in bed at the time; certainly nowhere near the scene of the so-called accident when the body was found. He was never even questioned. If he had been, his alibi was perfect.

Out of the hearing of others it had been simplicity itself to dare the other boy to come on a midnight swim with him. A broom lying by the poolside enabled Mark to strike one blow to knock his classmate senseless: thereafter holding him under the water had caused no problem. He had then washed the broom thoroughly in case there was blood on it then replaced it tidily back in the shed behind some other equipment. In the event no one had suspected foul play and a verdict of misadventure was recorded and the headmaster had gone to great expense to erect a fence round the area with a padlocked gate. Mark left soon after, having convinced his father the school was fast becoming a concentration camp and the teaching was below par. As his grades seemed to echo that situation Charles had taken the hint and Mark had been removed.

Mark was halfway down the slope with Annabel some distance in front when he sensed some people on the piste behind him and had the presence of mind to yell furiously to Annabel, knowing she would never hear him through her earmuffs. "Annabel! Stop! Wait for me-e-e!"

He raced frantically after her. But in spite of his desperate speed Annabel rapidly went out of sight. What the hell was he doing? This was stupid. He had allowed her to get too far ahead, completely underestimating the surface of the snow and the sheerness of the slope. He had no conscience to speak of but even he blenched as he considered his foolish action. This was utter madness! What in blazes was he about? Anyone with an atom of sense would understand one could not control a skier from behind. And, if one had to supervise like that then neither skiers should be on that part of the mountain. Experienced skiers would without doubt see his actions as criminal. He had seen her wavering once as though looking to see if he was beside her before disappearing round the next bend as he cursed his stupid action vehemently. Where the hell was she? She must be going much too fast to control her skiing. Bloody fool! Daddykins would be after him now when Annabel told him where she had been doing. That is – if she came out of this affair alive. Then, in spite of his fright, a solitary thought lingered temptingly in his mind – maybe his scheme would work after all? He just had to make sure he was not held to blame.

He came across her body at the end of a long deeply sloping drop leading to a nasty curve where the skier had to have his wits about him to stay on course. She had slammed straight into a huge rock and lay spread-eagled on the snow like an immense drop of scarlet blood in her brightly coloured ski-suit. When he reached her, he found that although he could see she was badly injured, she was still alive.

He wasn't able to finish the job for almost at once the two skiers following him came down the slopes behind and stopped to help. The Rescue Service went into action as soon as one of them trekked back up the mountain to phone for an Air Ambulance, while the other one, a Swiss National stayed with Mark as they both tried to make Annabel comfortable. Annabel, after a moment or two lapsed into unconsciousness while Mark prayed silently for her death. She hadn't spoken one word to him, had only once looked at him with those baby blue eyes that appeared to hold him culpable, to accuse him of trying to murder her.

"She is young, which helps, but it was a bad fall. You must be ready to accept she may not live, Mein Herr. We can do nothing until we have an expert doctor here. We heard you shout, did you not intend to use the run? It is well known for being difficult, did you not know?"

The Swiss skier was gravely sympathetic, if somewhat vexed with apparent carelessness.

"God no! She was ahead of me. I can't think why she turned down this way. We were going to Areitalm, but she's always been headstrong, always had her own way all her life." He groaned deeply, as if he had tried to keep her safe but she had slipped away from him.

The Swiss nodded with understanding. He saw the situation clearly. A wilful girl, a doting husband. There were many such people who came for skiing holidays, and accidents such as this, were the result of the lethal combination. "Ah yes, we saw you earlier. You were considering your route?" He said tactfully, "I saw you turn back, it appeared you did not want to go? Do not worry, mein freind, I will vouch for you and say what I saw. In some situations one is completely helpless. You have my deep sympathy, but take heart, our Doctors are very good."

It was late evening before Mark had the result from the surgeon. Annabel was barely alive but she was holding on grimly. She would never walk again for her spine was badly crushed below the waist. She also had a broken arm and extensive concussion, though these were comparatively minor in respect to the other grievous damage.

"Why she isn't dead, is beyond me." The doctor sighed with tiredness. He had spent many hours in the operating theatre and wondered if it would be in vain. "She has incredible strength and tenacity. If she manages to stay alive over the next few days maybe she will graduate to a wheel chair but at this foreseeable moment even that is out of the question. I also have to tell you she will never bear children. I'm sorry to be so blunt but it is as well that you know."

"Oh Jesus." Groaned Mark genuinely overwhelmed with the verdict. What had possessed him to act so foolishly? Why had he banked on a sudden whim killing her?

"I gather you haven't been married very long?"

"Only seven months," said Mark, his brain reeling over thoughts of the future. Of being tied to as cripple. How the hell could he get out of this one? Stymied! Bloody well stymied!

"Hmmm, you have a hard battle ahead of you. See how she goes then perhaps you could adopt a child to give her an interest in life. As for yourself, well, it won't be easy; you will have to make time in your life for an invalid. Still, I daresay it soon becomes a habit."

Not with me, it doesn't, thought Mark, who hated illness of any kind. Stupid silly cow, she couldn't even die without making a hash of it. What the hell am I going to do now? Annabel is sure to say it was my entire fault. How do I break the news to her father?

THIRTY THREE

It was the middle of May and Angus was three months old. He had lost the crumpled look of birth and his features were taking shape. Try as she may, Jessica could see no familiar likeness in him of her own family, neither to her relief was there any of Mark's. Instead, Angus had acquired a fluff of medium brown hair that was not unlike Luke's and his eyes had stayed a blue grey that also resembled Luke's. Recalling Mark's vivid blue eyes and dark wavy hair, Jessica breathed a sigh of pure thankfulness that there was nothing to remind her of the ordeal she had gone through. She found the love that had sprung up so fiercely when she had taken hold of him straight after the birth, had wiped all her bitterness and hatred away.

Luke, acting partly from knowledge with new-born lambs bonding with their mothers and the brief experience he had had with his own child knew it was important to get a swift bond within seconds of birth to encourage the growth of unity between a dam and her offspring. When Jessica was carrying the baby she might as well have had a stone inside for all she cared of the child. Luke had found her indifference difficult to combat. He continually wondered how he could overcome the loathing. In the event he need not have been concerned for despite the agony of labour when she had cursed Mark and what he had done, had wished death to free her from the pain, all was forgotten as she took pleasure in the rearing of her son.

"It's a good job we were able to buy Matilda? Her milk is a godsend while you are feeding Angus. Not to mention all those lovely rice puddings you make for me."

"Just as well you eat all those by yourself. I don't want to get too fat again now my figure is coming back. But yes, you're right as usual, Luke. I know I said she was a bit expensive but we would never have been able to drive to Invergarry every day for fresh milk. When I wean Angus he'll grow like a giant on her cream."

"Wait till he tastes your home-made cheese. Just think, Jess, if we get a licence sell..."

"Whoa back, boy! I manage to make it for us, but do not get carried away thinking I am a one-woman factory! Angus takes up all my time together with the housekeeping, let us wait until he is older before we go into production with a herd of Jersey cows. I am not against it, Luke; it is only because we need to consolidate what we have. You are so ambitious I can see you with an enormous dairy and sheep farm before long!"

"No I'm not really, honey. It's just I'm so proud of you learning to make butter and cheese, that's all." He gazed fondly at her. He had encouraged her every endeavour in the smallholding even when she had made some mistakes. She was a different person from the thin, pregnant girl who had first driven down the long road to Kinlochhourn although he was nervous to promote the deep attraction that was creeping over him. Much as he would have liked to say something he held back for her to give him a sign she was attracted to him too. So far she hadn't done so.

"You have no idea, Jess, how really thankful I feel meeting you. Making a go of things with me. I mean it, Jess, you have turned my life around completely. I bless you every day. I never knew life could be so fulfilling." His face grew solemn, the truth plain to see in his eyes. Overcome with sudden emotion she had taken his hand, but when she felt him draw her towards him, in an instant that afterwards filled her with regret as she saw the light die from his eyes, she said hurriedly,

"Oops, the potatoes are boiling over, I don't want a mess to clean up," and darted across the kitchen to pull the saucepan away from the heat. When she had looked round again the kitchen was empty; he had gone outside to lock up the chickens and see all was secure with their livestock. Well Jess that was a fine snub if ever there was. The least you could have done was not to flinch.

*   *   *   *   *

Angus was a good baby once he had made up the weight his early entry into the world had cost him. He lay content and gurgled in the Moses basket while Cladagh sat on the floor beside him, zealous in her continuing role of guardian. She no longer went out with Luke to work the sheep; instead, she enjoyed her life in comfort with Jessica. Her muzzle was quite grey and she limped a little with age but Jessica knew she would defend Angus with her life.

The slimness returned to Jessica and she looked a little like a teenager with her long fair hair pulled back in a ponytail and her fresh creamy complexion powdered with dark freckles until one recognised the shapely breasts of a nursing mother and saw she had matured into ripe womanhood. Luke saw it every day and wondered whether he would find enough courage to tell her he loved her.

They kept strictly to their partnership, dealing diligently with matters connected to the farm in a business-like vein, though Luke had been relieved to pass the paperwork into Jessica's competent hands. She slept in the back bedroom with Angus' cot beside her, the wood stove keeping the temperature warm for him. As she was still feeding round the clock Luke would rise early in the morning and go off to the sheep without disturbing her. At night he hurried home to be there for Angus' bath-time and Jessica was glad for him to take over the task while she prepared their supper. Once Angus was put down for the night they enjoyed a spell of quiet conversation over the food, always talking of how they could improve the holding. When it was time for bed Luke would long to join her but all he ever said was "Night, Jess, sleep well." and Jessica would retire with a vague feeling that he wanted to say more.

One Saturday morning he was still around when she came out into the kitchen carrying Angus and yawning sleepily. "Oh, you're still here? Taking the day off today?" She wished she had put on her dressing gown but it was too late to go back for it, so she sat down and put Angus to her breast. Luke glanced up from the task before him of cleaning his hunting rifle, to watch the two of them. The greedy, sucking sounds of the baby were extraordinarily erotic, Jessica's body scarcely hidden beneath the fine lawn nightdress. The image escalated and he felt himself harden with rampant desire and was most relieved the table was there to hide it.

"I'm going after that wildcat, Jess. I've just been down to the pens and a young lamb was killed last night. It's been almost eaten and the crows are after the rest but from the scratches on the wooden fencing I'd say they were cat. He must be a large one or he would never have dragged the animal beneath the fencing and away from the ewe. I'm very surprised we didn't hear anything, though I admit to being bushed last night. I don't think I'm over birthing the lambs yet."

Jessica frowned as she recollected the previous night.

"I've got a feeling I heard a noise or something. It was enough to waken me but as it didn't come again I thought it was Angus making the sound. I just kept very still after that in case he woke up then I must have drifted back off to sleep. I'm sorry I didn't wake you, that animal is eating our profits. We can't have that."

Luke chuckled cheerfully, "He could well find he is making us a mat for the floor. Some of them look rather attractive when they are skinned, dressed and properly stretched. Hunters back home take them along to the local store and sell them for a dollar or two."

"Luke, do you really mean to kill him? Isn't it dangerous? Suppose he springs at you?" She had a vision of a lion-like creature standing on a high rock waiting to jump on Luke. What if he was injured?

"Dangerous for him, yes. But at least I've got the gun. Seriously, Jess, I must get him or he could do untold damage frightening the sheep, also I'm sure he has a mate somewhere. There were too many tracks for just one cat. I've killed them before, love, in Canada. Pumas, cougars, lynx, they are all alike, and they get to be a nuisance. So don't worry, I'll be all right."

"Can't you get Jimmie Halverson to come over and help, I'm sure two guns are better than one and you can forget about a rug, I don't want any old mangy cat in here!"

"Yes, that's a good idea; I'll give him a ring. While I'm waiting for him I can have a decent breakfast. I don't see why Angus should have all the fun."

Unaccountably Jessica blushed red and pulled her nightie closer together but Luke had risen up and was reaching for a frying pan. "Bacon and eggs for you as well? Just dandy for a Saturday brekka. Sets one up for the day. My ma always used to have a fry-up then. She liked it better that day than a Sunday. Don't ask me why. Custom I guess."

"Yes, that would be lovely; I'll enjoy it with you. Angus will drop off to sleep now he's had his feed." She busied herself changing the baby's napkin then impulsively said, "Luke, tell me, how come you have a Scottish name when you're Canadian?"

"There are a great many Scots in Canada, emigrants from here in the early nineteenth century. My mother was a pure bred Scot, who went to Canada after the war ended, to marry a soldier she met over here, but he was killed in a road crash shortly before they could wed. She ended up with a French Canadian by the name of Pierre Lacoste. It was an accepted thing locally that he was my dad but he wasn't at all, I'm pleased to say."

"Then Fraser...is..."

"My mother's name, yes, that's right, I'm a bastard! However, not as big a one as Pierre Lacoste. He was the devil himself when he was drinking."

She stared at him with wide eyes filled with sorrow. So much was clear to her now, why he hadn't wanted Angus to be born without a father, why his mother had put up with a brute as a protector instead of being abandoned with a bastard child and nowhere to go. She thought she had had it rough but at least she had never been beaten, her parents had always been full of love.

"Oh dear, I'm so sorry I mentioned it, when it must bring back unhappy memories for you, please forgive me? Except you have made things a good deal clearer. I can see why it meant so much to you to give Angus a name."

He came over to her and pulled her up on her feet with the baby in between them.

"Listen honey, there's nothing to forgive; all that is in the past, same way for you. This place is here and now, this sanctuary, as your grandfather called it. There are only us and Angus and the farm and...and I'd better get on with the breakfast or I'll never get out." He had to let go of her quickly as her warm skin under his hands tempted him almost to despair. Retrieving his self-control he planted a great smacking kiss on her forehead and put her back in the chair.

"Luke, the baby's finished now, you burb him and I'll cook breakfast, I won't be a tick, I'll just get some clothes on." She dumped Angus with him and shot off into the bedroom, her cheeks on fire with the sudden urge to have him kiss her lips instead of her forehead.

While she dressed, she tried to analyse her chaotic thoughts that sent strange feelings racing through her body. Whatever was she thinking of? Luke was only interested in her as a partner not a lover. Hadn't she herself decided she would never want a man in that way ever again? Then why did her body tingle when he came near? What magic chemistry made her want him to touch her? It was useless to think so stupidly. Luke would have said long ago if he had wanted her. Wouldn't he? She sighed heavily with sheer frustration. Why oh why was life so difficult at times? Or was it her? Was she seeking a relationship that could never happen? She was soiled goods after all, at least in her own mind she was, though she knew most women of her age would laugh at her for being so prudish. If she had taken a lover when she had been at college would she still feel the same? But that would have been her choice, wouldn't it? What about Angus? Well she would have married the father, wouldn't she? Somehow that gave her no comfort at all. She didn't want anyone else as her husband except Luke.

The breakfast was rather more silent than Luke would have wished and he glanced now and then at Jessica's face trying to guess what she was thinking. Had she objected to his kiss? If the baby hadn't been between them would he have gone further and maybe frightened her? No, he mustn't do that. Their serene relationship depended on him keeping his desires in check. Once he lost the battle she would leave him, he had no doubts about that.

THIRTY FOVR

Two months went by after the accident before Annabel was judged by her doctor to be sufficiently out of danger to be flown back to England. It was most fortunate that Warren Seager's regular visit coincided with her release from hospital and he was overjoyed to be there to ensure all would go well on the flight home with his beloved daughter. He was eager to get her back to England to set her on the path for further treatment convinced that the doctor who had been chosen would work miracles.

Mark Welland was not a happy man. He stood in sullen silence in the sitting room, which had been put aside for their use, while Warren Seager's bitter castigating words fell yet again on his unwilling ears. How could he have been so stupid as to think Annabel's father would accept his arrogant attitude regarding blame for the accident? Warren had taken great exception to him attempting to slide from under, and his continual bleats about Annabel wanting her own way.

"Why the hell did you take her up so high? She's no skier, never has been, and doesn't even like it all that much. As for learning enough in a couple of days, well, three if you want to nit-pick, to attempt a black run and that bloody black run, of all runs, is beyond comprehension. You knew the danger; in fact I'm reliably informed you are very experienced. Enough to know the risks you can face on any mountain let alone in this area. You were also responsible for her safety, or should have been - she IS your wife after all, or did you intend to kill her?"

Ouch! That was hitting too near the bone for Mark.

"Certainly not! You know what she's like, once she gets an idea in her head she's off like a wild horse. You must have tried keeping her in bounds. It doesn't work, does it? In any case you heard what that Swiss bloke said. He was there, for God's sake! He saw it all happen. I didn't put words in his mouth."

"Yes, I know Annabel's headstrong, but she has to be given the idea first. I had you pegged for a wrong 'un when I first set eyes on you and nothing you've done since has changed my mind. Unfortunately, Annabel had her heart set on you; now look what's happened, you've ruined her life. It's a mercy she wasn't killed; though I daresay she will feel like dying when she gets to know the extent of her injuries and the fact she'll never walk again. Mark my words boy, mark 'em well!" He tittered, pleased at the unintended pun,

"You'd better devote all your attention to her well-being or you'll find yourself in dire trouble. Get my meaning or do you want me to spell it out?"

Mark shook his head in dismay, inwardly cursing his crass stupidity for causing the accident. On the other hand, to put it bluntly, attempting to murder her. It had been ill planned from the start. Christ! If he had succeeded her old man might have had him eliminated. He had the money for the job and he wouldn't have put it past the crafty old banker to fix him for good. He'd better put things right or he would be out on his ear, minus money, minus credibility and minus his own father's good will too. For Charles had told Mark in no uncertain manner, when Mark had phoned him the news from Zermatt, that he thought him a bloody fool not to have taken more care, he'd better be sharp at mending fences or they would both be back in disastrous trouble again.

The first time he had flown to Zermatt had been a frantic flight to a beloved daughter who was hovering on the point of death and Warren had been tight-lipped and frozen with grief and worry. In the interval of her amazing recovery he had time to think, time to analyse his feelings about Mark and the barely apologetic explanation of the whole affair. This wasn't the attitude of a loving, caring husband. Had he tried to kill her for her money? He wouldn't put it past him. The Welland's were a greedy pair. It was difficult to get at the truth but if what he suspected was true, Mark would need careful watching. Each time Warren returned to Zermatt he was riled enough to let fly at Mark repeatedly if only to warn him against ever trying to pull another stunt. The harsh words carried to the corridor outside the small private sitting room the hospital had put at their disposal while Annabel was readied for the journey. A private plane equipped medically for any eventuality was waiting at the airport and Warren anticipated few problems but he was still as edgy as a spooked cat and stood tense and angry as the doctor walked in. The surgeon took in the situation at once and decided to pour oil on troubled waters. He had taken in a deal of the events surrounding his patient's accident and he thought her father more than a little correct in his assumptions. However it was not his place to interfere. All he was concerned with was the health and safety of his patient. Now was not the time for recriminations.

"Ah goot, mein Herr, you are ready for the flight? I'm sure all will now go well with your daughter, she is a brave woman, Herr Seager, she's been very goot, you know? She will make a reasonable recovery, she has the will, you see. So many people give up when they think their life is ruined. You will keep her spirits high, yes?" His English was laced with a German accent.

"The nurse has been instructed and I myself will be going to London in a week to confer with your top Orthopaedic surgeon, Sir Archibald Dencer who has done amazing work with spines. If anyone can get her into a wheelchair, he can. Take heart, mein freind, the future looks brighter than it did at the beginning. Ja?"

Warren relaxed and continued to chat with the surgeon while Mark excused himself and went to see Annabel. She was being put on a special stretcher which in turn, fitted onto its own gurney, and her face showed the strain of being moved.

"Bear up, sweetheart, it won't be long before we have you back home, and then you'll feel more comfortable in the special bed we have arranged." Mark took her hand and kissed it.

She grasped his hand gratefully. "What a way to end up, I still can't think how I got into this mess, nobody's really explained. All I can remember is flying out to Zermatt - everything else is a blank. I can't even remember enjoying our holiday, Mark. Did we have fun?"

"Oh we did, darling, best ever. Now relax, it is all going to be fine."

Thank God for small mercies, she still can't remember thing, let's hope it stays that way and she never gets to wondering what she was doing on the dangerous run in the first place. He switched his thoughts to focus on being a loving husband just for Warren Seager's benefit, but the flight home was silent, with Annabel in a drugged sleep and the two men engrossed in their own thoughts. Seager's mind was surging, his mind concentrating on the two banks, regretting the union with the Welland's but knowing there was little he could do about it now.

Oh, they would be profitable, he would see to that, but there was no longer any pride in an association with two men he now knew to be second-rate villains; who would need continual watching to see they toed the line. He would be watching for an opportunity to have revenge. For though he couldn't prove it for the moment he knew these men had wronged him and he always took his dues. Sooner or later he would know. Villains always took one step too many.

Mark's thoughts were even deeper, more ugly, wholly concerned with his own comfort. How could he rid himself of such a stupid encumbrance? A detestable invalid, whom he would have to pander to if he wanted to continue in the luxurious style that he enjoyed, and felt that it was his by right. How could he rid himself of Annabel without causing trouble if he crossed Warren? Those thoughts filled his mind on the flight back and in the following months were never far from his continual deliberations.

THIRTY FIVE

Luke and Jimmy Halverson found themselves down near the end of Loch Hourn around midday, just as the light began to fade with a heavy shower of rain. It had been dry up until then and they had covered a lot of ground. There were plenty of tracks, rabbit, roe deer, a few of the bigger stags, though these usually kept away from the sheep preferring to find food in less crowded areas; and the usual tiny prints of weasels and voles. Jimmy was a very good tracker so Luke always learned something different when they went out together. They had stopped for a sandwich and tea, which Jessica had prepared, and were sitting out of the wind in a small gully halfway up the hillside overlooking the broad stretch of water across to Beinn Mhialairudl on the other side of the Loch. They watched the squall of rain sweep across the water in front of them hiding the other bank but well protected from its ferocity by the rocks on either side of them until it wore itself out and the air cleared, turning to a luminosity that was breathtaking.

"That's it then, ma bonny boy; ma feet are yearning tae gang awa back and get themsel's soaked. It's been a gye long walk for nothing, Luke laddie. Are we finished yet? It'll be dark afore we see yon pretty wifie o' yours, nae doubt she'll be lookin' oot fur ye?"

"Yes, Jimmy, she'll be looking out," said Luke, wishing it were as true as Jimmie hinted. He sighed as he heaved himself onto his feet then a second later his eye took in the grassy braes above him and he caught sight of a large black shape running over the rough moor towards a sheltering bush at the foot of a rocky crag. He brought his gun to his shoulder and fired; the sound echoing round the hills with the rumbling roll of thunder.

"Is that the cat, Luke? Did ye get him? Whaur is he, the varmint?"

"I'm not sure, maybe I only winged him. Come, let's go and see. God, I hope I did get him; he's a brute of a cat. Big as any I ever saw in the Rockies. Maybe he's from a zoo. Wouldn't fancy being up here on my own in the dark with him about. I'm grateful for your help Jimmy; I've a side o' mutton that'll eat well, waiting at home for you."

"Thanks verra much, Luke, you're a good man. I enjoy a bit of hunting' now and again, but rabbit, no' cat, eh lad? At least not for eating, though I suppose when it's in a stew it doesna hae its teeth an' claws. Mind you, it'll mak a grand wee trophy to boast about in Invergarry bars. You'll mebbe get it stuffed and be the talk of the town."

"You'll get stuffed, mate, if you don't stop cracking on." Good natured, they chaffed at one another as they climbed up to where Luke thought he had potted the animal but there was no sign of it not even a track or footprint in the coarse grass.

"He'll live a few more days, but not if he comes back near the sheep. Come on Jimmy, let's go home." They turned back down the hillside, taking a short cut through a copse of birch with Jimmie leading the way as before. A protruding branch suddenly whipped back to hook Luke across the forehead, knocking his hat off with the force of it. His searching hand smeared his face as blood trickled from the wound, before he bent to rescue his hat.

"Did I dae that, Luke? What a right clumsy beggar I am, a blooming auld fool. I mind the time I trod like an Indian and not a soul could hear me coming. Gie us a look at it."

"No, don't bother, it's only a scratch, I'll fix it when I get back. Let's get home, I've had enough of the hunt for today, there's not even a rabbit for our trouble."

"I got a couple o' partridge. They'll do you nicely in a tattie stew if you want them, Luke."

"You crafty old poacher! It's the close season."

"My stummick is'na closed. All these fancy rules aye keeps a man from a guid dinner, dae ye want them or no? You don't like to hang them as long as I do."

Luke shook his head. "Jess'll have supper waiting. You caught them, you keep them for yourself. Next time maybe."

It was quite dark as they reached the croft, Jimmy didn't linger but took straight off in his van after Luke fetched out the mutton from the freezer. Then Luke made sure the barn was locked for the night and its occupants safely penned before he opened the croft door to step in. Jessica was busy at the stove, where a rich smell of cooking wafted promise of a tasty meal. She turned to greet Luke and promptly screamed with fright as she saw the sticky trail of blood that still oozed down the side of his face from the long scratch on his forehead.

"You're hurt! Oh Luke, did the cat get you?" She rushed towards him and stared anxiously up at his bloodstained face.

"No, don't worry Jess; it was only a branch that caught me."

"Come and sit down while I bathe it, you must have it well cleaned with antiseptic or it will scar." Fetching the first aid box, she began to wash the blood from his face making sure it was cleansed of dirt. He enjoyed the fussing until she anointed him with antiseptic lotion, causing the wound to smart viciously.

"Jesus! What is that stuff? It's worse than a cut." He winced and grabbed her hand to pull it away from his forehead.

"How can I look after you if you won't let me clean..."

The nearness of her, the warm smell of her fragrant body was all at once too much for his long restraint. He gave up struggling with his conscience as he took hold of her arms and pulled her firmly down onto his lap. Barely hesitating he kissed her soft startled mouth.

For a moment, she wavered then as his kiss deepened, she gave herself up to him without a struggle. He allowed her a breath while he explored the rapidly beating pulse in her neck, his hand slipping under her cotton shirt to the soft outline of her breasts and hardening nipples. He sensed the awakening desire in her body. Was this the right time? Would he scare her for good? He paused for a brief second then took her lips again, burying himself in the honeyed sweetness. This time she responded eagerly, even returning his kiss with increasing ardour. Luke's passion flared white-hot. Subduing his feelings for so long had made him unaware just how strongly he felt about her. He wanted her desperately and now was surely the time to find out if she wanted him as well.

He rose to his feet still holding her in his arms.

"Reckon Angus will rouse?"

"No, he's fast asleep, tired out with teething."

"It'll have to be my bed, do you mind?"

She shook her head so he made for his bedroom holding her close to his chest. Now the moment had come she wished for some courage to calm her fears. She had vowed never to let a man near her again after Mark's assault. What was she thinking of? Was it wrong to run away from love and deprive herself of happiness? What strange alchemy had Luke worked on her that made her yearn constantly for his touch even in the most mundane of situations? He had kissed her deliberately before, once lightly, after the marriage ceremony then again just recently. Had he too, felt the urgent stirring of tightly held emotions, of attractions too strong to ignore? Or, was it just because a man was made that way and she was available? What if she made a fool of herself? Proved that she was useless and naïve? Let him love her and he was disappointed, so they went back to being just two strangers who happened to live together but who no longer shared companionship. How could she bear it after all that had happened? She felt her stomach clench with fear and tried to relax. If she did not concede, she would never find out the truth.

Racing through her brain streamed one scenario after another. Each one infinitely more terrifying than the last so she was scarcely aware of her surroundings until he gently set her on her feet in his room. Then she knew that at long last she would find out if she were going to be a true woman or just an empty husk that could not love or be loved ever again.

She need not have worried. Fear left her immediately her clothes dropped to the floor as Luke gently and very lovingly undressed her then quickly disrobing held her close against his warm frame. He ran sensitive hands over her back and down across her bottom, cupping the mounds tight to hold her against his erection and kissed her lips until they swelled with passion. His mouth went to a breast and closed on her nipple, licking and sucking until she writhed in anticipation. He was a consummate lover, sensitively tender one moment then sensuous and demanding the next, rousing her body to a state of ecstasy, which she never imagined would be possible after Mark. She couldn't believe she would feel such joy, such blissfully overwhelming passion, which made her respond so completely to him. She forgot her shyness, her terrors; she was only amazed that intuitively she knew how to please him in return.

When he entered her there was no holding back, and as he loved her, he knew the years of hurt and disillusion were behind him. This was where he belonged, wrapped in her arms, taking her as eagerly she was accepting him, welcoming the response of her body, which rose to an ecstatic rapture that neither had known before, but was there for them to cherish. As he brought her to fulfilment, he knew he had found a woman he would never part with. Aching long years had passed in the search but at last he had found love. The Wheel had finally come round to happiness.

Later, as they lay entwined together Luke said,

"Our son is going to have to get used to his own bedroom now, why waste a perfectly good double bed when we can make better use? You are never going to sleep alone after this."

"Yes," she said shyly. "I know. Did you have this in mind when you bought the bed?"

"Let's say I didn't think it was completely outside the realms of possibility, though you've taken a while to come to the idea we really are married. Legally, beyond any doubt, you are my wife, but more importantly you are my dearest love, forever and always."

"When did you find out you loved me?" She asked, bashfully curious.

"I guess it was when I saw you sitting on the floor trying to light the fire, your face was black and you looked so peppery you could have killed me. I believe I instinctively knew then I had found the right woman." He chuckled as she tried to slap him. He caught her hand and kissed it before taking her lips again in another long deep kiss.

"Oh, be serious, Luke, you couldn't have loved me then. I might have taken the farm from you. Or let you buy it and we would have gone our separate ways."

"Somehow it wasn't so important who had the farm, I just felt I wanted to know you better. Maybe Welland did us both a favour after all. You might never have come to Scotland if things had worked out differently; I might never have come here. I guess it was meant to be, still, it's kinda strange how we have both ended up at Kinloch Hourn."

"Darling, do you think Grandfather knows we're here?

"I shouldn't be surprised. He was a fixer all right. He might even have masterminded the whole thing. He had great faith in this croft and the land, said nothing could go too far wrong if you kept close to nature to let the gentle Lord heal your hurts in His own good time. I guess he was right there. It's taken a little time but our hurts are healed. The only real aim I had was getting my own back with that bastard, though my vengeance is fading now I have you. I have the feeling he will never be happy in this life no matter what he does, his evil ways will stay with him till death."

"What a terrible future he will have, Luke, if you are right." Jessica shivered abruptly as he gathered her up in his arms. Where was he now and who is a victim of his evil ways?

"Somehow I pity the woman he marries."

"As long as his future has nothing to do with ours we needn't concern ourselves. Our happiness is the only important thing, for I love you very much, Jess. So, if we go and eat the supper you were preparing, we can continue where we left off later. Consider your honeymoon has begun, my darling, for we have a lot of loving to catch up. How about if I take tomorrow off and we have dinner out? Mrs Stuart will have Angus, she'll be tickled pink."

"Oh yes, that will be great. Luke? I haven't said it before, it all came as such a surprise you see, but I do love you, I think I've loved you for a long time without knowing. I feel I'm working backward through life, having a baby first, making friends with you and then falling in love. It will be nice to start going in the right direction for once."

"Maybe we'll make a better go of it than people do who start off in the conventional way. At least we've known the pitfalls and the hard times, and coped amazingly well. You are right, we are good friends as well as being lovers; that is a plus in my book!"

His hand smoothed the contours of her body and she felt him harden again with desire and her own response rose with him. She smoothed her hand over his chest and gently pinched a nipple then was surprised as he flung himself quickly over her and pushed her legs apart.

"I've a mind to make love to you all night if Angus lets us. He's monopolised you for long enough, now it's my turn. On second thoughts, let's forget the food; I want to feast on you. Yes you sure as hell are my girl and you'll be mine for always. Never forget that, my darling."

She pressed upwards as close to him as she could manage, as he began to love her once more, feeling thankful they had reached their sanctuary and found each other, she would never be lonely again.

But the Wheel of Life keeps everlastingly turning. What will happen next?

THIRTY SIX

"Ma-ark." The voice was petulant.

"What?" His clipped voice betrayed impatience.

"I'm bored. Would you like to read to me?"

"Not particularly. I couldn't concentrate, I have to leave shortly anyway," he added hastily as ready tears sprang to her eyes. "Got work to do at the office."

"I thought Daddy said you didn't have to work if you were needed at home for me?"

The blue eyes changed to an icy inflexibility, which was daily becoming more evident.

"Now you are so much better, Sweetie, I'm sure you need time for yourself. After all, there's your Physio girl, your hairdresser, your beautician, all the people who are around to make you feel comfortable, I am only in the way. Besides I've got to earn a crust or two. I know you feel penned in, but you have to be a good girl for a little longer." He went on talking, for in spite of his inward rage he knew he still had to placate her. "Then you'll be in a wheel chair and life won't be so confining. You have to be patient and let things heal properly and you also have to realise we are all doing everything we can to make things easy for you until then. Sir Archibald said it wouldn't be too long before you could try to use a chair, probably by the end of August. Anyway, Annabel, it's late, I must go. See you later, all being well."

"Oh, very well. You seem determined to desert me; I might as well be dead, for all you care. You have no idea what it's like to lie here all day with nothing to do...I want you around, Mark dear. After all you have a lot to make up for, haven't you?" He froze, waiting for her next words. Would she choose this time? Or would the cat and mouse game go on until she was tired of playing it. He had been so completely convinced at first that she knew nothing. Now he was absolutely sure she remembered everything.

"What do you mean by that?"

"I mean, darling, you can walk and I have to lie in bed till my spine has finished knitting.

You know you being here always makes me feel better."

He relaxed. Not this time.

"Be reasonable, Annabel. I can't stay with you the whole time. I'll go stir-crazy."

She shrugged but made no reply. Strangely, the dangerous moment passed, for after staring at each other for a few seconds with hatred in their eyes, she closed hers and sank deeper in the bed. Nothing more was said.

Mark understood quite clearly then, this was his Sword of Damocles, ready to drop on him, when Annabel felt vicious enough to get her own back. Was this his punishment for the rest of his life? Oh no! Not if he could bloody help it!

THIRTY SEVEN

Hellfire, how am I going to stand you for however long you get to live? It's only been seven months and you're a bloody pain in the ass. Feverish thoughts filled his mind as he drove himself to Hampstead and a quickie with a convenient girl he knew. He wouldn't be able to stay long, Annabel could easily ring the office and check up on him; she'd done it before so many times before. He felt he was living on the edge of a volcano waiting for her to come out with the assertion she knew he had tried to murder her. What a bloody mess. He cursed the stupid folly that had pushed him to take action. He was trapped in a coil of lies and it had turned out to be a damned, awful situation. Was it worth it? No it bloody well wasn't!

He confessed to himself he was fighting a losing battle trying to stay sane and praying each day she would fall out of bed or take an overdose or just die, it didn't matter which way, just as long as she was out of his life. Between her and her father he was trapped. Warren Seager had both Mark and his father by the short and curlies and would not relax his vigilance for a second. What could be worse, total bankruptcy or marriage with Annabel? Even the money had paled into insignificance against that choice.

He had to plan a way of escaping from Annabel's clutches without Warren smelling a rat. If only she would get tired of life and commit suicide, anything! Except that prospect was not even a possibility as she was unable to obtain poison to do it. Now she was totally confined to bed following the intricate, incredibly difficult operation to strengthen the area of damage, which would enable her to sit in a wheelchair. She was paralysed from her upper waist downwards but up until recently she was mobile in her arm movements; however Mark had seen a tremor in her right hand causing her to drop things. Was the paralysis spreading? If it were then maybe it would carry on through the rest of her body. This made it even less likely she could manage to do anything for herself. So, if it wasn't suicide how could he kill her and convince Warren he was not to blame?

His brain ached as he went over one possibility after another.

He was determined not to make the same mistake as he had in Switzerland. The off the cuff, ill-planned and improvised attempt had been disastrous. He had been fortunate to get away with it, even if he had to put up with Annabel's veiled hints. Now his diligent attendance on his wife looked as if it had convinced Warren it had been just an unfortunate accident; but it couldn't go on for too much longer, he would explode with sheer hatred and ruin everything before long. How the hell could he rid himself of her, yet convince everyone he was totally innocent?

He guided his car through the city's afternoon traffic while his devious mind turned over a few possibilities but each plan was quickly discarded as being either far too risky for him or not feasible for her. He must try to be patient for he was certain something would turn up. He had always been good at extricating himself from many incidents in the past. Stupid occasions of carelessness or downright criminality, but he had always found a convenient scapegoat to take the blame. Even the trouble with the jet fighter when he was in the RAF, though bloody scaring at the time, had caused no lasting problem.

On his return, his Colonel, who had just returned from the Middle East and was intensely angered with the accident, was intending to make further enquiries but fortunately, for Mark, he was once again called away for high-level talks on a crisis, which had blown up elsewhere in the world. Mark prudently decided to get out of the service while he was still in one piece. No one remarked on the sudden exodus, certainly not to him, for his excuse had been his pledge towards the family firm.

"It's pater, you know, the old boy is feeling his age. I'll have to sacrifice my love of the service, of course, but it can't be helped, I'm not about to let my father down."

He left only a brief memory of his fun-loving air of bon viveur then was soon forgotten. But quite a few were glad to see him leave. Those, whom he had spitefully used, then tossed aside. Oh yes, they were extremely glad.

On Mark's arrival at the office, his secretary had some news.

"A Mr Golding rang for you, sir. He would not leave any message other than would you like to call back on this number?"

"Thank you, Deborah, I'll deal with it." He got rid of her and dialled the number through an outside line. He did not trust her not to listen in on his conversation with Frank Golding, who was a senior partner in a small, though reputable Detective Agency, whom he had hired to trace Jessica Meredith.

"No news as yet, Mr Welland, seems she packed up bag and baggage and took off after her mother died. The woman downstairs thought I was a debt collector and clammed up, though not before she let slip she thought the young lady had moved to Scotland. Perhaps she has family up there? Do you want me to continue the investigation?"

"Yes, yes, go ahead, I want her tracked down. But keep it strictly to yourself, don't leave messages in the office, they're a nosy lot. I'll ring you regularly at your office. Got it? I want the whole thing kept under wraps."

"Right sir. Give me a couple of weeks, I may have something for you then, okay?" He rang off. Privately, Frank Golding sensed he ought to have nothing more to do with the man, even if it meant turning down work. In the past, he had discovered it paid handsomely to find out as much about the client as possible before carrying out their orders, for it was surprising how it aided an investigation. His experience told him there was a lot more to this affair than just finding a girl.

It had been easy to put a history together on Welland, thought Golding. Typical rich man's son, officer in the RAF, playboy type, not too many brains...but there he stopped. Something about the man raised warning bells. Welland already had a wife, what did he want with the girl? Maybe she was an old lover? Maybe she owed him a debt? Whoever she was he did not think it would be a happy occasion when Welland caught up with her, in fact he preferred to say she couldn't be found but he had the feeling Welland would only hire another agency.

A couple of days later found him driving to Scotland having discovered from a woman down the street a crate had been brought out of the flat when the girl moved and put in a van belonging to a local removal firm. It was easy after that to find out it had been sent to Scotland and where it had been left at the local post office. It had been collected from there though he was unable to find out by whom or where it was bound. However whilst he didn't get the exact address he was given the general area. A man with his capabilities couldn't go wrong so he anticipated he would be finished with the case shortly. When the following Monday arrived and he was no nearer finding the girl he felt slightly aggrieved he had broken one of his rules by taking things for granted.

Golding was further irritated by the fact he was needed urgently back in London for another job so would have to leave this one on hold until later. On the other hand he could always send his junior trainee up to wander around, maybe the lad could unearth the young lady with a little more legwork than he felt inclined to put in. It would provide the youngster with valuable experience and save himself the trouble.

THIRTY EIGHT

Jessica, drowsy with sleep, watched the beam of sunlight slide slowly across the room warming the air as it went. It was nearly time to get up but she felt too comfortable to move. Luke's hand was curled round her waist and she fitted against the long length of him, delighting in his nearness and loving warmth, feeling safe and cosseted. How could she have guessed, all those dark hurtful months ago, she would end up in such an isolated spot and feel so protected and more at peace with herself than she ever had in London? Her ambitions to rise in her job and secure a good financial living had flown out of the window, all she wanted now was to make the farm pay a steady living, be a loving wife to Luke and rear their son to be a decent adult.

Her grandfather's croft was more than just sanctuary, it had become a symbol of security they could build on, preserve and pass to their children. For she was quite determined to give Luke a baby as soon her body had recovered from the birth of Angus and when he was old enough to cope with a sibling. A child of Luke's would show how deeply she cared for him, how glad she was to be married. Each day they grew closer to one another and happier.

The sun reached Luke's face and he stirred under the hot rays. Rousing, he stretched and slid a hand over Jessica's breast, feeling the nipple harden at his touch. Gently fingering the fullness he felt her move against him. His body responded with a surge of longing and he turned her over and gazed at the deep violet eyes glinting back at him, a half smile on her lips as he kissed her.

"Hello there, honey, awake early? What's up?"

"Nothing, I swear. I was listening to you breathing and wondering if Angus was awake."

"If you tell me I was snoring I deny it. I never snore." He grinned cheekily at her. "Hush, was that Angus?" They listened quietly for a moment. "No, he's still sound asleep. Anyway let's take advantage of the silence, I can't think of a better time." Pulling off her nightie he began to make love to her in the slow seductive way which she couldn't help but respond to.

"Darling, it's time to get up," she protested, though only weakly.

"Yes I am. I couldn't be more up if I tried! Now hush, lie still. Just enjoy the best start to a day I know, it beats porridge by a mile!"

"I will remind you of that later when you say you are starving!"

"If you're not too busy today there is something I would like to do," she said later, her voice sounding drowsy after the lovemaking, almost ready to slide back to sleep.

"Stay in bed all day? I think Angus has other ideas." The happy, chuckling sound was rapidly turning into a hungry wail as Angus felt it was time someone came to give him food. Jessica slid out of bed and went into his room to fetch him then handed him to Luke to keep amused while she quickly washed and dressed ready to start the day.

Later, in the kitchen, Luke asked what was it she had been going to say.

"Oh, I just wondered whether, if you weren't too busy, would you take me to see the Burial Cairns? I'd rather not go by myself. I was interested to find out more after reading about them in grandfather's book on the ancient antiquities of Scotland. Just imagine, they date back hundreds of years ago, to when this area was first populated, people like you and me scratching a living from the land. Grandfather knew a lot about the subject but I didn't realise we had one so near us until I read his notes."

"You mean the Cairns down our side of the loch? Sure baby, we'll go after breakfast and before Angus has his sleep, we'll put him in the backpack. It's a lovely day for a walk."

They strolled along the edge of the loch where dark green pinewoods clothed the hillside below the heights of Druim Fada, a towering bulk that helped to protect their glen from the worst of the northern winds. The air was soft, filled with the pungency of the pine trees and the red squirrels were busily gathering their winter stores before the advent of cold weather. Sunlight poured in pale beams through the branches, dappling the ground with lazy shadows. The weather was expected to break any day and Jessica was glad to be out in the fresh air while it was fine.

"I brought a bag with me; I thought I'd gather a few blackberries if there are any down here. I adore blackberry jam. My mother used to make it every year. It's so lovely on toast. I've denuded the bushes up by us and it's a really good year for the fruit, they are so juicy."

"Ah, I see the plan now," said Luke, "You don't want any cairns, and you just want me along to help with picking. Oh the trials I have to put up with." He sighed dramatically.

"Of course not, still, you might as well be useful now you're here; after all you eat the pies I make," she retorted, her lips puckering with amusement. "Of course I don't have to do them."

"Well I could be persuaded. At a price you understand? Which we'll agree later." He pretended to leer at her. In this way they jested and teased one another as they walked and Jessica scarcely noticed the distance, so happy did she feel while Angus contentedly drowsed on Luke's back. They came out of the belt of trees to see a wide grass area backed with steep crags that rose from the flat ground like huge giant steps quarried out of the mountain. It wasn't until Jessica got close to a series of moss and grass covered rock hummocks she perceived they had reached the cairns. She stood staring at them in puzzlement.

"Oh, I thought they were covered in stones?"

"Well if you'd laid here a couple of thousand years or so I guess you'd have a few weeds on your back. I don't reckon there are many gardeners in this neck of the woods."

"Luke! Be serious and tell me all about them, for I am sure you know a bit. Grandfather told you all about them, didn't he?"

"Yes, William was a great one for yarns, here, I've got a torch, I'll show you what they look like inside." He led the way to a low entrance and sliding the baby off his back told her to stay with Angus until he had checked that it was okay to go in. He was gone for a short while then giving her the torch told her keep her head well down till she reached the end of the passage guarding the main chamber. He followed close behind with Angus in his arms till they both stood erect in a circular area ringed about with tightly packed stones. The air had a musty, gamey smell as though beings still inhabited the place. Everywhere was dry even to the rough floor beneath their feet.

"Early Bronze Age this is, according to William. He said he got the information from some archaeologists who happened by some twenty years ago. Apparently they were doing the rounds of all the ancient finds to make sure they were still preserved and in good order. Then they were going to produce books for libraries and museums. They must have got on well together for they camped by the Croft for a few days."

"According to his notes Grandfather had a lot to ask them. How far back is the Bronze Age?" Asked Jessica, eagerly intrigued with the thought of an ancient tribe living so close.

"Maybe two thousand years, more likely three. The earliest bronzes were discovered in the Middle East about 4000 BC. People were roaming all over the world by then and a great many hut circles were found in this area of Scotland, probably because it was a good place for hunting and fishing. Therefore, where you have humans you have burial grounds and the start of religion. The sun, moon and the stars as well as animals and nature all contributed to making up stories, passing on legends and protecting oneself from evil."

"What are these holes?" She asked, pointing to some low openings into the main chamber.

"Those lead to small burial or storage chambers but they are mostly walled up. This central place was kept clear for visitors. Not that there's been any recently. It's a long way off from the town and I guess you'd have to be real keen to come out here." At that point Angus took exception to the dark strange place and began to cry, so they crawled back outside.

"I suppose the houses people lived in would have been like this, mostly underground and well away from the cold?"

"Yes, but these dwellings ten had wattle roofs instead of stone and were only used during the cold weather or for storing food. They were called Briochs. If the Clans felt safe then during the warm weather they lived outdoors under temporary shelters. But that was only if they were on the move. Mostly they lived in wattle huts surrounded by a fence, or in big round towers 40 feet across, if they were in danger of raiding by other tribes. Life was full of peril then, with each tribe vying to be top dog."

"How come you know so much history?"

"It was lucky William saw what happened when my plane crashed for I came down in the woods over there," he pointed to the end of the loch. "Your grandpappy, having seen the plane accident searched for me then carried me back to the croft on his back. No mean feat, I tell you, though he was a strong man. I'd broken my leg and had concussion. It was a while before I made any sense as to who I was and who to contact to fetch me. He avoided cops like poison, you see."

"He set my leg, made a good job of it too, so the doc' said, then waited till I was rational and could tell him. I lay reading his old books till I was taken back to the station, then when I came back here afterwards I carried on reading the rest and listening to him talk; he had a rare fund of knowledge for one so isolated. It's a pity you never knew him, you'd have got on well."

"I've often thought it," said Jessica sadly. "I feel cross with my father for never bringing me back here to meet him. Why are people so short sighted?"

"Selfishness mainly, I guess, for the majority are only concerned with their own needs. Perhaps your father only wanted you and your mom, nobody else mattered."

"Oh Luke, you are too forgiving, think of all that's happened to you, most folks only have one bad thing in their lives but you've had so many, don't you feel like hitting out at the world? You seem to have gone from one disaster right into another.""

"Yeah, honey, but it has a habit of hitting straight back at you. No, I've had my share of grief I reckon. From now on it's all down hill, unless of course we get blight with the sheep that knocks us off our perch, so I'd better not be too complacent. I'm happy, but are you? You have a rare talent with finance that's being neglected. You could easily get a real fine job. I don't want to shut you away from life in this backwater just because of my needs. Let's get through this winter then we can talk about where we are. Angus will be that much older and we'll know if we want to stay. How's that for an earth-shaking decision on such a beautiful morning?"

Jessica nodded and laughed, "The only decision I need to make is to walk home and decide what to cook for dinner. Let's go, Luke, or one baby will be grizzling before we get too far and spoil the peace of the day. Besides this place gives me the creeps, it's too quiet. Have you noticed the birds stopped singing as soon as we came out of the forest?"

"Maybe because there are no trees to sing in."

"No, that's not it. This is either a Holy place or a spooky place and I can't make up my mind which. I think I'll leave it to its ghosts and we'll go home. Okay?"

"Whatever you say. Personally I can't feel a thing."

Her cheeks dimpled with mirth as she murmured softly,
"Ol' wooden head." Then shrieked with laughter as he sped after her to grab and kiss her soundly. They made swift progress homewards as the baby took exception to the boisterous play and was determined to make his presence felt; the blackberries forgotten in their race to get home before Angus got upset. Still, thought Jessica later, it had been a lovely morning and she had learned more about her grandfather. Now she knew education didn't necessarily happen in school. It was what you taught yourself after that counted the most. And she wanted to learn everything she could. The next thing we must try building is another extension where we'll have a study. We can collect our own small library. I want Angus to read everything he can lay his hands on. Maybe, as we live so far from schools I can teach him at home. She hugged the thought to herself. It was a long way up the road as yet, but there was no harm in planning for the future.

THIRTY NINE

It was just after Angus' midday feed a week later, after he went down for his afternoon sleep that the post van turned up with Andy Keiller grinning from ear to ear. They were old friends now and Jessica asked if he would like to join her in a coffee and sandwich lunch.

"Aye, that would be fine, I've no much tae deliver the day, I can afford to tak' a wee while tae rest." They chatted inconsequentially of all the local affairs in the neighbourhood and Jessica realised anew the importance of the role he played bringing news and unity to the scattered farms. He was a born raconteur and knew just what would interest his listeners, changing topics to suit.

All at once, he threw out a surprising question. "Would you ken anyone who would be looking fur ye? Someone who didn't know your address?"

Jessica chilled at the seemingly innocent question and panic lanced through her like a sword. Who would look for her? She had no family, no friends other than those she'd made locally and her past life was behind her. More than that, she had no wish to resurrect anyone from the South. Was it Henry? Or could it be Mark?

Had he found out about Angus? No, surely not. Her mind totally denied the possibility. Henry would never have told him; even had he fully understood the hidden meaning in her letter. Mrs Watts would have had no idea; she had never left a forwarding address, making an excuse when she left that she would write when she was established. She never had. It had been so long ago it was difficult to remember those dark, dreadful hours when she had been on the point of taking her own life. As for Mark, he was married, and probably just as eager to forget the incident as she was. He would have no desire to check up on her. She was just being foolish, letting imagination run away with her. After a moment's strained silence, reason prevailed, and she relaxed. She was brainless, allowing daft thoughts of disaster to have their way.

"What do you mean, someone looking for me? Who is looking for me?"

"Och, it was an Englishman who was asking, a Mr Golding. Wanted a Miss Meredith not a Mrs Fraser. Those he asked did not associate one with t'other, ye ken, so he has not got far in his inquiries. Ye can mak' up mind if ye do want to see him. I never let on about other folk's business ye ken unless they say so."

She shook her head violently before she could stop herself saying weakly in a voice not her own, "There's no one I want to see from London, no one at all Andy. My life is here with Luke and Angus, and only them. Don't say anything, will you?"

He looked at her considering. She had something to hide; he'd thought that from the first. Funny she had never introduced herself as wife to Luke Fraser but simply granddaughter to Willy Meredith. But his personal rules were inviolate; never look too deep below the surface, one was aye likely to stir up mud no matter who it was. So he replied with droll assurance:

"Naebody will ken from me you're a Sassenach bewitched away from they dirty streets o' London, but I canna answer for the rest o' them biddies at Invergarry, mebbe one o' them will let the cat oot o' the bag. They are a wee bitty chatty if someone gets them going."

"There's not a cat to let out, Andy." she was firm. "When my mother died I was left on my own. I had no other relatives, you see. I knew I had to start a new life so I left my job and came here. I wouldn't go back to the old life for anything in the world and I'm sure there's no one down in London who would be interested in me after all this time."

"Quite right too," he said approvingly, "Ye canna beat the Highlands for guid clean living. Well, I'll just squash any mention o' you if I should come across Mr Golding. Dinna fash yersel' lass I'll nae let on yer' whereabouts. Now I'd better gang awa'. Thanks fer ma dinner, Jess, you tak' care o' yer' twa men and gie Luke ma regards, I'll mebbe see him in the Royal Oak one o' these days for a dram. D'ye ken he has a rare wee touch with a dart. Ower team fair miss him."

Jessica blushed at his parting words. Since she and Luke had begun making love Luke had given up his weekly visits to the local inn, preferring to keep Jessica company each evening. He had also embarked on carving wooden toys for Angus and the quiet domesticity of their life together had deepened the love that was ever growing stronger. Jessica was completely content but she wondered if perhaps Luke missed the company of his male friends in Invergarry.

"Andy was asking after you today, said he missed you," she said, when Luke came home.

"Oh yes?" He was preoccupied with opening the letter the postman had brought for him. Jessica noticed it looked official but she didn't attempt to ask what it was. She waited until he had finished reading it then said:

"Missed you playing darts - apparently you are very good, I think he wanted to know why you had stopped, I wasn't sure what to say. I don't mind in the least if you want to have a night off playing darts. I'll be all right by myself..."

He rose from his chair, caught her up in his arms, kissing the soft lips he could never have too much of. "Thanks Kiddo, but I'm happy here with you...unless you are tired of me?" He raised his eyebrows in question.

"Of course not, I just didn't want to be selfish; I've taken over your life..."

"Exactly how I love it," he concluded. "Now my darling, if that's all that's worrying you,
forget it, if there's anything to enjoy we'll enjoy it together, okay?"

"There is just one thing," she added doubtfully. "Andy said there was someone roaming around Invergarry asking for a Miss Meredith."

"Christ!" Luke's rare expletive dropped like a stone into the sudden silence which followed her words. "Who do you think it is?" His contrived quiet voice after the initial outburst did not calm her at all for she knew him well enough now to know he was disturbed with her news. The foreboding which she'd felt like a dark shadow all the afternoon sharpened into a real threat.

"I did wonder if it might be Mark Welland," stammered Jessica.

Luke's lips tightened angrily. "How could he possibly know you had come up here?"

146

She blushed as she explained about the note to her boss.

"Well, perhaps it's your boss, maybe he wants to know how you are..." His voice trailed off as she shook her head, her eyes bright with unshed tears.

"Look Jess, our marriage is perfectly legal; Welland can't prove Angus is his child or if he did there isn't a court in the land would grant him paternity rights, anyway."

"It's not that, Luke, I'm just terrified of him coming up here and spoiling our lives."

He took her in his arms again and held her close.

"Jess, you know I wouldn't let him hurt you, I'd kill him first. You've nothing to fret about for Mark-bloody-Welland will have more on his plate sooner than he wants; he's gonna be very busy answering questions about some of his other evil ways."

"What do you mean?" She gazed at him wide-eyed.

"That letter is from my old Colonel. It seems he's not happy about the case of my buddy getting killed. They want me to give more evidence, and boy am I gonna do just that, and this time they'll have to believe me. I'm not hiding the truth so Welland can get the benefit."

"Luke, if you are declared innocent regarding the accident will you go back to flying?" She had watched him many times wearing the wistful look on his face as he stared at the high-flying jets. When they flew overhead he would gaze at them until they were out of sight.

"You miss flying, don't you?"

"Yeah, sometimes, but no I wouldn't. I have a whole new life with you and Angus, what do I want with service life all over again, it's no fun for the wives, you have to move around wherever the pilots go and put up with crummy accommodation. No Jess, we're fine where we are. We may not have as much money but it's a peaceful life." She stared at him for a moment to see if he was telling the truth, then she said seriously,

"If you want to go back you only have to say, Luke, I would be okay about it. In fact I can cope with most things these days except you being miserable. Now don't you forget? Promise?"

"Yes, my darling girl, I promise. In any event there's no use speculating, they might decide there's no case to answer after they've spoken to me. I only had a split second to avoid the plane coming in on me and I could have been wrong about the pilot..."

"But you don't think so," concluded Jessica. "Besides, grandfather saw the plane too."

"He's dead, Jess." Luke said gently, "What I need is someone who actually knows something of flying and who can tell it as it was. There's no one like that or they would have come forward before. No love, it's all water under the bridge, I can't see them believing me."

"When do you have to go?"

"Next Monday, I'll be gone maybe two days, will you be all right here on your own or do you want to stay with Mrs Stuart? I can drop you off easily as I drive through."

"Of course not, I'll be just fine."

"What if you-know-who turns up?" Luke said, frowning at the thought.

Jessica grinned and said jokingly, "I'll bar the door and shoot him through the window!"

"Come on Jess, be serious. Your safety is all that matters to me."

"Seriously Luke, you don't think he's going to make the same mistake twice. It would be a jail sentence with out a doubt, and they would throw away the key!"

"I wouldn't take his word if he swore on a hundred holy books. Once a rat, always a rat. Besides, you'd never face him without being reminded again and I'm not having that, so keep the door locked. Okay Honey?"

"Yes, Luke, I'll take care, I promise. However, I've been thinking about the man who was supposed to be looking for me, maybe it was the Glasgow solicitor just curious as to what we had done about the farm. He must have been mad at me for doing him out of such a large sum of money. I wonder how many other people he's diddled along the way?"

"No." Luke reminded her. "Andy said he was English. As for Macfarlan, he was lucky to get away with only losing the money. I'd have taken it a great deal farther."

"Yes, and probably ended up in jail for punching him on the nose." She gave him a sudden hug. "Let's forget all the ifs and buts and go to Invergarry, I need some stores, also some driving practise to pass my test."

Luke shook his head in sorrowful pretence.

"Ah yes, there'll be no stopping you after you pass, I'll have to hide the keys or I'll never get the car. You'll be off lord knows where, swanning all over the countryside."

"What makes you think I'll pass? Not everyone does."

"Jeez honey! Look at all the things you set your mind to. You've learned so much since you came up here - how to burn cakes, how to set the chimney on fire! Now there was a grand sight, nearly gave me a heart attack thinking the croft was burning. I beat every miler on record to get here." he grinned mischievously again.

"Luke Fraser! If you don't stop mocking me I'll..." As he stopped her mouth with a penitent kiss he reflected on the change he could feel looming ahead. What would his visit to see his Colonel bring? Trouble? And who was the stranger who was seeking Jessica? More trouble?

Suddenly he felt icy shudders run down his back. The quiet glen was not safe any more. Maybe there was no security anywhere in the world for the likes of him. Was he forever doomed to setbacks and disasters? His light-hearted mood vanished, and although she tried hard, Jessica could not shake him out of the doldrums.

"Don't worry, Luke. It will be all right I'm sure it will. It will give you the chance to set the record straight, put your side of the story with the facts, as you now know them. Cheer up, darling, I hate it when you are miserable, really I do."

"I'm sorry, hon, it's just I can't see an end to the trouble and it makes me feel uneasy. Anyway, I'm not really down. I've got you and Angus...and the farm...and the sheep! Hell, we're rich, baby! There's nothing to worry about."

But there was.

FORTY

A couple of days later Mark called the agency for news and was told Frank Golding had left a message for him. Finally, Golding's trainee was successful. He found out Jessica had married an American at the end of September. According to records, the child had been born the following February, which puzzled Mark for a moment when calculating the dates as he would have expected the baby to have been born in March. Without doubt, she was a virgin when he took her so it might have been an early birth. He had not been so drunk as to mistake the signs, or misread the dates. Married! Hell and Damnation! Mark flopped back in his office chair, his thoughts whirling angrily as the news of Jessica, now married and living on a farm in Scotland, penetrated. Not only married but she also had a boy child who was, by all accounts, about nine months old.

Turning the event over in his mind, he was fully convinced. Jessica had given birth to a son whom she had fostered on some Yank. He would lay odds it was his son and he was going to claim him in spite of Annabel's antagonism. Suddenly Mark's face twisted with rage. HIS SON was being brought up by a damn Yankee. Well, my lady, we'll see about that! There was only one answer to this mess. Annabel had to die and the sooner the better. But how could he do it? For pity's sake, brain - think, can't you?

He stopped himself reaching for the phone again. Hold it boy, you can't see about a thing. You're married! To a bloody cripple maybe, but still married. You have no proof the child is yours, so what can you do? He calmed down and began to go over the options he had. He now knew for certain that Annabel would never give him a child. She was able to use a wheelchair for short intervals but the pain she suffered made it an agonising exercise. Consequentially he had ventured to speak to her once or twice about adopting a child to give her an interest in life. Finally she had stared at him with venom.

"Adopt! Who would we adopt? One of your by-blows?" Her face was hard and cynical, the suffering of the last few months etched in pain-drawn lines across her face. He mumbled something about wanting an heir then she screamed back at him, "You'll just have to wait until I die, won't you and that might take a long, long time, Mark darling. I don't want a child to get in the way or distract you...I want all your attention...every last little drop!"

Her face twisting cruelly with spite she snarled, "You did this to me and now you have to look after the dire results. Not pretty are they? Moreover, I need looking after meticulously or Daddy will not be pleased. Got it? Mr high and Mighty Mark Welland?"

At last! It was out in the open at last. So she did know. Had likely known all along. All the months of waiting and wondering - if she, would she? *And what would she say?* Particularly to her father. A wall of silence grew between them and for a long uneasy moment, they stared at one another.

Then he said softly, "Blackmail Annabel? It hardly becomes you." She just shrugged at his words without answering, her face bitter and ugly. He had left things like that and walked away. The time for recriminations was past. It was time for action now.

"I'm going fishing at the end of the week, Annabel."

"So." She was in a surly mood again.

"So, I'm telling you, that's all. I shall be away for a few days, probably a week. It'll give you a rest from my company. I rarely seem to please you at the moment."

"Where are you going?" She didn't protest at him leaving her, it was too much of an effort.

"Up to Scotland. With an old school chum of mine," he added." He has a hunting lodge above Loch Ness and gets a party together for the Salmon run. I missed last year for obvious reasons but I'm sure you won't mind if I go now,"

"And if I do?"

"Annabel, sweetie, try to respond a little more kindly. I know you feel angry at life but truly we've done everything possible to make you comfortable. Try and be a good patient."

"You don't have to lie here all day bored to tears and in pain most of the time. I'm sick to death of platitudes I wish I were dead!"

"Now, now, Mrs Welland, that's no way to talk or wish you dead. There's plenty worse off than you! A little less self-pity and a bit more effort in your exercising will work wonders for your spirits. You are managing more time in the wheelchair and your father has promised to take you away on holiday if we can get you mobile." Annabel's resident nurse was both cajoling and firm and with a tip of her head, she motioned Mark away as she began to coax her patient back to a better humour. "Let me give you a back rub and I will soothe those unpleasant aches and pains that are such a trial. A face massage would be just the thing too. We can't have you getting wrinkles on your face from bad thoughts, now can we?"

Annabel's attention was immediately redirected at that terrible thought and she picked up a mirror from the bedside table and surveyed her face.

"Mark! You don't think I'm looking old do you?" But Mark was gone and Annabel flung the mirror down with a thud as she faced the truth. Why in the world had she married him? It didn't matter whether she looked old or young it was patently obvious her husband did not want any part of her now; finally, she asked herself - had he ever.

Mark made good his escape thinking that at last she had admitted she wanted to die and in front of a witness. Though what good that would do at this moment was hardly worth bothering about, Annabel could not get out of bed without help and when she was out was unable to guide her chair very far at all. It would have to be devised and as reluctant as he was to cause her more grief the only solution that had come to mind was to burn the house down around her.

He had caused a fire before when he was in the RAF. He had been in charge of the mess funds and when the time came for the annual audit, he had been unable to pay back the missing monies, which had unaccountably strayed into his pocket. He had been sick with desperation till an idea came to him. He had always been good at Electro-technology at school. Hopeless at written work and exams but gifted in setting up apparatus in the lab to enthral his classmates with his ingenious experiments, his strange spurts of genius coupled with ignorance might have been labelled Dyslexia had anyone known the facts or taken the trouble to analyse his odd behaviour at the time. He had an amazing memory and an ability to recall what people said but the written word confused him. He could read after a fashion provided it was not complicated and he had time but mainly he relied on his memory and imitating others parrot fashion. His form master, who disliked him intensely, decided he wasn't worth the trouble of delving into his psychological quirks. He had neither the knowledge nor the inclination to try to help Mark. Only a young enthusiastic science master encouraged the boy in play-acting until the Head eventually said, with an eye to Mark's father and school fees, that he had to concentrate on his regular schoolwork.

However, he never forgot how to use the knowledge he had acquired at that time, when much later, and entirely for his own ends, he had successfully burnt down the building where the camp's records were kept, with no one being any the wiser. Happily it was also at a time when

he as was usual, had a watertight alibi. Needless to say he evaded an inquiry or any accusation of misappropriating funds, for the evidence was gone, and once again he escaped retribution. He decided to use the same method, carefully arranging a cast-iron alibi to prevent his father-in-law from accusing him of murder. His annual trip to Scotland was an ideal excuse.

Fortunately, their new home would provide the ideal combination to get rid of Annabel. Warren had given Mark and Annabel the house when they got married. Mark had wanted an old stone place near Cookham, but *they* had decided on a large newly built residence in Sevenoaks, which was close to Warren's home.

Mark, of course, gave in, he hadn't paid for it so what did it matter? However, at the time he had some telling remarks to make about the shoddy workmanship they had found.

The night before he planned to leave for Scotland, he made sure the nurse was in her own quarters and Annabel fast asleep, before going into the enormous garage. It could hold three cars, though at present there was only his Jaguar; various crates of books which he had not bothered to unpack; odds and ends of furniture; and some builder's rubbish consisting of wood, half-used tins of paint, rolls of paper and a tin of brush cleaner. Items which were all beautifully inflammable.

He donned the rubber gloves he had purchased earlier in the week and found the mains electricity cable where it entered the house before going into the meter. Without turning off the current he carefully removed a lead seal the Electricity Board had fixed to the cable and opened the meter. Leaving the wires still connected inside, he slit the cable apart for a short distance then warily bared both live and earth wires to expose a tiny area adjacent to one another, taking the utmost care not to touch one wire with another. He closed the meter, adjusted the seal as though it had never been touched and arranged the paper and paint tins to lie close to the cable where he knew the fire would start. Once the cable was smouldering and melting the plastic wire, it would not take long for it to ignite the paper. Then bingo it would soon spread to the inflammable material and hopefully the garage would go up like a bomb, taking, if he was lucky, the house with it.

When he was done with the preparations, he carefully inspected the garage to make sure there was nothing left to incriminate him. He replaced the tools in their box and put the rubber gloves in the boot of his car. He would lose them en route to Scotland.

Satisfied with his work he retired to bed.

*   *   *   *   *

Early the next morning he bade farewell to Annabel and just before he climbed in his car, he gave a slight twitch to the mains cable. The two wires made contact and he could hear the small popping sound as they arced. No one else would hear it, as there was only the nurse and his wife in the house that day. Her father was not due to make his visit and the housekeeper was away on holiday, so no one would notice when the cable began to overheat and smoulder.

For once, the M25 was reasonable and he made good time getting to the M1 and driving northwards keeping his speed within bounds until he was past Birmingham and well up on the M6. Pulling into a service station at Preston he rang his secretary to remind her to give his father some notes which he had deliberately forgotten the previous day. He made sure the girl in the newsagent's shop remembered him as he flirted with her and he also ensured his secretary knew exactly where he was. Filling up with petrol he went on his way with a song in his heart. This time tomorrow he would be free, and this time he would stay free.

Mark stayed overnight in a hotel near Edinburgh where he was known and the next day wasted no time driving to the lodge at Cannich, to spend a holiday with his old school friend. Peter Frewins was waiting impatiently when he arrived, trouble writ large upon his face. Mark was to phone his father-in-law immediately, as there had been a serious accident.

"What kind of accident, Peter, did he say?"

"Not really, you'd better call him, he sounded very upset, something to do with a fire." Keeping his face straight and praying his plan hadn't gone awry, Mark dialled his father-in-law and was told the news that Annabel and the nurse were dead, the house was burnt to the ground and where the blazes was he, when he ought to have been at home with Annabel.

Mark swiftly retaliated. "Christ in hell, Warren, what the fuck happened? The whole house burnt down? I can't believe such a dreadful thing. On the other hand I told you over and over again we shouldn't have bought that bloody place, I knew it was a bodge-up. Damn you, now my wife's dead and it's all your fault!"

FORTY ONE

Charles Welland finished his work on some bank matters then turned his mind to the matter that had been irritating him all day. He touched the intercom switch. "Has Mr Mark returned from his holiday yet, Marie?"

"Yes sir, I believe he's in the building. Do you want him?"

"Yes, ask him to come see me when it's convenient." Although the times, which were convenient to Mark, as far as his job in the bank, was concerned, were subject to argument. He had departed to the continent soon after his wife's distressing death. Distressing that is, to her mourning father, and in consequence, to Charles, who had been made to feel he was a party to all sorts of trickery, not the least of which, was the mere fact of being Mark's father. With the upward lift in the economy, and the backing of Warren's firm, the troubles over the loans had receded. Charles had just began to feel, with a sense of relief, that his financial affairs were coming back into order when out of the blue Annabel's accident ensued and any normal kinship between the two families sank once again to a low ebb. Mostly he left things to the employees who conducted the necessary affairs of the banks.

The months passed and things went on as usual for the banks and again Charles was feeling more optimistic when lightning struck again, but this time Warren was not to be placated. He had investigators take the burned ruin apart looking for signs Mark had been responsible for the fire. Though nothing was revealed, Charles instinctively knew Warren suspected his son. He kept a very low profile himself, pretending he was still very grieved about his daughter-in-law. Despite minute searching all that was uncovered in the parts not totally destroyed, was faulty wiring. This was put down to shoddy workmanship on the part of the builders. He began to relax once again.

The Electricity Board vigorously defended their part in connecting power to the house, quoting the stringent rules and regulations, which governed their actions. No sign was ever discovered of Mark's work on the fuse box for the garage was completely demolished, so too was the main bedroom suite, where Annabel and the nurse had lost their lives. The fire, fiercely blazing by this time, shot up the lift shaft, which Warren had installed after her accident to allow her to be taken downstairs to the garden, then had engulfed the suite where she spent most time.

The Coroner noted the nurse had endeavoured to save her patient, rather than only her, for their bodies were found together beside the overturned wheelchair, near the bedroom door. He assumed the nurse had attempted to wheel Annabel to another part of the house but the massive explosive rush of flames must have driven them back. He duly commended her loyal bravery. When it was further revealed the builder had been on the edge of bankruptcy, had skimped on building materials, Mark knew he was home and dry.

The verdict was accidental death, which, coupled with extreme negligence on behalf of the electricians sub-contracted by the builder, led to strong criticisms about the use of short cuts to save money. The electrical firm had since gone out of business and Warren, much as he felt like suing the builder, knew it was useless; nothing would bring his daughter back. His only solace, he need not pretend regard or further kinship with his son-in-law ever again. He would have relished proving Mark the guilty party, but had to admit there was indisputable evidence that the man was in the clear. Far, far away from deliberate intent, a cast-iron alibi in fact, having left home long before the fire started, according to the experts, who had spent hours piecing together the evidence and finally adjudicating on the results. Though how do they really know these things, he wondered?

Days after, whenever he snatched a moment or two to be by himself, he would puzzle over the enigma, for deep down his hard headed instincts still felt murder had been committed. How, he had no idea, but so well, and he had tried hard enough to find sufficient evidence, God knows he had striven hard, no one could prove that Mark was culpable.

Despite the lack of evidence in naming Mark a killer, Warren knew he'd managed to 'fix' the so called 'accident' just as he had contrived the fall in Switzerland. His daughter had been impetuous but never downright stupid. He credited her with having far more sense than to go blindly into danger on the spur of a whim. Mark must have got her up there then dared her to try the run knowing full well she would fall. Perhaps he had meant to ski behind and complete the murder but had been followed too quickly by the other skiers. At least, Warren thought bleakly, it would have been more humane, would have saved his beloved daughter from the months of pain and mental anguish, to be followed by the appalling death in the fire. Once more his throat contracted painfully as he shed inconsolable tears of bereavement.

After a moment, he dried his eyes. He must stop this maudlin weeping; he had a bank to run money to make and two Welland men to keep a close eye on. He would bide his time, let the bile of vengeance curdle a little more. There would come an opportunity, he felt sure, to wreak his revenge on Mark, for it was all he had left to him. His wife, an invalid herself for most of her life, mourned the passing of her daughter but Annabel had been daddy's girl so her absence caused only a ripple in the fabric of her pain-ridden days.

* * * * *

Vague disquieting thoughts were still milling around in Charles brain when the door opened and in strolled Mark. "Hullo Father, how are you?" Mark looked rakishly fit; his sun tanned skin shining against the dark hair and white teeth added a slightly foreign cast to his usual good looks.

"Not as well as you by all accounts. Your mother told me you phoned her last night to say you were home at last. Thanks for letting me know." Charles tone was dry.

"Yes, I had a great time, the weather was perfect," he said, ignoring the sarcasm. "I feel a trifle better now," he added, determined to keep up the illusion he was still suffering from the bereavement. "Fortunately I've had time to think about things while I've been away and I've come to a decision about the bank."

"Oh, a decision?" His father looked at his son with searching eyes. Now what?

154

"Well, I really don't see myself as a banker, plodding the straight and narrow, keeping office hours etc. You know what I mean, Father, it's a bloody tedious business."

"One that kept you at good schools fed and housed you in the lap of luxury and has kept me in employment all my life. Don't denigrate it to me, Mark, I'm proud of what we have here, proud of what I, mostly single-handed, have accomplished."

"Don't get me wrong, its fine for others, for you, but not for me. I have other fish to fry, but not in this country. I've the chance to buy into a restaurant-cum-night-club in Marbella, that's where all the best people go...."

"What with?" Charles interjected swiftly, his mind as ever on financial details.

"Come again? What do you mean, what with?" Bloody miser, always wants to know how much and where the money's coming from. "Are you talking about the cost? Well, this time you don't have to worry, Father. I'm not dropping on your head. It's worked out rather well I think, in the circumstances. I've got Annabel's Trust money to use."

Charles sat rigid, silently gazing at his only son. His grim face belied any humour. He was rather in the mood to kill Mark himself. He had quite forgotten Warren had told him on the day of the wedding that he had bestowed on Annabel a hefty sum of money in her own right. To be kept for a rainy day, when the kids were all grown up and perhaps the happy couple wanted to go around the world or something. His beaming smile indicated he imagined it would be roses all the way. Even then I knew he was only kidding himself, he thought. Another even darker thought entered his mind; twisting and squirming like a monster fiend from some nightmare. No! He dare not even think it, surely it was impossible, not his son!

He stared intently at the man before him, a transformed man, wholly unlike the sulky, irritable husband of a month ago and knew it was perfectly possible, indeed even probable Mark might have killed his wife. A cold shudder froze him to his marrow. What kind of monster had he spawned? He shook himself mentally; he must put the idea away as if it had never been lest his wife drag it from his mind. It would kill her if she ever knew the truth.

"Lucky chap, you've really fallen on your feet, Mark," he made the effort to sound normal.

"Haven't I just. Course, I'm still missing Annabel. I shan't ever marry again but don't despair about a grand-son, I think I can surprise you in that quarter."

"What? What surprise?" Charles couldn't grasp the way the conversation was leading. He was still embroiled in trying to rid himself of the fearful soul-destroying thoughts.

Mark coughed self-consciously, perhaps he was jumping the gun but his parent suddenly looked very old and down in the mouth, he must cheer the old buffer up somehow. He had taken Annabel's death very hard, poor old beggar.

"You'll remember Jessica Meredith?"

His father stared at him fiercely, his eyes steely with intent at the unexpected words.

"Yes. I remember Miss Meredith."

Mark hastily went on. "Well, father, I've just found out that coincidentally, she produced an infant last February and amazingly he's my son! What do you think of that?"

"Not a lot, Mark," his father managed an even tone. "It's a great pity you go about life in the way you do, I can't pretend you're an example to the human race. Not that I'm suggesting you ought to have married the girl, but you could have been a lot better off, had a nice family..."

"Come off it, dad, you paid the girl off, besides, you talked me into marrying Annabel. It was all done for financial reasons. Bloody business as usual. I wasn't keen, if you remember? Still, things have a way off working out, and talking of working out...that money you gave Jessica...one could say we've virtually bought the child..."

"Christ Almighty, Mark! Enough is enough! I did not buy anything except your freedom from prison! I am beginning to think I should have left things to take their course. Now leave things alone, leave the girl alone. You've probably got bastards from here to - to - all over the place. Go off to Spain, marry or not as you wish but if you have a child make sure he's yours and legitimate, for I'll not look at anything else. Now get out, I've work to do. Make sure you see your mother before you leave. I've nothing more to say. Goodbye Mark."

"That sounds a bit final, father, don't know what I've done to upset you." Mark's mouth was sulky. He had been ready to discuss a way to get his son back so he could take him off to Spain. He had thought his father would co-operate but it was apparent the old boy had acquired strange ethics. Too bad, he would do the job himself. At least he could rely on himself to do things right. And there would be only one alibi to manufacture.

Charles opened his mouth to tell Mark exactly what he had done to upset him then closed it. What was the use in stirring up more trouble, if he fell out with Mark then his wife, Muriel, would want to know what had caused it. How could one calmly say, oh by the way your son is a rapist and a foul killer? Put like that it seemed impossible to even contemplate it for a second let alone voice it. But Charles had the chilling feeling if the police knew half the facts that he knew about his son's life, they would discover a great deal more.

For Mark had spent his life always on the edge, but somehow never quite implicated, in any amount of scrapes and accidents that happened with increasing regularity as he grew older. As a child it was always someone else who was blamed for the misdemeanour, never Mark. As an adult, he usually managed to disappear from an awkward situation without people ever realising how or why. Time after time, small incidents, usually most painful to the victims, but scarcely notable in themselves, seem to happen in his vicinity.

Mark gazed at his father with irritation, why couldn't the silly old fool retire, go and put his feet up, he was past it, ought to leave things to younger folk. One of the reasons he had turned his attention to other pursuits was the thought of having his father on the one side and Warren on the other.

Besides, living in the South of Spain would be like being on holiday all the time and getting paid for it. His share would not amount to much at the start, but just you wait, he promised himself, he'd acquire sole ownership before long or his name wasn't Mark Welland.

That would be something to boast about to his father who had seldom, if ever, patted him on the back for an achievement, invariably querying the deed as though Mark had made things up. In the end, Mark had given up trying to impress his father, choosing instead, to impress others. But deep down he felt the lack of approval, was unconsciously forever thinking of ways to be a hero in his father's eyes. Bitterly he glared at his father's bent head. "Well if that's all you've got to say then I'll be off. Don't bother to see me out. See you sometime...maybe."

He went back to his own office to find his secretary, Deborah, waiting with coffee and a pile of unopened mail.

"I only opened the ones which were obviously to do with the firm, sir, as you requested. If you would like to go through them you can let me know what else you want doing." Her voice was distant, uncaring. He was a swine to work for, changing his mind from day to day on the turn of a whim, but she needed the job. Life had been easy in the last month while he'd been away, now she would have to cope again with his sulky ways. To her surprise he spoke kindly, turning the famous charm on like a waft of perfume from an atomiser. The air in the office brightened.

"Thank you, Debby. My, this coffee is good. Okay, let's see what we've got here, I'll call you shortly to deal with the letters when I've digested this lot. It surely piles up. Can't say I'll miss it when I return to Spain. Ah! That's in confidence. Not a word to you-know-who till I've had a chance to tell him myself. Had enough of Banking. Sun and sea are more my style, yet I'll miss your fair charms, my dear."

Will you hell! Thought Deborah. Miss being chivvied by your father likely. And I'll have to see about another job, worse luck, while glamour boy is off, swanning in the sun, I only hope the firm can still find room for me here. At least my next boss should be a darn sight better than this one, if I'm lucky. He could never be worse.

FORTY TWO

Colonel Phillip Haskins leaned heavily back into his chair, the soft leather creaking gently.

His eyes closed and his brain began ticking over like a computer. At last the pieces of the puzzle were sliding into place. Anomalies identified; half-truths and lies giving way to facts and truth. It had taken him some while, for the demands on his time were enormous, but it proved his keen intuition had not led him astray, for pains-taking as usual, he unearthed the rotten apple among his staff. The officer in question was lazy and negligent. No wonder men like Welland had been able to get away with devilry. The outrageous tangle of lies and dishonesty in his group angered him, yet at the same time the discovery of it gave him great satisfaction. He wasn't quite over the hill yet. He could still cut it, as the Americans were fond of saying.

He had been temporarily seconded to advise on air strategy in the Middle East, specifically to do with Iraq, when the trouble in Scotland blew up. The inquiry on the accident was finished and various participants moved on before he returned. Shortly afterwards he read the transcript of the accident investigation, but with his mind on other things he didn't pick up the significant detail that Welland shouldn't have been playing war games in the first place for he was hardly a good pilot. In fact, he should never have gone to go to Scotland, and certainly not fly.

The squadron had apparently drifted into lax ways while he had been absent and although he tightened up the discipline on his return, he knew he had been at fault with his choice of a second-in-command. With so much work to do he had missed the signals, which with hindsight were patently obvious, that the shirkers and dodgers in this world will find cosy billets and dig themselves in happily to the detriment of all concerned. The ADC was moved on and out of the service but it still left a bitter feeling in his gut. It should never have happened at all.

It was a stupid thing really, which had first set him puzzling again. He attended a farewell party at RAF Dishforth for an old friend who was retiring and the subject had arisen in the half-drunken group of comrades relaxing at the bar with a last drink, after a tasty gargantuan meal. It concerned the burning down of the records office on one of the satellite 'dromes. It was only one of a number of topical oddities they laughed at that evening but the name of Welland came up together with the ribald jest that he had covered his ass in ashes by burning the evidence. The remark had triggered a question in his mind and Haskins began by asking a few pertinent questions the next day then had rung the Colonel in the US Army Air Force who carried out the inquiry into the Scottish disaster. To Colonel Schafer's surprise Haskins raised vital issues that had never been discussed in the investigation. His probing questions touched on matters that Schafer thought were buried for all time. Eventually they agreed to have a meeting to discuss things. Haskins also agreed to keep things low key between them for Colonel Schafer had been deeply reluctant to raise the matter again.

Haskins caught on to his embarrassing dilemma when the Colonel confessed he had tried to make Luke Fraser put in a different report, concerning the death of his wingman.

"He told me to go stuff the one he had given me up my fanny. If he had to lie to get on in the Force, then the hell with it. So he took back his report and refused to say another word and we had no choice but to ground him. It could have been worse but I managed to swing the disciplinary hearing so that his pension wasn't affected. Not that it did any good, as far as the dead pilot, Mike Whitman, was concerned, he was gone. But I lost another damn good pilot through my own stupid fault. But jeez Colonel, you've no idea of the pressures we Americans have over here, God-damn-it, Haskins, you Brits are as touchy as a bunch of old hens."

Phillip Haskins laughed, "I know just what you mean, and it's the same for me. Anyway you're sure he recognised the third pilot and that it was our man Welland? I must say Fraser's reactions appear to be excellent. He would have had only a couple of seconds to eject once he touched his co-pilot's wing. It was a damn shame the other chap didn't make it too."

"Yeah they were both great guys, always flew together. I know it broke Fraser up to lose him. It's probably why he didn't care any more. See here, Colonel, to hell with keeping our heads down below the fence, if you can get something out of this creep, let's go for it."

"I hoped you'd say something like that." Haskins grinned conspiratorially to himself. "Right, I'll get the case reopened this end and we'll put it together. We'll try a little digging first; one never knows what will come out. Even if there's no chance of a prosecution after all this time I'd still like to give him a bloody good fright."

"I'm with you all the way, buddy, but it had better be quick, my tour of duty ends in a couple of months and I'm home to good ol' US of A. Be in touch. Bye Colonel." Haskins rang off with a feeling of lightness. He had not in fact mentioned the fire in the Records office, only that he had known Welland was not cleared to fly solo, nor to be precise, to fly anyway. He had a pilot's licence but that was as far as it went. He was ground staff and not too bright an officer in that field. At least not as far as his work was concerned. Haskins had heard rumours of other pursuits, which enhanced his feelings that Welland was a villain in more ways than one.

Nor did he say anything of the latest news article he had read of the unfortunate fire in Kent, which had killed two people; a cripple and her nurse. The name Welland, was coming up again and again, each time in situations which by themselves would not cause a second thought, but put them together and one had a nasty feeling a sewer would be too clean to hold a man with such a capacity for lies and skulduggery. Haskins felt it was imperative to put him where he could never kill or hurt anyone ever again.

FORTY THREE

Mark went through his largely insignificant mail, a long overdue tailor's bill, a final tally of the contents of his ruined house, which would be dealt with by insurers and solicitors from now on. A bill from the detective agency, too steep by far, he'd have to write them a sharp letter. Then he picked up two Air Ministry envelopes. What the hell were these?

He slit them open and ran his eyes quickly over the words. The first one, signed by his old commander, merely asked him to ring a number. The other, which by the postmark had been sent first, stated 'That further enquiries were being raised in the accidental death of a US pilot, and also the loss of two US planes, whilst engaged in practical manoeuvres over Scotland in March 2001.

It would be appreciated if he could produce more evidence, which might aid a secondary hearing'. A meeting of the respected officers involved, was to be held on (the date was long past, he had been in Spain then) could he arrange to be present? Yours etc... Bloody hell!

He sat thinking of what to do. Should he just ignore the whole thing and take off for Spain? No, perhaps not, they could still request him to return for questioning and it would look as if he'd been trying to evade a meeting. He tried to remember what he had said in his evidence but the details were dim with the passing of time. How could they discover he hadn't been where he said he was? Radar? No, he had gone below the screen like the others. Extra fuel? No, surely not, or if they did query anything, all he had to do was look perplexed.

After all, he had not taken a plane up since that time so it would naturally follow he could forget. In any case it was only by the merest chance he had been sent on the exercise instead of the usual combat pilot who was away on extended sick leave.

"Wanna have a buzz, Mark, old boy?" The ADC was feeling magnanimous. "It'll cost you a box of ciggy's but I'll put you down for Scotland if you want it."

He had thought it would be a lark to do a spot of flying. He hadn't actually said to the US staff he wasn't clued up with jets and barely up to flying standard with props except for being able to recall the position of various controls whenever he had taken the opportunity to examine the latest plane. Perhaps he could get someone to talk him through the cockpit arrangement just in case they really meant him to take a jet up. Not that he cared particularly. He would get a trip out of it, see new faces, have fun; and at the same time, he hoped to bluff his way through as he usually did. In the end, as his orders were to act as a lookout for the incoming Tornadoes, he was given a BAE Hawk Trainer, which he knew he could mange well enough without guidance. And, more to the point, without waiting for the designated co-pilot, who had been delayed, and whose presence would put a stop to the germ of an idea he had floating in his brain.

In fact, nothing happened to him at all. It was the other guy who hit his wingman, not him, so why worry? He was in the clear, not a damn thing to be concerned about! He lifted the phone to dial and when the base operator answered, requested to speak to his ex-Commanding Officer, Colonel Haskins. It was a while before the Colonel came to the phone but when he answered, the voice was terse.

"Haskins."

"Er-yes sir. Mark Welland speaking, I understand you wanted a word with me."

"Who did you say?"

"Er-Welland sir, I WAS Captain Mark Welland."

"Oh, what are you now?"

Damn the fellow, grumbled Mark to himself, was he trying to be facetious. He must know I'm a civvy now. What's he on about? "I'm a civilian now sir, left the Force several years ago. I've had a letter from you to asking me to call." Funny how one got back to calling an officer sir, Mark thought with irritation.

"Took your time surfacing, Mr Welland. The meeting we wished you to attend is over - Ah, good, nothing to worry about. "- however, I personally would like to see you, I still have one or two things I'd like answers to, could you make it tomorrow?"

Unexpectedly Mark felt a shiver go through him as though someone had walked over his grave. He shouldn't have rung the CO; he should have kept quiet and ignored it. Haskins was continuing in a persistent manner, blast him!

"It would help me tremendously if you can make it then; I have a full schedule this week. It won't take up much of your time and it should see an end to this enquiry." Mark was tempted to say no then he reflected the CO would likely set another time and spoil his return to Spain.

"Er - Let me see, yes, I can make it."

"Good, catch the 10.10 am out of Liverpool Street, we'll have a car waiting for you at Newmarket. I look forward to meeting you. Goodbye Mr Welland."

"Er - yes. Goodbye, sir." And I wish it were goodbye to you, thought Mark unhappily.

There was a smile on the face of Phillip Haskins as he put the phone down; the fellow was dammed reluctant. So he ought to be, the arrogant swine, one man killed; another fine pilot out of the US Force obviously still grieving over the loss of his friend, reduced to sheep farming of all things. Two expensive planes lost and an embargo put on a good flying area. All because of this man's stupidity. What was worse they couldn't pin anything on him unless they could get him to confess. Even so Haskins knew they would not be granted another enquiry unless they had a watertight case with the new evidence clear and concise. It would be like opening a can of worms, all sorts of things would surface which might affect not only this ex-officer but his own future career in the RAF. Perhaps his present group superiors would assume he had been at fault in his choice of men. Well so be it, it wasn't going to stop him doing the right thing now.

FORTY FOUR

Haskins' mind went back to the day he had encountered Luke Fraser. He had liked him the instant he'd met him. Liked the frank, open eyes and pleasant smile. His handshake was firm and altogether Haskins rated him a reliable chap, not one to lie and cheat in a cowardly fashion. It was natural he had been a trifle withdrawn at the start of the meeting, considering what had happened. He was slow to give answers; almost waiting to be called a liar. Then as his story unfolded and the only two men Colonel Schafer had been able to get hold of, out of the original eight base technicians who had co-ordinated the whole set-up, agreed with everything he was saying, Luke cheered up considerably.

"Why didn't you say this at the inquiry?" Asked one of them.

Luke reddened. "As I recall we didn't have AWACS overlooking as it was only the first dummy run and it is difficult to define things over the glens in low-flying. He appeared out of nowhere and it was my word against him so I felt it was useless. Welland had it cut and dried. I heard him sounding off in the bar about stooging around waiting for planes that never turned up. Besides, Mike was gone, I'd hit him. End of story; what was there to say after that."

The men round the table fell silent; they all knew the importance of losing a buddy. There was an unwritten code of loyalty that said it all.

Colonel Schafer sat easily back in his chair, his nerves at rest, as relief flooded through him. Fraser could have dropped him right in it with a vengeance for thwarting his report; but he'd said nothing of his last meeting with his Colonel. Schafer owed him one.

"Let's go back to the moment when the intruder came in on your right, did you get a clear identification?" Haskins prompted Luke again.

"Yeah, I spotted the Hawk, all right. I've flown it before in the States. We call it the Goshawk and use it on Aircraft Carriers or as trainers like you. It has a distinctive cockpit, windows large and clear. That was how I was able to see the different flying suit. He was also wearing one of those World War 1 white scarves. He looked a right prune."

"Then what?" Haskins smiled briefly at the quip as the rest of the men chuckled.

"I yelled and slid off to the left."

"You tried to warn Whitman?"

"Correct, sir, I heard him on the RT." said someone. "I was absent from the hearing and to be honest I was never asked for my opinion until now."

"Okay, then what?"

"I can't remember pressing the eject handle, I must have blacked out with the speed. Came to with the ground coming up damned quick and hit the trees like an express train. Passed out again then came round again to find myself hanging thirty feet above the ground with a broken leg. I had the mother and father of all headaches, which I learned later, was concussion. I didn't know how the hell I was going to get down. I sure was mad. All that training on parachute jumping and then I go into the bloody trees. If it hadn't been for an old guy who got me down, jeez I'd be there still. It is very easy to get lost in that sort of wilderness miles from anywhere. Anyway, Willy Meredith saw it all, rescued me an' everything. Even saw the three of us up aloft, and my evading action. I discovered what he knew when I went back to see him again, but it was too late then, I was out and...what the hell..." he shrugged helplessly. "The poor ol' soul falls off the bloody roof and can't give any evidence from where he is now so it's still no use. I haven't anyone else to corroborate my story. Welland would be a fool to come back and own up, just like that. So, like I said, does it really matter now?"

"Yes, Mr Fraser, the truth always matters." Colonel Haskins said abruptly. "Lives have been needlessly spoilt and changed, though I hope not ruined entirely," he smiled at Luke. "All because of inconsiderate negligence. At least I hope it was merely inconsiderate, it's a new ball game if it was deliberate." The men round the table looked at each other in astonishment. They hadn't given a thought that the accident would be anything other than irresponsible flying.

Leaving that thought in their minds Colonel Haskins closed the meeting. "There's nothing more we can do now until I see the person in question and find out if he can shed any more light on the case. Thank you for coming here today, gentlemen, your explanations have been clear and most enlightening. I am puzzled the inquiry did not go further but I understand at the time you did not have a lot to go on. Now Colonel Schafer and Mr Fraser, could you spare me a few minutes of your time before you leave?"

The two men rose with the rest of the group and Haskins led the way into his private office. Once there he waved them to seats, waited till they were comfortable, and then pulling out a bottle of whisky said: "Scotch, okay?" They both nodded and he poured three tots before sitting down himself. He gazed at Colonel Schafer his eyebrows raised in query.

"Shall I talk or do you want to?"

"No, go right ahead, you're doin' okay so far." Martyn Schafer grinned conspiratorially at Haskins. "That meeting was a real jackpot as far as I'm concerned."

"Nice of you to say so but we're not there yet. However we're going to have a go." He turned towards Luke who was nursing his whisky and looking kind of bemused at the other two.

"Well, Luke, as this is informal do you mind me using your Christian name?" He carried on at Luke's nod. "We only wanted to know if you had any thoughts of coming back to flying.

Joining up for another term, that's if we're able to clear the air, so to speak."

"You were a dammed good pilot, Luke." Schafer interrupted, "And probably still are, if a little rusty maybe. I'm sure you haven't forgotten a thing, though."

Luke shook his head deprecatingly. "Haven't thought much about it for a while."

"I'm wondering if you would like to join the SAS."

The words fell abruptly into the conversation like a pebble being tossed into a quiet pool, the ripples racing through Luke's mind, of opportunities, adventures and above all, of flying again. He had missed flying, yearned for it with an aching pain which mustn't be allowed to master him or he would always be only half a man, it wouldn't be fair to Jess.

Ah, Jess. For a moment he had forgotten about her.

"There's one problem, sir, I'm married now."

"Is it a problem? I wouldn't have thought it would disbar you from that particular unit.

They are all ages, nationalities, varied expertise; the one thing each must have is an outstanding ability in their own particular speciality. Martyn would certainly vouch for your proficiency while you were with him. Understandably, you will need a refresher course but as the SAS put the men through a stiff training regime, I expect it could all be incorporated. What do you say?"

It was a time for honesty. These men were trying to help him. Trying to put right the injustice of him leaving his flying career. He could never go back to his own unit but they were offering him a top job in a crack team, which went anywhere in the world where they were needed. He was still young enough to relish the danger and excitement. Could he have flying and Jess too? Or did he have to make a choice? He knew Jess wouldn't mind so he began to tell them the truth.

"...So we think someone is looking for her but we're not quite sure who and if it's Welland then I daren't go off and leave her on her own. She would be terrified if he came near her. I would also have to sell the sheep, I couldn't just walk away. As far as the croft is concerned we could keep it and use it when I had a long leave. I'm tempted to take your offer but I have to go with an easy mind and have my wife and kid with me or I wouldn't be any use to you."

Luke stopped speaking and there was a long silence while the two Colonels digested his words. He had been frank, telling Jessica's story as it was, their meeting, about the child, falling in love and their resolve to make a good marriage. Schafer shook his head and stared at his feet. For Chrissakes! What a load of shit to get dumped in. He had heard some stories but this one sure took a lot of beating. Haskins took the initiative again.

"Thank you for being so open, Luke, I'm grateful for your honesty, it will be a big help in deciding how we shall act." Schafer nodded his agreement. Haskins continued. "The man is very astute, and also I suspect, extremely evil. The facts you have given us today means the more knowledge I have of this villain the better I can deal with him. As far as the offer to join the SAS is concerned, it still stands, but you have to talk it over with your wife very carefully. She has suffered a great deal at the hands of Mark Welland. It would be a crime if she had her happiness spoilt again. However, if she agrees that is another matter altogether. I would suggest nothing be decided until we have put away Mark Welland for good. One way or another he has to be prevented from ever harming anyone else again. I am glad he was not here with us today; he might have slipped the net. I need to review my strategy thoroughly before I get to see him."

The meeting ended at that point and as Luke made his way back home, he reflected that although Mark was still at large he himself felt better for airing the truth. He had kept it bottled up for so long it felt as though a weight had lifted from his mind, leaving him free to decide the future. What it would be didn't matter, the great thing was his integrity had been given back to him and he could face the world with honour.

"I hope you don't mind, darling, but I felt I had to be square with them. It's meant telling your story as well but there is so much involved, I didn't want to turn their offer down without explaining why. After all they didn't have to make it..."

"Why do you need to turn the offer down?" She cut in.

"Because we're happy here..."

"We can always come back when you've had a spell playing war games," her cheeks dimpled with a smile, hoping to lighten his solemn face. "You will enjoy a bit of fun and a chance to get back in the air."

"Blast it, Jess, be serious. One does not *play* at war in the SAS. One can easily be killed dealing with dirty problems all over the world. They are peacekeepers but they have to fight to keep the peace, if you know what I mean, just the same as in a genuine war."

"In that case, stay with the sheep, the worst that can happen is falling off a mountain! Just don't ask me to make your mind up. Consider yourself as free as if you had never met me." She spoke sharply, her anger showing. Feeling deep down that she wished he had never gone to the meeting. Oh why couldn't their happy life go on without disturbance?

"I thought we'd moved on since then, isn't there some thing about loving each other? Being together? Deciding together what we should do?"

"Yes, I love you very much, but I'm not using that to blackmail you into staying here when you'd rather fly. Don't you see, Luke? It's been something you've always lived for until fate put you on the ground. If you change your nature then it will have to be because you really want it that way. Maybe in a couple of years you will regret turning down the offer and blame me for it. No, Luke, you have to make the decision. I may not like whatever it is but I'll accept it and back you up. The point I'm making is that has to concern you. You are the only one to decide if you want to fly again." She wasn't about to give way and soothe his ruffled feathers. They glared at one another, each thinking up a further cutting remark until Luke said,

"Why are we fighting?"

"Perhaps because we are frightened of change?"

"That's a very profound remark. Are you frightened?"

"A bit. A lot!" She admitted. "I hadn't realised how deeply I had burrowed into safety here. Outside is a big frightening place after this haven of peace."

"Then we shall stay."

"No! I couldn't bear to think I'd stopped you doing the thing you love best. Stopped you flying. Every time you look up at a plane, I see it in your face. You light up somehow then look sad as though it's an impossible dream. Well now it isn't, you can choose what you want to do."

"Jesus! Am I so transparent?" He scowled at the thought.

She nodded. "Yes, my darling Luke, but it is only because I know you so well. I really do not mind, especially if Angus and I can come with you. At least that is what you said, isn't it? I could not stay here by myself. But you know that. Let's wait and see; like the man said, there's plenty of time to decide."

"Yeah, I guess so, but it will be tough not knowing exactly what to decide." Luke frowned anxiously. "Our lives were all set and now I've gone and upset the whole caboodle. I still think it's a choice we have to make together."

"Don't think about it, you'll know when the time comes." Jessica said, more cheerfully than she felt. There was going to be a great upheaval ahead when Haskins began investigating Mark. He would be furious with everyone and, she intuitively suspected he might try to take revenge on those who had stirred the mixture. She prayed his anger would not be directed at Luke, but a shiver of presentiment ran through her. They could be in the firing line of his vengeance!

FORTY FIVE

It had been raining the night before and the sky was an overcast of uniform grey with no beginning or ending. The countryside seen from the window of the train seemed to disappear into the same gloom, hiding itself in the damp, drenched air. Mark's spirits were as low as the weather forecast; he felt apprehensive at the forthcoming meeting though deep down, a spark of anticipation yearned to revel in the new challenge. He'd got through every other hurdle, why should he let a bloody timeserving Colonel intimidate him. He wasn't in the service any more so he did not have to answer to the Air Ministry's authority, they had had their damned inquiry once and nothing had come of it so what was all the fuss. Nevertheless, he would be relieved to be on the way back to London.

He was shown into Colonel Haskins office and offered a seat as the officer entered from another door. Haskins greeted him pleasantly and after a brief exchange of how Mark had fared on the journey and what a dreadful day it was, he sat down behind his desk. In front of him lay a pile of papers though the Colonel barely glanced at them. He began by reviewing the period when Mark joined the RAF, his ambitions and proficiencies. The various stations he had been on until he had come under Haskins command. All fairly innocuous questions but they were beginning to tax Mark's ability to remember what was true and what wasn't. It reminded him of being hauled before his headmaster. He would have to watch his tongue, he told himself, no snide answers, just play it straight, boy, and you'll do okay.

They were halfway into the interview and Mark was glad of a respite when an orderly brought in coffee. He glanced around the office during the pause while the Colonel, apologising, excused himself for a moment to take a telephone call in the outer office, taking in the crowded bookshelves with various service mementoes and awards crowding the shelves. The walls held all sorts of framed photographs showing events, sports teams and friends. They showed the man had extensive tastes, and furthermore, Mark was realising his mind was as sharp as a rapier and as deadly. Mark turned to face the Colonel as he entered again looking at his brown, deeply lined face, the steely grey eyes, which bored through him.

"Shall we continue?" Suddenly the voice matched the eyes, precisely biting, each word distinctively pronounced. "We will gloss over the fact you knew perfectly well the Americans were expecting an experienced officer and that you lied to get yourself sent up to Leuchars to take part in the exercise. It was lucky for you they didn't require you to be one of the raiders. You hadn't a clue what was expected. A sandwich short of a picnic when it comes to flying? Or did you think I wasn't aware of your problem with words? Another fact that has emerged. Dyslexia isn't it? How you passed your entrance exams for this service I'll never know but I'll be making some inquiries, bet on it. A watching brief off Cape Wrath, those were your firm orders. So how come you squawked your radar transponder over Loch More?"

"I'm not sure; I guess it was wind drift." Mark shifted uneasily with embarrassment.

"Then you guess wrong. The wind that day was SSW, the weather a little cloudy but despite that, visibility was good. You would have seen the Isle of Lewis clearly?"

"Yes, I did; very clearly, I recall I said so on the RT. They also confirmed my position."

"Then how come you missed the drift in over the coast from your scheduled rendezvous?"

Watch it Welland! He is sharp, very sharp.

Coming on the jets so suddenly like that had scared the wits out of him as he had flown rapidly south with a vague, and in hindsight, stupid idea of putting a scare into the Americans. He thought their lack of expertise in a strange plane would give him an advantage. Instead, he had had the fright of his life. Added to that, he almost forgot how to operate the controls of the Hawk. Nothing appeared familiar and it had taken him long seconds to react to the emergency and streak for safety in the north. If the American pilot hadn't evaded him then there would have been a mid-air collision without doubt. He still sweated to remember the close call he had had.

"Truth to tell, sir, we'd had a heavy night in the mess, my attention must have wandered."

"Wandered far enough to take you across country to the south where the men were starting their run in for the phantom raid. Did you perhaps want to put a scare in them? Teach our American Allies a lesson? Show them how the RAF can fly? If so, you won't be the first, nor the last I'm afraid, despite it being utterly stupid. Nevertheless, a man died, very expensive equipment was lost, was it worth it?" Haskins' tone was bitter and scathing.

"Are you accusing me of being the cause of his death?" Mark was now beginning to sweat in earnest. Haskins was too near the bloody truth for comfort. Don't worry, he can't penalise you for it now; it's history. Done and dusted. Keep your cool, Mark, my boy.

"I'm not as yet accusing you of anything at this moment. Why? Is it possible you have something to confess?"

"Not a bloody thing, neither can you prove anything!" Mark answered violently.

"Oh yes we can, Mr Welland, as it happened, you were recognised."

"I don't believe you, you're bluffing!" *Christ! What had he walked into?*

"Recognised? What! By a bloody angel floating along at 600 mph? Go on tell me another one! That fairy tale stinks!" Mark sneered viciously.

"No, Mr Welland, I'll just tell this one, if you'll be patient. You were recognised by US Tactical Air Force Captain Luke Fraser before he ejected. You forced him on to his wingman's plane. Before you deny it, do you want me to describe the flying jacket you wore, with the scarlet chevrons on the sleeves? Quite a unique jacket by all accounts. I'm sure you still have it at home in your wardrobe? And the white silk scarf! Would you like us to check? Easy done!"

The jacket and scarf weren't in his wardrobe, for most of his belongings had been burnt in the fire, those, that is, he had left to be burnt. The rest of his things were in two suitcases in a lockup at Paddington Station waiting on his collection. Included was the flying jacket and scarf, which he had won in a card game from an ace pilot. "Check if you want, you will find all of my clothes were cremated recently when my home burnt down. All I have left from that misfortune was a suitcase of holiday clothes I took to Scotland."

"Oh yes, your house burnt down, didn't it? Quite a tragedy by all accounts. Are you fond of fires, Mr Welland, they seem to follow you around?"

"What the hell do you mean? I'll have you know I've just lost my wife in that fire; I don't need your sarcasm. And it was a tragedy and I'm still devastated. Call the police if you think I'm lying!" This time the sweat was tinged with fear, what else did this sadist know? And if he knew, why didn't he call the police? As he had recently discovered in a law book the Air Ministry could easily instigate a civil action as well as a Military one.

"We will, if we think it necessary, Mr Welland. At the moment I am merely getting things clear for the reopening of this inquiry. What actions transpire from it remains to be seen when all the additional facts are collated."

Ah, he is only bluffing about all this, Mark my boy, relax, he can't do a thing, he has no evidence, nary a jot for you to worry about. "So that's what this meeting's about, just buggering around, hoping to incriminate someone who had nothing to do with the accident? I imagine you are most disappointed you haven't established more proof. Never mind, you can't win 'em all, as they say. Now if you are quite done with this bloody useless and extremely tedious exercise, I would like my ride back to the station. I've much better things to do with my time than stay here to be bored to death."

Later Colonel Haskins reported to the American officer.

"He's as guilty as hell. It was all I could do to keep myself from pressing him too hard. I had to pull right back in the end and the beggar's gone home thinking we're stymied. His eyes gave him away over the coat. He's still got it. I'll lay a pound to a penny or in your case, Martyn, a dollar to a dime it's hidden somewhere he can easily retrieve it. This affair is beyond our remit or even our combined Services. It's definitely a case for the civil police and I shall go to London and raise a top man there who is a personal friend of mine. I don't want it to get bogged down in the rank and file of another Ministry inquiry. They might shelve it for lack of evidence, particularly as it's already had a hearing with us. What we need is an undercover man to discover where the coat is. Or other things, given a little luck."

"What do you mean, other things? Don't tell me there's more to come than the rape?" Martyn Schafer frowned with dismay. "You know more than you've told us, don't you?"

"Yes, a lot more, but it will take some getting at. I'm not capable of doing it myself, I've no time to spare for one thing and I'm sure you're in the same boat. No, we need expert help on this case and quickly too, before he gets away. I'm thinking of a Criminal Psychologist."

"What the hell! Is the guy nuts or something?" Schafer said, stunned at the thought of a pilot with murder on his mind. This case was looking blacker than ever.

"Could be. That interview was dammed queer, almost as though he was provoking me." Haskins shook himself as though casting away a shiver.

"Anyway, I won't take chances, in fact I don't dare. I'll get the right man on the job. You agree?"

"Sure do, my friend. You are in charge of this nasty episode and rather you than me. My brain doesn't like dealing with nutters. Sides, I'm up to my neck in clearing my desk. I've reached the finish of my Tour in the UK. I'm back to good old US of A by the end of the month. Still, I trust you will keep me posted won't you?"

"Yes, I will. I hope my next report means we've got the man safely put away. Bye Martyn, it was nice meeting you." Haskins clasped hands with the US Colonel feeling he had gained a friend. "Maybe see you in the States one of these days when I'm Globe-trotting."

"Sure thing, look me up. I'll give you a taste of real American coffee, if nothing else!"

FORTY SIX

Mark travelled back to London in a state of white-hot fury. So, it was the sodding Yankee flyer that was to blame for all this. Mark wondered at the time why he had given no evidence at the inquiry. He presumed the pilot was ill or something, or that his own good luck of evading reprisal was still with him. He thought he'd screwed up when he'd tried to put the two fliers off their stroke. It was just meant as a prank. He was going to fly over them but had miscalculated his speed and height. Coming on them so suddenly like that had scared the wits out of him. He'd fled back to his former position to pretend it had never happened. However it seemed this Yank had spotted him so clearly he could identify his jacket, and worse still, he was the guy who now had his son. He was not having that, no siree. What a pity he hadn't died when his plane crashed. Well, it could be remedied, would be remedied. Later, when he had fixed things he would hightail it to Spain where there was no extradition. He had better get on to it right away, while there was still time.

There was no telling when this Haskins bloke would start on the next part of the court proceedings. If his luck held good as usual, he assumed he would have at least a few days. No Ministry moved quickly and he couldn't see this one going anywhere. Certainly not without the evidence of the coat, and that was going to stay safely hidden until he went to Spain.

Nevertheless, his anger continued to mount; his lifelong psychosis of always having to be at the top, never to be found at fault in any way had changed over the years. It had begun as a small boy, when he found he could never do enough to please his father. He never really got his approval or even a well-done commendation for his efforts. He had given up trying in the end but the sore rankled still within him. The psychopathic behaviour, which emerged and gained strength as he grew to adulthood, needed not only to feel superior but also required he must subject his inferiors with pain to make them realise they were as dust beneath his feet. His jokes, laced with spite, turned sadistic.

"Mark Welland! You are an evil little boy. If you bring any more spiders or slugs into the nursery I shall tell your mother!"

Nanny had found the last spider in her bed, almost scaring her into hysterics. Still upset, she boxed his ears. As luck would have it, his mother chanced to visit the nursery just then and she had been sacked on the spot. It was useless to explain.

She left with the sight of Mark grinning from ear to ear at his victory, and how easy it was. Growing up, his ability to avoid discipline appeared his prerogative as he moved from one crime after another easily evading punishment. He continued living as he pleased, ridding himself of obstacles as they appeared and answering to no one. However, there was one exception, as he recalled distastefully. An American boy at one school refused to give in to his bullying and raised a huge fuss. It had caused the headmaster to recommend to his father that his son would be better off elsewhere. It coloured his thoughts against Americans after that and was the basis of the plane crash. Only now, as he felt the world closing in on him bent on meting out justice over an act he considered trivial, and due payment for the former slight he had undergone, did it seem grossly unfair. Furiously angry, at what he took as persecution, the latent schizophrenia, which governed his freakish moments, rose to look for vengeance and gleefully he selected his next victim and his route to Scotland.

The moment he reached the London hotel, where he had been staying since the fire, he hurriedly packed his clothes, settled his account and headed for Paddington where he picked up the rest of his gear including the jacket and scarf. He had immediately decided the best thing was to flee the country. What did he want in England anyway? His father couldn't care less. As for a job at the bank – forget it. He had better things to do. But before he went there were things to finish. Scores to settle, and one infant to collect. It never occurred to him he couldn't just remove a child from its mother and take it off like a parcel. The mere fact it was his wish to do so was good enough. The interview with Haskins had tipped him further to the edge of mental instability. His mood was one of desiring satisfaction. He wanted something, ergo - he would have it, come what may. He had got away with so much in his life, even murder. Three, if one counted the prostitute he had beaten up one night in Marseilles. As for the dead pilot, he felt that might only count as half a murder. In all, he was omnipotent.

Once he'd settled his score with Jessica and taught that Yank he'd be off to freedom in Spain with his son. They lived in the backwoods so he had been informed; it would be easy to deal with them in such a remote place. Just let anyone try and stop him. With his good brain he had always been ahead of people anyway!

FORTY SEVEN

Meanwhile, Phillip Haskins arranged to meet his old school chum two days after his session with Mark. They lunched at Simpson's in Piccadilly, afterwards sauntering through St James Park, while Phillip gave Commander Harry Patterson, a man in high office at the Yard, the gist of the story. "The trouble is, Harry, though I've dabbled a little in psychology, because I've found it helps when I'm assessing a man, I'm out of my depth here. Ordinary codes of conduct mean nothing to this man. It's why I backed off when I smelt a whiff of hellish sulphur. I hope to god I backed off in time. I sense he is not just a villain but is completely amoral. I did not want to spook him before I had help in catching him. This is more your field than mine, Harry, will you take it on?"

Harry rubbed his chin thoughtfully, feeling the hard rasp of his beard. It had been a six am shave and he was feeling the strain of the long hours he worked. He had a while yet to do before retirement but he felt he was ready for it now as he ruminated on Phillip's tale.

"You think the collision was deliberate mischief, not just careless flying, or being in the wrong place at the wrong time? Did he say something that made you feel that way?"

"Yes. I don't know how to describe it but it was almost as though he was daring me to find him guilty so he could crow over me when there was obviously no real evidence. He looked sick once or twice when I got close, but I got the distinct impression he thought it was all a big joke and I was the mutt who had fallen for it. He's a real bastard, Harry. One needs to be extremely wary how this affair gets tackled."

"Sounds as though he's schizoid, though a third of the population is either that or manic so you don't want to place too much reliance on name-calling. I'm sure you are right in one respect, one fire is unlucky, and two fires and especially serious fires are rarely a coincidence. I'll see if we can discover what he has been up to in the last two or three years, that should give us a clue about his mental stability."

"Luke Fraser mentioned his wife worked in the merchant bank owned by Welland's father, it seems he was being groomed to step into the old man's shoes." Haskins added.

"Banking? Ah. That means his father is Sir Charles Welland. He's one of the London City Father's, if you know what I mean, supposedly cleaner than clean, though I did hear tell he got his shirttails dirty a while back - overreached himself in lending money. Almost on the edge of money laundering so I'm told, but pulled back in haste to amalgamate with another Merchant Banker by the name of Seager. Then, if I recall correctly from an item in the press, Welland's son married Seager's only daughter. Well, well, so that's who he is. Didn't he lose his wife tragically just recently in their house fire in Kent?"

"Yes, he did. It was that, and other things that got me thinking."

"Well, it was a perfectly straightforward accident, according to a report I saw. But come to think of it, Phillip, the girl had a bad fall in Switzerland last winter and was bedridden. For life, I believe. Her personal nurse died with her. Hmmm, I don't like the sound of it when one starts to add it all together. You may be on to more than just a flying accident. Right, I will be working on it soon as I get back to the yard. I rather feel it would be advisable if we pick up chummy pending further inquiries, or at least take away his passport. We do not want him high tailing off to foreign parts. Phillip, thanks for the lunch, I will be in touch as soon as I hear anything. I have a strong feeling you won't need to begin any more inquiries your end, I bet we will have him for being a villain in Civvy Street. Oh, one more thing. Thanks for tipping me off. I appreciate it. If there's one thing that gets me going it's someone who thinks he is above the law and can get away with crime, time after time. I love to stop them in full pelt!"

Phillip laughed at his friend's newly found enthusiasm. "Good hunting then, Harry, I hope you find him quickly, especially for the Fraser's sake."

"Yes, they don't need any more grief from someone like him. Okay then, Phillip, I'll get my driver to drop you off at the station after he's left me at the yard." He waved to the dark saloon car, which was following slowly behind them. The driver caught them up and they climbed in. Harry left when he at his office and the car then took Phillip to his station. The journey back to base was not tedious as Phillip mentally went through every detail of his interview with Welland then his conversation with Harry. With luck, the pieces would fall into place and one undoubted criminal would get his come-uppance.

FORTY EIGHT

Jessica was finishing her work in the barn extension, where she had been milking the cow and feeding the two young heifers they had bought cheaply at auction in the Summer Sales. The cattle had been thriving on the lush grass that was to be found on the hillsides above the farm but the weather had begun to turn cold so they had been brought inside. The worst of the snow was not yet imminent but icy rain and heavy winds made the treks outside to attend to the livestock unpleasant and the barn was a godsend to use for the necessary tasks. Inside, the warm sweet smell of animals contentedly chewing the cud gratified Jessica enormously. Could she bear to leave it all behind?

As she did the chores her mind went back to the close of summer and the building of the extension. Luke had borrowed a large mowing machine to take a large crop of hay for their winter-feed which, with the supplement feed would ensure the animals enough food to last them until spring. This had been stacked nearby. All the sheep were growing strong and healthy and Luke was well satisfied with their improvement and even the profit from the spring sale of Lamb had been better than usual. Luke felt elated at his fine progress since he had married Jessica, and was convinced that together they had achieved great things. In fact, so much convinced were they, he and Jessica had decided to spend some of their savings on yet another extension to the barn. Excited, they agreed on the plans and before long the schedule was ready to be started.

When the work began, the weather turned warm and the sheep healthily grazed without a need of too much supervision. Luke would drive along the loch as far as he could once a day, find a spot where he could survey his flock through field glasses and see if there were any problems, but the rest of the time he helped the builders where he could. It enabled them to save on labour charges but more than that, it gave him a great sense of achievement working on his own home. Over the months he had changed from the withdrawn taciturn individual he had been most of his life into a man able to turn his hand to most jobs and relish his ability to get on with his fellow men. He had also toughened up and could tackle any of the strenuous farm jobs.

With the support of Jimmy Halverson and two Invergarry friends in the building trade, Luke set up a prefabricated shed, which could accommodate the stock throughout the poorest of winter conditions. Jessica, taking tea out to the workers, would see him perched high on the extended roof joists holding the wood in place as it was firmly anchored to the rest of the house. He would swing down with agility, give her a hug and smacking kiss in front of the other men and drink his tea with gusto. Later one evening while she was praising his efforts of that day he had held out his hand, looked at her gravely then said, "It's for us, our little family. I feel it's a miracle, Jess."

Was that miracle about to end? Surely not? Would it matter if they had to move away? Would things change that much? They would still be together – at least some of the time. But not like it was in this valley. She shook her head in despair trying to rid her mind of the dreary depressing facts, which she could no longer ignore. Oh such brave words she had said. Do what you want; go where you want, I'll tag along like a good little wife. But did she mean it, honestly and sincerely? Reviewing all the facts once more she decided she did mean it because she truly loved him. It would be hard to leave but she would gladly do it for Luke's sake. He ought to have another chance although she was terrified of him going into danger. She mustn't think of the risk, only that he would do the things he'd been trained for, flying planes again, revelling in the thrill of being thousands of feet above the earth. He had tried to explain what it was like and for a brief moment she envied him the joy of it then she had quickly shaken her head.

"Rather you than me, I prefer to have my feet safely on the ground, thank you."

"That's my Jess, always with your feet on the ground. Quite right, too. It's safest." He had teased her gently. "Can't have my financial wizard deserting me."

"Jess, Jess? You finished yet?" She heard Luke's voice calling from the croft. "I'm starving and the smell from the kitchen is getting to me. Hurry up, love."

"Just coming," she called back. Then with a last look at the animals she latched the door as firmly on them as on her thoughts, knowing her mind was finally made up

"I've just had Jimmy on the phone, Jess. Guess what?" His excited voice made her smile. She slipped her coat off looking at his eager, bright face, reflecting how much she loved him. In spite of their quiet existence life was never dull, never humdrum. He was always thinking up new things to please and surprise her, showing in countless ways how deeply he cared.

"Go on, tell me." Was this another surprise? Yes it was, but hardly what she expected.

"You remember ol' Matheson dying last month? Well, Jimmy tells me his son David isn't going to run the farm any more. He wants to be off travelling. He's had enough of farming, says he's turning into a form-filler with all the paperwork he has to do these days. So, rather than pay an auctioneer to get rid of his stock he's going to sell off locally to his neighbours put the land into 'set aside' and go off and enjoy himself. If he doesn't like it he can always come back to carry on with farming." His eyes sparkled as he went on, "This means Abraham is for sale!"

"I thought you were giving up sheep farming?"

He looked at her like a small boy who had been caught with his hand in the cookie jar.

"Ah...well, yes, but we hadn't actually decided yet, have we? Though if we do decide to go I could advertise them as complete flocks, rams and all, couldn't I?"

"What's wrong with David selling a complete flock?"

"Hmm, he could do that, I haven't spoken to him yet so I don't know what's in his mind. I just thought I'd have a word with you first to see if you'd agree. But just think of it, Jess, having Abraham would increase our sale of wool for the tweed market and maybe we would get other requests. There are plenty of customers both here and abroad that want good quality wool."

Instantly she guessed how his mind was working. Jessica thought of the huge Blackface Highland horned ram, which David's father had bred some years earlier. It had sired a good part of their flock and numerous fine specimens of others in the area. It had always been a healthy, reliable animal and passed on its genes to enhance the quality of their sheep. If they acquired the ram it would save them extra tupping fees.

Jessica thought of the difference between the numbers they now had and the small flock in her grandfather's time. As of this year they now ran too many ewes for the rams to cope with but if they had to sell would they recoup the money they'd have to pay for the Blackface ram?

"Abraham would be fearfully expensive, Luke, far beyond our means. We agreed we wouldn't spend any more money this year after building the extension." His face fell and she hated her words of caution, for when it came to his sheep he was all too liable to go overboard.

"Yeah, I guess you're right, it was only an idea. Maybe not such a good one at that; after all, he is old for a ram, perhaps that's why David wants to get rid of him locally, banking on his reputation. Outsiders, who won't know his bloodline and what he is capable of, might think the old chap is past it. Forget it Jess, it was a crazy idea. I'll just forget the sheep and stick to flying, the money's better."

She studied his circumspectly arranged features and knew he was caught between two ambitions, his love of flying on one hand and his happy life in the Scottish hills with his sheep. What was he thinking of behind that reserved look? Was it because she had made it plain he had to choose for them both? Or blaming her because she refused to involve herself in the decision? She wouldn't choose for him, he must make his own mind up. All she prayed was when he did it would be the right choice for both their sakes, for if he were wrong then it would bring heartache and misery into their hitherto contented lives.

FORTY NINE

Harry Patterson put the phone down with a muttered oath. He had just been informed his men were too late to bring Mark Welland in for questioning, for he had packed and left his hotel the day he met Colonel Haskins. Harry didn't blame Phillip, it could have been just an innocent remark which alerted the former RAF captain, but what ever it was, it had sent Mark high-tailing off to God knows where, for his men hadn't a clue where to start looking. He gave the usual orders for Ports and Airports to be alerted but he felt it was a wasted effort. There were so many ways of leaving the UK without going through the usual exits and this man had shown himself to be wily. It would not be possible to keep him in the country if he was intent on getting away. Scowling fiercely, he told his secretary to order his car and throwing on a jacket left the office. She watched his retreating back with relief. Heaven help anyone who got in his way in this mood, he looked as though he would tear them apart. Harry made a brief visit to a doctor friend of his to corroborate some facts then an hour or so later, he was sitting in Sir Charles Welland's office facing the shrewd banker.

Charles was signing some letters and thinking it was about time to stop for the day when his secretary knocked and entered his office. "I have a Commander Patterson outside. He would like a word with you if it's convenient, sir."

"Commander? A naval officer? "What's it about?" Charles was puzzled. He was certain he didn't know any navy chaps who might call on him and the name Patterson didn't ring a bell.

"It's a policeman, Sir Charles. He's from Scotland Yard."

He sensed her inquisitiveness and smoothed his face to blandness.

"Send him in. I've a few minutes to spare before I leave."

So it had come at last. He was not unduly surprised at a visit from the Police. He felt in his bones it would come one day; but he wondered which subject would be raised. Had Seager found something else he was not happy about and decided to take action? Was it Mark? The latter was likely, he thought; his son had a way of encouraging trouble like a magnet to iron.

All his suspicions rose again as he thought over that last meeting with his son. Then, it was almost as though he talked to a stranger, a man he didn't know any more. Perhaps he had never really known his son or even, dare he say it, liked him very much. But what did surprise him was the rank of this man. Why should a Commander take an interest in Mark? What new devilry was he up to now? Yet it mightn't concern him at all. Likely, he may have come about something quite different.

The introductions over the two seated men faced each other.

"I would be most grateful, Sir Charles," began Harry, "As we are at the present moment unable to locate your son, if you could tell us his whereabouts or alternatively the place he might head for. He might be able to help us with some inquiries we are dealing with."

Charles shook his head firmly.

"I really don't know where he is. In fact I'm as surprised as you are; he was due to come to work today to host a set of meetings. While he is in the process of retiring from the Bank there are a number of duties, those that he was personally responsible for, that need passing on to others. His absence today has been inconvenient." Charles scarcely concealed his annoyance, for he had been forced into gritting his teeth as barely veiled sarcasm from his staff pointed out Mark's absence yet again. It finally occurred to him that his staff hated both himself and Mark. Had it always been so? How could he tell? Once he had ruled with an iron hand that forbade anyone lifting his or her head to look him in the eye. Now it was different. The coming of Warren Seager had changed everything. Some of his staff had even requested to be moved over to the other bank. Away from him or away from Mark? His intuition fell to a new low as he thought about it.

Charles forced his attention back to the Commander. Patterson was looking puzzled with the pause in the conversation; or was he only pretending? One never knew with these men.

"Oh? Retiring to where?"

"Spain of all places; supposed to be buying a wine bar. I can't think of a more stupid thing to do at this particular time. However, he is over twenty-one, it is his own money, and I can't stop it." He sounded, thought Patterson, definitely aggrieved with the situation.

"Do you know if he's already left the country?"

"Well, he wasn't due to go for another fortnight." Charles answered slowly. Something was jogging his memory; what the hell was it? "He certainly hasn't said goodbye to his mother yet. My God, my wife would be most upset if he left before seeing her. She dotes on him and him on her." But not on father, Patterson noted.

Good. He might be able to coax him to be a little more forthcoming.

"How well did you know your son's wife?"

"Hardly saw anything of them in the last year, she was an invalid, you know, had a fall and couldn't walk." Charles paled a little, so this was why Mark was wanted.

"Yes, we did get to hear of the nature of her injuries. It must have been a terrible blow to your son so soon after his marriage? It can't have been easy for him to learn she would never walk again nor have children."

Charles swallowed hard. His mind had leapt onwards to the next dreadful accident. It filled him with sheer horror as he imagined the scene in a blazing house, of two people frantic to escape. Christ! He thought, if my son's had a hand in that then he is definitely a raving lunatic.

What the hell am I supposed to do? Tell this man I suspect Mark of being the cause of the first incident and I'm none too certain he wasn't involved in the second one? That he has always been evil? Always mixed up in questionable events that never proved him the culprit.

Patterson watched him carefully; he could read his acute discomfort like a book. He kept on with questions which Charles parried as best as he could. Then came a question, which slid quietly into the conversation, so innocently put, but so damming. Charles replied too soon.

"It would be perfectly natural, of course, if he hated to be tied to a cripple, it's no life for an active man, I wonder why he didn't just divorce her."

"Oh, he couldn't; his father-in-law would have been down on our necks like a ton load of bricks." It was out before he could stop it. He bit his lip in exasperation at the slip. Instantly he realised it dammed him as well as Mark. It could easily have been a scheme between the two of them to rid Mark of a crippled wife, a nuisance to all except a doting father, who it appeared, already had a hold over them. And what might that hold be I wonder? Patterson almost smiled as the words were said. Ah! Got him! But not by so much as a quiver of his eyes did Patterson betray his inward satisfaction.

"Perhaps you'd explain that remark, Sir Charles. Why would Mr Seager take exception to a divorce? They are quite normal these days, according to the statistics."

Charles stuttered. "Well - er - any father would hate - would have hated to have his daughter er-er..."

"Got rid of?"

"What the hell are you saying? I wouldn't put it like that," he declared disapprovingly. "No way would I put it like that."

"How would you put it, Sir Charles?" Patterson watched as Charles seemed to lose track of things and gaze on something only he could see. He repeated his question.

"How would you put it?"

Charles raised his head in shocked stupefaction, his mind still filled with a scene of a blazing fire, of two people caught in an inferno without means of escape. An appalling death! What was the question? Oh yes... "Divorces happen; they're unfortunate, of course..."

"But not to people like Warren Seager? Why should he take a strong view on divorce?"

"She was his only child. He er...he wasn't happy with her terrible accident in Switzerland, naturally he didn't want her to have any more grief."

"Like being burnt to death?" The raw words struck at Charles like a blow. He stared at the Commander with horror-filled eyes, his face grey and strained. How had the conversation turned from divorce to the house? What had he said? He'd answered so many odd questions but none of them was about the fire, at least he didn't think so. Suddenly he felt he was being silently accused along with Mark. It was too intolerable. He hastily gathered himself together and tried to answer. "Of course it was dreadful, we were all very sorry, but surely it was an accident, wasn't it?" Charles saw Patterson slowly shake his head. God, the man knew Mark was guilty. More than that, the Commander was trying to implicate him as well.

"Look, I don't know what you are trying to imply but I had nothing to do with their house, ask anyone, I hadn't been there in over a year. Seager was a difficult man to get on with; it has been bad enough working with him in business..."

"I wasn't trying to imply anything, Sir Charles; it's not my way; if I suspect something then I come straight out with it. I think you know who started the fire, sir, and it would be better for us all if you were to get it off your chest. Knowledge of any death is an intolerable burden to carry; when it's someone you know like a cripple - unable to save herself from burning to death – just think of those two women - trapped inside a blazing inferno?"

"Stop it! It's bad enough suspecting, but to actually point a finger! Blast it, man, put yourself in my shoes! He's my son! My only son - I've no more children."

"That's exactly what I've been trying to do. Imagine what it is like to be you. I can't pretend I'd like it. In fact no way would I like it nor have anything to do with the position you are in. You have a heavy responsibility, you know, hiding a murderer, but one thing you may be sure of if he's done it once he'll do it again, do you want that on your conscience?"

"But I don't know if he's done it, it's only a hunch." Despite his protests Charles knew it was useless to continue evading Patterson, he had to be straight with him.

"Who are we talking about, sir?"

"My son, of course! Dammit man, I haven't lost my wits yet. He has had a lifetime of shirking problems; lying; forever sliding from one accusation to another and never being caught. If my son wants something badly enough, he always gets it. With hindsight, you understand, I suppose I always knew. Maybe it's why I kept putting obstacles in his path. I think I resented him always getting his own way. What a sorry mess we make of our lives, Commander, I don't think I can ever trust my own judgement again," he shook his head miserably. "What happens now? Will you want to question him?"

Patterson watched as he bowed his head. Strangely, despite the contempt he felt for the man, he also felt sorry for him but he couldn't and wouldn't stop until he had it all.

"When did you change? When your son raped the girl?"

"Bloody Hell! Do you know about that too?"

"Among other things. It's a criminal offence! Why didn't you do something about him then? He would have been able to get help, medical help; surely, you could see he had a problem? One needing vital and immediate attention, if not communication with the police."

"No, I didn't see it clearly, didn't want to if the truth be known. His mother would have been so upset if I'd even hinted...I couldn't tell her anything about that incident...she wouldn't have believed me...she dotes on him, you see."

"She's going to be a lot more upset now, Sir Charles." Patterson gazed sternly at the Banker who had lost his upright bearing and was looking small and wrinkled in the huge leather office chair, ageing rapidly before his eyes. "Right then, let's go through it all again. Try to think of any detail that you might have missed to give me a clue where he is now. For his own sake he needs to be in custody to stop anything else happening...what's the matter, man?"

Charles was staring at him as though he had seen a ghost.

"I've just remembered something that came up at our last meeting; he wanted me to help him take his son away from Miss Meredith. To actually kidnap him, I suppose. I told him not to be so bloody stupid; I wouldn't countenance that at any price. But...oh dear God, maybe he will try all the same. How could I have let him go without trying to stop him?"

Harry Patterson felt a chill run through. Welland had two days start on him. Where the devil was he now. What were his intentions? He'd thought he merely had a runaway to contend with but if the man was after a boy he thought was his son, would he kill to get hold of him?

If his past history was anything to go by of course he would.

"Miss Meredith is now a Mrs Fraser, the wife of a former pilot in the American Air Force whom your son very nearly killed in a plane accident. Sadly, his Wingman and close friend died instead. Mark's subsequent lies cost Fraser his career. Add to it the rape of Mrs Fraser when she was your employee. An extremely serious fire, damaging Air Ministry property, and probably, though it could never be proven, details of missing funds. This all happened when your son was in the service. An enquiry will begin again connected with your daughter-in-law's accident in Switzerland, plus an even bigger one concerning her ensuing death in the fire at her home.

Sir Charles, you had better believe me when I say there is going to be bloody mayhem with you unless my officers can get to the Fraser's home in time to stop a dreadful tragedy. Is this enough proof for you to establish we've a very serious situation on our hands? Now, are you absolutely sure he would go to Scotland to try to get his son back? I have to know everything to take immediate action." Patterson almost snarled as the bitter words exploded out of him.

Charles face turned the colour of putty. What had he closed his eyes to all these years? He nodded his head. "It doesn't bear thinking about but yes, I believe he will try."

"May I use your phone?"

Charles groaned in agony. What had he closed his eyes to all these years? He had taken his son's part on every occasion so he was as much to blame for Mark's sins. He hastily nodded his head then numbly listened as Patterson got through to his office and began issuing directives to discover the location of the Fraser's home from Colonel Haskins, then another call to set the wheels in motion to trace Mark before he did any more harm. Nothing had gone right for the banker in the last two years ever since he had tried to make some easy money. It had all seemed so simple at the time but now he would have the unenviable task of trying to explain to his wife, her son was a rotter. There would also be the task to find a really good counsel for Mark. For of course he would have to be defended, wouldn't he? Heaven only knows how much that would cost. Charles wondered if it was worth it. In the end Mark would be found guilty. Still, his wife would never countenance anything else. He sighed heavily as he thought of the trauma to come. Life was a bitch!

FIFTY

Jessica glanced at the clock. Luke was late. He was probably gossiping to Jimmy and had, as usual, forgotten the time. Those two were worse than women were when they got together.

"Come on my little cuddly bear, time for bed, Daddy's not home yet, sweetheart, and you are a tired little boy. Up you come; it's time to go beddy-byes." She picked up Angus who was playing on the floor with some of his toys and took him through to his bedroom to tuck him up with all his soft toy animals, his favourite teddy and a small blanket that he liked to hold until he went to sleep. The little boy, drowsy from his bath, closed his eyes and Jessica stood watching him in the soft glow of the dimmed bedside light, filled with a love she still felt was miraculous after all that had happened since his birth.

She never deliberately, thought of the very beginning. Only of her complete disregard while she was carrying him. How could she have ignored such a wonderful event? It would be different this time, she thought, for she was almost sure she was pregnant again. Another week to wait and she would take herself off to the doctor's for his opinion. Would it be another boy this time or maybe, just for a change, a girl? A girl would be wonderful for her but Luke would want a son.

Luke would be over the moon. She would have to find the right time to tell him, perhaps when they had just finished making love. Jessica was looking forward to the surprise and joy when he found out. She wondered how he had acquired his ability to be a good father. Nothing in his past childhood would have shown him how. Must be in the genes she decided, thinking of his forbears. Funny how both them had ancestors in Scotland. How strange it was that each had travelled a long way to meet each other yet it seemed as though they were merely coming home to what had always been their blood-tie. Do we really decide our own fates? Or are we the instruments of others who rule our lives. Moving us around like marionettes on a stage. Some earmarked for joy, others fated for sorrow. She shivered all of a sudden. How silly she was, to think such strange thoughts. Luke would laugh at her, for in spite of his past he was a very level-headed man not given to fancies.

Ah, there was the car. She turned back to the kitchen and hurriedly scooped up the toys to put in the wooden box, which Luke had especially made for the purpose. The table was set and the meal keeping hot in the oven. Now Angus was asleep, they would have the time together to eat in peace. He was gorgeous but come evening Jessica was glad to get him off to bed.

Abruptly there was a knock on the door and she stood transfixed, caught with surprise, her heart beating with the suddenness of the unexpected sound.

"Who is it?" She called through the door. The voice, which answered with the short word: "Me." sounded so like Luke she didn't hesitate. Yes, it was Luke. Very likely, he had his hands full of whatever Jimmy had given him for their freezer. Jimmy was an inveterate hunter, always augmenting their supplies with all sorts of game he had just happened upon. Or so he said!

She flung open the door with a flourish, then seeing who it was; she caught her breath in terrified dismay. Standing slackly, very much as he had outside the cloakroom door, on that fearful celebratory evening, stood Mark. The same black lock of hair fell across his brow into one eye; the same cheeky smile lay on his lips. Outlined in the darkness it could even be the same place. The nightmare she had endured over and over again was never going to end.

"Hello sweetie, how are you?"

She felt her stomach turn over with nausea as she stared at him. He still had this air of superiority as if no one could better his handsome looks, his desirable body. How many females, she wondered, had fallen for him only to discover the trash beneath?

"Wha-what do you want?" Her heart began to pound furiously.

"That's no sort of a greeting after driving all the way up here. You HAVE tucked yourself away. It's taken me two days to find you. Aren't you going to ask me in?"

"I said - what do you want?" Jessica did not intend to be hospitable. She only wanted to get rid of him before Luke turned up. Heaven knows what Luke would do if he found Mark here. There would be a fight for sure.

"Only to talk to you, to apologise, to say I'm sorry for what happened, and see my son."

"Your son! He's not your son! Go away! You are not welcome here and never will be!"

"Oh but I think he is. Shall we have a blood test to decide or are you going to be a good girl and let me in. I promise you I'll leave after I've seen him. But I must see him this once."

She hesitated. Perhaps he was telling the truth. Maybe he would just look at Angus then go without a fuss. Angus didn't look at all like him. Maybe she could convince him he wasn't his son. If he didn't know his date of birth it might be all right. What else should I do? Oh, where was Luke, he would know what to do. No! He had vowed to kill Mark. Oh, please God, don't let him come yet, don't let there be a fight. She swallowed hard, wondering what to do.

"Angus is asleep now, why don't you come tomorrow when he is awake. You can see him in daylight. Perhaps you will then realise he's not your son. Anyway it's not convenient now." Hastily she manufactured the excuse hoping it would give her time.

"After coming all this way, NOW is when I want to see him, not tomorrow or the day after. Move out of the way, I'm coming in." He hardly raised his voice but Jessica felt terrified. She was alone, no one for miles and panic filled her mind, it sent reason and common-sense flying.

If she tried to stop him, what would he do? Hurt her again with his powerful strength? She had no doubt he was capable of doing that, but Angus? Surely he wouldn't hurt a baby? If he just came in for a minute to peek at Angus, would it do any harm? Perhaps that was all he wanted. To look, then go away? But why now, at this particular time? Why did she feel it was all wrong? In an agony of indecision she stood silent desperately trying to weigh up the odds.

One part of her mind was shrieking NO! Don't let him in. The other trying to figure out how many steps it would take to grab a sharp knife from the drawer in the kitchen. But what if she did? Could she raise the enormous courage to kill him or at least incapacitate him until Luke came home? Would it be counted as self-defence? She thought not. Oh what should she do?

"Well! What's it to be Jessica? Come on, what are you waiting for?"

She jumped at his curt words. He had said something like that before. She had placated him then look what had happened. Disaster! She licked her lips and began,

"I really don't think..." Just then the sound of an engine reached them and Jessica breathed a sigh of relief, thank goodness, it was Luke at last, he would sort it out.

"There's Luke, he's the one to say if you can see Angus." Mark turned immediately to see headlights illuminating the slope to the quayside as the car headed down to the loch before swinging round to the right to drive to the house. Silently he stood watching as Luke expertly backed the Landrover into a carport, switched off the engine, shoved opened the door and slid out. Then bending forward out of sight of Jessica he picked up a rifle and unexpectedly and to Jessica's horror lined up on Luke, took aim and fired straight at him as he emerged into the open. Caught, as Luke was in the glare of the outside lights, he never stood a chance. Mark's aim was true and at once Luke flung his arms up in the air and slumped immediately to the ground.

Jessica, appalled at the sight, screamed shrilly as Luke fell, and she went to push Mark out of the way so she could get to her husband. In an instant her world had crashed in dreadful ruins.

"For pity's sake, Mark, you're crazy! A rotten evil brute. Move out of the way! I have to see what you've done to him! Please god he's still alive!"

Mark, his eyes glittering with hatred, barred the way, stopping her from going outside.

"You've killed him, haven't you? You swine; you unutterably foul, devilish swine!" Jessica screamed at him. You're mad, do you know that? Stark raving, bloody mad!"

"So what! You should have let me in the first time. Now I *will* see my son."

Cold shock raced through Jessica's body as she listened to the uncaring, childish words as he put a foot over the step to go into the kitchen. He was crazy! Worst of all with Luke dead there was no one to protect little Angus or her. She would never be able to reach the phone. What could she do? Swiftly, hardly timing the move, the only consideration in her head that of getting to Angus, she thrust violently at his chest, knocking him off balance and shoving him back from the step.

Then she tried to shut the door, only to find he had rapidly recovered and was forcing it open from the other side. Leaning against it with all his might the door was slowly opening and she was powerless to stop it. Realising she had no strength to beat him she whirled round and made for the inner door. Once through into the tiny hallway, she slammed it shut and pulling a chair round from Angus' bedroom, jammed it under the doorknob to clamp it tight. It would not hold for long but it might give her a chance. For what? For pity's sake what was she to do now?

Oh God, help me! Hardly knowing she was praying, she at once darted into their bedroom and grabbed the first garment she could find. It was cold outside and she might be out for a long time. Flinging on Luke's sweater, she went back to the other room and carefully but swiftly took Angus up from his cot, folded him tight in a blanket and cuddled him close to her. He gave a small mew of protest but was too sleepy to cry.

Going back to their own bedroom she quietly opened the window and pulling another chair beneath it, climbed up to sit on the sill while cautiously holding her son. Opening the window quietly she swung her legs round until she was sitting on the outside ledge balancing her and Angus, blessing the fact their croft walls were thick and the window shelf deep. She was able to wriggle her way forward until her foot touched the bare area behind the house; then she jumped the rest of the way to the ground. Jessica reached forward and softly shut the casement window before edging along the narrow alleyway to the back of the barn. Here, the going was difficult, for nettles and weeds blocked the way, but without making too much noise, she managed.

Back in the croft she heard the slamming of a body against the inner door and knew it wouldn't be long before Mark discovered she was gone. By some means she had to get back to where Luke lay, to see if he was really dead. If he was, then her only hope was to take his car and race to Invergarry and the protection of her friends before going to the police. Could she run fast enough to reach the car, start it and be up the road before Mark caught her? She would have to try. It was the only thing she could think of.

FIFTY ONE

Except, what would happen with Mark? He would chase her, no doubt of it. The road was bad enough in daylight, but at night it would be treacherous and she'd only just learned to drive. What if she killed Angus? Oh, dear God, what was she to do? And Luke! Suppose he was still alive? He'd need help, though she couldn't imagine him to be alive after the way he had flung out his arms, falling straight down on his back, to lay still, oh so still. Nor had he moved again in the seconds she had stood helplessly stunned at the suddenness of it all. Luke was dead, she had lost her love, and all because of a vicious, ghastly man who thought it was his right to take anything he wanted. If she was to ensure he was punished for his dreadful acts she must stay alive to let the police know, and she had Angus to consider too, she must protect him at all costs. But how? Dear God help me to get through this.

He wanted her son! She could hear him bellowing out at the top of his voice:

"Jessica! Jessica! Give me my son. I'll leave you alone then, you'll be safe, I promise. I won't hurt you; it is not you I want anyway. But I'll have MY SON. He's mine, I'm taking him to Spain, and he'll have a great life. Believe me, Jessica! I'll give him everything! "

Believe him? She would never believe him if he swore on every bible in the land. Angus was hers. She would protect him with her life right to the very end. Then all at once the place turned as bright as day. He had found the switch for the extra lamp fixed outside the croft. He was standing in front looking down the path to where she was hiding. There was no way Jessica could get past him back to Luke or the Landrover, for the shed where it was parked was built hard up against a niche carved out of the steep hillside which protected the back of the croft. She would have to come out into the open where he would see her.

She supposed he would not shoot her while she held Angus but she knew she was not strong enough to fight him once he took the baby from her and he dare not leave a witness. It might be days before she and Luke were found, giving Mark ample time to make his escape. The tragedy would be put down to misfortune, a mad killer? Possibly roaming the hills? No one would know it was Mark. He would be away overseas, no reason to even dream up an alibi. He would be gone and little Angus would be at his mercy. The idea of her son all alone with Mark filled her with horror. She felt physically sick at how cruel he would be to her baby.

The sobs that Jessica had so far held back spurted from her throat and she buried her face in the baby's blanket to keep Mark from hearing. Angus began to stir and lest he give away their hiding place, she knew she must go further into the woods to hide and trust Mark would get tired of waiting and go away. Slowly and quietly, she began to inch away from the cottage.

Mark caught sight of her in the distance disappearing into the trees. Ah, he had her now. She wouldn't get far carrying the child. Once he had hold of her the rest was easy, he'd make her come back and pack her and the baby's things then he would get rid of her somewhere else. The police would think she had killed Luke and run off with the child. He wouldn't be blamed at all. Oh very clever! But then, he had always been so, hadn't he!

He yelled after Jessica that he had seen her. That it was no use running, she'd better come back before he got very annoyed. His voice echoed strangely across the water and Jessica, hurrying for her life, tried to increase her speed, but it was hopeless with the baby in her arms.

Mark went back inside the house to search the kitchen for a torch. Blasted woman, she was being stupid, why run that way; there was no road out there. The nearest hamlet was miles away, too far for her to reach; he had already noted it on the map. The land around was bare and desolate. She would die of exhaustion and cold long before she got to safety.

The only way out was past him and she had better do as he said was told, and quickly, or else he would kill her here and be done with it. Grinning to himself, he began the chase, supreme in his egotistical confidence he could overtake her easily. The torch shone intensely, lighting up the forest with a white glare, now and then glinting against the ghostly eyes of the few nocturnal inhabitants, which were abroad at this time. Mark wasn't happy about searching such a wild area but at least he had the consolation that it wouldn't take long. Physically fit, his powerful legs could cover the ground more easily than Jessica could, especially as she did not have a torch, and she was carrying a baby.

She could readily trip over a root and the cry of the baby would bring him hot on her heels.

Jessica was thinking that very same fact and blessing her recent visit down the stony path she was treading with such care. She couldn't go fast, in any case, for Angus was weighing heavier with every step and her breath was coming in exhausted pants. Each time she looked behind her she could see the torch coming on remorselessly. Mark would not give up and she knew there was no place to hide where she was. How far was it to Arnisdale? If only she could reach it, she would be safe. Then she shook angry tears from her eyes as she faced the truth.

Jessica stepped off the path and leaned against a tree to get her breath back. Her heart was pounding in her throat like a steam engine. Angus moved restlessly in her arms, she felt him inhale ready to burst out with a loud and revealing cry and quickly hushing and snuggling him close she managed to avert the danger, but she knew she could not quieten him much longer. Poor little chap; it was no fun being jounced about in the woods late at night. She set off again at half run, her legs feeling wooden with fatigue but she knew all her efforts were useless, the village was miles away, a day's hike in her condition, and one she wouldn't normally attempt. Even without carrying Angus it was totally impossible in the dark. What was she to do? Think woman! Think of something!

The torch was gaining on her when she remembered the burial cairns. Was there a place to hide inside? She would have no light, she would have to feel her way blind and holding Angus would make it difficult. Surely Mark wouldn't know what they were. Maybe he would go past without searching them. It seemed the only chance for her and Angus, she couldn't think of anything else. She must forget her nervousness for the baby's sake. There would be spider webs – oh the hell with them – she would just have to forget her fear of creepy crawlies. She hurried on through the trees, fighting her weariness and praying her strength would last out till she was able to hide.

All at once, she heard Mark cursing behind her. He had tripped on a root and fallen heavily. His yells of anger reached her as she struggled along the winding shore path. Perhaps he would give up the chase, leave them alone, and escape while he had a chance? But then she recalled he couldn't afford to leave a witness. Jessica had to die or she would name him as Luke's murderer and once dead what hope did her baby have? None whatsoever in his hands.

FIFTY TWO

Luke raised himself slowly, putting a hand to his head and feeling the sticky mess at his forehead. Jesus! He felt as if he had been hit with a ten-ton truck. What had happened for Pete's sake? He sat for a moment until the dizziness subsided then got warily to his feet. His head was thumping with the fiercest of headaches and briefly he felt like throwing up. Slowly the vertigo died away but he still held onto the car bonnet in case he toppled. After a moment or two he was able to look about without fear of falling and realise where he was. Suddenly he recalled the sound of a gun. Hellfire! Of course! He had been shot at. Had someone tried to kill him?

Lights were blazing in front of the croft but not a soul was around. This wasn't like Jess. Reeling to the open door, he listened. Nothing! Not even the vestige of a sound. He called quietly before going in, but hardly expected an answer, it was all too quiet. He knew she would never leave Angus on his own or an open door, so where were they? He searched the place rapidly but as he expected it was empty. Oh Jeez, Jess - where are you, for Pete's sake?

Then he recalled the car that had been parked someway back in the lane and the fact there was no one around. A visitor? Surely not at this time of night. Despite the insignificant hint of uneasiness rising in his mind he had no thought of danger as he emerged from the shed where he parked his car. He caught a glimpse of someone standing in the light from the open doorway but there was no time to react before he was hit. Only now did he remember the familiar face that was engraved on his memory for all time. That bastard Welland! How dare he bloody park his feet on my land? Fucking bastard! He would order him off in short order. Then it hit him with incredulity.

Not only had he been at the croft, HE was the one who had shot him! It was only sheer luck he had missed a vital spot and creased the side of Luke's head. Quarter of an inch over and he would have been a goner. He went back outside. Welland's car was still there so he wasn't too far away, but where was Jessica and Angus?

A second later, he heard an echoing sound, someone was yelling. The still waters of the loch carried the noise clearly back to him and he ran to the edge of the loch and stared seaward, at once catching sight of a torch held by someone making their way through the trees.

The light was easily seen as it waved back and forth in a searching pattern. Jess and Angus! Mark must have the torch and was searching for them! That meant they were still free. Oh God he hoped so. If Mark was crazy enough to shoot at him, whatever would he do to Jess and Angus?

Luke clenched his fists in agony of apprehension. Jessica was still free from the looks of things, but for how long? She must have got away from Mark and was running with the baby for he knew she wouldn't have gone without him. How could he get to her in time to help save them? He was quite certain he knew one person would die for he would kill Mark with his bare hands if necessary, but he had to ensure the safety of Jess and Angus first. Wasting no time he ran as best as he could back to the house for his gun and ammunition. His torch was missing, but he guessed Mark had it.

Wisely, he took a few seconds to phone Jimmy Halverson to get the police double-quick.

"Don't ask questions, man! Just do it, damn you! We're in trouble here; there's a madman loose who's trying to kill us. Tell 'em to come armed."

His only answer was a growled, "With you soon, ma bonny!" Then Luke set off after the others in a half run that covered the ground easily. His head was still aching but he forgot the pain as he concentrated on minding his feet. It was fortunate he knew the path so well for the darkness was intense but the gleam of water from the loch on his left helped to guide him.

He had to get to Jess before Mark harmed her, he just had to. Christ! What a thing to happen when they were so happy. Was it his fault? Why was his life filled with one tragedy after another? Give me a break will yah Lord? Haven't I done enough penance in my lifetime to please yah? Or am I gonna have shit for evermore?

FIFTY THREE

Mark eventually reached the open space where the burial cairns lay, his knee throbbing from the hard fall. Bitch! It was all her fault for being so contrary. Just wait till he had her in his hands. He'd show her who was master! Dimly he saw the wide stretch of water leading out to sea and heard the sound of the surf breaking on the shore. A few stars glinted here and there but it was the dark of the moon and there was little else to see except in the rays of his torch. He shone it around letting the beams drift over an empty landscape. She had vanished!

Where the hell were they? Suddenly he heard the tiny cry of the baby, swiftly muffled but somewhere off to his right. He shone the torch over and saw to his surprise a number of what appeared to be hillocks. What the hell were they? Ah yes. Some sort of cairn, he remembered now, they were marked on his map. So, she was in one of the cairns was she? She mightn't have realised it but she was nicely trapped, he thought with satisfaction. This stupid farce of running across the wilds of Scotland was soon going to be over. He would catch her and his plans could proceed without hindrance once he killed her, but not before he taught her another hard lesson.

He was beginning to feel quite exhilarated, man chases woman, man catches woman, man rapes woman! Would that he lived in the olden days when life was meant to be taken by the throat and enjoyed. He quite fancied himself as a wild Scottish Chieftain. He would have done rather well with his own clan. Fighting and looting! Plenty of blood and adventure. And the spoils of war! What a bonus! Enough women to satisfy him. Oh yes, life was meant to be lived to the full, but not in present days, and never in England. Ah well, enough of exotic dreams - now to business.

"Jessica! I know where you are, come out and we'll say no more about your stupidity, if I have to come after you, you'll pay dearly, my girl, I promise you." There was an uneasy silence, even the wind had dropped and the dark night was filled with a waiting stillness. He played the light over the cairns and realised most of the entrances were blocked with weeds and bushes. Only two looked as though they were accessible and he bent down at the nearest one to look inside. A small fall of earth at the start of the tunnel ruled that one out for it was not marred with footprints, though he was not to know that it was the one Jessica and Luke had gone into when they had come before. Mark turned to the other one. Stooping down, he roared loudly into the tunnel for her to come out but there was no reply, nor did he expect one. She would be difficult to the last and would never know how it gave him all the more pleasure. There was silence. Nothing, not even the cry of the baby. Oh, he would hurt her, yes indeed, hurt her very much, but it would serve her right, she should learn to do as she was told. Just like his son would learn. Oh, yes, in time he would also learn to respect his father's wishes.

With a reluctant shrug for Mark hated small confined places, he bent to crawl inside. He had to go slowly for there was no room to manoeuvre or to stand fully erect. He'd hardly gone a yard or so when something heavy and furry hit him violently in the chest and instantly clung with a savage, immovable force against his upper thorax. Terrified at the sudden assault he screamed wildly as he backed out rapidly to the open air, dropping the torch as his hands went up to dislodge the vile thing, whatever it was, which was gripping him so tightly. His attempts were in vain, the object held on and a nauseating smell filled his nostrils.

"Help! Oh God, help me! Someone...help...aaah!" He screeched again in frantic terror. But it was no use he could not prise away the frenzied demon at his throat that was kicking, biting, and scratching with an unbelievable ferocity. His vainly clutching hands were useless!

Lethal claws were raking the skin off his bare throat and upper chest as the tee shirt was torn asunder, causing a white-hot fire to leap through him. Long feral teeth sank their sharpness into his jugular vein, tearing and ripping till he was covered with spouting blood. It was going everywhere, in his mouth, in his eyes, gushing over his hands that were unable to wrench away the fiend that held him in a vicious clutching grip that he was totally powerless to tear away.

For God's sake, what was happening? The brute was trying to kill him. All at once it struck him he was actually in danger of dying! How could this be? How could life stop like this when he had it all figured out? Was this was the end of his life? In that case he'd been cheated! Bloody well short-changed! It was too late to get to the top, to be a winner. His marvellous plans were all useless. He would die a loser just as he had been all his life. He tried to call again for help but the words bubbled in his throat as he struggled to take an impossible breath and knew he was drowning in his own blood.

As the last seconds ticked away, the sudden recollection of Henry Fowden filled his brain. Why Fowden? Why think of him? Was he here watching? Did he know the agony Mark was feeling? Had HIS chest hurt like a thousand knives? Had he felt just as helpless to stop the agony? There had been no one to help Henry in his dying, no one around who felt the slightest pity or regret for him, who would put out a hand to save him, least of all Mark Welland, who was now paying the same price! Henry's curse had come home to roost. Fate decreed there would be no help at all for such a villain as Mark Welland.

The Wheel, as always, turns a full circle.

"That what goes around, comes around. What goes up must come down. You reap what you have sown, thus you must think ahead and consider your actions, whether you find yourself on top or at the bottom of the wheel."

And what of the whims of the Gods? Ah, they are nothing but cruel players. In the end, they too must bow their heads to Fate and allow Mark to work out his dreadful Karma in another life. The soul of Mark Welland left him. He had merely been a self-styled playboy and trifling adventurer, whom nothing had touched too deeply except for the claws of a wild cat, himself fearful of the echoing voice, booming through his lair and most anxious for his mate, who had given birth to two more kits. The animal had launched himself against the unknown enemy, and filled with fierce resentment against all interlopers, had the power and ability in his puma genes to retaliate with all his might to defend his home.

Luke saw the body in the light of the still shining torch as he emerged from the forest and also the black silhouette of the cat. He had no idea whose body it was and lest it was Jessica's and she was still alive he fired once and it was all over. There was silence from the heap on the ground. Silence was everywhere, save for the wind keening through the trees behind him. Were they dead?

"Jessica! Jess love, where are you, speak to me Jess!" He cried out in an agony of dread as he reached the two bodies on the ground and saw in the torch light, the terrible damage the cat had inflicted on Mark. He could scarcely recognise him. He felt the bile rise in his throat as he stared down at the mutilated body overlaid with the dead cat. Thank God, it wasn't his Jess, but where the hell was she? Please don't let me find the cat has killed her first.

"Luke?" A quavering voice came from the stony cliff some distance away. "Luke! I'm over here! Oh darling, is it really you? You're not dead after all? Oh my dearest, I can't believe you are alive. I thought he had killed you after that shot! You were lying so still..."

She had balked at crawling into a dark hole at the last moment, deciding to take her chance in the open, thereby saving her life, for the wild cat, having had a brush with Luke's gun was filled with anger and terror at being cornered once more.

Luke scrambled over the rocky ground to clutch his wife and son safely in his arms where at once their mingled tears washed down onto Angus. For the first time since he had been rudely snatched from his bed Angus protested. What an indignity for a fellow. He was wet, he was cold, he wanted his teddy, and he wanted out of this darkness and to go back home. His howls brought them to their senses. They had fought a duel with the devil but life must go on and one frightened small infant must be lovingly and so carefully cared for.

"Come, Jess, my love, let's go home. We'll let someone else clear up the mess." Luke, with Angus on one arm guided his wife back through the trees to their sanctuary. It had been disturbed for a while with evil but it was still there to nurture them.

FIFTY FOUR

The arrival of Jimmy and the police coincided with a number of men, who had flown up from London by helicopter. Luke reflected to himself how enormously lucky he had been to avoid a lethal hit and to get to Jessica in time. For all the police in the United Kingdom would have been powerless to help him had Mark's aim been accurate, or save her and Angus if Mark had got to them first. It went a long way towards making his mind up on rejoining an army unit. A very long way indeed.

Days later, Commander Patterson sat in his office, coffee in hand, soberly discussing the case with a colleague. "You know, Jack, for all the time I've been in this job I am still amazed at the way some things turn out. Take this last situation, for instance. As devilish a scenario as you are likely to come across. Here is a woman badly treated, a pilot's career wiped out, a dead pilot and his grieving family, a man full of revenge for his murdered daughter, a Colonel looking for a scoundrel, a father who did not like his son and me, tail-end Charlie as usual but very determined to see justice done. All of us were seeking retribution of one sort or another. Yet in the end we were all stymied by a wild cat that just wanted to protect his family. He knew nothing of the sins of the man; the dreadful things that can happen in this world, he was merely the instrument of divine justice.

"Divine justice?" Exclaimed Jack perplexed.

"Yes, pure and simple justice. For I am reminded most strongly of the words: "Vengeance is mine; I will repay", saith the Lord.' Romans 12.19. It's an old favourite quotation of mine. I have found it applicable in so many cases I no longer think of as coincidence. I'm not a church-goer as my wife will attest. She never tries to get me up on a Sunday morning to go with her; but I have a great respect for the teachings of the few impressive men the world has known and the miracles and mysteries that have stemmed from them and the bible. Incredibly, the instrument He used in this case was a wild cat. Certainly not one of us, for all our efforts. Life is infinitely more mysterious than we ever realise."

"At least you'll agree He's saved the taxpayers a mint of money in prison fees?"

"Amen to that, Jack. In addition, the chance of a parole. I have also heard that the Welland name has gone from the City. Seager has taken over the place now old Charlie Welland has retired for good. Will Charlie ever have second thoughts, I wonder, and recognise his grandson? Will the Fraser's ever let him? Who knows? But if I were them I'd never allow it."

* * * * *

The room was warm, the loving had been powerful and sweet and Jessica was preparing to tell Luke her news, when Luke lazily wrinkled his nose, giving her a rueful smile. Puzzled, she stared at him, pulling back suspiciously. "Go on then, tell me."

"Tell you what?" Then he grinned contritely, she'd rumbled him again. "Jess, I hope it's okay but David's dropping Abraham off tomorrow. I checked the bank balance and it seemed reasonably adequate. I did a deal. I thought you wouldn't mind too much, especially as we agreed...well... I thought it would be okay..." Luke stammered lamely as he tried to confess what had been on his mind all day.

"So it should be," she replied tartly. "I paid the egg money in. It topped it up nicely."

"Oh Jeez! That's your money. It's not for the bank. You should have said."

"Come to think of it, Luke Fraser, though I'm not sure you deserve it, I might just have some odd cash to contribute towards Abraham. Part of a legacy, one might say, I was keeping for Angus. I think he'll be proud to have a small share in his Dad's business, especially if you are going to train him as a sheep farmer. If Abraham is as good as his reputation Angus will have a high gain. Now tell me, does this mean what I think it does?"

"Yeah, I guess so. It has sure been on my mind since – well you know, since all the trouble erupted. I don't ever want to leave this valley till they carry me out, is that okay?"

"Yes, my darling, it's more than okay with me."

Jessica grinned mischievously and snuggled closer to Luke. "Now here's a bit of news you've got a definite share in! How about another son or maybe a daughter?"

"You know honey, I'm gonna spend a lifetime trying to figure out where you come from. You always surprise me no matter what I do."

She giggled as he pounced on her.

"It couldn't be better," he continued. "With the profit on Abraham we'll build an extension to this place then we can have another baby and another..."

"Hey there, whoa down, boy! This is not a flock you are talking about, this is me! Let's take them one at a time. For now, thank goodness, I am only having one baby. And don't you dare, Luke Fraser, if you value your life, count on calling him after your ram!

Printed in the United Kingdom
by Lightning Source UK Ltd.
120438UK00001B/349-378